### Praise for *Tomorrow I Become a Woman*

'Aiwanose Odafen has written a gripping story that holds a mirror to society, reflecting the harsh realities of gender inequality in our society. The book forces us to reckon with the pervasiveness of violence against women and girls, which remains one of the most significant human rights violations impacting millions globally. Yet rather than perpetuate a victim's narrative, *Tomorrow I Became a Woman* is a survivor's story of self-determination, reminding us all of the strength and resilience of women and girls everywhere.'

Elizabeth Nyamayaro, author of *I Am a Girl From Africa*

'Searing and beautifully rendered, Aiwanose Odafen's writing acutely speaks to intimate experiences at the crux of race, gender, class, culture and tradition.'

Koa Beck, author of *White Feminism: From the Suffragettes to Influencers and Who They Leave Behind*

'Odafen writes with compelling craft of a world where certain expectations are put on women. Her exploration of the Nigeria her characters inhabit is unflinching and cuts to the core. It lets no one off the hook. *Tomorrow I Become a Woman* is ultimately a celebration of the irrepressible strength of its protagonist. This is a necessary book.'

Chika Unigwe, author of *On Black Sisters Street*

'*Tomorrow I Become a Woman* is an accomplished and emotional triumph. With deft language and in-depth characters, the book explores female friendships, difficulties and loss. It pulses with life, and taught me a lot.'

Louise Beech, author of *How To Be Brave*

'Uju and her friends may be fictional characters but their stories are real, and they are women that I know, women that I love, women that will stay with me forever. This isn't an easy read, there are triggers of domestic violence but it must be read and shared.'

Di Lebowitz, author of *The Marks Left on Her*

# TOMORROW
# I BECOME
# A WOMAN

## AIWANOSE ODAFEN

SCRIBNER

London · New York · Sydney · Toronto · New Delhi

First published in Great Britain by Scribner,
an imprint of Simon & Schuster UK Ltd, 2022

1 3 5 7 9 10 8 6 4 2

Simon & Schuster UK Ltd
1st Floor
222 Gray's Inn Road
London WC1X 8HB

www.simonandschuster.co.uk
www.simonandschuster.com.au
www.simonandschuster.co.in

Simon & Schuster Australia, Sydney
Simon & Schuster India, New Delhi

A CIP catalogue record for this book is available from the British Library

Hardback ISBN: 978-1-3985-0611-4
Trade Paperback ISBN: 978-1-3985-0612-1
eBook ISBN: 978-1-3985-0613-8

Typeset by Palimpsest Book Production Ltd, Falkirk, Stirlingshire
Printed and bound in Great Britain by CPI Group (UK) Ltd, Croydon, CR0 4YY

*For my family*

*'She's a woman now. A true mother,' I heard them
say as they scattered the dust on my grave.
'She'll watch over us from the other side.'*

# PART 1

# YESTERDAY

## 1.

## *I'm going to marry him*

We stood side by side in March of '94, arms around each other with milky pasted smiles, displaying all our teeth for the cameramen shouting, '*Oga*, please look this way,' and 'Madam, please move closer to *oga*,' as we cut the ribbon to the factory Gozie was opening in his hometown. Our pictures would appear in the glossy pages of society magazines, above flowery articles of the business exploits of Chigozie Azubuike, a respected member of the community, and his dutiful wife, one Obianuju Azubuike née Nwaike, who'd stood by him through the toughest of times. Mama would buy dozens of copies and distribute them to all her friends and members of *Ndigbo* Women's Association of Lagos and show every visitor that crossed the threshold of her and Papa's household; her daughter, her own Uju, was now a star.

Church members would approach me with timid smiles to say, 'I saw you in "so-and-so" magazine,' and compliment my expensive wrapper and head-tie, my designer shoes. And I would smile with just the right blend of pleasure, humility and satisfaction, tilt my head elegantly and say, 'Thank you.'

Just days before, an expensive earthenware vase with hand-painted red roses, the one Gozie had bought on his last trip to China, cracked on the wall just above my head and shattered in an icy rain around me.

'You're a witch!' Gozie screamed. And I knew I'd dream of those words, the letters dancing in circles around me – you're a witch! You're a witch!

We met at church – the perfect place for an upstanding Christian girl to find a husband – on a Sunday in August of '78. I was a student at the University of Lagos at the time, with only a few months left till graduation.

The church was alive that Sunday, the air electric with fate. The atmosphere bubbled with music and people. Smiling women in floor-length skirts and colourful headscarves stood at the entrance distributing flyers, and men in oversized trousers directed us to our seats.

My friends Adaugo and Chinelo had pestered me to attend service that day, and I finally caved when they threatened to report me to Mama. Nothing was scarier than Mama showing up at school, wearing that frown of hers that would make even the devil quiver. I could picture Mama in the matching wrapper and head-tie she always wore for her *Ndigbo* women's meeting, with wafts of her hair sticking out the open top. 'Obianuju! Obianuju! Tell me what I heard isn't true!' she would yell. No. I'd have rather faced the devil himself, and my evil friends knew it.

The three of us had been inseparable since we were waddling about in diapers, and our mothers had the black and white photographs

– showing tiny chubby versions of ourselves and flashing toothless grins – to prove it. There was a story to this. Our mothers had met in the late forties at the back of a packed bus. The three of them were young and newly married Igbo women on a one-way trip, from the southeastern region of Nigeria to Lagos, to meet the husbands their parents had chosen and married for them in absentia. Terrified of their unknown futures, they had created an unbreakable friendship at the back of that bus, one so thick it had withstood time and all its tests. Mama always said she would never have survived the city without them by her side: they were her godsends.

It wasn't a very large church but a branch of the new Pentecostal wave that was sweeping through the country. The pews were arranged in a semi-circle and faced a wooden pulpit with a microphone at the front of the hall. And the room was coloured in a warm glow from the overhanging orange lights.

My agreement to attend church had been temporary until I could come up with a good enough bargain to get myself out of it the following Sunday. I'd even made sure to dress rebelliously – my skirt was an inch above the acceptable length, and my makeup was more heavy-handed than usual. But walking in there that day, I knew I'd be back.

Instrumentals blared from the side of the pulpit and out through the building and its open doors and windows as the service started. Men and women danced and shouted and waved their hands above their heads in rhythm with the music, a strikingly different form of worship from the solemn assemblies of the orthodox churches we'd been raised in. I watched in surprise as my friends joined in, dancing and screaming like everyone else, encouraging me to do so as well.

But the session ended abruptly, before I could fully absorb the goings-on around me.

A young man with striking features approached the pulpit, his hair combed out in a soft Afro. I thought he looked like he'd walked out of one of the myths of African gods. He picked up a microphone and opened his mouth to let out the most beautiful sound I'd ever heard. His rich tenor rang throughout the auditorium, enunciating each word and hitting all the right notes. I sat, rooted to my seat, and watched his lips move, moving mine as well with lyrics I'd known my whole life but with a different subject of adulation in mind.

> *Let angels prostrate fall;*
> *Bring forth the royal diadem,*
> *And crown Him Lord of all!*

Shuffling to my feet, I looked around to confirm I wasn't the only one mystified by this angelic creature. A lady in the row behind me was smiling so wide, I knew her thoughts were unfit for a church service. Even the choir members behind him seemed to be enchanted, their eyes darting back and forth between the heavens and the mortal before them, seemingly unable to make up their minds who mattered more.

The hymn ended before I was ready for it to, and I followed as the man who'd arrived out of my imagination walked off the stage. A solemn man with large reading glasses slowly climbed up the steps to the stage to take his place and cleared his throat to begin the sermon.

He spoke for an hour with vigour and power, sweat pouring down the sides of his face and moisture gathering round the chest and armpits of his shirt. Around me, people jumped to their feet and shouted 'Hallelujah' and 'Amen' at the top of their lungs. But I was lost in another world, where the only people that existed were myself and the handsome man with the voice from heaven.

'Who was that?' I asked Ada and Chinelo that evening in our small shared university room.

'Who was who?' Chinelo replied, not bothering to look at me as she rolled over on her bed, flipping through the pages of a novel. On the front cover, a man held a woman from behind as she arched her back in an exaggerated display of passion. I wondered if she'd quarrelled with Christopher – the cute Chemical Engineering student she was dating – again. Every time they had an argument, she would return to the university hostel with a new romance novel, where the men were perfect and acted the way she wanted, and would complain of heat in her chest, saying that she could feel the heartbreak. The last time, I'd told her it wasn't heartbreak but heartburn from the peppery food she consumed so often.

She stretched out her arm to pick from a bowl of *chin chin* beside her and filled the room with the *kra kra* of her chewing.

'You know who – the guy. That guy!' I insisted, my hands on my hips.

'Which guy?' Ada asked obtusely, her own eyes fixed on the glossy magazine in her hands. ABBA's 'Dancing Queen' filtered through a small radio beside her, and she hummed the lyrics underneath her breath. 'Do you think she had surgery done?' she said, pointing at a celebrity whose nose had become slimmer overnight. It was one of the many old magazines we collected from our classmates who regularly went to the United States over the summer. Sometimes they brought back wedding magazines as well, and we admired the expensive dresses we knew we'd never wear and imagined grand weddings that would never happen.

Ada flipped the page over, not bothering to wait for a response, and clapped her hands together. 'Ahh, ahh! The latest hairstyles.' She turned the open magazine to face me, a wide smile on her face. 'What do you think? Which one will suit me the best? This one or this one?' The first hairstyle was a bob with a fringe that could only have been achieved by the tortuous application of heat, the second a head full of tiny cornrows braided with extensions and decorated with colourful beads and cowries, so many that I feared for the model's neck.

Ada rolled her eyes. 'Answer me now; I need to change my hairstyle. Or can't you see?' She patted the large pink rollers in her hair for emphasis.

Chinelo stretched her neck away from her book to peep at the magazine. 'The braids look good o.'

'Can the both of you please pay attention!'

They both turned to stare at me. '*Nne*, what is it?' Ada asked.

'I asked who was that? And before you say "who" again, I mean the choir guy with the voice.' I silently inserted 'heavenly' before 'voice'.

'Oh! That one?' Chinelo replied nonchalantly. 'He's the lead chorister o. What's that his name again? Go—Gozie. Yes, Gozie, that's his name.'

Ada giggled. 'If you're interested in him, you better join the queue because every girl in church is gunning for that one. I don't even know what they see. Fine boy, no *kudi*. Fine face cannot buy food.'

8

We all laughed; it was such a Lagosian statement to make – the city was a melting pot for several tribes, from Igbo to Yoruba to Igala, and so we threw words around that weren't indigenously ours and forgot that *kudi* was Hausa for money and *ode,* another word we often used, was Yoruba for a daft person.

I smiled, wide and big. 'I don't care what you say; I'm going to marry him.'

They burst into even more riotous laughter.

'What is it? *You dey go clean church?'* Adaugo demanded through bloodshot eyes after I tapped her awake the next Sunday. It was three hours before service.

Chinelo eyed my sober attire of ankle-length skirt and long-sleeved blouse, with a matching silk scarf. 'Mother Mary!' she shouted before bursting into laughter, her fair skin turning red.

I ignored her. I was determined to look the part.

'You better wake up this early for class tomorrow,' Ada grumbled minutes later as we left our room.

'I don't know what you mean. I always wake up early,' I retorted, not meeting her eyes.

The early-morning Sundays and loitering around the church premises long after sermons became a ritual, until even my friends, having reached their limit, abandoned me to my endeavours. 'If you wake me up early again, I'll break your head. I'll see you in church!' Ada said to me in a voice that told me she meant every word.

I carried on like a pagan worshipping its god from afar, lighting a candle at its altar; I watched him, listened to him sing, and tested out how our names sounded together.

The day I finally summoned the courage to approach Gozie, the pastor spoke about perseverance and determination. 'Go after what you desire. Faith without work is dead.' He'd barely finished saying 'Amen' when I dragged Ada and Chinelo in the direction of the choir, stretching my long legs to cover as much ground as quickly as possible. But there were those ahead of me who'd heard the message as well. They surrounded him like ants on a sugar cube, fluttering their lashes and waving their colourful handkerchiefs like butterflies.

Finally, after several minutes of waiting, it was our turn. At this point, I was sure I didn't stand a chance, but I had nothing to lose. He moved closer, a charming smile stretched across his face. He was even more arresting up close. His skin glowed like polished wood and his dark eyes sparkled with intelligence. His features were epicene – angular and strong enough for a man but soft like a woman's. He stood taller than I'd expected and had shoulders so broad they pulled at the material of his starched white shirt.

Ada stretched out her arm to shake his hand. 'Brother Gozie, we enjoyed your ministration today.'

His smile widened. 'Thank you. I try my best.'

Ada pulled me forward. 'Have you met my friend? She's new to our church. She really enjoyed your ministration too.'

He turned to look at me and all the words I'd so carefully prepared disappeared and my voice was replaced by something little above a whisper.

'Hi. Obianuju. U-Uju for short,' I mumbled, gripping his outstretched hand.

He smiled again; he was used to this, the effect he had on people. Chinelo prodded me in the back to say more.

'I really enjoyed your singing; it was heavenly.'

10

'Thank you,' he replied graciously. 'I hope you'll keep coming to our church.'

'She'll keep coming,' Chinelo jumped in enthusiastically before I could utter a word. 'She's our good friend and a really nice girl . . .'

I stood quietly as she extolled my virtues, like a market woman trying to sell off her goods.

He nodded politely when she was done. 'It's nice to know that. Hope to see you next Sunday,' he said, then moved on like we were a kiosk at a colourful carnival.

Ada faced me with a frown. 'What happened?'

'I don't know,' I mumbled and lowered my head.

Chinelo tapped my back. 'Don't take it personally Uju; he is a very popular guy. Who knows, he might talk to you another day.'

'Another day' came many weeks later. Service had ended, and we sat talking with Sister Chinasa, the head of the ushering unit I'd just joined. She was explaining the many complexities of ushering – standing like statues throughout service, collecting offerings, quieting rude chatty teenagers. Gozie sauntered over confidently, his hands in the pockets of his grey trousers, and rested against a pillar beside us quietly. I pretended not to see him. Sister Chinasa paused the moment she noticed him. 'Brother Gozie, good afternoon,' she said with the same dazzled smile every woman sent his way. I felt jealousy curl like a hot ball in my chest.

'Good afternoon, Sister Chinasa,' he replied evenly. 'Do you mind if I speak with Sister Uju for a few minutes?' he asked. It took Ada pinching me to make me realise he was referring to me, Uju. Brother Gozie wanted to talk to me?

Sister Chinasa giggled nervously. 'Of course, of course,' she said pushing at my shoulder a bit too forcefully. Chinelo winked at me as I slowly got to my feet, stunned.

When we were far enough from the group, he stopped at a pillar and turned to me. 'Sister Uju, how are you?'

I blinked. Was that what he'd called me aside to ask?

'I-I'm fine,' I stuttered.

Then he said the words I'd imagined but never thought possible. 'Sister Uju would you be free on Tuesday after mid-week service? I'd like to take you out.'

'Yes! Yes!' I near screamed.

## 2.

### *Only a foolish rat dances with the lizard in the rain*

It was at the newly opened restaurant across the street from the church that we had our first date, our booths facing the image of the cross at its roof centre, staring at us, daring us to sin. Nat King Cole's 'Unforgettable' wafted out of the speakers in the background, spinning us in its web.

I mouthed the lyrics, the music clinging to me just like the song said.

'We should get to know each other instead of staring like this, don't you think?' Gozie said, raising a perfectly arched brow.

I blushed but still said nothing. I wasn't often alone in a strange man's company because Mama had told me it was indecent for a girl to spend too much time alone with a man that wasn't a relative or a close family friend. 'Only loose girls are seen with men all the time,' she'd said. And I'd always wondered how she expected me to find a husband when I was never to spend time alone with one.

He talked about himself and I listened. He was a lot older than I'd anticipated, thirty-one – ten years my senior. He'd been raised in the eastern parts of the country and had only moved to the city following graduation. He had a degree in Mass Communication from the University of Nsukka and worked as journalist at a popular national newspaper, *The People's Voice*. He'd lost both parents in the civil war and was responsible for the welfare of most of his family.

I absorbed every detail, watching the movement of his firm lips. I even missed his parents, these people that must have been just as beautiful, lost forever. I knew what it was like to lose loved ones to war.

'What about you? Tell me about yourself,' Gozie said some minutes later, another dazzling smile on his lips, after we'd taken enough bites of the cold food served by the waiter.

And so I told him I was twenty-one and a final-year Economics student at the University of Lagos. His raised eyebrows told me he'd expected me to be slightly older. I spoke shyly about Ada and Chinelo and our long-term friendship. I talked about Mama and Papa and my three much older brothers: Kelechi, Ugochukwu and Ikechukwu. He laughed at my stories, smiled where appropriate, and hung on my every word. We'd ended the date with a chaste hug and a slight peck that brushed the side of my face and made it tingle well into the night.

'Do you think he's too old for me?' I asked my friends that night, my face scrunched in deep thought.

Ada chuckled. 'You worry too much. There's nothing wrong in him being much older than you. In fact, it's a good thing. It is a man's job to lead his woman and teach her,' she said.

I frowned; she made me sound like a pupil dating her teacher.

\*

Akin looked up slowly as I bounced into his office the next morning unannounced and lovestruck. His lips were drawn in a smile that radiated through his dark eyes, the same smile he'd worn the very first day we'd met in the library three years before.

'Good morning to you too, Smallie,' he drawled as I sighed dreamily. He insisted on calling me that even though we were the same height.

'I met someone and I'm going to marry him,' I said.

He raised a brow slowly and shut the book in front of him. I had his attention now. Something flashed over his eyes, but it passed before I could decipher what it was. 'Really? Shouldn't you be thinking of your upcoming final exams?'

I wrinkled my nose at him. 'You just had to remind me. Well, you could help by providing hints on where the exam questions will come from,' I replied with a cheeky grin.

Akin's smile widened, exposing white, even teeth, and I was reminded once again that he was also handsome – maybe not god-like like Gozie, but good looking, with his chiseled cheekbones, perfectly symmetrical nose and dark loose curly hair. 'He should have been a model with his fine shiny skin. I don't know what he's doing in this university,' Ada had commented once.

'You should try trapping him,' Chinelo had added then with a mischievous wink and I'd knocked her on the head. What Akin and I had was different, a special type of friendship that made me feel safe, like I could be whoever and say whatever without ever wondering if I was deserving of a marriage proposal. Besides, he was Yoruba. Mama would never agree to such.

'Who knows, you might fall in love over economic theories and calculus,' Chinelo continued adamantly. But he'd never shown that sort of interest in me, except one time and we'd never spoken of it again.

He'd watched me that day in the library try to convince the librarian of my supposed entitlement to more books than my student card allowed. I'd barely noticed until the exasperated librarian had turned to someone – him – standing beside me, eager to escape from my clutches. 'Sir, do you need help checking that out?' Her eyes pleaded for him to say yes.

He shook his head slowly with a wide smile and waved for us to continue. Rolling her eyes ever so slowly back to me, she said. 'Listen, I have told you—'

'But ma,' I interjected, and we started all over again.

Somewhere around the third re-run of our back and forth, throaty laughter interrupted us. It burst out like he'd been struggling to contain it. 'Put the extra books on my card,' he said to the librarian, stretching a brown card forward. 'I'll make sure she returns them.'

'Thank you,' I mumbled with a shy smile as the bespectacled woman looked between us before grudgingly penning down the book titles on a card.

'Akintunde Ajayi,' he said, flashing another charismatic smile as we strolled out of the library, books in hand, and waited for me to introduce myself.

'Obianuju Nwaike,' I replied. 'Thank you for helping me with the books. I'm not always like that,' I quickly added, remembering Mama's complaints about unladylike arguments. It made me self-conscious that this stranger had met me under such circumstances.

'Obianuju Nwaike,' he said slowly, as though testing my name on his tongue, then raising a bushy brow. 'Always like what?'

I stared down at my platform shoes. 'Always arguing and stuff. I just really needed those books. I have a test coming up. If you don't mind me asking, how come you were able to get so many books on your card?'

He laughed, long and loud. 'I like you, Obianuju,' he said finally. 'I like your spirit.'

Then he walked off, leaving me standing there thinking he was the strangest person I'd ever met.

I wouldn't see him again for a long time, but I made sure to return the books when they were due, afraid to break the unprecedented trust this strange man had placed in me. The librarian had looked over her glasses at me as she'd collected the books, her mouth set with disapproval.

The following semester, Akin walked into a lecture hall and introduced himself as our Econometrics lecturer. 'Obianuju Nwaike. We meet again,' he said to me after the class with a smile.

A bond was formed that day – he a twenty-three-year-old genius with a PhD and well on his way to becoming a professor, and me a nineteen-year-old student in need of affirmation and direction. 'You're always welcome to stop by my office for anything you need,' he said that day and I took those words seriously, partly because I was really and truly fascinated – I'd never met anyone like him.

I stopped by when I needed a textbook I couldn't find in the library, when I had an assignment I didn't understand, when I needed to rant about a difficult lecturer. He was easy to talk to; he listened like every word mattered, something I wasn't used to.

It was in his office that I cried the day I received a test script with fat 'F' circled in red pen; my first experience with failure.

'You're smart Obianuju, this is just one of those things, a small bump in the road,' he reassured me with a hand on my shoulder then offered to buy me lunch. At the cafeteria, we traded football banter between spoonfuls of rice, and I told him what the class thought of his teaching style, to which he replied, '*Ehen? Is that so?*' with a mischievous smile. There were many lunches after that, dinners and brunches, random outings and silent walks back to my hostel in the middle of the night surrounded by chirping crickets. We never pressured our connection with questions; we were too busy just being.

'People probably gossip about us,' I said one day as we neared my hostel gate. It was not 'probably'. The whispers had already gotten back to me – why would a student and lecturer spend so much time together if nothing untoward was going on?

He turned to look at me with a perplexed expression. 'Gossip? Why do you say so?'

I stared at the gate ahead and shrugged with faux nonchalance. 'I don't know. I'm a student; you're not. I'm a woman; you're a man.'

He laughed long and hard, and I smiled because I liked his laugh – it made me want to laugh too. 'Obianuju, people will always talk,' he said finally. 'It's your choice whether to listen or not. I don't listen because I don't care. We enjoy spending time together and that's what matters.'

I wanted to ask other questions – *Do you see me? Do you like me?* – but I remained silent.

'No exam questions for you Smallie. Go and read,' Akin said and stuck out his tongue like a little boy.

'Well I have to try at least. I mean, the class is depending on me.'

18

He laughed. 'Are you going to tell me about this wonderful Mr. Right or not?'

I clapped my hands together, my excitement returning. 'Yes! So, Chinelo and Adaugo invited me to their church about a month ago,' I began.

'Really?' he said with exaggerated enthusiasm. 'Tell me more.'

I wrinkled my nose at him again and continued talking.

That weekend, I went home to see Mama.


Mama never got tired of telling me the story. She'd been married for many years to Papa, and her position was safe: she'd had sons, three strong boys. But Mama had wanted a daughter; she'd prayed and begged for one. Someone to share her stories with, to pass on the recipes her mother and grandmother had given her, to teach all that she knew about life, to take trips to the salon with and gossip about the things only girls cared about.

Mama always said I was punishment for her mixing ancestral worship with her Christian faith. She'd sought the counsel of native medicine men, worn amulets, and prayed to *Ala* and other deities to give her a daughter, even though she'd been an active member of her church. Her father still had a shrine in his compound although he had sent all his children to the missionary school in their village. And so, in anger, the gods had connived and sent her a daughter identical to her in looks but nothing like what she wanted.

How else could she explain my disinterest in everything she loved – cooking, cleaning, taking care of the home – and my determination to be anything but the person she'd endlessly tried to mould me into? Then I'd inherited Papa's height and long limbs, hovering inches over every other girl my age and many men, aka suitors. 'I can't introduce your daughter to my son o. She's too tall for him – in fact, she's probably taller than him. When they argue, she'll just give him a knock,' one of Mama's friends had joked once.

By the time I was a teenager, Mama had thrown away all her amulets and other relics of pagan worship she'd been brought up with, and dedicated herself fully to the church.

Mama was busy when I arrived, hard at work on a pot of *ogbono* soup. 'Uju, go and sit in the parlour, I'll come and join you. I'm almost done, or I would have asked you to help me,' she said to me when I walked into the kitchen that afternoon, her eyes set on the pot she was stirring. She slapped the spoon she'd been using to turn the pot on her palm and wiped the traces of soup it left behind with her tongue. 'More salt,' she said to herself.

I walked back to the living room and settled on the long sofa, looking around at the familiar setting. Nothing had changed in over two decades. There were still three 1950s brown Scandinavian-style sofas and Papa's special chair in a corner close to the veranda so he could relax and read while fresh air cooled him. The chair had been specially carved as a gift by the best carpenter in Papa's village, whose boy Papa had helped send to university.

The box television with the sliding door still stood on the storage unit, and beside it was Papa's precious gramophone. When we were children, Papa would slide the door shut, lock the television in, and keep the key as punishment whenever we misbehaved. He would touch the sides of the television to make sure none of us (Ikechukwu in particular) had found the key in his absence. In the evenings, after listening to the news, Papa would pull records out of the storage and play them on the gramophone. Jazz, blues and rock would fill the house. Nat King Cole had been my favourite, his baritone voice soothing and hypnotic, and many evenings I'd crooned along to 'Smile', floating in the magic of its lyrics, imagining what it was like to live smiling with an aching breaking heart.

Our pictures still decorated the wall; the one with us together as a family during Easter after church service, one of me smiling with missing teeth on my seventh birthday, and right beside it was the only odd picture of the lot. The black and white image of the man who still haunted us with his charm and smile – Uncle Ikenna. Mama said the picture had been taken just before he left for England to study.

I looked away and tried to imagine Mama's reaction when I told her about Gozie. She had been waiting eagerly for me to bring someone home. I needed to marry early, she said. I lacked the traits and beauty to attract many suitors, thus, I had to make do with what I had before I was too old and educated to catch a decent man.

'Maybe I made a mistake by letting your father send you to the university. That's why you like arguing like this; too much book is inside your head,' she'd lamented one day after interrupting a heated conversation between me and my brothers. 'Today, it's politics; tomorrow it's football. Instead of you to come and join me in the kitchen, you're shouting up and down the house like a street boy. My grandmother used to say, "Only a foolish rat dances with the lizard in the rain." You're a woman! Your brothers will have wives to cook for them. *Akuko abughi nri.* After all this book, better make sure you come home with a husband. You better not bring just a certificate home. Adaugo has that young man Uzondu; even Chinelo has somebody.'

Mama had been born in a time when education had been a luxury, if not a waste, for a girl child. But my grandmother had been a troublemaker; she'd insisted her husband send all their daughters to the local primary school to learn to read and write. Mama had spent the years afterwards learning to be a wife and then her father shipped her off to be married long before she'd turned eighteen. I had other ambitions, desires she didn't understand, to be something other than a wife.

I hoped telling Mama about Gozie would restore her faith that I would be married someday. I was tired of being introduced to friends' sons, cousins, uncles, friends, tired of Mama telling me every time the daughter of someone we knew got engaged or married and the *aso ebi* they all planned to wear, tired of congratulating others and watching as they responded with oily smiles of those who had achieved all you aimed to, saying, 'Don't worry. God will do your own.'

'Obianuju, how are you?' Mama asked, a grin on her face as she wiped her hands with a towel. 'Sorry I took so long; you know how much your father likes food. I had to make sure it's done before he gets back.' She relaxed into the sofa beside me, pulled a three-legged wooden stool from the corner and threw both feet on it. 'How's school?'

'School is fine, Mama.'

She asked about my friends, my lecturers, even the hostel matrons that she knew. Everyone knew Mama. Then she leaned forward. 'So, any news on . . .' She didn't complete her sentence but instead shook her head and blinked her eyes quickly to indicate that I should know what she was talking about.

I didn't hesitate. I told her about Gozie, 'a man I just started seeing,' I called him so she wouldn't raise her hopes too high. I'd barely finished speaking when Mama jumped to her feet and broke out in song and dance. The stool in front of her clattered to the floor.

I laughed, holding my stomach as I fell to my side on the sofa.

'You're laughing at me instead of dancing? You better dance. God has answered your mother's prayers. My enemies have been put to shame.' Mama always spoke of enemies, beings that monitored her every step to ensure that she never got her wishes. She prayed against them, fasted so that their plans would not succeed, and celebrated all good news as a sign that they had failed. Real or imagined, Mama took them seriously.

Mama stopped dancing, as if something important had crossed her mind. 'Wait first. Uju, what part of Nigeria is he from? Is he a Lagos boy? Please tell me he isn't a Yoruba boy or one of those Northerners,' she pleaded.

'No, Mama he isn't. He's Igbo. His name is Chigozie,' I assured her. I wondered what she'd do if she knew of my friendship with Akin – a Yoruba man. It had been less than a decade since the war ended and our wounds were still fresh. Those three years accounted for the only period in my life that I'd lived outside Lagos.

'Thank God!' Mama exclaimed. '*Hei!* I can't wait to tell your father,' she said, smiling.

'Tell Papa? But there's nothing to te—' I started to say.

'There is o. There is something to tell. Anyways, that is not your concern,' she said. 'Tell me more about this man. Where exactly is he from? Which town?'

'Well, he isn't from our village,' I replied hesitantly.

Mama waved her hand dismissively. 'That's okay, at least he's Igbo. I've already told your brothers that if they like, they should bring Yoruba girls home. If they think I and your father – a red cap chief – will follow anybody to prostrate in the name of marriage, they are dreaming!'

She clapped her hands together excitedly. 'This news calls for celebration. Finally! I was beginning to worry when no single man was interested in you,' she said cheerfully. 'Let me ask Mama Sikira next door to bring two bottles of chilled Coke.' I wondered if she realised that Mama Sikira was Yoruba or if she was trying to pass on a message: we were to live in harmony with the Yorubas but never to marry one.

Minutes later, Mama returned with bottles of soft drink wrapped in a black nylon bag and placed them on a stool. The bag clung to the wet bottles. She picked up the steel opener and proceeded to open them. As she hooked the corner of the red bottle cap, she stopped and turned to look at me with imploring eyes. '*Nne* please behave yourself with him; don't drive him away. Don't talk too much, and don't be doing *I-too-know*. Even if he is wrong, just smile, at least until he pays your bride price. I know you're stubborn but please do this one thing for your mother. *Biko*. Promise me Obianuju.'

'I promise Mama,' I replied solemnly.

Mama opened the last bottle with a smile.

## 3.

### *This one is a strong woman; only a strong man can handle her*

I followed Mama's advice; I feared I would lose Gozie if I did otherwise. I was careful not to talk too much, counting my sentences and pausing dramatically. I gave my opinions carefully, picking my words and watching his reaction. I made sure to sound neither too smart nor threatening. I listened to what he had to say and never insisted on my way. Most important of all, I was careful never to mention a politician's name, past or present, dead or alive.

During the weekends, I visited his small apartment to clean and wash his dirty clothes. I prepared pots of soup, stew and rice until the air and walls had a lingering smell of my sweat and blended spices. Mama said it was the only way to keep such a man: to show him a glimpse of what he was to get when he married you. 'Let him know that there's a woman in his life; show him that you were brought up well,' she said. 'And let me tell you a secret,' she whispered conspiratorially. 'It will keep other women away.'

Gozie reminded me of Uncle Ikenna, and with his easy laugh and charming smile, he brought back painful memories of the first man I'd ever fallen in love with.

I was five the day Uncle Ikenna showed up on our doorstep. He'd been studying on a government scholarship in the United Kingdom for many years and had returned a vibrant young man. I stared at him that day, perplexed and wondering about the identity of this man that looked like a taller, masculine version of Mama and made her squeal and dance like a little girl, that made the hardest woman I knew soft.

Uncle Ikenna was a magnet; people could not help but be drawn to the field of charisma he created around himself. My brothers and I worshipped him, and we fought like female rivals for his attention, but soon it became clear that I was the chosen one: Uncle Ikenna's favourite. He would come visit with sweets and hair ribbons hidden in his pockets and would hand them over to me when he thought my brothers weren't looking. 'This one is a strong woman; only a strong man can handle her,' he used to tell Mama.

After Uncle Ikenna got a job at the ministry, he and I became regulars at Leventis stores, where I'd stare, from behind the glass, at the array of confectionaries on display while he ordered my favourite strawberry ice cream and sugared donuts. On other days, he took me to Kingsway stores to pick out a new dress and would wait patiently as I tried them all on and decided on which made me look the prettiest. And so I fell deeply in love with this man who treated me like a princess and made my little heart flutter like a trapped bird. The feelings grew each day until finally they burst out, refusing to be hidden anymore.

'I'm going to marry Uncle Ikenna when I grow up,' I announced to Mama some months before I turned ten, my heart in my eyes. She stared at me, shocked into silence for a moment, then she laughed and laughed, until I demanded to know what was so funny.

'You, my daughter, you're so funny,' Mama responded, still giggling. 'Don't you know you cannot marry your own uncle?'

The war came that rainy season, expectedly and unexpectedly. Talks of it had flown about for months: disgruntled Easterners feeling sidelined and persecuted by the state of Nigeria, and the killings in the North had raised tensions to an all-time high. I would sit in a corner and listen as Papa, Uncle Ikenna and my brothers analysed what was happening and how our country was no longer for all of us. But even then, few actually believed that Ojukwu would be brave enough to announce the secession of Biafra.

They gathered around the radio, heads bent over its speaker. Even Mama, who was never interested in such things, wrung her wrapper nervously as Ojukwu's sonorous voice came on air, his accent seasoned by many years of study outside the country. *Fellow countrymen and women, you, the people of Eastern Nigeria . . .*

Uncle Ikenna was to marry that year. A nice, quiet girl from our town was to be his bride; he'd met with her family already. Mama didn't inform me until the day of the announcement. I cried and cried until the soon-to-be groom himself was forced to comfort me with ice cream and the reassurance that I would always be his Uju. But everything changed that evening, as those words flowed from the radio. It was in the heavy silence of afterwards, in the way Papa cleared his throat uneasily, in the way Mama stared at the floor, and in the way Uncle Ikenna's eyes lit up – I knew our lives would never be the same.

27

Papa did not play his records on the gramophone that night, and there was no Nat King Cole to tell us to smile when we needed it the most.

Uncle Ikenna disappeared not long afterwards. Mama told us he'd gone to the village to prepare for his wedding but I overheard her and Papa saying he'd gone off to join the Biafran army.

Papa instructed us to pack our things and get ready to leave for the East; Lagos was no longer safe for us. We locked the doors and windows and put a large padlock on our gate, and Mama asked our neighbours to look after our home.

We returned three years later, when it was over. We'd lost it all: the war, Papa's properties and businesses, our friends, family members, my innocence, but at least we had our lives and our home. We'd seen blood, hunger, devastation. I was no longer the girl who believed in people and fairytales; I'd seen with my own eyes what humans were capable of.

We would hear different accounts of Uncle Ikenna, from those who claimed to have been there – the survivors of the massacre. He was last seen alive at Asaba, stranded with a leg injury. His comrades, having escaped by crossing the bridge to the other side of the Niger river, had blown it up to prevent the enemy from following them. The federal soldiers had gone from house to house searching for Biafran sympathisers. They'd shot him on sight. His body was never brought home to be given a proper burial; he became just one of the many unidentified casualties of war. Others claimed he'd survived and disappeared shortly afterwards, crossing the border into Cameroon. Mama held on to the latter; her Ikenna couldn't be dead. But years passed and we heard no word of him.

When the dust of war settled, Mama sent letters far and wide, and travelled across the country every time there was a claim of a sighting of someone fitting Uncle Ikenna's description. Papa checked the official records of the dead, hospitals, mental clinics and refugee camps, but still, Uncle Ikenna remained gone. When Mama began compiling newspaper clippings of those who'd had relatives return to them many years after the war, I worried she'd finally caved and lost her mind.

They say that those who have seen war never recover from it. I watched as we all struggled to return to our normal lives, even though normal had become an aberrant reality we no longer identified with. A light went out of Mama's eyes and new lines appeared on the sides of her face. She would sometimes sit outside all by herself and sing songs in Igbo of war and death or stop in the middle of something she was doing to wipe away tears she didn't know had fallen.

For me, nothing and no one could fill the hole Uncle Ikenna left, and for years I compared every man I met to him – his smile, his laughter, his heart – until I gave up hope, accepting I was searching for the impossible. Well, there was Akin. Akin made me feel heard, understood, and then I met Gozie and he made my heart flutter again.

I wondered if they'd tell future generations the true story of what had happened, the gory details of how countrymen had risen up against countrymen, of how millions were killed and others starved to death, of the millions that were forced to move on with nothing after losing all they'd held dear. Or would they gentrify the tales, and paint them in brief paragraphs of meaningless words in thick textbooks and tell only the colourful stories of the victors, just like they'd done with colonialism: covering up its many atrocities and failing to emphasise the role it played in creating the warped democratic union our country had become.

On a cold night a few weeks after the announcement, I had woken up to make a cup of tea when I heard two familiar voices arguing in the living room. Uncle Ikenna's was the loudest; I'd never heard him speak so indignantly.

'No, brother!' he told Papa. 'We cannot sit and do nothing. War is coming; it's a matter of days. We have to fight for the country we want. Does it look like this one we're in is heading anywhere? Let us tell ourselves the truth!'

I pulled the blanket tighter around me; the cold had suddenly become frigid.

That was the last time I heard Uncle Ikenna's voice.


With time, it became obvious that Gozie was serious about me. We spent after-church hours on Sundays together. The restaurant across the street was our spot where we brazenly stole kisses in the face of the cross and revelled in soft jazz and the redolent lyrics of rhythm and blues. On weekdays, he dropped by my hostel to visit or take me and my friends out for lunch or ice cream, so often that his blue *tokunbo* 1972 Volkswagen Beetle became recognisable by others, and they would run to my room screaming, 'Uju! Uju! Your husband is here.'

Church was no longer a friendly place. I'd done the unthinkable – I'd snatched the most eligible bachelor. Sisters stopped talking to me, and many made malicious remarks. *Where did she come from?*

*When did she start attending this church? She is not even that fine; she must have used other means to trap him. Ashawo!*

The holidays came and I formally introduced Gozie to my parents. He would often visit afterwards; to share a drink with Papa, chat with my brothers or listen to Mama's endless stories. Other times, he would stop over before going to the office, sometimes as early as five in the morning, 'just to see my face.' Mama would shout my name till the whole house was awake and I wondered if she kept vigil, waiting for his car to appear.

'You should be grateful that you have someone like this. Not many men are like that,' she told me one morning. 'He reminds me so much of Ikenna. In fact, that was the first thing I thought the day I met him,' she added in a whisper, her eyes welling up with emotion.

Gozie instructed me to dress up one sunny Saturday morning: he was taking me out. To a special place. It was four months since we'd begun seeing each other and things were moving smoothly, like the locomotive of a well-oiled machine.

The sun chose to come out that day, and just like everything else in Lagos, it showed itself in full force. After several hours of deliberation, I decided on an ankara skirt-and-blouse ensemble with red and blue triangular patterns, then I stretched my thick natural hair with the aid of a hot-comb, packed it into a bun and tied it with a leftover strip of matching ankara material. Next, I patted my face with powder and put on bright-red lipstick.

He drove to the city park and stopped under the shade of a large tree. He'd barely spoken on the drive there and I worried that something was wrong. There was no bouquet of roses, no flowery declarations of undying love like in the movies and books. Just three words: Marry me, Uju. I stared, frozen in disbelief. My thoughts scrambled frantically in all directions: *This was it, everything I'd ever wanted, and it would make Mama scream and cry and dance for joy. Wait. But it was all happening too fast. Was I even ready? It'd just been a few months, after all; I hadn't even graduated yet. What of my ambitions? I loved research; I wanted to travel. Akin and I had even spoken about him recommending me for the university's master's programme. Wouldn't marrying so soon disrupt everything? I'd thought I had more time!*

'Uju!' Gozie called, after several minutes of silence, interrupting my muddled thoughts.

'B—but I haven't finished school yet – my graduation is in a few months' time.'

'I know.'

'And I have national youth service after that.'

'I know.'

'And—'

'Obianuju do you want to get married or not?' he snapped. It was the first time he was anything other than sweet and good-natured. My eyes showed my surprise. Did I really know him?

Gently, he took my hands in his and rubbed them lightly, affectionately. I felt my skin tingle with awareness.

I swallowed nervously. 'I want to, but can't we wait just a little bit? Don't you think it's too soon?'

'What are we waiting for? None of these things you've mentioned are important. We already know we're suited for each other, plus we cannot give sin the opportunity to creep in.'

I had no response to that. He'd chosen the perfect comeback;

I couldn't still say I wanted to wait – that would have been equal to saying I wanted to live in sin, against all I'd been raised to abhor.

'Alright, but please give me a few days to think about it,' I replied nervously.

'Okay, fine.' That was obviously not the response he'd expected.


Gozie didn't come in to see Mama and Papa that evening; he zoomed off without a word as soon as I stepped out of the passenger seat.

Mama, hawkish as ever, made the observation immediately as I walked in.

'Uju, where is Gozie?' she asked, her eyes turning into slits.

'He has gone home,' I responded, not meeting her eyes.

'Why? What happened? What did you do?'

'Nothing happened,' I replied quickly. Too quickly. I realised my mistake immediately.

Mama folded her arms across her chest. 'Obianuju! You better stop lying to me. What happened? Did you argue with him?'

Still, I said nothing, altering my expression to give nothing away.

I watched Mama as the lines of her face transformed with each emotion, from confusion to anger to disbelief and finally, panic. 'This girl has finally done it. She has chased away the only man that will marry her,' she shouted, throwing her hands on her head and looking to the ceiling for divine intervention. She turned to me with anguish. 'But you promised me *ehn*! You promised your mother that you would behave, that you wouldn't argue or insult him or talk too much. Oh God! My enemies must be laughing.'

'*Nna-anyi! Nna-anyi!*' she shouted in the direction of the rooms, calling for my father. Mama only called Papa when she felt she could no longer handle me, and her tone always seemed to say, 'See what your beloved daughter is doing.'

It was my turn to panic. I moved to block her path. 'Mama, there's no need to call Papa. Nothing important happened.'

'You're still lying? Move out of my way now.'

'I'll tell you. Please don't look for him,' I pleaded.

'He asked me to marry him,' I mumbled reluctantly a few seconds later, when we were seated.

'He what?'

'I said he asked me to marry him,' I repeated, louder this time.

'Marry him?' she asked excitedly, her face brightening. '*Hei!* My God has done it. My enemies have been put to shame!' she shouted then broke into song and dance, moving her waist vigorously, in beat to imaginary instruments. *Mmama dirigi, Chineke-e, Mmama dirigi-o. Onye oma.*

I stared at her dejectedly; there was no going back now. My fate had been sealed.

She stopped, suddenly. 'Uju, why aren't you singing and dancing? This is good news! Or didn't you say yes? Please tell me you told him yes,' she said, panic creeping back into her voice.

'I told him I'll think about it,' I confessed, and waited for hell to break loose.

She stared at me for a while, eyes dilated like I had suddenly taken leave of my senses, then she exploded.

'Are you mad?! What is there to think about?!' she screamed at the top of her lungs.

34

'I have to think about it; it's an important decision. I'm just twenty-one,' I rushed to explain.

'*I'm just twenty-one*,' she mimicked. 'I married your father at sixteen!'

'Mama that was then, this is the seventies. I haven't finished school yet.'

'And so? Are you the first? Don't you have married classmates?'

'Mama, I'm not them. Besides, Dr. Akintunde told me my grades are currently one of the best in the department, and that he plans to recommend me to the head for a direct admission into the master's programme. He thinks I shou—'

'*Kpuchie gi onu ebe-ahu!*' Mama yelled, switching to Igbo immediately, the veins on her neck standing. Mama always switched to Igbo when she was upset. She expressed herself better in it, her words flowing easier and faster as if her tongue had been loosened from the bondage of a tightrope.

'Will your professor marry you?' She crossed her arms across her chest. 'It is my fault. I knew I let you spend too much time with your brothers; now you're thinking like a man.'

'But Mama I'm not saying I won't marry him. I just want to wait a while. I'm not ready. That's all.'

'What is there to be ready for? Have I not brought you up well? Have I failed as a mother?' she asked, obviously perplexed by the words coming out of my mouth. 'Uju, a woman should marry when the man is ready. And when a man is ready, he is ready.'

I thought of another angle. 'But can't we wait for the both of us to have more money? I should at least get a job first.'

'Did he say he cannot take care of you? Do you think your father and I had plenty of money when we started out? Your place is to help him build his wealth for both of you,' she said, her tone brooking no argument.

I sighed dolefully, and wondered what Akin would say. He always knew what to say. 'He didn't even propose in a romantic way,' I grumbled under my breath. 'No flowers or chocolate, nothing. Just asked me to marry him like that.'

Mama heard. 'Roma-what?' She burst into raucous laughter. 'My daughter, forget all those things. At least he asked you; your father didn't even talk to me – he went straight to my people. That is even our tradition. I don't know where you are getting these *oyinbo* ideas from, but *ekwensu bu onye asi*. My enemies are trying but they will not succeed,' she said with a smile, her good humour back in place. 'Listen to me. Tomorrow you will go and meet Chigozie and accept his offer. Do you hear me? And better pray he hasn't changed his mind or you won't have a home to come back to. I cannot share the same roof as such a foolish daughter. God forbid.'

## 4.

### *Are we cartons of milk? Ehn Ada?*

'I'll marry you,' I told Gozie after church service the next day. We stood at the front of the building, in the intimidating shadow of the cross. People milled around us noisily – calling to friends, gossiping, discussing the sermon, pretending to ignore us. I wondered if he'd heard me; my voice had been barely above a whisper. A smile played at the side of his lips and began to light up his face, and I knew he had.

'I'm sorry for not saying yes that day,' I added, then stared pointedly at my toes.

He held my hands in a firm grip and nudged my chin upwards. His smile widened as I raised my head, and I questioned what madness had caused me to hesitate. 'It's okay,' he said. 'You're young; it's normal to be nervous. Don't worry – everything will be okay. Getting married won't change anything; we'll just be living together. I won't stop you from doing anything you want.'

'Anything?' I asked, searching his face.

'Yes – school, work, whatever. Anything,' he reassured me, and massaged my hands soothingly.

Our eyes met and held. The man I saw wasn't Gozie, but the one who would never lie to me, the one I still missed dearly.

By the end of the week, news of our engagement had spread widely, and Gozie beamed as people rushed to offer congratulations; even the church ladies who'd had not so nice things to say behind my back offered their well wishes, although grudgingly with tight smiles pasted onto their faces as though they suffered from severe cases of constipation.


Sally Agboga was a different breed from the rest of us – she lived fully and committedly on her own terms. She was heavy-handed with her powder and dark-brown eyebrow pencil, her eyelids always shone with bright eyeshadow, making them appear like moving disco balls, and her plump lips were forever coated in a deep wine colour. She wore whatever and whenever, trousers so tight you could make out the contour of her buttocks, sundresses that rode up her thighs, and big hair that blocked the sun.

The first day I sighted her outside the hall, just before class in our first year of university, I stood transfixed, my eyes on her bare thighs underneath the dress she wore and the cigarette she casually puffed on. Mama would have fainted at the sight.

'What is it? Never seen a girl like me before?' Sally asked in a low sultry voice then crushed the stick of cigarette she'd been puffing under the large block heel of her knee-high boot, a sardonic smile curving the side of her cheeks. 'Going for the class?' she asked, gesturing towards the classroom with her head. I nodded mutely. She laughed, tapping me lightly on the shoulder and pushing me towards the door. 'The lecturer will soon be here. You should go in or you won't get a good seat; the class is already very full. What's your name?'

'U—Uju.'

She smiled brightly, exposing small yellowish teeth. 'I'm Salome, but my friends call me Sally. You can't be staring at people like that; this is university, you will get tired of staring,' she said just before we walked into the classroom. She was right.

We spoke regularly after that, and she would often invite me to join her at a bar where a live band played highlife music on Friday evenings and the resident cook served the best goat-meat pepper soup and palm wine in Lagos.

The week after I became engaged to Gozie, Sally smiled when she saw me walking down the corridor, on my way to Akin's office.

'Uju baby! You were going to get married without telling me personally? I had to hear from others by myself. You no try o! Anyways, congratulations,' Sally said good-naturedly.

'It's not like that, my dear, I've just been so busy preparing for our final exams, I haven't had time to tell all my friends. Besides, who needs a town crier when one has Chinelo and Adaugo.' We both burst into laughter.

'So, you're really getting married? Just like that?' she demanded with her hands on her ample hips once our mirth had died down.

'Like what?' I asked, confused.

'Just like that! Straight out of school. You should enjoy your single life a little, you know. Flex, go out, meet people. You know, your Gozie is not the only man alive, even if he looks like those drawings of Greek gods.' She rolled her eyes dramatically and I laughed.

'I'm serious. You should meet other people and be sure if it's him you want first. You're only twenty-one.'

'Or,' she lowered a voice to a whisper and leaned closer so no one else could hear, 'are you pregnant?'

The laughter burst out again. 'Sally,' I said in between breaths, 'please, I'm not pregnant o.'

She grinned slyly. 'Okay o, if you say so. Just make sure you remember to invite me to eat rice at the wedding, if you decide to go ahead with it.'

'She asked if I was pregnant,' I recounted to Chinelo and Adaugo that evening, cackling.

They didn't find it funny; they'd never understood my friendship with Sally. 'That Sally *sef*, she too talk! What is her business if you decide to marry today or tomorrow? Will she give you a husband if you lose this one?' Chinelo said.

Ada nodded in agreement. 'You better ignore her Uju. Men don't marry women like her, and she knows, so she's trying to spoil your own. You better grab this one you've seen now before it's too late and you expire on the shelf like she will.'

I giggled. 'Expire? Are we cartons of milk? *Ehn* Ada?'


It had taken me thirty minutes to muster the courage to knock on Akin's door that day. Thirty minutes of pacing, panicking and handwringing. Eventually, I folded my sweaty palms and knocked ever so lightly, hoping he wouldn't hear or that he was absent from work that day.

'Come in,' he responded, his deep voice carrying through the door, and my chest grew heavy.

I turned the door handle slowly, scolding myself. There was nothing to be nervous about; we were friends. Just friends.

His eyes warmed as I walked in. 'Like liquid caramel,' a classmate had observed once. And I realised he hadn't heard the news. He never listened to gossip, this one; I was the one who brought him all the news. Like when a lecturer whose office was just down the hall from his was escorted from the building for throwing punches at a student and I'd walked in to find Akin peacefully reading.

'Didn't you at least hear the noise?' I'd asked, puzzled.

He'd shrugged casually and grinned at his book. 'I was busy.'

'You're too carefree,' I said.

'That's why I enjoy life.'

'Hi,' I said with a shaky smile, shutting the door carefully behind me.

'Hey! Your friend Sally just left my office,' he said. 'You know I've always liked that girl. She's so – for lack of a better word – cool.'

My stomach cramped with unexpected jealousy. When did he have the time to notice Sally? And why was he talking like everything was normal?

Akin didn't seem to think anything strange of my behaviour. 'She says the funniest things and is so blunt,' he continued with a soft laugh.

My mouth tasted grainy, like I'd chewed on sand, and I felt the sudden urge to puncture the bubble of normalcy he resided in. Why was he so happy when my chest felt like it was on fire?

'Smallie, is everything okay?' Akin asked, grinding my thoughts to a halt. His brows were furrowed in concern.

No, I wasn't going to pretend. 'I'm getting married!'

'What?'

'I'm getting married,' I repeated, watching his face carefully.

It was flat and devoid of emotion; only his dilated pupils and the sparse gap between his lips gave him away. I'd well and truly shocked him.

I stared at his lips, a dust of pink at their centre. I'd felt them once, during that night in my third year we never spoke about, as though it never happened. Sally had invited me for a fun night of pepper soup, palm wine and sweet highlife music. Akin was restless that day, worried about a paper he was writing for an important journal, and I pestered him to join us to take his mind off it.

Sally never showed up – she'd been stuck in a campus meeting, an explanation I never understood. We'd barely noticed amidst several jugs of palm wine, bowls of pepper soup, drunken stories and the relentless crooning of the bar band's lead singer. When the piano banged the intro chords to Nelly Uchendu's 'Love Nwantinti', Akin pulled the both of us to our feet for an inebriated swing and sway. He was different that night; uninhibited, free.

Thoroughly crocked by the end of the night, we hailed a taxi and stumbled into its backseat before it zoomed off for the campus. A cool breeze slapped our faces through the rolled-down windows and Marvin Gaye's voice came over the radio. Akin turned to me and sang along – *I've been really tryin', baby, tryin' to hold back this feeling for so long*. I giggled and joined in. Just before the chorus started, he reached across the seat, pulled me to him and crushed his lips on mine. I was aware in that moment that something was happening, something that neither of us could control – a shifting in the orbit

– but I was distracted by our lips moving, gliding over each other and Marvin Gaye's singing – *Let's get it onnn*.

'Why?' Akin asked.

'What do you mean why?'

'Why the hurry to marry?' he asked.

We'd joked once before about getting married to each other if we both failed to find a partner.

'I can't marry someone that wouldn't even give me exam questions,' I'd retorted.

'Well, it would be years from now so you would have forgiven me by then,' he said and winked slyly.

'Years from now? You want me to grow old waiting for you? My mother exists, you know.'

'It has to be years or the department would have my head. Thank God you don't always get As, or how do I prove I'm not helping you?'

I frowned. 'What do you mean? I get As!'

'Not enough in my opinion; go and read!' he said, and my response was a slap on the shoulder with a book. We giggled.

'I mean, I think I love him, my parents are in agreement, what else is there to wait for?' I told Akin, but my voice didn't sound convincing even to my own ears.

'Do you even know him?'

'I know *you* – are *we* getting married?' I countered before I could stop the words.

I didn't have to second guess the emotion in his eyes this time – I recognised it: pain. 'Is this what you want right now or is it what your mother wants?' He'd sidestepped my question.

'It's what I want,' I said with finality and jumped to my feet before I could do something embarrassing like burst into tears.

His voice called to my back as I turned to leave. 'Obianuju?'

'Yes?' I answered, waiting in the silence for him to say something, anything.

'Take care.'

The days afterwards passed in a blur as many traditions were observed. Gozie formally paid a visit to my parents' home with his uncle for the *ikuaka*, or 'door knocking', to inform them of his intent to marry me, bearing palm wine and kola nuts. He called on us again weeks later, accompanied by more relatives, this time for my bride-price settlement. Uncles and elders from Papa's village were present as witnesses.

'Gozie, my son. I hope you are prepared to pay. This is my only daughter. And she is very smart, educated and beautiful. Don't expect me to give her to you cheaply,' Papa jested as they mock-haggled over the bride price. It brought to mind a story Mama had once told of a village not far from hers where the women staged a protest against the exorbitant bride price set by the village elders, complaining that they were getting old because the men could not afford to pay.

A list of requirements was presented to Gozie and his family and a date was set for the *igba nkwu*; the church wedding would be many weeks later in the city. Relatives far and wide were informed and preparations went into full gear.

The morning of the *igba nkwu*, I was awakened by the acrid smell of firewood burning, the *tap tap* of pestles and a cacophony of disembodied voices screaming in Igbo at the back of my father's house in the village.

*'Bring the tomatoes!'*

*'Where did you put the utazi?'*

*'Is Uju still sleeping?'*

Mama burst into the room as I tried to gather my wits; she smelled of sweat and firewood. 'Obianuju! Get up! There is a lot to do. You can't be lying around in bed on your wedding day. Your friends are already up, and the women have started cooking.'

Hours later, Gozie's family arrived at our large family compound, already packed with canopies and people, bearing drinks and gifts: tubers of yam, kegs of palm oil, kola nuts, gallons of palm wine, bags of rice, crates of drinks, bundles of wrappers, goats, jewellery and more. Members of my family went out to greet and welcome them. Minutes later, Mama informed me it was time.

Dressed in bright-orange Hollandis wrappers, a gold blouse and matching orange *ichafu* that Mama had painstakingly tied for me, and large red coral beads, I danced out to the sound of drums, the whistle of the *oja* flute, the bass of the *udu* and the rattles of the *ichaka* with my cousins and friends. Our relatives and well-wishers stood up to spray banknotes on us as we moved.

Next, Gozie and his family presented their gifts to the elders for inspection. Where they found fault, Gozie was asked to compensate with money. The gifts were accepted and kola nuts were broken and shared.

Moments later, I danced out again, in a change of outfit, with my group in tow, this time to kneel for my parents' prayers and blessing. Afterwards, Papa poured palm wine into a wooden cup and handed it to me to go find my husband, who'd hidden himself in the crowd.

'Fine girl, I'm the one you're looking for,' one of the guests called as I walked through them to find Gozie.

'Don't mind him, bring that cup here, I'm the one,' another joked.

I found Gozie at the back of the crowd – it was almost impossible to miss his distinctive features and the shining dark-purple *isiagu* with intricate gold patterns he had on. But the face in front of me wasn't his. Uncle Ikenna looked back with an affectionate smile. His eyes bore the same twinkle of mischievousness of youth, like we shared a secret no one else knew; a replica of the one he'd given me every time he'd said, 'My strong girl. My Obianuju.'

My feet iced over, my hands began to vibrate and droplets of palm wine splattered across my wrist.

'Obianuju!' Mama's voice called from somewhere, bringing me back.

I blinked and Uncle Ikenna was gone. I turned to frantically search for his face in the crowd but none resembled his.

I exhaled to calm myself and plastered on a smile as I danced in Gozie's direction, until I finally stood in front of him. I knelt and offered him the cup. The crowd went wild with applause as he sipped from it and then pulled me to my feet to escort me to the elders for their blessing.

The feasting began as we danced together, our families and guests moving vigorously about – Mama being the most joyous of them all – and pausing every few minutes to spray banknotes, which stuck to the sweat on our foreheads.

\*

At my graduation ceremony a few days later, we stood to take pictures. Mama pulled me to stand beside Gozie, while she and Papa stood on either side of us. Gozie's arm stretched across my shoulder to pull me close, his hold on my arm unyielding, possessive. As the light of the photographer's camera flashed, Mama's smile was the widest. I'd made her proud; I hadn't returned from school empty-handed.

# 5.

## *You're going to be a woman tomorrow*

I was four and a half when Ebuka from down the street returned home for a visit with his girlfriend – his *oyinbo* girlfriend. He'd been away in America for years, studying to become a doctor. When his mother received the letter informing of his impending arrival, she'd gone around the neighbourhood with it tucked in the corner of her wrapper, ready to be pulled out at the slightest provocation to remind all and sundry that she had a son training to be a *dokita* in *obodo oyinbo,* and was thus of a higher social status than they were.

His girlfriend's name was Sarah. She was slender and wasp-waisted with a freckled nose and waist-length hair the colour of a burned-orange sunset, making her head appear as though it was on fire. Every day, she and Ebuka would walk down the street hand in hand as he pointed at places. Then one afternoon, she stepped out on her own wearing fitted denim shorts that stopped mid-thigh. Older children from the area followed her around town, calling her *ashawo* and other vile names and throwing stones at her back until someone rushed to find Ebuka. He came just in time to save his weeping girlfriend from her assailants.

Later that day, I narrated what had happened to Mama and questioned why the children had behaved that way.

'It's against our culture to go about half-naked,' she replied, not taking her eyes from the *ugu* leaves she was chopping.

'But Ebuka wore shorts yesterday. I saw him,' I countered naively.

'Ebuka is a man; a woman cannot go around dressed like that.' Years later I would look at ancient pictures of our people in skins and cloth that barely covered their crotches and with beads that left their breasts exposed, and wonder what culture Mama had spoken of. That day, however, I awoke to the consciousness of womanhood.

Our games were different. The boys played with make-believe guns and pretended to be superheroes; we played mothers to dolls, dressing and feeding them, subconsciously preparing for what was to be our future. We learned to skip rope and took turns playing *When Will You Marry*, purposely tripping when we heard 'doctor' and falling down in fits of laughter when others missed their steps at 'carpenter' or 'plumber'.

Our rules and upbringing were not the same. My brothers were given a freedom of life that I could only dream of, and every time I questioned it, I received the same response: you're a woman. And for that I felt resentment – towards them and the universe – that I'd been born a woman.

My brothers could barely boil an egg, whereas I started joining Mama in the kitchen the moment I turned eight, learning to cook at her feet. By the time I was ten, I could make a good pot of soup without any help. Once I was tall enough, Mama started to send me to the market for food-stuff and taught me how to bargain for the best price.

Every complaint Mama and Papa had about my behaviour and actions was linked to the imaginary husband and children I would one day have to impress.

Whenever I complained too much, I was warned that I was in grave danger of becoming a nagging wife; the one the scriptures had described as worse than a leaking roof.

When my cooking didn't turn out as intended, it was, 'Uju, is this the poison you will serve your husband and children when you marry?'

And God forbid that my skirt was deemed too short. Papa was always the first to ask, 'Uju, why are you dressed like a prostitute? Which decent young man will see you now and want to marry?'

My brothers were allowed to be home by midnight, while I pled my way to a strict 6 p.m. curfew because decent young women 'do not jump around town like antelopes'. And on Friday evenings, when our neighbours blocked the street and threw parties that lasted till the early hours, my brothers joined in the fun while I watched from the prison of our living room window.

No one ever asked Ikechukwu if he planned to be a wife-beater when he pummelled me for touching his precious ludo game. Or asked Ugochukwu which decent woman would marry him whenever he ate his food open-mouthed like a goat chewing cassava. Neither did they question Kelechi's morality when he started chasing everything in a skirt. Mama only quarrelled with him over his escapades when he began dating Sikira, our Yoruba neighbour Mama Sikira's daughter. Mama threatened to kill herself if he dared to contemplate marriage to her, and Kelechi broke up with her the following week. Mama Sikira found out, and she and Mama wouldn't speak to each other for days. For the next two weeks, visitors to our home had to make do with bottles of cold water because Mama Sikira, the only soft-drinks seller on our street, would not sell to us.

'In my next life, I will ask God to send me back as a man, let me enjoy life small,' I grumbled to my brother one day as I angrily pulled *ugu* leaves from their stalks for dinner.

Kelechi laughed and stretched his legs further across the length of the sofa, his arms folded behind his head as he concentrated on a football match on the television. 'Do you think it's easy to be a man? Don't be deceived; nothing in this world is easy.'

I wouldn't know it till I stepped outside in April '79, but I'd chosen one of the worst days possible for my wedding. It was hot, the kind of hot that made you want to tear off your clothes and jump in a cold stream, and the roads were blocked. My wedding dress, floor-length with a silk skirt, high neckline with pearl beadings and a long satin veil, clung to my skin. Mama's hairdresser had curled my hair with a hot comb and piled it up in a regal style held in place by tiny pearl pins. I worried that all her hard work would collapse under the intense humidity.

After two hours of traffic, I stood outside the church with clammy palms and a heartbeat as fast as the rhythm of the new yam festival drums. I looked around for an escape route. The choir started singing before I could actualise my thoughts.

'Obianuju, it's time,' Papa announced, and held out his arm.

My bridesmaids went first, dressed in long-sleeved pink chiffon gowns with matching wide-brimmed hats, and clutching mini-bouquets of flowers. Then the marriage march began and I hooked my arm in Papa's as he walked me down the aisle. As though sensing my trepidation, Papa rubbed my arm reassuringly, but I refused to look at him. I was afraid that if I did, I would break down.

At the other end of the aisle, Gozie stood beside the head pastor of our church, looking breathtaking in a fitted black suit, white shirt and black bow tie. He'd cut his hair to an attractive low Afro, with faded edges and a side-part. I felt my doubts melt in a puddle.

We passed by Mama, shining in her matching gold wrapper, *ichafu* and coral beads. Her *ichafu* was tied differently; she'd gone to Mama Sikira for assistance. Everyone in our neighbourhood knew Mama Sikira's head-ties were special. She wove them until the hands of the fabric came up in beautiful styles like wings. Mama flashed me a dazzling smile. I thought of her words to me the night before, when she'd pulled me into a fierce embrace and whispered excitedly, 'My Obianuju, you're going to be a woman tomorrow.'

'Yes, Mama. Tomorrow,' I replied with a smile, trying to match her enthusiasm.

Her eyes grew misty, and she seemed to wander into another realm. 'Your Uncle Ikenna would be so proud of you. He always said that whoever married you had to be special. You know that's one of the reasons I've always liked Chigozie. He reminds me so much of him, always happy and smiling, so kind and caring. Or don't you think so?'

I wasn't sure if she expected me to respond as she didn't look at me as she asked, but I answered anyway. 'Yes, Mama. I think so too.'

She continued to stare into the air, lost in her memories. 'You were so in love with him, you know.' She laughed but it was not a happy one and her voice broke at the end, like she was about to cry. 'Then you found out he was going to get married and you cried and cried like a baby. I was so worried during the war. But you stopped talking about him on your own.'

I couldn't tell Mama that I'd stopped speaking about him because the mention of his name made her cry. That I'd never been able to express how his disappearance had affected me for fear of reopening festering wounds.

Mama wiped her eyes with the end of her wrapper. 'Gozie will take good care of you. You're in good hands.'

I looked at Mama again as I walked down the aisle, my hand gripping Papa's arm tightly with all the uncertainty I felt. Yes, I was doing the right thing.

'We're gathered here today for the joining together in holy matrimony of Chigozie Azubuike and Obianuju Nwaike,' the pastor declared when Gozie and I finally stood before him, his voice resonating throughout the large church. He would have made a very good town crier in the days of old.

He launched into a sermon on the sanctity of marriage. 'For this cause a man shall leave his father and his mother and cleave to his wife . . .' Mama nodded slowly in agreement, moving the colourful flower-patterned fan in her hand up and down.

'If anyone can show just cause why these two should not lawfully be joined together in holy matrimony, let them speak now or forever hold their peace,' the pastor announced.

Gozie held my hand in a death grip and turned his head to the crowd, his hard stare almost daring anyone to say something. From the corner of my eye, I observed Mama looking around apprehensively, like was she expecting her enemies to make an appearance and ruin the happiest day of her life.

'I now pronounce you man and wife,' the pastor declared at last and the congregation broke into deafening applause.

The celebration would continue until the late hours of the day at the reception, in the cavernous rental hall Papa had booked for the occasion, in the benevolent presence of spicy jollof rice, hot pounded yam and *ofe nsala*, chilled bottles of cola and the wonderful tunes of Oliver De Coque. People would come forward to offer their congratulations and present their gifts, Ada and Chinelo would share an exaggerated version of our love story to the enjoyment of the crowd, and Gozie's best man would raise a toast in our honour. Papa would give the closing remarks: 'Our people say, "*Onye jee obodo a n'ebe nti, o bere nke ya tinye*," meaning, "If one goes to a land where they cut off ears, he should cut off his own and contribute them." Obianuju, as you've married, you now belong to another family; whatever they're doing there, you must do. There is no going back.'

'Obianuju, my daughter,' Mama said on the evening of my wedding day, pulling me into another hug, the lace of her blouse making crinkling sounds. Her eyes shone with unbridled joy.

We were at Papa's house waiting for the car to take Gozie and me to our new home. I could hear the *iya alase* in the kitchen interrogating her helpers about the cooler filled with fried pieces of meat she'd left in the house that morning.

'Uju, let's go to your room and talk a bit,' Mama said and headed in that direction. I got up to follow her.

'I hope you know you are a woman now,' she said once we were seated.

I nodded dutifully.

The first time I'd heard those words, I was fifteen and I'd just run to Mama in panic, clutching my bloodied underwear. Mama smiled, then she sat me down and recited those exact words to me, handed me a pack of thick sanitary pads and told me not to let any boy touch me 'funny' or I could get pregnant. I nodded, not fully understanding what she meant, but hoping that when 'funny' came around, I would recognise it. That was the closest Mama would ever get to discussing sex. In fact, she never used the word; she only referred to it. It always sounded like a taboo, a forbidden fruit – eating from which meant there would be no turning back.

Womanhood was something to be cherished, a sacred cult I'd joined. I learned to keep a calendar, counting and monitoring the dates with anxiety, and to hide packets of pads in my school bag in case the visitor came unplanned. And when the cramps came, I would swallow painkillers and go about in a state of constant discomfort but pretending everything was alright – writing my tests and speaking up in class – even though it felt like someone had my uterus in a punishing grip and would not let go. In many ways, I felt betrayed by my body, this shell I'd taken care of so diligently all these years, only for it to turn around and treat me so badly. But when I lay alone in my bed, curled up in discomfort, Mama would remind me, as she handed me paracetamol tablets, that I had to be strong as I was yet to face pains of the bigger demon that was childbirth.

'You have to be a good wife to Gozie,' Mama continued. 'Remember all that I have taught you.'

'Yes, Mama.'

She cleared her throat and shifted awkwardly. 'Also, from this night, you now have to start thinking about children; hopefully in nine months' time, you will have your first child. We don't want your husband's relatives to start saying that you're barren and we married a man for their son.'

Mama's words rang in my ears that night as I nervously waited for Gozie in our bedroom, wishing I knew more about what was to come. What little knowledge I had, I'd learned from old romance novels and biology classes on reproduction.

I should have been better prepared for the pain, the vulnerability. For the joining, the grunting and groaning as he moved in and out of me. And the loneliness after it was over, when he quickly turned the other way and snored his way to slumber while I lay awake unfulfilled, staring into the plaster of the ceiling and wondering if I'd done it right. I felt an errant tear slip down the side my face and wiped at it hastily.

I would not cry. I was a woman now. I thought of another time instead, in the back seat of a taxi, Marvin Gaye blaring out the windows as my body came alive.

## 6.

### *If you don't want him, find a way to chase him away yourself*

Mama had been waiting, eyeing my stomach every time I visited. And each time, her expectant smile would slowly dissolve into a grim line. 'Uju, what is going on? Don't you and Gozie plan to have children?' she asked finally. I was surprised she'd taken so long to bring it up. 'Look, your father and I want to see our grandchildren before we die,' she continued.

'Mama, please don't say such things. You and Papa are not dying any time soon,' I replied calmly.

'Thank you and amen. But we still want to see our grandchildren. You've both been married for a while now. Please, what is happening?'

'Mama, we've been married for only about a year, and we're both still young,' I said.

'Tah! "*We are still young. We are still young*",' she said, mimicking my voice. 'That is how the both of you will say until you're too old to have children. Don't you know that thirty is not far away for you? See, tell him to stop travelling so often, so the both of you can focus on having children.' She was referring to Gozie's new position as a travelling reporter.

'But Mama, we need the money. They pay him more when he travels to places no one wants to go to. He's a journalist; that's his job.'

'*"Travels to places no one wants to go."* And you're letting that happen? *Hei* God!' she exclaimed and clapped her hands. 'Don't you know that if he dies now you're in trouble? *Ehn?* You have no children, talk less of a male child to carry on the family name. Adaugo just got married and I won't be surprised if she's pregnant before the year end. How do you even know Gozie's people aren't planning to get him a second wife? Obianuju, think! Think!' She pointed a finger to her head.

We prepared for Adaugo's wedding to Uzondu in early '80. Like me, Ada was the first daughter after a string of sons, and Mama always said Ada's mother must have done something great for her people in her previous life; it was the only reason God would send her such an offspring – a daughter who was beautiful in every sense of the word, outside and within.

Ada's perfection had never been a question, with her flawless skin, sculpted, oval-shaped face, light-brown eyes and teeth like coconut meat. She was tall but not too tall – just the right height for a woman; slim but with just enough curves in the right places. To crown it all, Ada was intelligent – 'beauty with brains', they called her, as though the two were mutually exclusive – but never spoke in a way that was intimidating to her listeners. She acknowledged her duties and never complained. The perfect daughter. And she knew it. By the time we got to university, the other girls would say, 'Ada tell us your secret; we want to be like you,' and Ada would smile with the fake modesty of one who knew she'd been given naturally what others desired.

Adaugo's romance with Uzondu started in our second year at the university. The two of us and Chinelo were on our way back from class when a flaming red '76 Olds Omega pulled up beside us and a fair-skinned man with striking amber eyes poked his head out the window.

'Hello,' he said to Ada in particular, his voice honeyed.

'Hi,' the three of us chorused.

'My name is Uzondu,' he said, a smile plastered on his face.

We stared blankly. We were raised never to speak to strangers, especially men. Human sacrifices were common for money-making rituals.

'Do you know the way to Moremi Hall? I am on my way to see my sister and I'm not sure I'm headed in the right direction,' he said, again looking only at Ada.

'It's just over there. You're going in the right direction,' I responded, not giving Ada the chance to reply, pointing at a building straight ahead.

He sent me an irritated glance, as if to say, 'Who asked you?' and turned back to Ada. 'Since it seems we're headed in the same direction, why don't I drop you off?'

'No, thank you,' Ada replied immediately.

'Alright, do you mind if I escort you back then? You know there are many dangerous people around,' he insisted. 'You don't have to enter the car; I'll just drive beside you.'

Ada shrugged her shoulders nonchalantly and started walking, her hips swaying smoothly. Chinelo and I followed behind, casting wary glances at our escort.

Accurately guessing that Chinelo was the most amiable of the three of us, Uzondu turned to her and tried to make light conversation.

'So, I've told you my name and even a little about myself, but you've not told me anything. That's not fair,' he said, noticing his charms were taking effect.

Chinelo didn't waste any time. 'Oh! Sorry about that. I'm Chinelo, that is Uju, and this is Ada,' she obliged, already convinced that he was harmless. I was tempted to slap her, like her mother would most likely have done that very second. She was so easy to sway.

Uzondu smiled triumphantly. Unsurprisingly, a few days later, a female student with familiar striking brown eyes was at our room to inform us that her elder brother was outside the hostel waiting to see us. Ada and I turned to stare pointedly at Chinelo.

We would forgive Chinelo as we came to realise that Uzondu was not the type of man that one easily said no to, or that took no for an answer. He visited regularly, each time bearing gifts: ice cream, food, books, jewellery, anything he thought would win us over. It wasn't long before Chinelo and I would turn on Ada.

'See, Ada, you're being too stubborn. Your *shakara* is just too much. This guy really likes you, plus he's a nice guy. What is the problem, exactly?' I confronted Ada in our hostel room, in a planned intervention.

Chinelo nodded. 'My sister! He is fine, funny, friendly and he has money. Or didn't you see his car? You're the one always talking about marrying someone who can afford you. *Biko*, madam, what else are you looking for?'

Ada rolled her eyes petulantly and turned her attention to her nails. 'Did I say I didn't like him?' she grumbled.

Chinelo was not having it. 'When he is around, you suddenly become silent like a woman mourning her husband. When he cracks a joke, you keep a strong face.'

'What is the problem? Tell us so we can understand,' she added, convinced Ada had a reason we weren't privy to.

'Nothing is the problem,' Ada said, refusing to take her eyes off her nails.

I lost my patience. 'See, don't allow me get angry this hot afternoon. Better open your mouth and talk because I've already collected enough gifts to be arrested by the police as an accomplice in this matter. So, if you know what is good for you, you better talk.' The police were always looking for a reason to detain people in order to extort bail money; the other day the newspapers had carried a bizarre story of how a man's goat had been arrested for eating a neighbour's yam.

Ada laughed and looked up at us with a relaxed smile. 'It's nothing,' she said, seeing the overt scepticism on our faces. 'I'm serious; there is nothing wrong. I just don't want it to be too easy for him. Mama always says that you must make a man work for it.'

'Ada, it is called hard to get, not impossible to get. You should only act like this if you don't like him, and we will support you one hundred per cent in that instance, help you chase him away, even,' Chinelo said.

'If you like him, this behaviour doesn't make sense o. So, you better wake up before I inform Mama, who will definitely inform your mother that you're about to chase away a very good potential husband,' I threatened.

Ada's eyes popped out on hearing her mother mentioned. 'Wait, wait. It has not gotten to that level now. Why must the both of you be so wicked? Okay, I will be nicer to him. Are you happy now?' she acquiesced.

Chinelo grinned. 'Better, or if you don't want him, find a way to chase him away yourself because we don't have the energy for such. I can't be refusing free *suya* because of you.'

Ada eyed her. 'It is enough. I already said I have heard you,' she snapped.

Uzondu's visits after that required less and less input from me and Chinelo, although that didn't stop our regular supply of gifts; our people say that a man must appease the gods to get his heart's desires, and Uzondu knew we were the gods in this matter.

When it was time for Ada's traditional wedding, Gozie accompanied me on the long journey to her father's village. He sang when we sang and danced when we danced, even though I knew he'd rather be somewhere else. We'd settled into life as newlyweds, like the first weeks of wearing brand-new shoes – tight pinches and painful chafing, until eventually they took on the perfect form of the feet of their owner.

Living together had a way of exposing one's worst habits and I would find out that my reincarnation of the gods was no different from my father and brothers. He would return from work and throw his belongings about like toys in a playpen. And after eating his meals, he would recline ever so casually in his seat, rub his filled belly and pick at his teeth with a toothpick, then say, 'Thank you, my wife,' as I cleared the dirty plates in front of him – something he'd never done in our dating days.

During the weekends, he and his friends gathered around the television watching football and screaming at the players. I would busy myself serving drinks and fried peppered snails, and picking up the empty bottles when they were done.

He hated to be argued with, and it became increasingly difficult to hold my tongue as the days went by. But Mama said to never criticise a husband's faults as it may have been those little imperfections that stopped him from getting a better wife.

The first time he raised his voice, I stared unblinkingly at him, stiff with shock as the sound reverberated in my ears. I'd forgotten his food on the stove and fallen asleep on the living room sofa, exhausted from a day at the market, only to be awoken by the acrid stench of scorched beans and the screech of Gozie's voice. 'Are you mad? Do you want to burn down the building?' I wondered if the neighbours could hear us and equally if they wondered what sort of newlywed couple we were, and worried I would end up like those women Mama spoke of, whose husbands returned them to their parents' homes after just a few weeks of living together because their mothers had failed to raise them properly.

I'd also started my compulsory one-year youth service, teaching at a local primary school. In '73, the military government had introduced the scheme to purportedly promote peace and unity. The government had left but the initiative had remained, and every graduate was to spend a year post-university serving the country in whatever capacity assigned – usually in a posting far enough from home to encourage a better understanding of other cultures. Mama made sure, through Uncle Uzoma, her distant relative that worked in the Corps, that I was posted to Lagos.

And Gozie and I learned to press out the kinks in our relationship, like the rumples in an unironed shirt.

At the white wedding weeks later in Lagos, Gozie sat beside me, massaging my fingers, kissing my palm, reminding me of ours, as Ada glided down the aisle – her beauty and joy radiating for all to see – and Uzondu looked on like a man who'd just won the lottery.


With Ada's marriage, Chinelo's singlehood was cast into a harsh spotlight, the emptiness of her ring finger glaring beside the perfection of our wedding bands. 'So, when are you getting married? Should we start preparing to come for your wine carrying?' people asked.

'You should talk to your friend to get married,' an aunt whispered, her breath brushing the back of my ear, as though Chinelo had refused the possibility of marriage.

'Uju and Ada have left you behind. You people are no longer mates,' another loud-mouthed relative quipped at Ada's reception and I was tempted to ask him if he had a barn full of suitable men for her to pick from.

The questions stung, I knew, even though Chinelo tried to hide her reaction. Her road to marriage was blocked by intertribal differences and her parents' insistence that she marry a man of their choosing – her boyfriend, Christopher, wasn't Igbo.

Then Gozie broached the subject days later and I began to see things in a different light. We sat on the open veranda of our ground-floor apartment, chewing boiled groundnuts and enjoying the evening breeze. 'Your friend Chinelo, doesn't she plan to get married?' he asked suddenly, almost nonchalantly, but I could tell from the slight tension in his shoulders that he was very serious about the subject.

'Why would you ask that?' I replied evenly, as I cracked a groundnut shell open between my fingers and threw its contents in my mouth.

'Because you are married, and Ada is married. Shouldn't the both of you be encouraging her to do same?'

I turned a wary eye in his direction. 'I didn't even think you noticed such things.'

The tension in his shoulders moved to his face. 'Well, I noticed because you're my wife and it is my responsibility to know who your friends are. As a married woman, you should have married friends, so you can encourage and learn from each other.'

My emotions roiled together and melted in a steaming pot of anger. 'I've never bothered to monitor the marital status of your friends,' I retorted. 'And for your information, there is no way I will abandon Chinelo even if she decides to become a nun!' I got up, brushed the residue of the shells off my skirt and stormed into the heat of our apartment, leaving him to eat the groundnuts alone.

'She's single,' Mama said as though that were explanation enough, when I complained to her as we walked round the busy Yaba market pricing foodstuff the following weekend.

'And so? Does that make her an outcast?'

Mama shook her head as though she couldn't believe I was her daughter. 'Don't you know having single friends can lead you astray? They know nothing about marriage and they'll always give you the wrong advice. Many of them even become jealous and bitter and they try to scatter their friends' homes. Also, your husband should be your ultimate friend! If you know what is good for you, you'll protect your marital affairs from outsiders,' she said.

# 7.

## *We girls have to take charge of our bodies*

I knew I was pregnant that long rainy season in '80 when I could no longer swallow goat-meat. I'd always loved goat-meat – fried, roasted, boiled for pepper soup, sautéed in pepper sauce as *asun*. Even *isi ewu,* the infamous goat-head meal, was a favourite of mine. And so, when all of a sudden the mere aroma of the meat made me queasy, I knew it had finally happened.

Before then, I'd had no way of telling Mama or Gozie that I was unready for a child. And when the constant harangues and questionings wouldn't stop, I took matters into my own hands and visited a pharmacist to prescribe birth control pills. It was my body, after all. I'd first heard of birth control pills in secondary school, when our Biology teacher had given a lecture on family planning. But the first time I would ever seen them was in my second year at the university, a transparent packet of small white pills on Sally's bedside drawer.

'What is this?' I asked, holding it up.

'You don't know what that is?' she replied, a hint of surprise in her voice.

I shook my head, and she laughed. 'You really don't know? You've never seen birth control pills before?'

I nearly jumped off the bed. 'Birth control pills? What are you doing with birth control pills?'

'What do you think I'm doing with them?' she drawled sarcastically.

It shocked me how easily she admitted to having sex, as though it were an everyday activity like bathing or eating and not an act to be spoken of in hushed tones and coded tongues.

Sally laughed again. 'Oh, my dear Uju, you're so naive. We girls have to take charge of our bodies. These men don't care. They won't be there to suffer with us as we carry the children, not to talk of the effort to raise the child afterwards. I'm only protecting myself from unwanted responsibility.'

I hid the pills in my underwear drawer, a place I knew Gozie never looked through, and took them secretly.

Then one day, Gozie couldn't find a document. 'Uju, do you know where I kept it? I think I left it here the last time I came home,' Gozie called from the room.

'No, I haven't seen it. Check the drawers!' I yelled from the kitchen without thinking.

For several minutes, there was nothing but silence, then Gozie yelled, 'Obianuju, come here!'

'Is everything okay? Have you seen it?' I called in the direction of the room.

'Obianuju, I said come here!' he shouted in response.

Abandoning what I was doing, I walked obliviously into the trap I'd set for myself.

'Uju, what is this?' he asked, raising my packet of contraceptives and taking menacing steps in my direction. His face was a hard mask of rage. I'd never seen him like that.

I felt cold creep up my spine and took a self-preserving step backwards, unsure of what to make of this Gozie.

'Uju, I said what is this?' he demanded again, his voice rising threateningly with each word.

'I-I-I.' That was as far as I could get; I was shaking all over. Cold sweat formed on my forehead and slowly dropped down the sides of my face.

'So, this is why we don't have children yet? You've been taking pills behind my back?'

'I-I-I,' I stammered, internally pleading with my brain to conjure a response, but it had deserted me in my time of need.

'Answer me!' he screamed, the veins in his neck and face jutting aggressively against his skin, just before his palm descended with crashing force on the side of my face.

I fell to the floor, shocked and shaken, clutching the stinging half of my face, hot tears rolling down. 'I'm sorry. I just wasn't ready,' I mumbled in between sobs. He'd never hit me before.

'How dare you! How dare you!' he screamed over my bent head, then stalked out of the room, his feet banging on the floor tiles. A few seconds later, I heard the front door crash in its frame, the sound reverberating through the empty space.

I remained on the floor curled in a ball, confused, heartbroken and terrified I'd destroyed my marriage.

After what seemed like hours, I heard the front door open again and I got up to see who was there. In my living room were Gozie and a raging Mama. 'Obianuju! Please tell me what your husband said is not true. Please tell me those tablets aren't yours. I didn't even tell your father because it might kill him.'

I bent my head, ashamed.

'So it is true? Why would you do such a thing?'

'I'm sorry,' I croaked.

Mama stared at me in shock. 'Are you sure you fear God? How can you marry and not want to have children? How can you be this evil? You even prayed with me and Mrs. Anosike the other day! This is witchcraft!'

'I'm sorry,' I whispered, tears starting to run down my face again.

Mama wasn't appeased. 'You deserve a dirty slap! Sorry for your-self. And what is that on your face?' she asked, pointing at the purpling bruise from the heavy hit I'd taken from Gozie earlier.

I paused, unsure of what response to give. I decided on the truth. 'Chigozie hit me,' I mumbled.

'Good!' Mama said. 'Maybe that will teach you some sense. You're lucky he didn't beat you very well like other men would have done. Instead he came to call your mother to talk to you. How many men would have done that? *Oya* kneel down! Kneel down and apologise to him. Tell him you won't do that again,' she instructed, pointing at the floor.

Slowly, dejectedly, I obeyed: I knelt meekly in front of Gozie. 'I'm very sorry. It won't happen again, I promise. Please forgive me.'

Back in May '80 Mama hadn't yet accused me of witchcraft or wickedness. She'd been blissfuly unaware, chewing boiled corn and *ube* in our living room. I'd stayed home that day because I had no classes and Mama had come over 'to keep you company', she said. But it was more for herself than me.

'Your brothers are barely around these days. Kelechi has gotten his own place and Ikechukwu is always travelling to the East for business; your father and his fellow old men always have one meeting or the other. That house is too empty.'

I laughed. Who knew this day would come?

'This corn is so sweet. Where did Gozie find good corn like this in Lagos?' Mama said, pulling out a chunk of grain with her teeth.

'He has someone he buys from that brings directly from the North within days of harvest; it's why it's so fresh. Do you want more? I boiled plenty today. Gozie likes corn.'

'No wonder. I'll definitely eat more, but let me finish these ones first,' she answered jovially. 'This is why you need children – how can only the two of you be enjoying life alone? Come on, don't be selfish.' She cackled at her own joke, and I joined her.

'*Ehen*. That reminds me, Mrs. Anosike, the women's prayer leader, said to tell you that she submitted your name to the leadership of her women's prayer group. They will be praying for you. God will come through for you.'

'Amen,' I said.

Her eyes brightened. 'You should come and visit our church once in a while, even though you now attend your husband's church. So much has happened since you left.' Mama had all the latest gossip. The pastor's daughter had gotten married and was already heavily pregnant, and many were counting the months until the birth to make sure it was actually nine months post-marriage. Sister Chidebere had just opened a new clothing business and Onochie, the choir-master, was finally getting married at the ripe old age of forty-five.

'Turn on the television; let's watch something,' Mama said when she'd exhausted her stories.

*BIAFRA: THIRTEEN YEARS LATER* flashed across the screen in bold white letters.

I picked up the remote control quickly to change the channel, conscious of Mama's presence.

'Wait!' Mama instructed, pausing my finger on the button. Her eyes were glued to the screen.

'Biafra, thirteen years later, and ten years since the end of the war. What lessons can be learned?' the moderator started. 'Today, with us, we have experts and survivors of the war to discuss this very important subject in our history.'

'Mama please, let me change it,' I begged.

'No.'

For the next hour, the panel broke down the events that had led to the war and the horrific happenstances afterwards. My attention was focused on Mama – she watched the programme quietly, her eyes fixated and unblinking, nodding vigorously when a panellist said, 'We did terrible things to ourselves.'

It wasn't until they began to play clips from the war that the tears came quietly, until they were so heavy that she covered her face with her hands. 'Ikenna,' I heard her murmur in between sobs.

'I'm going to start looking for Ikenna again,' she said suddenly into the silence when the programme was over. She wouldn't look at me.

'Mama—' I started to say.

'I know it's been many years since he left, and if he was alive, he should have come back by now, but I can't just give up like that. Maybe he's a refugee somewhere and he's waiting for me to find him. I won't give up on him. I can't. I-I promis—' Her voice cracked. 'I promised my mother before she died that I'd take care of him.'

I put my arm around her shoulders. 'It's okay, Mama, I understand.'

We sent out letters after that, far and wide. Gozie included Uncle Ikenna's details in his newspaper's Missing Persons column; their newspaper was read around the country, someone would know something, he reassured Mama. But our efforts were met with the same results as the last decade – silence.

Chinelo received her parents' approval when she finally defied them. 'Please can I stay here for a while?' she said, as she pushed past me lugging an enormous suitcase, not waiting for a response.

'What's going on? Did something happen?' I asked the empty doorway; she was already on her way down the hallway to our spare bedroom.

'Chinelo, what is happening?' I shouted, shutting my door and following her.

'I'm taking my life into my hands,' she declared, breathing hard from the effort. She kicked the bedroom door open, dropped the bag in a closet and bounced on the bed.

'I'm not going back to that house. I'm tired!' she announced.

'Tired of what? What happened?'

'They won't let me live my life. So what if Christopher isn't Igbo or from our village? So what if he's from the North? His parents aren't even Hausa or Muslim you know; they're Nupe and they go to church like us. They think every Northerner is Hausa. Even if they were, I would still want to marry him, not that fellow I've never known from Adam they're trying to shove down my throat.'

I laughed. 'And you decided my apartment was the best hiding spot?' I mocked, joining her on the bed.

'Your mother won't expect you to hide your single friend in your marital home now. She thinks you have sense.'

I threw a pillow at her and she bent to the side to dodge it.

Chinelo looked around the room as if searching for something or someone, and lowered her voice. 'Where is your husband? Is he around? I know you said he travels a lot. Please help me talk to him to let me stay, just for a bit. *Shey* you won't abandon your friend in her time of need? *Nne biko.*'

Gozie was out of town; we'd barely spoken since the pills incident. The air in our home had been stilted afterwards, awkward with falsity, as we both tried to pretend it never happened. It was a relief when he announced a posting to cover a riot deep in the South West. I scrunched up my face and pretended to think. 'Mm. Well, he's around o, and he might not like strangers. You better prepare to move under the bridge.'

The pillow I'd thrown connected with my face. 'You think I don't know when you're lying? Your voice sounds high-pitched like a singing mosquito.'

'You're the one who sounds like a mosquito,' I returned, and we began a tussle of flying limbs and high-pitched laughter.

I was not laughing when Mama's stony face appeared through my keyhole a few days later. 'Obianuju! Open this door!'

'We're in trouble,' I whispered to Chinelo and motioned for her to run inside.

Chinelo's mother was weeping in the crook of Mama's arm and her husband was solemn. 'Good morning, Obianuju,' he greeted her. 'Can we come in?'

'Yes, yes. Please come in. Is everything okay?' I responded, and moved to make way for them. Mama's eyes narrowed suspiciously on my face as she passed.

'Good morning, Mama,' I said.

'Obianuju, we've been searching for Chinelo for days now and we're very worried. We were wondering if you had any idea where she is,' Chinelo's father said when they were properly seated.

'Obianuju, you better tell the truth; I'm ready to search this place,' Mama warned as I opened my mouth to speak. I shut it immediately.

I was surprised by their shock at Chinelo's refusal to leave my home. 'Chinelo, when did you become like this?' her mother demanded tearfully. It made me wonder if they knew their daughter at all or if they had spent their lives grooming a stranger separate from the person they built her up to be in their heads.

This was Chinelo; she was as nice as she was tough, quiet as she was loud, easy to win over as she was stubborn, complex as she was simple. She operated on different sides of the spectrum daily, constantly choosing which side to exhibit. She'd been that way for a long time.

When she left that evening with her parents, it was with their agreement to put all wedding plans on hold, for the time being at least.

'I'm getting married!' she announced at church the following Sunday, jumping up and down. A kangaroo.

'To who?' I asked, confused.

She laughed. 'Who else? Christopher, of course.'

'It's a lie!' I screamed.

'It's true!' she returned, and we jumped up and down like we'd done as girls when our mothers had sent us out to play.

'Wait,' I said, pausing mid-jump. 'How come? How did it happen?'

'I heard them talking. My mother said it was better to let me to marry who I want, since I'm so adamant, than wait for me to grow old in their house.'

I thought of another man, one my parents would have objected to if I'd ever broached the subject. I damped the treacherous thoughts immediately; there was no use thinking useless things. I was supposedly a happily married woman.

For weeks afterwards, Mama would not speak to me.

# 8.

## *God has taken away my shame*

Gozie wore his joy at the news of my pregnancy on his sleeve, proudly, like a coat of many colours. My Joseph.

He bought baby clothes – colourful and tiny onesies, bodysuits and rompers – and he would put them to his chest and ask with a childlike smile, 'What do you think?' I returned home from school one evening to find him assembling a cot, hammer in hand and pencil behind his ear like an actual carpenter.

'What are you doing?' I asked, stunned, dropping my handbag on the floor.

'What do you think I'm doing? Will the baby sleep on the floor?'

The nurses at the government-owned hospital at Apapa had sent pitying glances my way when I showed up without my wedding ring – forgotten in a fretful hurry – to confirm my suspicions. I could picture their thoughts: a young unmarried woman asking for a pregnancy test could mean only one thing – she was promiscuous and stupid, and her stupid promiscuity was about to cost her any hope of a profitable future and a good husband.

It rained as I waited for the results, heavily, the torrent coming down in a monotonous roar, leaving behind the overpowering scent of moist earth and the stench of the exposed city sewage.

'Your result is ready, madam,' a nurse called to me.

I vacated my seat by the window, where I'd sat watching, listening and smelling the rainstorm to go pick up my envelope. I knew the answer without opening it, the same way I'd anticipated Gozie's unbridled excitement. The victorious shout he let out, lifting me above his head like a trophy he'd won at the World Cup. And I laughed and laughed, the joy flowing from my belly to my throat. I was happy as long as he was.

'We should tell Mama,' he said, when he finally put me down, slowly, as if lowering an egg crate.

We were on our way to my parents' house minutes later, Gozie singing along to gospel tracks in the car. I could see why he and Mama were friends.

Mama laughed, then she danced, then she sang to the ceiling. '*He has done for me, he has done for me, what no man can ever do, my God has done for me.*'

'Obianuju, won't you dance? God is good. You're ungrateful o,' she said and pinched my cheeks playfully.

'Obianuju, my daughter! You're now a woman,' Papa said in his characteristic gravelly voice, a satisfied grin on his face.

'Small Uju of yesterday is now a big girl,' my brother Ugochukwu, who happened to be home, said with a sly smile, before adding, 'Congratulations, Chigozie.'

Gozie and I were instructed to kneel for blessings and prayers.

'Father God! Let the enemy not see them, keep the eyes of the

evil ones away from their child! Protect them! Let this be the beginning of more to come. Male and female! Bless them with more!'
Mama shouted, her right arm outstretched over our heads.

'Amen!' I responded in time with Gozie, the strong tenor of his
voice overshadowing mine into the background.

I no longer had the National Youth Service Corps as an excuse. The
headmistress was already organising the send-forth party for corpers
posted to the primary school, and our pass-out day was pinned to
the notice board at the state secretariat. People spoke about the
upcoming march-past with delightful anticipation – the crowning
parade by the select few, the synchronized movement of arms and
feet to the band, the official salute of the corps, the great applause
and whistles from the crowd. Everyone made plans for life post-
service: Christopher had already gotten a job at an oil company – we
called Chinelo 'Madam Oil Money' – and Chinelo received an
interview invitation from a pharmaceutical firm. Uzondu did not
want Adaugo working: she was too beautiful to be surrounded by
lecherous men who wanted to steal his prize. She was fine with that;
he had money enough for the both of them, and more.

Before Gozie, I'd planned to return to research, to work in the
university, to be like Akin. Now I had others to think about. Gozie
wanted me to wait. It was our first pregnancy; my body was unused
to that sort of strain. He did not want us to lose risking the baby.
I agreed with him, reluctantly.

But now I had no excuse to keep avoiding Akin. I'd last seen him
at my wedding reception, wearing a brown suede jacket with elbow

patches that looked like it'd been thrown on in a hurry in a last-minute decision to attend; the same jacket he'd had on when he received his promotion letter to full lecturer status.

'Oh my God!' I'd screamed, reading the words over his shoulder on my toes then throwing my arms around his neck in a congratulatory hug. This was his dream.

He seemed oblivious of my presence as he held the paper in a frozen stare. I screamed again and he blinked, then slowly turned to pull me into a long embrace.

'I can't believe it,' he said into my hair.

'You better; you're a genius,' I told his neck.

I wasn't expecting Akin to attend my wedding, even though I'd been the one to slip the invitation between the tiny space separating his door from the floor, too cowardly to face him.

'Congratulations, Obianuju. You look absolutely stunning,' he said with a smile that seemed too cheery to be genuine. It was the first time I'd ever seen a false smile on his face.

Most of the crowd had dispersed and Gozie was outside the hall, checking on the car that was to take us to my parents' house.

Akin pulled me into a firm hug, one stiff enough to be shared between friends but far from the warmth of ones we'd shared before.

'*Stunning*,' I mimicked, trying to match the lightness of his tone. 'Since when did you start speaking like the British?'

'I see you're still as mouthy as ever, Smallie.' He pulled my nose and we burst into laughter; the tension broken. We fell into the easy chatter that always seemed to flow between us.

'Is this what you want? Are you happy, Obianuju?' he asked suddenly, searching my eyes. I looked away, taken by the surprise at the question, feeling uncomfortable, exposed. He'd always been able to see through me. It wasn't a question I'd asked myself in recent times. Was I happy? What defined happiness? Did it matter?

'He's the perfect man,' I said instead.

'That's not an answer, Smallie,' he murmured. His eyes glistened with unspoken words.

A discomfited *ahem* sounded and I sensed the owner even before I turned with a fixed, bright smile. Gozie was staring at us owlishly.

'This is my friend Akin; I think I've told you about him,' I hurried to explain.

'Pleased to meet you,' Gozie said, stiffly extending his hand, his eyes hard.

'Likewise,' Akin responded quickly, his radiant smile back in place. 'I have to go now, Uju. Congratulations once again,' he said, pulling me into another quick hug. 'I'll miss you, Smallie,' he whispered into my hair. Then he was gone.

'I went to our university today. I saw Dr. Akintunde – he asked of you,' Ada would say in the months after, watching my face carefully.

I'd already registered to begin further studies, thanks to a merit-based fully-funded scholarship granted by the university. Akin had been one of the lecturers to recommend me. Now I had to go tell him I planned to defer.

'Obianuju! It's been forever!' Akin exclaimed excitedly when I walked into his office, jumping to his feet and rattling his table in the process. He eyes roved quickly over me. 'You're pregnant,' he added in a deadpan, matter-of-fact tone and I felt my stomach sink.

I smiled sheepishly. 'Hi Akin. Longest time.'

'I guess I should say congratulations,' he responded.

'Thank you.'

He cleared his throat and forced a smile. 'How have you been? I assume you're here to see me concerning your programme,' he said. His voice was polished, professional.

I nodded, checking for signs of the Akin I knew, the one who had appeared briefly when I walked in.

'I was hoping I could defer my admission till next year,' I replied.

'Why?' He seemed genuinely perplexed. 'Is something wrong? Are you having a troubled pregnancy?' he asked, his voice laced with concern.

'No, no. I'm fine; my baby is healthy too.'

He closed his eyes and when he opened them slowly I could see beneath the veneer he kept in place. 'Is this about something else, Obianuju?' he whispered carefully.

I opened my mouth to respond and he raised his hand to stop me. He'd never shushed me before; he was my sounding board, he'd said, sent to the earth to make sure I didn't torture others with my talkative ways.

'Smallie, I know things have been awkward between us lately, but you shouldn't give up on your dreams because of that. You've always wanted this. I'll stay out of your way; you wouldn't have to see me if you want. I—' He reached out to place his hand on mine on the table and I snatched my hand quickly away. The last thing I needed was for him to touch me, to remind me.

I'd wounded him; his eyes said that much.

'No, my husband just thinks it's best I don't stress myself much since it's our first child,' I said.

The professional mask went back in place. He cleared his throat again. 'That's fine, Obianuju. Please stop by the registrar's office to submit a formal request for deferment and I will speak with the head of department. He should be able to pull some strings so you don't lose your scholarship,' he said finally.

'Thank you very much, sir,' I said, grateful.

'No need to thank me, Obianuju,' he replied softly. 'You know I've always thought highly of your abilities; you were a star student. I really do think you have potential to do a lot more than you've already done.'

He shook my hand at the door. It felt cold, just like our new friendship.

Outside, the tears welled up slowly, clouding my vision, then floated down the sides of my face, wetting the top of my dress as I walked to the bus stop. Passers-by stared or tapped me and asked, 'Madam, are you okay? Is it your baby?' in concerned voices.

We bonded over our bellies, Adaugo and I. We went shopping for baby items, giggling at their tininess, and shared tips we received from our mothers and well-meaning aunties and church mothers.

'See your big stomach,' she said, pointing at my jutting belly, cackling.

'You're one to talk. You look like you swallowed a palm-wine-tapper's gourd.'

We laughed and laughed at each other, then breathed heavily from the effort.

I watched my body transform drastically with obsessive

fascination. I could no longer fit into any of my clothes, my back ached and my feet were always swollen. I tried not to look at the stretch marks on my belly – squiggly faded lines that seemed permanently tattooed onto my skin – or whine about the fact that I could no longer see my own toes. My body had been taken over by the creature growing within.

'Dem don knack this one. Shakara don end,' a street tout shouted one day as I passed, and I complained tearfully to Gozie that evening. I seemed unable to stop crying these days.

The congratulations came now that my condition was evident. Gozie received each one smugly, satisfied with his efforts. But he would always add a murmur of 'God is good' and 'His name be praised'.

In harmattan November, amidst the dry, cold breeze and occasional dust rising, Chinelo got married to Christopher.

It was a big affair. Chinelo's father was a red-capped chief, just like Papa, and his daughter's wedding had to be befitting. But I sensed an overcompensation for their dissatisfaction at the choice of the groom, as if to say, 'As you can see, we can take care of our daughter. Please return her to us if you cannot do same.'

Despite false pretences, there was a clear divide at the wedding – the bridegroom's guests on one side, and the bride's on the other. It became even more apparent when the time came for the groom and his people to present items from the bride price list.

'What kind of nonsense is this?' one of the elders complained in Igbo, staring at the bleating animals in front of him. 'Are these goats or puppies?'

'As if it's not bad enough that we're giving our daughter to a

Northerner, they insult us with this. These yams don't even look like they were harvested this year,' another chimed in in English, daring to offend the visitors.

'We reject the gifts. The wedding will not hold,' the oldest man in their midst declared and made to rise up. His counterparts followed.

But Chinelo's father would not be embarrassed in front of his guests, and so he called the elders aside for a brief chat. A few minutes later, they returned wearing oily smiles, to announce that the events would go on as planned. And I suspected that he'd wetted their palms with bank notes.

The wedding carried on after that, but a few weeks later, at the large reception for the church wedding, each family hired their own set of caterers for their guests. Trays carrying varied tribal dishes passed by me – *eje boci* for the Nupenchizhi, and pounded yam and *ofe oha* for the Igbos present – amidst snide comments and regurgitated stereotypes.

'God has taken away my shame,' Chinelo said to me later, flashing the bold gold band on her ring finger.

# 9.

## *Na her first pikin and she no even born boy*

Ego came in March of '81, wailing at the top of her lungs and wrapped in skin the same shade as her father. Her eyes were mine – the same uninteresting black irises.

I'd nearly given Gozie a heart attack. He was in the shower, at home on temporary desk work, when I screamed. 'I don't want to miss it,' he'd said. *It* being the birth of our child.

He rushed out, clad in only his towel, soap suds covering most of his face. I would have laughed were it not for the pain coursing through me. 'What? What happened? Is it the baby?' he asked, his voice wobbly with fear.

'I think it's time,' I squeaked out.

'Let's go!' he said, running to our room to grab his car keys.

'Go where? Like that?' I shouted after him, pointing at his towel.

'Doesn't matter, there's no time,' he replied as he returned with his keys and dragged our bags to the front door. We'd had our luggage packed for weeks, like soldiers awaiting a call up from the government.

'They won't attend to us. They'll think you're mad. Please put on clothes. Don't worry, I'm fine, I can wait for you to change,' I pleaded, ready to cry.

'Okay, okay,' he acquiesced. 'Don't move!' he ordered as he returned to the room, like I had plans for a trip. He put on the first pieces of clothing he found – baggy khaki shorts, an oversized red t-shirt and white rubber slippers.

Gozie drove like a man chased by evil spirits, nearly getting the both of us – and several motorists and pedestrians unfortunate enough to be on the roads at that time – killed in the process. 'Your head no correct!' one elderly man shouted out of his car window.

At the hospital, I was handed over to two nurses, who wheeled me quickly to the labour ward even as Gozie screamed, 'Obianuju, don't cry; I'm here,' behind us, his croaky voice sounding like he was ready to succumb to tears himself.

Then began the most traumatic experience of my entire life.

'PUSH!' the nurses shouted in my already-ringing ears, throughout the next twelve hours. My back was propped up and legs wide open, and I desperately wondered why I'd decided to have a child anyway. I was ready to throw in the towel. 'Let me die, let me die. I'm not doing this again; I'm tired,' I cried.

'Ah, madam, you can't give up now; you're almost there. You know you're a woman; you have to be strong. We can already see your baby's head. You just need to push a little more,' the younger of the two nurses encouraged.

'Why are you begging her?' the older nurse, hardened by years of rounds in the delivery ward, asked without a hint of compassion. 'When you were doing it, were you not enjoying yourself? Now you're here crying like a small girl. My friend, open your legs and push.'

'It's a girl!' I heard the young nurse announce later as I collapsed in the bed. The room rang with an infant's cry. She was handed to me later, after she'd been cleaned, and I stared into her angelic face and knew I would never love another being more.

'Is this your first child?' the older nurse asked, interrupting my thoughts.

'Yes,' I answered with a small smile.

'Congratulations. No wonder you were shouting like that. Sorry. Let us go and bring your husband in,' she said, then turned to leave with the younger nurse. At the door, she whispered, '*Ehya*. Na her first *pikin* and she no even born boy.' But she was gone before I could properly process her words.

A flustered Gozie burst into the room seconds later. 'Obianuju! I was so worried,' he said, running his palm along the side of my face.

I smiled at him and directed his attention to the little bundle in my arms. 'I think there's someone that would like to meet you,' I said, grinning as he looked down at our little princess.

Gozie bent to have a closer look. 'Hello,' he whispered. 'She looks just like you,' he said, sounding like a disgruntled child, and I laughed.

'I nearly died from worry, hearing your screams outside,' he said, his voice raspy as he pulled a seat close and clutched my free hand. 'We won't have any more children, I promise.'

My response bubbled in my belly until it burst out in a squeal of laughter.

'What's funny?' Gozie demanded. 'I'm serious.'

We left the hospital days later, with the doctor's stamp of approval. Our apartment was full when we arrived – Mama had started her own little party in our living room, distributing plates of sweets, kola nut, bitter kola, groundnuts and bottles of soft drinks to our visitors. Mama Chinelo and Mama Ada passed *nzu* around for people to rub on their necks.

'*Erimeri na adi mma erimeri e. Erimeri na adi mma erimeri e. Onwu egbule nwanyi n'af'ime k'omuora anyi nwa, tara okporo, nuru mmii ngwo,*' Mama sang as we entered; her friends chorused along with her.

There was something about someone singing in our local language that always excited them. Papa said that the best way to get a man on your side was to speak to him in a language he understood. 'This English is not our language; it is the white man that gave it to us. We must not speak the white man's tongue and forget the one our fathers spoke. We must teach our children – just like we have taught you and your brothers; you must teach yours as well. When you see an Igbo man, greet him in Igbo; let him know he is your brother. That is the only way our culture will not die out.'

'Uju, my daughter. You're now a woman, and you've made me a grandmother,' Mama said to me that night when all the guests were gone, her voice light and airy. Her prayers had been answered, her enemies put to shame. She had officially begun her *omugwo*. I shared in her joy.

On the eighth day after our daughter was born, we announced her name: Nwakaego (Ego for short), meaning 'child is greater than wealth' – we had no money, but we had a child, and that child would bring us wealth.

\*

Adaugo said I'd gotten too used to living like a woman without a husband; that it was why Gozie and I clashed so often after his permanent return to desk work.

'I don't know what you mean,' I complained. 'I just go about my business as usual.'

'*Oho!*' she replied, as if to say, 'You have your answer.'

'It is a woman's job to build her home,' she added and continued cooing at her baby.

Whenever a dispute between a young couple was brought to Papa to settle, he would always say, 'When a young man lacks money, he complains that his wife's manners are not good.' The economy was worse than before under the new civilian government, and with an extra mouth to feed, life had become much tougher for us. Prices were up, and the National Labor Congress organised one strike after the other demanding that the government act as promised. People marched in the sun and carried placards, screaming for change. Then the government called for a closed-door meeting with the congress leaders. The strike was called off the days after, with the leaders claiming to have reached an agreement with the government, but nothing changed.

There was a tanker explosion the following week, and the news showed charred bodies being removed from the singed skeletons of vehicles on a road I'd passed earlier that day. There were no protests afterwards to hold the government responsible; lives were expendable, and prayers had long replaced our systems. The roads were full again the next morning as the people of the city rushed about their business; they were wary of being used for protests, for the benefit of a few to enrich their pockets.

Mama and Papa spent any time together reminiscing about the good old days. 'This country is going bad. Things were much better when I was a young woman. Money used to be so valuable back then; now everything is so expensive,' Mama would say, then launch into stories about how much simpler life had been living in the village and feeding mostly off the land.

'This oil has ruined this country. Nobody wants to farm again; now everybody is looking for oil bloc. Agriculture used to be our major export; now no one is talking about all the farms lying fallow. The oil is polluting our rivers and killing all our fish but they aren't doing anything. They say democracy is of the people, by the people and for the people, but I do not see how they are better than the military government,' Papa complained.

I wondered if we were ever great as a nation or if it was just human nature to romanticise the past, blurring out the evil and focusing solely on that which had brought them joy.

'I didn't do anything wrong this time,' I protested. 'I only offered to work, you know, to make things easier for us. Ego is old enough to be left with Mama. Next thing, he was asking if I didn't think he's man enough to take care of the family.'

'Who sent you to say such things? Did he complain to you? Mind your business,' Ada said.

'Any news about your uncle?' Chinelo asked – I suspected, to prevent Adaugo and I from descending to blows. We were in her apartment, after all.

It was more than a year since Mama had started looking again. I sighed, heavily. 'Nothing yet. But Mama is hopeful that something will come up.'

'What do you think?'

I did not know how to answer that question. I sighed again. Did I truly believe there was any hope of Uncle Ikenna returning after all these years? But saying I didn't would mean I'd given up on him, and I could never betray Uncle Ikenna that way.

'I don't know,' I started.

Adaugo's high-pitched squeal crashed through my thoughts. We jumped and turned to her.

'What? What happened?' Chinelo asked, already panicking.

Ada danced and pointed excitedly at her baby. 'See. See,' she said. And we both got up to go look.

'Can't you see?' she asked when we continued to stare at the wide-eyed baby, confused.

'See what, Adaugo?' Chinelo demanded, annoyed.

'Her first teeth!' She raised the child's lips to give us a better view. 'Can't you see? It's just there.'

'It must be ghost teeth,' Chinelo mumbled and hissed, returning to her seat. 'How old is she that she will even have teeth?'

'Adaugo, leave that child alone. How will she get any sleep if you're always hovering over her like that? *Abeg* don't use your shouting to wake up my own baby. No put sand for my garri. Let me rest small,' I said, laughing in Ada's sulking face.

'What about you, Chinelo?' Ada said, settling in a seat close enough for her to keep an eye on the makeshift bed. 'Do you plan to have children soon?'

'We just got married now. I just started at my job, too. Allow us to enjoy ourselves a bit. We're still young.'

'Love in Tokyo!' Ada hailed, alluding to a Bollywood movie that had made waves around the country in our teen years.

'Does your mother know? She might have a different opinion o,' I said. And we all laughed.

'Marriage is sweet o,' Chinelo said. 'You people didn't tell me this was what you were enjoying. Do you know that my mother's hairdresser addressed me as 'Ma' and served me soft drinks when I went to get my hair done the other day? And that Mama invited me to join her married women's association? Me?'

'That one is standard now. Are you not a married woman?' Ada said.

I chuckled. Adaugo was right. That was very standard behaviour.

'Wait until you have a baby and tell me if it's still that sweet,' Ada added.

'What?' she asked when we just stared at her.

'See my body now,' she whined. 'All this fat has refused to go *ehn*. I even jog around my street every morning. A beauty queen like me. And I have constant back pain.'

'Mama said it's normal for your body to change after childbirth,' I replied, helpfully. 'At least you're not forgetting everything, like me.'

'Who said I'm not?' she retorted. 'They should have told us everything beforehand; they waited till afterwards so we would agree to have children.'

'Don't worry, Adaugo,' Chinelo said, slapping Adaugo's thigh playfully. 'You're still the finest person I know. *Omalicha!*'

# 10.

## So, the rumours are true?

It shocked me how quickly my daughter grew from a tiny infant to a chubby six-month-old rolling from her back to her stomach and making gurgling noises. Adaugo's daughter was teething and crawling about with so much zeal that Ada had to block corners and build fake walls to keep her from harming herself.

When Ego was three months old, we held her *ije uka nwa* and *onu nwa*. And Chinelo's father had bought her a car – a black shining BMW, the seats covered in the clear plastic of brand-new vehicles.

'We heard something and came to confirm with our own eyes,' Adaugo announced as we entered Chinelo's living room.

'What did you hear?' Chinelo asked, sounding like she already knew.

'Whose car is that?' I asked, pointing at the vehicle glistening in the sun through the window.

Chinelo smiled, a mischievous twinkle in her eye. 'Your mothers gossip too much,' she said.

'Your mother too,' I quipped.

That was not Adaugo's concern. 'So, it's true? *Hei.* Were you planning to hide it from us?'

'I just got it yesterday o,' Chinelo said. 'My father said, as a married woman it's only responsible that I have a car.'

'*Oya,* bring out the key; let's take it for a drive,' Ada instructed.

'But you won't believe that Christopher isn't happy about it. He said my father should have asked for his permission, or at least informed him out of respect, before buying such an expensive gift for his wife. Do you think I should return it?' Chinelo said as we buckled in.

'Return *gini?*' I said.

'Nonsense,' Ada added. 'Tell him to not worry; one day he'll be able to afford to buy you a car. He shouldn't be jealous. For now, enjoy the one your father gave you, my sister. Christopher will be alright.'

'Na your type dey spoil marriage,' I told Adaugo.

'Na my type get sense,' she retorted.

We stopped at a station to buy fuel then zoomed down the highway, urging Chinelo to go faster as we rolled down the windows to let the wind blow against our screaming voices.

Chinelo raced past a red traffic light and a police car sped around the corner and moved to block us.

'You should return the car. Your father doesn't know you're not responsible,' Adaugo mumbled.


I stepped into our compound as Gozie parked his car; I'd perfectly timed my return to coincide with his. The policeman and his notebook, demanding we follow him to the police station – 'You must write statement today!' – had nearly derailed my plans, but he'd finally let us go with a mere warning when Adaugo had flashed her prettiest smile and told him we were rushing to the hospital to meet a dying friend.

Angry faces, travelling bags at their feet, greeted me at the door. 'Where have you been?' they demanded the moment I came into view.

Ego started to cry, and I rocked her gently to calm her. It was time for her feeding. They turned their eyes to Gozie, who'd just squeezed out of his Volkswagen. 'So, the rumours are true?' the group's self-appointed spokesperson said. 'We come all the way from the village to Lagos for your child's *onu nwa* and this is what we find? You allow your wife to gallivant about Lagos without any control? *Ehn* Chigozie? *Tufiakwa!*' He snapped his fingers. Elder Ibekwe, my husband's uncle. I'd last seen him at our wedding, smiling as he gulped down bottles of beer.

'And you! How can a woman that just gave birth be jumping around town like an unmarried girl? What sort of mother carries a little baby around in this hot sun? And who is the owner of that car that dropped you off?' he continued. 'Chigozie, does your wife now have boyfriends?'

I rushed to unlock the front door, bending my knees and murmuring words of apology as I moved. 'These young girls of nowadays. Very irresponsible.'

Over the next week, we made do fitting Gozie's relatives into our cramped quarters. The chairs in the sitting room were moved back against the wall to create space for mats and mattresses for those who couldn't fit into the second bedroom. We took turns taking baths in our small bathroom and cooked food in batches.

I felt, consciously, the constant presence of eyes following me: watching me as I bathed Ego, as I fed her, as I cooked, as I took in breath; like one of those specimens our Biology teacher in Form 4 regularly put under the school's only microscope for the class to study.

We gave an open invitation to the *onu nwa*. It was a waste printing formal invitation cards – such things applied only to the *oyinbo* man and the rich. Our people attended events when they heard about them, not when they were invited.

'This child has a good head. See the number of people that came, when we told only a few people,' Mama said, staring out of our window at the crowd of people gathered in our compound on the day. It would soon be time for us to make our appearance. When we finally did, it was to an onslaught of greetings.

'Congratulations o! You didn't tell us, but we came,' Ogechi said. I hadn't seen her since secondary school. But I'd heard through the grapevine that she'd married a wealthy businessman not long after we'd written our final exams, and moved to Ikoyi, where only those who employed gardeners and drove Land Cruisers lived. She had two daughters now and had recently given birth to her third child – a boy. Her husband had killed a cow, thrown a big party and opened a big boutique to celebrate.

She dripped with expensive jewellery – her wrists, neck and ears were covered in it – and her embroidered lace attire complemented the fairness of her skin that was enhanced by the foreign products she used. A part of me envied her; here she was, living a life I could

97

only dream of, with a Senior School Certificate, because she had married right.

'No, it's not like that. You know—' I started to explain.

'I'm only joking. When did you lose your sense of humour?' she said, and giggled like a little girl, showing tiny teeth. 'I know it's not easy being a new mother. Even with the nannies and maids helping me out, I hardly have any time for myself. These children just take over your whole life.'

I plastered on a smile and thought of what to say. 'How are your children and your husband?' I said eventually.

'They are fine. We thank God. I would have brought the children along to greet you, but they travelled with their father for a short visit to America. I will be joining them in a few days.'

I nodded. I had never been outside the shores of the country, and nothing in my life indicated that that would change soon. Ogechi's attention switched to Nwakaego, who was still in my arms. 'Your daughter is very pretty. She looks just like you,' she said.

'Thank you,' I replied, still smiling, my jaw beginning to ache from the effort. But for the shade of her skin, Ego was my spitting image, which meant she was also Mama's spitting image (a fact Mama pointed out at every given opportunity), and Ogechi wasn't the first person to notice.

'Don't worry, God will give you a boy next,' Ogechi continued. I was tempted to retort sharply, to tell her to mind her business.

I'd heard several variations of this prayer, in patronising tones and expressions: 'This one God has given you is okay, but He could always give you better.' But she meant well, I knew: her husband had treated her well on the birth of a male child; only a good friend would wish the same for me. And so, like the other times, I murmured, 'Amen.'

That evening, after the festivities were done – the canopy dismantled, the chairs packed and the excess food distributed – Gozie was pulled aside by his relatives for a family meeting.

They left for their hometown the following morning. But whatever was discussed at their meeting remained like an invisible man.

Our discussions became stilted and controlled. Gozie became watchful of my activities, and demanded I let him know where I was going every minute of the day, and when he wasn't home, I was to give him a breakdown when he returned. Our country had a democratic government, but my home began to feel like I lived under a military one. This was what it meant to 'have control' over one's wife.

Things got worse one late afternoon when I realised I had run out of detergent. Ego was asleep so I searched in my drawers for change and rushed across the street to buy a new packet.

Chike, the shop owner, was a talkative and self-appointed jack of all trades – a plumber when your pipes were leaking, a painter when your walls peeled off – who sought every opportunity to sell his services. When I returned, twenty minutes had passed and Gozie was back, glowering at the front door.

'Where are you coming from?' Gozie demanded in a growl as soon we stepped into our flat, his arms akimbo.

I laughed. 'Where do you think I'm coming from in slippers and jeans at this time?'

'Obianuju, where did you go and leave our daughter alone in the house? Who were you with?'

I blinked. 'Wh—what are you talking about. She's asleep. And I wasn't even gone for that long.'

Gozie's eyes bulged. 'Obianuju, you've not answered my question. Who were you with?'

'I wasn't with anyone, I just went to b—'

'Was it him?' he asked.

'Was it who?'

He paused. 'That man you were with at our wedding. The one you kept looking at like your lover. You think I didn't notice? Or that I'm blind? Are you seeing him again? Are you sleeping with him?' His eyes were fearful, watching, waiting for my answer.

*Akin.* I hadn't seen him since that day at his office door. 'Chigozie, what are you talking about? I wasn't with anyone.' I held out the detergent. 'Look. I just went acr—'

'You must think I'm stupid. My people even noticed when they stayed over. Just a week and they noticed that you were always away from home, doing God knows what, seeing God knows who.'

I hissed, quick and dismissive. 'So that is the cause of this inter-rogation this evening? Is that why you've been acting like this? How won't your people notice when they are always following me every-where with their eyes? Your people need to learn to mind their business!'

Gozie's eyes narrowed. 'What did you just say?' he whispered dangerously.

I was too stupid to notice. 'You heard me. Your people need to learn to mind their business!' I re-echoed, then made to move around him. I didn't get very far – my arm was seized in a death grip. I was turned around and a fist landed on the side of my face in a sharp blow that was immediately followed by another.

My arm was released, but only to make it easier for his fists to find their target. 'Today, I will teach you to have some respect!' And the blows continued to rain, blocking out my cries as I begged for him to stop.

Nwakaego's wail rang out suddenly, belligerent and demanding attention. It was only then that the blows ceased and Gozie stalked out of the house, slamming the door behind him.

I pushed myself to my feet and hurried to our room to pick up our daughter. As I comforted her, silent tears fell down my face and into her curly hair.


My brothers visited in the morning. They shouted my name at the door like debt collectors pursuing an unrepentant defaulter – Ikechukwu's voice was the loudest. I rushed to open the door before our neighbours would hear them and to confirm that I was indeed home. I opened the front door and watched the smiles on their faces die slowly, one after the other.

Blatantly ignoring my greeting, they pushed their way in and shut the door with a bang. Kelechi grabbed my jaw and turned my face from side to side for them to inspect it better. 'Uju, who did this to you?' Ikechukwu demanded, his eyes already brimming with fire. He'd always had a short fuse, so bad that he'd once been suspended in secondary school for beating up a teacher who had dared to flog him for not tucking in his shirt.

'No one,' I said, trying to pull my face out of Kelechi's grasp. My brothers had always been protective of me, and on several occasions had dealt severely with anyone outside of our family that had dared to lay a finger on me. They were also taller than Gozie and built like village wrestlers. They would kill him and leave his scattered remains for vultures to feed on.

'Uju, what happened to your face?' Ugochukwu asked, calm, too calm.

'Nothing,' I said, trying to cover my face with my palm.

'Obianuju, you better start talking now, before we take matters into our hands. We will not listen to you then,' Kelechi threatened.

I looked between them, and by the stoniness of their expressions, knew there was no way out. I narrated the events that had taken place the previous day, taking great care to leave out the worst of the details.

Ikechukwu was the first to react. 'I'm going to kill that bastard. Does he think that because you're married, he can do with you as he likes? You might no longer belong to our family but I will show that idiot that we're not powerless,' he announced.

I moved to block his way. 'No, please. It's my fault. I was rude. I deserved it,' I pleaded, grasping his shirt. 'Please don't do anything. Please, I'm begging. Mama won't like this. Please.'

'Has something like this happened before?' Ugochukwu asked.

I turned to him. 'No, I swear! It hasn't,' I replied, placing my finger on my tongue and pointing to the sky in an oath.

They were quiet for a short while. 'Since it's the first time, we will give him a very stern warning. We're only doing this because you're begging on his behalf. If it ever happens again, we will send him to meet his ancestors,' Kelechi said finally, breaking the silence with his deep, rumbling voice, deciding on their behalf. Ikechukwu looked like he was about to protest Kelechi's decision, but instead thought better of it and nodded in agreement.

That night, just as the sun descended on the city's horizon, Gozie was given the kind of warning that would put the fear of God in the filthiest of sinners. And it was in that moment that I knew we would never remain the same.

# PART 2

# TODAY

## *11.*

## *Someone needs to speak for the people*

Gozie and his friends from the newspaper were playing Fela's music again; it had become a favourite pastime of theirs. They crooned along in loud, discordant voices and stamped their feet to the beat of the drums, *shekere* and melodic bass guitar riffs. This time, they'd chosen a favourite song of theirs: 'Zombie'.

I could hear them sing in time with Fela's distinctive voice and his band of scantily clad dancers, the verses likening the ceremonial drills of military men to mindless zombies. They weren't the only ones singing along to Fela in April of '84; everyone had dusted off their cassettes, ready to communicate their feelings about our rescission to military rule through the defiance and criticism in his music. At the markets, when the soldiers made inspection rounds enforcing the government's price ceilings, the market men and women took it a step further, shouting 'Attention!' 'Quick march!' 'Slow march!' and demonstrating with their hands and feet. The soldiers didn't have much of a sense of humour, and so the market holders spent their afternoons doing frog jumps and kneeling in the sun like children caught stealing meat from the pot.

It had happened on the thirty-first day of December, the day we always dressed in our Sunday best and gathered at church with the rest of the faithful to usher in the New Year. Gozie got up to switch off Ego's television programme, ready to leave, when the national flag flashed across the screen of our new colour television and the Nigerian anthem began to sound. We exchanged worried glances.

'I hope it is not what I think it is,' Gozie murmured, sounding rather anxious.

The scene was all too familiar. Our new head of state appeared on the screen dressed in full military regalia and began to speak in a heavily accented Northern tone. 'In pursuance of the primary objective of saving our great nation from total collapse, I . . .'

'No! No! No!' Gozie said over and over, holding his head and slumping back into the seat he'd just vacated. I followed suit, sinking into an empty chair. Journalists were always the most affected by a military regime, thrown behind bars for the slightest criticism of those in charge.

This couldn't be happening to us, not when Gozie had just been promoted to assistant editor. We'd gone on stage the following Sunday to testify of God's goodness, crafting our voices with humility so it would not be said that we were taking the Lord's glory. We'd purchased a colour television and Gozie had gotten the Peugeot 504 he'd always wanted.

The rounding-up started, closely followed by corruption charges, whether true or false. The newspapers responded with criticisms of abuse of human rights, and their columnists were sent to join those rounded up. I pleaded with Gozie to remain uncontroversial. The newspaper had already received several warnings and threats but Gozie would not be denied this act of defiance. Even Mama became worried. 'Chigozie, these soldiers are not like the civilian heads of state o. They will not laugh at your insults; they will just throw you in jail. Please stop writing these articles. Don't you care for your life?' she said to him.

They had gotten closer after she'd called me and my brothers for a family meeting to reprimand us accordingly. '*Ngwanu*, what is this rubbish I hear about you interfering in your sister's marriage?' Mama inquired, and my brothers looked away with guilty faces. It reminded me of the time they had been suspended from boarding school for stealing yams and a goat from the principal's farm to roast with friends. They'd had the same expressions on their faces as Mama questioned them, just before she launched into a diatribe about their path to hell. Then Papa whipped them severely to ensure that the message sunk in.

'Is it not you people I'm talking to? What carried you to Uju's house to go and interfere in her family matters? Have you not read that what God has joined together, let no man put asunder? Do you want to scatter her marriage?' Mama demanded, her voice dangerously high-pitched. She looked ready to spank the lot of us like we were still children.

'Mama, we cannot sit down and watch another man beat our sister. You should have seen her face. She might no longer belong to our family but we needed to remind him that there are men in our family too, just in case he forgot. He's lucky we didn't send him to the grave,' Ikechukwu finally responded heatedly, unable to keep his cool as usual.

'And so? Do you know what she did wrong that her husband beat her?' she flung back, clapping her hands in his face. 'Instead of you to start thinking of marriage, you're putting your nose in your sister's own. Does a man whose house is on fire go hunting for rats?'

'Mama, you cannot blame us. Have you seen the list of things our people demand for before you marry a girl? Goat, cow, palm wine, cartons of beer etcetera. Just to marry! We don't have that kind of money please,' Ugochukwu said.

Mama turned to face him squarely. 'You! 1, 9, 8, 1 minus 1, 9, 5, 0?' she asked, and we all stared at her like she had completely lost her senses.

'1, 9, 8, 1 minus 1, 9, 5, 0?' he repeated with the perplexity we all felt.

'Yes. What is the answer? Or didn't you go to school?'

He paused for a few seconds to work the numbers. 'Thirty-one,' he said eventually. The rest of us looked between them, wondering where this new line of questioning was going.

'Yes! Thirty-one! That is how old you are. Your mates are getting married and you're here saying "I don't have money." Mister playboy. You better go and find money.'

She faced Kelechi next. 'You! You're the eldest. Look at your head next time you pass a mirror; you're almost bald and you don't have a family of your own. Don't you have any shame?'

'And you,' she continued, turning to me, not giving my brothers a chance to respond. 'Why would you go and report such delicate matters

110

to your brothers? Are you the first to get married? Don't you know there are people going through worse? Couldn't you have to come to meet me or your father so we could settle this matter like adults, instead of making your brothers threaten your husband like touts?'

That evening, she followed me home to make sure I apologised to Gozie. My brothers would not come along.

'*Biko* be careful. Think of your family,' Mama said to Gozie. 'What will they do if these soldiers lock you up?'

'Someone needs to speak for the people, Mama,' he replied in response to her concerns. 'We cannot be deprived of our fundamental human rights!' And I wondered if he preferred to exercise his human rights behind bars.


The War Against Indiscipline (WAI) initiative was launched in March '84, and interesting things began to happen. People lived in fear of retribution: they no longer pushed their way onto buses or crossed roads illegally; motorists drove sensibly; and the price of essential commodities began to decline. Soldiers were everywhere, and you never knew when one would appear to mete out strict punishments for breaking the law.

Gozie and his fellow journalists assembled weekly in our sitting room like religious faithfuls, bickering and crooning.

'Why should they start a war on indiscipline? Are we goats or sheep that need to be told what to do?' Gozie would ask.

'No!' they would chorus, the veins in their necks sticking out like tattoos.

'But we cannot deny that our people can be disorderly; maybe the soldiers are not too bad after all,' a timid voice in their midst said one evening.

'What nonsense are you saying, Obinna? That we should accept our current situation?' Gozie demanded, angrily dragging the cap off a cold bottle of beer with the side of his teeth. He took large gulps and the lowered the bottle to glare at the skinny young journalist. He'd only just joined the office, fresh out of university.

Obiora, a much older man, nodded, his large bald head moving up and down. 'Maybe Obinna has a point. The other day, I saw Izunna, the civil servant, running early to the office like a bush animal being chased by the hunter's gun, and we all know Izunna would rather spend his mornings occupying his wife,' he said, and loud guffaws echoed throughout the living room.

Gozie was not in the mood for jokes. 'Good or bad, the military must go. A democratic government is what we need. Just look at America – see how well they are doing with their government,' he said, swerving the discourse back to the serious path. He spoke of America with admiration – the ultimate example of a democracy.

'My brother, this is not America. Look around you: what has democracy done for us?' Obinna insisted.

'It's "dem-all-crazy" we were practising. That is why our system was bad,' Obiora quipped, and more loud guffaws followed.

Festus, a seasoned journalist like Gozie, was also in no mood to smile. 'Nigerians are too docile; we must fight to take our country back from these people, military or democratic. How much longer are we going to allow this country to continue like this?'

I almost fainted where I'd hidden to eavesdrop. Fight? Was his plan to get all of them killed?

'We should never have been put together as a country in the first place. The colonialists knew what they were doing when they forced all of us together,' Obiora said, serious for a change.

The questions had become more concerned. 'Uju, hope all is well?' they asked, their faces twisted with worry.

Of course, they'd started out as jocular queries. 'Uju, don't you want to give Ego a brother or sister? Or have you people started living like the white man that has only one child?'

'Uju, how far now? We're expecting to hear another cry soon o.'

Then the suggestions began to flow in; there was a doctor I should see, a powerful pastor that would pray for me or a concoction I could drink that would get me pregnant, just like that.

When I finally became pregnant, Gozie lifted me up like the first time and we went to a nice restaurant to celebrate. But a few weeks later, I woke up to a soaked bed and blood running down my legs. He held me while I sat on the bathroom floor and mourned the loss of our baby; he said everything would be okay, that we could always have another.

Months later, I was pregnant again. Then I wasn't anymore. The cycle continued, a revolving nightmare I couldn't wake up from – the crushing disappointment, the frustration, the anguish. Gozie seemed helpless, unable to reach me in my ever-present shroud of grief.

After a while, he no longer reacted when I told him I was expectant; he gave small smiles that seemed to say he had no hope left. And when the eventuality happened, his 'sorry' felt monotonous, useless. I could tell that he blamed me for whatever I did to make my womb ineffective, and I wondered if he wished he'd chosen someone else. I was suddenly alone in my battle.

Mama became worried when Adaugo had her second child; Chinelo had had her first in '82. 'Uju, nothing yet?' she asked, feeling my belly for signs of a bulge. She recommended herbs, roots and tinctures, and I took each one faithfully. We visited pastors, prayer warriors and doctors. Nothing happened. Mama said God was punishing me for not wanting to have a child the first time around, for taking pills and being dishonest in prayer. She said I needed to beg for forgiveness and mercy. And when I did as Mama said, crying and pleading for mercy, Mama said I didn't have enough faith.

I returned to the university, registering to take advantage of the scholarship and admission I'd deferred. And when I ran into Akin, I greeted him stiffly, murmuring 'Yes, sir' at every juncture to establish the distance between us. 'I'm glad you came back, Obianuju,' he said once.

School was fulfilling. The arguments, trading ideas and solutions, laughing at jokes, meandering between the serious and unserious, discussing things outside the monotonous scope of childbearing and prayers, shored a gaping hole within me.

Had I known what would happen next, I would have cherished the feeling harder, marinated myself in it until I could perceive its scent long after it was gone. Halfway through the first year, I returned home one evening to find Mama and Gozie deep in conversation. Ego was strapped to my back, sound asleep. Adaugo helped me take care of her during the day. 'Stop embarrassing me. That's what friends do for each other,' she'd said when I'd thanked her profusely.

'*Ehen*. Thank God you're back, Uju. We were just talking about you. Put Nwakaego to sleep in the room and come back. Let's talk,' Mama said as soon as I walked in.

I did as instructed and returned to the living room. 'Hope everyone is okay: Papa, Ugochukwu, Kelechi and Ikechukwu?' I asked, worried that something had happened to a loved one. Such visits were usually precursors to announcements like 'Your Uncle Ugonna passed away.'

Mama smiled, deceptively serene. 'No, everyone is fine. We thank God,' she said.

I breathed a sigh of relief. It would be short-lived.

'Uju, your husband and I have been talking and we think you need to put your school on hold for now,' Mama said.

'What? How? Why? Did something happen?' I looked at Gozie, tears of betrayal in my eyes. He looked away.

Mama folded her hands together and leaned forward. 'It is distracting you from what's important. We think the stress is one of the reasons you've not been carrying to full term.'

'But—but . . .' I stuttered, unable to formulate an argument.

Gozie's eyes hardened with determination. 'No "Buts", Uju. We need to focus on what is important. And what is important right now is Ego having a brother or a sister,' he said, and Mama nodded in agreement.

Mama and Gozie spoke for a while afterwards – what more we could do, treatments we could try – while I remained in shocked muteness.

Then Mama rose to leave. 'Let me start going to my house. Your father must be worried,' she said. 'Chigozie, come and escort me to the bus stop.'

'Ah no, Mama. Let me get my keys and I will drop you off.'

'Thank you, my son.'

When he stepped out of the room, Mama turned to me anxiously. 'Uju, see how lucky you are. How many men treat their wife and mother-in-law so well? He isn't even considering taking another wife. Please just forget about school for now. What will you do if you lose your husband? Focus on what is important. The person with a burning house does not go catching rats,' she whispered rapidly in Igbo, eager to be done before Gozie returned with his keys.

Gozie was back before I could respond. Mama stroked my cheek affectionately and followed him outside.


Akin held my hands as I cried, our knees rubbing clandestinely against each other as he stroked my back, murmuring, 'It's okay, Smallie.'

'I don't know what I'm going to do,' I blubbered, my tears merging with my running nose. He handed me a handkerchief and I blew into it desolately.

A knock on the door and a brief communication of my withdrawal from the programme had been the plan, but the tears would not stop coming and Akin would not let me go until I explained why.

'I can talk to him for you,' he offered. 'He might be willing to listen to an academic.'

I jerked up apprehensively. 'NO! Please.'

His handsome face creased in confusion. 'Why?'

I looked down at my hands, mumbled, 'He already thinks we're having an affair,' and waited tensely for his reaction.

'WHAT?'

116

'He said we looked at each other like lovers at my wedding.'

Akin laughed loudly, but it did not seem born from mirth. 'Doesn't he know who he married? He should at least trust you,' he declared.

I continued to stare at my hands, ashamed at the imperfections of my marriage.

Akin's thumb nudged my chin. 'Obianuju, is there something else you're not telling me? Did something else happen?' He knew. I knew he knew, and he knew I knew he knew, but I would never confirm it verbally.

I started to shake my head no and our eyes connected. And I felt it again – that nameless something that flowed between us. A puppet on the strings of invisible hands, waiting for something to happen – a miracle to take place. Nothing. Not even the miscarriages I'd gotten used to. Nwakaego chattered about the house; she was older now, her words clearer and her mind sharper every day. With each new sign of development, I dreaded the day she would leave me; wave goodbye at the front of her classroom, holding her teacher's hands, depending on someone else other than her mother.

## 12.

### *Is there another Chigozie Azubuike?*

Adaugo's face told me something was wrong before she opened her mouth in May '84. I was bent over a basin at the back of our compound, my arms deep in soapy water, vigorously scrubbing dirty clothes, when she and Chinelo ran over screaming my name.

I laughed. 'Who is chasing the both of you that you're running like this?'

Then I saw their faces and my heart stopped. 'What happened? Is it Papa? Is my father dead?' It couldn't be Mama; God would have a struggle on his hands before he took her.

'Obianuju, have you seen today's papers?' Adaugo asked solemnly, still breathing hard.

Chinelo thrust a torn-out newspaper page at me and I could tell it had been pulled out in a hurry. 'Everyone is talking about it. Christopher is worried.'

It was a movie moment, one where I watched myself as I read the editorial my husband had written.

'Or is there another Chigozie Azubuike working at this newspaper who we don't know about?' Adaugo asked.

I stared at the page clutched in my fingers in confusion and terror.

The article accused the military government of corruption, injustice and suppression of human rights. Each sentence dug a grave deeper than the last. Referring to recent arrests, it spouted claims of tribalism, nepotism and false accusations without proof. Of recent executions by firing squad, it said, 'Why should human beings be made to face the barrels of guns of men who are no less unscrupulous than they are? Since when did it become proper for men to be declared guilty with evidence produced only by the accuser? Are we no better than the animals we slaughter for our daily bread? Is this what our beloved country has come to?' It went on to accuse the government of theft and far worse decay than the civilian government.

Befittingly, it concluded, 'And if by any chance you support this anarchy or believe that this government has succeeded in any way in righting the wrongs and corruption of the past government, you, my friend, are a fool.'

I collapsed in tears and Adaugo and Chinelo gathered around me like I was a widow in mourning.

'Leave the country for a while – go to Cotonou or Accra,' Adaugo suggested when I finally paused my crying. 'The government cannot arrest your husband over there; they are too busy trying to catch those officials that stole money under the civilian government. They won't have the time to chase a small-time journalist outside the country. Stay there, at least till things die down.'

'But Gozie will not agree; he'll say it's cowardly of him to run away from his country. You know how our men are; pride is everything to them,' I said dejectedly and started weeping again.

'What do you mean he won't agree?' she responded, looking at me like I'd lost my mind. 'Are you not a woman? Convince him!'

I nodded, unwilling to admit that I hadn't yet attained such heights of womanhood.

Gozie wouldn't hear it, and he made sure to enunciate just how much of a coward he thought I was. 'I did not do anything wrong. I will not leave my fatherland,' he obstinately declared.

The newspaper was shut down temporarily; the editor thought it best to let the noise die down before resuming publishing activities as usual. It seemed no one had been prepared for Gozie's article to receive so much attention from the public, not even Gozie himself. The hope was that somehow the government would be too busy chasing ghosts of the past to care about a small-time reporter.

A day passed, then two, then three, then a week. Hope began to sprout, a tiny blossom from a place of desperation, that perhaps everything would be okay after all – life would go on as usual.

They came for him two weeks later, dressed head to toe in the distinctive black uniform of the Nigerian Police Force, wielding heavy assault rifles, looking like they'd come for a dangerous criminal, an enemy of the state, not an ordinary reporter.

Gozie did not struggle or argue; he went with them calmly and I followed behind, hysterically begging to know where they were taking him. An officer finally took pity on me and informed me that

I could come visit him at Kirikiri Prison, the nation's largest maximum-security prison. Just before he was thrown in the back of the Black Maria police vehicle, Gozie turned to look at me and said, 'Take care of Ego.' Then he was gone, in a cloud of dust left behind by the battered vehicle. The government meant business.

I received a letter from Akin days later. He was leaving the country.

*I thought it best to do it this way, Uju. Your marriage means a lot to you and it's best that I respect it. I do not want to be the cause of any more problems between you and your husband. The military government has cut the funds available to the university for research . . . innovation and growth cannot thrive in such a stifling environment. I have decided to take up a postgraduate position at the Massachusetts Institute of Technology . . .*

*By the time you get this, I'll probably be out of the country. I've written my US address and phone number below. Please do not hesitate to contact me if you need anything at all. Anything. You know I'll always be here for you. Your admission and scholarship with the department are still very much open, I've made sure of that. I strongly believe in you and in your abilities Obianuju.*

*I remain sincerely yours,*
*Akintunde Ajayi*

*He hasn't heard about Gozie,* I thought, then held the letter to my bosom and wept.

\*

After Gozie's arrest, Papa contacted his friends with military connections. They all gave the same response – they needed time. Gozie had created such a stir that the government used him to warn off others who might be contemplating revolting against the administration.

'The government is still very upset about that article. In fact, I was told that the head of state said that people like Gozie are distracting them from their work and he must be made an example of. We need time to pass so they can forget about him and go after others that have committed more serious crimes. Then my friends will try to use their influence to get him out before his trial because once he's tried by the military tribunal, he would have to serve whatever sentence they give him,' Papa explained, his tone resigned.

'But Obianuju, how come you couldn't convince your husband to behave himself during such dangerous times?' Mama said as she escorted me to the door, like I was somehow to blame for Gozie's actions. 'Don't you know we women are the voices of reason when men want to do stupid things? Or haven't you noticed how I always advise your father?' *Biko* talk to Gozie. Tell him to behave like a good prisoner and not make any noise. You know our people have short memories. Before you know, they'll be talking about something else.'

Days later, I paid my first visit to a correctional facility – Kirikiri Prison – to see Gozie. The high exterior walls both fascinated and intimidated me, and the fading yellow interior walls and battered doors made me wonder where all the budgets for our prisons went – probably straight into a senior official's bank account.

At the check-in point, I asked to see the second-in-command like Mama had instructed, the brown envelope she had prepared for me in my handbag.

Officer Musa's uniform was crisply ironed and his head shorn of every follicle of hair. 'Good morning, madam. What can I do for you today?' he asked as I stepped into his office. He was seated behind a wide mahogany desk that took up most of the room; the empty organisation of its surface starkly contrasted with the piles of files stacked in slumping towers in a corner. I wondered about the identity of the people whose names filled those files.

'Uhm, yes, sir. I'm Chief Nwaike's daughter. I'm here to see my husband,' I replied, smoothing my palm over the sombre black dress I'd chosen for the occasion. Rumours were that military men liked women and I was determined to attract as little attention as possible.

'Ah! Chief Nwaike! My good friend,' Officer Musa said, his harsh features transforming into an expression of pleasant surprise. 'How is he doing? And your mother?'

'They're both very fine, sir.'

He nodded slowly. 'Good, good. Yes, your parents already informed me that you'd be coming to see your husband. Please take a seat. I hope you brought my package along,' he said, smiling slyly.

'Yes, sir. It's right here,' I replied, settling into the mahogany armchair facing him and handing over the brown envelope.

'Good, good,' he said as he tucked it away in a drawer. 'You see, we try our best to keep things going here but we don't get enough from the government to compensate our efforts. They keep sending new prisoners every day, accusing them of one thing or the other, and they refuse to increase the allocations. Do they expect them

123

to eat dust? It is people like your father that encourage us,' he lamented.

I wondered why he felt a need to explain himself to me.

We were interrupted by a knock on the door. 'Come in,' Officer Musa instructed, and a lower-ranking officer scurried in, holding a newspaper.

'Your morning paper, sir,' he said, handing the paper over with two hands and a melodramatic bow. This was what it meant to be an *oga* in Nigeria, to be treated like the reincarnation of a king.

'Thank you, Dayo,' Officer Musa mumbled, staring at the front-page headline. It said, '*TROOPS STORM MARKETS TO ENFORCE LOWER PRICES*' in bold black letters. Dayo bowed once more before rushing out of the room.

Officer Musa continued to peruse the front page while I waited patiently for him to be finished. Finally, he grunted, dropped the paper on his desk, shook his head and looked up. 'Where were we, madam? Yes. Your husband. You'll need to talk to him. He's giving us serious problems, always talking to the inmates about human rights and the like. The commandant is already suggesting that we isolate him from the other prisoners because we don't want a riot on our hands,' he said.

'I'm sorry, sir. I'll talk to him,' I replied anxiously.

He nodded again. 'Good,' he said, then yelled, 'Idris! Idris!' and a tall lanky officer materialised at the door to perform an exaggerated salute.

'Take her to see the activist.'

'Yes, sir!' Idris responded, saluting once more. It worried me to hear Gozie addressed as 'the activist', and even more so that the junior officer immediately knew who he was referring to.

124

'Okay, madam. Greet your father for me; tell him his gift is well appreciated,' Officer Musa said as I rose to leave.

The door to the small, dark visiting room shut behind me with a clang. For a moment, I panicked, afraid that I was trapped in. How did people survive in there without going mad?

At first, Gozie and I stared at each other in silence. Then I began to speak. I told him about the effort my parents were making to get him out, encouraging him to be patient, and he listened attentively, making no contributions.

I left the prison walls that day in good spirits, buoyed by the knowledge that our problems would soon be behind us.

A week later, the newspaper front pages carried the story of one Chigozie Azubuike, who was transferred to solitary confinement as punishment for organising a hunger strike amongst the prisoners at Kirikiri Prison, Apapa.

I stopped by the barber's shop on a whim weeks later. I watched, entranced, as his clipper buzzed through my thick Afro, levelling it to a low-cut that exposed the prominent ears underneath. At the photographer's studio, I requested several shots so I could choose the prettiest one, the absolute best to send to Akin; I penned Mama Sikira's house number as the return address.

*What do you think?* I wrote in the letter attached, the same one that said, *Nigeria was stupid to let a brain like yours go.*

I'd learned to stand on my own two feet, to live without a husband; to worry about the rent and the water and electricity bills. I'd asked the mechanic with a shop on our street to teach me to drive so I could make use of Gozie's car.

There were days I wished I had a husband, like when a man hit my car in traffic and asked me to take him to the man who must have bought me the car, as he did not discuss such issues with women. I cried on my way home that day, wondering where I would get the money needed to fix the broken tail light.

We visited Gozie when he was finally removed from solitary confinement, but only during the regular visiting days; no one was willing to risk their jobs by allowing us to visit a prisoner who'd caused so much trouble.

Our savings began to dwindle, and I knew it was time to get a job. I didn't want to collect any more money from Papa and Mama; I had to finally become my own woman.

I picked up application forms at various offices, and while Ego played, I sat at our dining table and diligently filled them out. In the evenings, Chinelo and Adaugo visited bearing cooked food. 'Things will get better,' they said, and I would nod, wanting desperately to believe them.

Nwakaego did not understand the word 'prison', but I said it to her anyway because I thought it unfair to lie to her about her father's whereabouts. She loved him in the way children love their parents – wholeheartedly and without question. And in return, the innocence of her affection brought out a different side of him. Before his arrest, he would come home with biscuits and small boxes of juice and glow with blissful contentment as she said, '*Tank* you, Daddy.'

The year she turned one, he'd bought her a colourful cake and a frilly dress with the trendy sailor collar, then he'd invited a photographer to take a picture of the three of us squeezed together on a small couch.

'*Pwison*,' she said after me, her eyes squinched in innocuous confusion, and I knew she would ask me the same question the very next day until I gave her an answer she understood.

I told myself it was the right thing to do, to create an acute consciousness early on of the state of the world we lived in, but, in doing so, I felt an inherent selfishness in bringing her into the harshness of reality, in initiating a comrade because I didn't want to feel alone.

A month and little more into Gozie's imprisonment, we passed a shop with a large pink teddy bear just about Ego's height displayed in its window.

'Mummy, teddy!' Ego shouted excitedly, pointing at the bear.

'No, Ego, we can't buy that now,' I said calmly but sternly.

'Mama, teddy!' she insisted, then burst into tears as I continued to drive, the teddy bear getting further away from her.

At home, she cried for her daddy and demanded to know where he was in high-pitched screams, because Daddy would have bought her the teddy bear.

The tears came for me then, and when she noticed, she paused hers so she could rub my shoulder and say, 'Mama sorry, don't cry.'

# 13.

## *I told you things would get better*

Gozie had been away for over four months by September '84. Four months of uncertainty, of helplessness and hopelessness. He never said much when I saw him, just sat with bent shoulders as I told him about our lives since he'd been taken away, each time feeling like a little more of his humanity had been stripped away. I only spoke of the positives, words to assure him that there was no need to worry, that somehow our world wasn't upside down.

It made no difference. He always turned away and focused on the plates of food I brought along, his cheeks swelling as he stuffed them with rice and his teeth grinding loudly. Even Ego's enthusiastic chatter and whining of 'Daddy, Daddy' failed to draw him out of his reticence.

Perhaps he was suffering from a guilty conscience, knowing full well he'd brought it upon himself, upon us all. I'd warned him but he hadn't listened. His friends said he was a martyr, a patron of democracy, that I should be proud to be the wife of such a great person, a person willing to die for his beliefs. But they weren't present when I had to explain to Ego why her father couldn't come home with us, or why she couldn't get her teddy bear or an extra packet of butter biscuits. All they did was talk while they walked free.

Sikira, Mama Sikira's daughter, had taught me Yoruba – *ookan* was 'one' and *oloriburuku* was 'a cursed person' (literally meaning owner of bad head). It was why, when my neighbours screamed at each other one evening, I understood what was happening.

We sat outside discussing headlines, a newspaper open between us as we studiously flipped through the brown pages. 'Just look at that,' Chinelo said, pointing at a snapshot halfway down the page. Three men and a woman stood side by side in a black and white photograph. The caption read: Mr. Mustapha Abdullahi, his wife, Mr. Benjamin Akintola and Mr. Goodluck Okoro at the Annual Stockbrokers Conference. 'What does "Mr. Mustapha Abdullahi, his wife" mean? Does the wife not have a name?' she complained.

'Well, she's his wife. Maybe they didn't have enough space for her name,' Adaugo commented.

The compound gate was thrown open with considerable force, and a fuming Mama Ifeoma marched through. She resided in the building next to ours, same as Mama Bidemi, with whom she had a tumultuous relationship.

Mama Bidemi strolled out of her apartment at the exact same moment and relaxed in a seat at her veranda.

'You're evil! God will punish you!' Mama Ifeoma screamed.

AIWANOSE ODAFEN

Mama Bidemi rose to her feet immediately. 'It is you that God will punish!'

Fearing that the altercation might soon degenerate into blows, I rushed to squeeze myself in between them and pushed them apart, even as my friends shouted for me to mind my business.

Mama Ifeoma eyed me. 'Uju, get out of my way!' she commanded, her face mutinous. And for a second, I was tempted to grant her wish.

'Let her come; let me give her the home training her mother forgot to give her!' Mama Bidemi shouted behind me.

'Please wait,' I pleaded with the two of them. 'Let us sit down and settle this the mature way. We're all adults here; there is no reason for us to act like children.'

'Now that everyone is calm, please can someone explain exactly is going on?' I said when we were seated. I turned to Mama Ifeoma. '*Nne,* why did you enter the compound and start screaming like that? At an elder, for that matter?'

'Obianuju, you won't believe what this *elder* did to me,' she said, echoing the word 'elder' sarcastically.

'What did she do?' I asked.

'So, you remember my Yoruba tailor? Her daughter gave birth a few weeks ago.'

'Congratulations to her o! God is good,' I said, clapping my hands together.

'Uju, that is not the matter!' Mama Ifeoma growled.

'I'm sorry. Please continue,' I said, duly chastised.

She nodded and continued. 'Like I was saying, my Yoruba tailor's daughter just gave birth. I decided to buy some baby clothes and

130

go and visit her. Before I left, I said, let me learn some Yoruba sentences that I will use to greet them when I get there. You know, to show that I am a good friend. I approached Mama Bidemi to teach me some words. And you won't believe what she did,' she said, then paused dramatically.

'What did she do?' I asked, giving her what she expected.

'She told me that when I get there, I should first kneel down and greet the elderly women with *"Ekaro o. Oloshi ni gbo gbo yin."* And that I should turn to the daughter and ask *"Sisi, obo yin ko?" Good morning o. You're all foolish. Young lady, how is your crotch feeling?*

I screamed with laughter and Mama Bidemi did not hesitate to join me, enjoying a recounting of her mean-spirited joke. It was later I would realise that that was the first time I'd laughed since Gozie's imprisonment, and my heart would feel lighter.

'It is not funny!' Mama Ifeoma grumbled.

'*Nne*, I'm sorry,' I choked out in between fits. 'But you're alive and in one piece, so what happened afterwards?'

'My sister, the women nearly beat me o. If not for my tailor that intervened and begged on my behalf, who knows, I might have come back with one leg,' she answered, looking ready to cry.

'Thank God,' I said, holding back another bout of laughter.

Mama Ifeoma shook her head in distress at the memory. 'Yes o, thank God for her. She told them she was sure that I didn't know what I was saying, that I've been her customer for a long time. She even asked me to repeat what I said in English, and when I couldn't, she translated for me. That was even how I found out that this "elder" had sent me to my own funeral. So, *nne*, please tell me, don't I have a right to be angry? Is this woman here not a witch?'

'Ah, you do. You have every right to be angry,' I replied.

I turned to interrogate Mama Bidemi. 'Mama Bidemi, why would you do such a thing? Please apologise.'

'I thought she was joking o. I didn't think that this one that is always abusing Yoruba people could have a Yoruba tailor. And I thought she would know I was joking when she heard *oloshi*. Who doesn't know the meaning of *oloshi* in this Lagos?' Mama Bidemi said, without a hint of remorse.

Days later, I would spot them seated in their usual spot on Mama Bidemi's veranda, laughing and chewing coconut pieces as though nothing had happened.

I was ill the day a job offer finally came in the mail – the postman grinning sunnily like he knew what was contained in the envelope – throwing up the contents of my stomach into the toilet bowl until Chinelo said, 'It's enough! You're going to the hospital,' and pushed me into her car.

'Madam, please have a seat,' the doctor said when I stepped into his office. He was a middle-aged man with a full head of black hair sprinkled with tufts of white, and a pair of giant glasses carrying the thickest lenses I'd ever seen.

'Madam, so we conducted various blood tests, as well as a test on the urine sample you provided, and we can't seem to find anything wrong with you,' he said. He looked up from the paper he held in his hands, and I stared at him in confusion, waiting for him to continue.

'But I'm sure something is wrong,' I pushed.

'Yes, yes,' he replied in an all-knowing tone, looking down once again.' You see, we didn't find something wrong with you, so we decided to test for something else. Madam, there's no other way to say this – you're pregnant.'

I couldn't have heard right. 'Excuse me?'

'I said you're pregnant, madam.'

'How?'

He frowned. 'What do you mean "how"? I should be asking you that question.'

'But my husband is in prison,' I countered.

'Well, I'm sorry to hear that.' Then on second thought, he asked, 'How long has your husband been in prison for?'

'Two months,' I responded automatically; I'd counted every day like a believer awaiting the second coming of Christ.

'Well, you're three months pregnant. I hope this sorts out your confusion,' he responded with finality, and got to his feet. 'Now if you'll excuse me madam, I have other patients to attend to. Please see the nurses for a copy of your results and further details on payment and antenatal care.'

Chinelo drove me to my parents' home. On the way, she chattered non-stop about how good the news was: 'Finally! I told you things would get better.' *I don't have money for a baby*, was all I could think.

'Obianuju, what is it?' Mama asked as soon as she opened the door. She'd always been able to read my body language, perhaps because it was so much like hers.

'I'm pregnant,' I blurted out. Perhaps telling a third person would somehow convince me that I wasn't mad.

Mama's scream penetrated my foggy mind as her band-like arms enclosed around me. I was let go after several seconds, but only to create room for a celebratory dance. 'My God answers prayers!' she declared, then rushed me in to sit. 'Did the doctor say anything else?' she asked.

'No. Why?'

'You're not excited.'

I sighed and rubbed my palm across my forehand. 'I finally got a job; I was supposed to start work on Monday. What am I going to do now? I don't have money for a baby. And even if I do start, how can I take maternity leave so soon?'

Mama looked ready to slap me, and she might have if I wasn't pregnant. 'What nonsense are you saying? *Eh*, Uju? Instead of you to be thanking God that you are finally pregnant after how many years. What nonsense job is more important than having a family?'

'But Mama we need the money.'

Mama pointed her finger in my face. 'See, you're not resuming at any office on Monday. You will not lose this child God has finally given you. God forbid!' She snapped her fingers and passed them over her head.

'But Mama . . .'

'Don't Mama me anything. If it is about money, your father and I will get the money for you to open a shop. You can sit there every day and attend to customers if you're looking for something to do.'

I had to stop myself from rolling my eyes. 'Mama, I'm no longer a child. Allow me do things the way I want,' I protested.

'What kind of woman abandons her primary responsibilities to pursue a job? Adult my foot!'

The next day, I submitted a letter politely rejecting the job offer.

Papa opened a provisions store for me on our street like Mama had promised. It wasn't much, but I no longer had to dread our landlord's monthly visit, or that of his wife.

Independence Day of '84 came on 1 October, and by 7 a.m. I was seated in the living room, waiting to listen to the address I knew was coming. It was a ritual performed every year, and I knew this year would be no different, military government or not.

The image of the head of state splashed across the screen once the last words of the national anthem were sung, and he began to talk about his government's numerous achievements. I had already started to tune out the address when he spoke the words I'd been waiting for: 'Thus, we have to come the decision that all members of the press currently in custody be released, to celebrate . . .'

With those words came a renewed hope, an expectation and desire for tomorrow. Our lives would indeed change for the better. Any time now. Any time soon.

It was while we waited for Gozie's return that the first letter came – someone finally knew of Uncle Ikenna's whereabouts during the war.

# 14.

## *It was the wrong time for such things*

*Cute.*

*I hate it because I loved your hair, lush and full. But you'll always be beautiful – hair or no hair.*

Akin's words fluttered and settled around my heart, cushioning it in a cocoon in January '85. Our letters took far too long to get to one another thanks to the slow postal service, and by the time they did, our lives were much removed from the words on the pages. He'd signed his letter differently – *Love always, Akin* – and I ruminated over it, over its significance.

The picture he'd tucked in between the folded leaves was a Polaroid – I'd heard of them but never seen one. In it, he flashed a casual smile in a baggy jumper and fitting denims. I wondered if he'd taken the picture just for me. He would love my hair now; Mama had made me grow it back not long after I'd cut it – 'Your husband will come back soon; you're not a widow.'

I waited till I heard the familiar grunt of Gozie's snoring, then I snuck to the living room to write my response.

He'd come home unexpectedly in November, when we'd given up on the government ever keeping its word. I was seated in our worn-out living room sofa, counting the proceeds of the day, and Ego sat on the floor playing with her toys. I shoved the money in my handbag when I heard the knock, struggled to my feet and waddled to the door. My belly made it impossible for me to move any faster.

'Who's there?' I called out.

'It's me,' a familiar voice replied.

Recognition came, tangled with hope; I worried my mind was playing tricks on me. 'You, who?' I responded.

'Me. Gozie,' the voice responded. I unlocked the door as fast as my jittery fingers could work.

The man in front of me was very different from the one that had been taken months before. His clothes hung in tatters from his body and his bones stuck out of what was left of the flesh under his skin, like those we saw in documentaries of survivors of war and famine. It was a miracle that he hadn't been one of the unfortunates who had mysteriously died behind bars and had their names published in passing in the daily newspapers. I would think of those changes much later, when we were settled, and I followed him around the house like a shadow to convince myself that months of worry and grief hadn't made me imagine his return. But in that moment, I grabbed Gozie and enveloped him in my arms, happy to be able to do that again.

We cried, we laughed, then we cried some more. Nothing could dampen the pure joy we felt. Mercy had shined up on us and we were finally together again. My heart and shoulders felt lighter; a burden had been lifted off them. Ego danced around us shouting, 'Daddy. Daddy,' then squeezed herself into our embrace.

The woman – the one who had known Uncle Ikenna during the war – lived in Lagos, right under our very noses. Nneka Onwuka was her name and she'd seen our advert in the newspaper.

She was thickset with large bones and wide, swinging hips; the type of body my brother Ugochukwu referred to as *I dey here*. When she smiled, which was often, it revealed fine, even teeth. I could tell she'd been beautiful as a young woman.

Nneka welcomed me and Mama into her living room like long-lost relatives, with warm hugs and plates of fried chicken and bottles of soft drinks. Our feet sank into the fur of her living room carpet, reminding me of the days of walking in the lush sands of Bar Beach – soft and soothing.

Mama smiled and nodded mechanically through the pleasantries, saying the right things at appropriate moments, but I could tell she was only waiting to get to the purpose of our visit.

'I met your brother in Enugu,' Nneka started at last, and Mama leaned forward eagerly. 'Just before the war started, in '67. Everyone was moving back home then; they said the North was no longer safe for our people. My father was at home on leave from work in Kano in '66 when the whole moving thing started.

'When his leave ended, he said he had to return to Kano to take permission from his place of work, and that he'd return home and wait till things settled down.' She paused and the pain in her eyes told me what happened next before she did. 'That was the last we

138

heard from him. They say he was killed during the riots. Burned alive.' A tear slipped out the corner of her eye and she wiped at it.

'After my father's death, I stopped school to help my mother take care of the younger ones. I was nineteen then. We used to make soap from palm oil – *ncha nkota* – and sell it in the marketplace. Everyday my mother would share the soap between me and my siblings and we would walk miles to neighbouring towns to sell it to make money so we could eat.'

'That was how I met your brother. He was a Biafran soldier.' Her eyes were glazed over, and a smile played at the corner of her lips. She was no longer with us, but back in '67 with Uncle Ikenna. 'He used to come to the market to buy *ncha nkota* from me twice a week without fail. He would even buy more than necessary sometimes just so I would have money to take home.

'He was not like the others. He was so handsome; a refined gentleman. He spoke the Queen's English too. I always asked him what he was doing there.' She looked at us. 'He didn't belong there you know.' I nodded, understanding her meaning.

'He was too good. He used to tell me jokes and stories – about his life, his time in England, his family. He told me about his sister and her children. He said he'd had a fiancée but her family had left Nigeria just before the war started. They said he was a fool to fight for Biafra.'

She stopped and I had a feeling her next words were going to be heavy. 'We fell in love.' She shook her head slowly, and laughed a humourless laugh. 'It was the wrong time for such things. Not long after I found out that I was pregnant, they – the federal troops – attacked Nsukka. Bullets fell from the sky like rain. Bombs were dropping everywhere. People were running. We didn't know where we were going to, we were just running.

'We ran deep into the forest – that was the only place we were safe. They were shooting people on sight. They were raping women, too. There were dead bodies everywhere. I lost two sisters and a brother that day. They were just selling soap.' Her voice cracked and she cleared her throat to drive away the tears.

'We walked and walked until we got to another town. But they attacked that town too and we had to run again. There was no food; we ate whatever we could find in the bush – rats, lizards, even cassava leaves. We didn't even have salt; we used to go to the river to fetch river salt to cook. My mother died not too long after. She was too old for that kind of stress.

'I had the baby, but she died less than a year later from malnutrition: her stomach was big but the rest of her body was all bones – kwashiokor. I tried my best, I really did. She starved to death in my arms.' Nneka covered her face with her hands, and her shoulders shook as she wept for her lost child. Mama moved over and wrapped her in a tight hug and soon they were both in tears. When she'd composed herself enough to answer, Mama asked Nneka detailed questions to piece together information about Uncle Ikenna's whereabouts.

He hadn't died in the attack on Nsukka; he'd led many civilians out into the forest to their safety. He'd even left a note for her – which wouldn't reach her until the end of the war – that he would be back for her and their child. She'd not heard from him since.

As we stood up to leave, I noticed that there were no pictures of a family of her own hanging in her living room; no husband, no children. I wondered if, like us, she was haunted by the ghost of the man Uncle Ikenna had been.

Our euphoria about Gozie's return was short-lived, rudely interrupted by reality's harsh knock. Nothing had changed with Gozie's homecoming; if anything, we had one more mouth to feed. Gozie couldn't get a job. The newspaper he'd worked for had shut down since his imprisonment, and other press houses weren't willing to take the risk. He returned home daily, after hours of roaming the streets, forlorn and dejected. His moods got darker and he lost his temper often. It was as though prison had unleashed a violence within him that wouldn't be controlled, and no matter how many times I asked, he would never tell me all that had happened there. Then he began to take solace in the bottle. On some days, he stumbled home in the early hours, words slurring and barely aware of his surroundings.

February came quickly. We'd settled into our pattern of living – I worked at the shop; Gozie spent the money. Nothing had changed except my burgeoning size. Then one morning, while Gozie was out with friends, I went into labour. A customer found me in the shop and drove me to hospital.

They came out within minutes of each other. 'It's a girl,' a nurse announced as she held her, smiling sweetly.

Another contraction hit almost immediately. 'Maybe it's a boy,' another nurse said excitedly. A few minutes later, another baby girl came.

Gozie found his way to the hospital hours later. A nurse put one daughter in my arms and handed the other over to Gozie. He peeped at the bundle in my arms and back at his. 'They are both girls?'

'Yes. Didn't the doctor tell you?' The nurse seemed caught off guard by Gozie's question.

'No, he only said my wife had given birth to twins.'

'Okay.'

'And both are girls?' He sounded incredulous.

'Yes, they are,' she responded, this time with a little more emphasis. She walked out shaking her head.

I held my daughter closer and turned away from him.


When the time came, I chose the names Nkechinyere (Whichever God Gives) and Nwamaka (Child is Beautiful) myself – my children were as good as any.

'Uju, you should start trying as soon as you heal,' Mama said. I stared at her, expressionless.

'Why are you looking at me like that? Don't you know your position isn't safe with only girls? His people might tell him to take another wife. Is that what you want?'

'Mama, please. I can't be thinking of such things now. I just gave birth. We barely have enough money as it is,' I said wearily.

'Forget about money; God will provide. You better start thinking of *such things* before you find yourself accommodating another woman in your home.'

With the babies here, I expected Gozie to fully focus on finding a source of income. But if anything, he grew more agitated. He always had time for choir practice. And on Sundays, he sang as he'd always done, sending melodies to the heavens.

I hired Grace to run the shop while I recovered, a tall, thin young lady who needed the money to pay for her night classes to further her higher education. She was a hard worker, too, and brought in more sales than I'd managed to. But even then, we were barely surviving. Our stews were watery and disappeared in rice, with more pepper in them than anything else; tomatoes had become too expensive. I washed our clothes with soap until my knuckles and palms were raw, and carefully mended and ironed them to avoid buying new ones. When the landlady's son came demanding the rent, I begged for an extension until he threatened to call the police.

# 15.

## No matter what happens, you're subject to him

A picture of Uncle Ikenna came in the mail that day in June '85 that Mama nearly lost her legs, with a return address that read: *83 Upper St, London, N1 0NU.* 'Who's writing to me from London?' she asked no one in particular as she turned the letter over, squinting as if to see through the opaque envelope.

We'd left for the market at dawn to shop in preparation for Papa's birthday; he was to turn seventy in a week and Mama had a small party planned. 'Don't forget to add *atarodo,* those small peppers, to the list. We need to cook extra in case the caterer doesn't deliver as planned,' she said over her shoulder as she marched through the jostling bodies at the marketplace like a bulldozer.

'Yes, Mama,' I replied from behind her, as I narrowly avoided an elbow to the head.

An ache had formed at the back of my feet and wormed its way up to my thighs by the time noon came around, but Mama was only halfway through her list. 'We still have to buy half a cow,' she announced, counting what was left of the money in her purse as we arrived at the junction to cross to the other side of the market.

We'd barely made our way across when a wheelbarrow overloaded with cartons of goods slammed into us from behind and its contents toppled onto Mama as she screamed and screamed.

'Ask Obianuju. I could have died! I nearly lost my legs,' Mama said to Papa as we settled in the living room hours later, telling a story she would repeat frequently over the next weeks. He smiled and patted her shoulders in comfort as he murmured, '*Ndo*.' He was used to Mama's exaggerations and embellishments.

'A package came for you,' he informed her and got up to pull out a medium-sized envelope from the television cabinet. Mama almost never got packages; her world was atomic, revolving around the sheltered confines of our family, church and relatives.

The photograph was from Uncle Ikenna's time as a student in the United Kingdom. 'See his full Afro,' Mama said, staring at the picture with teary eyes. There were three people in the black and white photo: a bespectacled young man with a toothy smile, a lanky woman with hair upswept in a poodle clip, and Uncle Ikenna, leaning into the middle, his dark arms around them, a contrast against their fair skins. An air of youthful mischief and nonchalance shone through and his smile lit up the frame. Papa and I exchanged worried looks.

It had been months since we visited the woman who had known Uncle Ikenna during the war and Mama still spoke of it like it was yesterday. Our trail had run cold and yet she held out hope that he was still alive, hidden somewhere in the vast world, waiting to return.

'Do you think he's over there? Maybe he sent this?' Mama asked, her eyes sparkling with child-like excitement as she turned the picture around. Papa's widened even more.

'Let's check; a letter might have come with it,' I said quickly and turned the envelope upside down. A slip of paper fell out.

*Dear Obiageli,* it started, and I wondered how they knew my mother's name.

*You may not know me but I heard of your search and know your brother would have wanted you to have this. He was a beautiful human: selfless, loving and always looking out for others. A wonderful friend with the heartiest laugh. I miss him. Hoping he's somewhere out there.*

*Sincerely,*

*Rebecca*

The tears in Mama's eyes spilled over and she wiped at them with the back of her hands. Papa and I listened in rapt silence as she began narrating stories we'd heard before: of the time Uncle Ikenna had sacrificed his food for her, of when he'd taken a punishment in her stead, how he'd sent her money as a poor student. She painted each tale with detail – his laughter, his energy, his heart.

'Gozie reminds me so much of him, you know,' she said when she was done. Her eyes were a bright shade of crimson.

'Yes, Mama, I know,' I replied. But I'd already begun to wonder if we'd been wrong all along.

\*

My resentment began to grow. I grew tired of being docile, of handing over money, of excusing Gozie's irresponsibility, of pretending everything was well. Then one day, all hell broke loose.

Grace had just stopped by the house to drop off the sales proceeds for the day, and I sat counting each note diligently and humming *Amazing Grace*; the choir had rendered it the previous Sunday, Gozie their lead chorister. Nkechi and Nwamaka were fast asleep and Ego sat watching her favourite cartoon. It was my idea of a perfect evening. I'd just tucked the counted notes in my handbag when Gozie unlocked the door from the other side and casually strolled in.

'I saw Grace on the way here,' he said. I kept mute.

'So I'm assuming she brought back money from the shop.'

I said nothing.

'I see you've suddenly gone dumb. Anyway, hand it over.'

Ego stopped watching her cartoon and turned to look at us.

'Please lower your voice; the children are asleep,' I said finally, weary.

'Don't tell me to lower my voice! Give me the money!'

I sighed. 'I'm sorry, I can't.'

'You what?'

'I can't. I need to buy baby food and nappies and foodstuff for the house. Ego's school fees are due soon, and we need to save as much as possible or we won't be able to pay.'

His right eye began to twitch, and the vein in his forehead throbbed dangerously. 'So, because you're feeding us, you think you're now the man of the house *ehn*? I'm asking for money in my own house and you're listing all the things we need like you're talking to an idiot. Did I say I wasn't aware?'

'It's not like tha—' I tried to explain.

His voice covered mine. 'No wonder! When people told me you didn't act like a woman whose husband was in jail, that you went about your merry way and you were even driving my car up and down, I didn't believe them. Now the evidence is before my eyes. You were happy I was in jail so you could be doing whatever without anyone questioning you. And how do I even know those brats are mine? I came back to find you pregnant. How do I know they don't belong to that lover of yours? Why didn't you just marry him?'

'What is that supposed to mean?' I screamed, all thoughts of not waking the children gone.

'It means what it sounds like! You're a cheat and a whore. And those children are not mine.'

The last vestige of control I had on my temper slipped, and I raised my hand to strike him. His instincts were sharp, even in his drunken state, and he grabbed it roughly and pulled me to him. 'Don't even think about it. I said give me the money!' he roared in my face.

'I'm not giving you any money,' I yelled back. 'You will not waste money for my children's food on beer and rubbish talk. I will not let y—'

A brutal slap cut my words short, my ears vibrating from the impact, and before I had time to react, I was knocked to the floor.

'How dare you talk to me like that? You think because you're the one feeding us, I'm no longer a man? Don't worry, I'll show you today how much of a man I am,' he promised.

I was careful not to scream, afraid to alert the neighbours; people rarely intervened when they heard raised voices – arguments between couples were normal – but screams meant something else. What would they think of us?

Blows were replaced by furniture, and the last thing I remembered before the darkness claimed me was the serving stool I used to entertain visitors connecting with my temple.

'Mummy, Mummy,' the familiar voice called from a distant place, and I used it as an anchor to battle the oblivion.

My eyes opened slowly; my lids felt like they'd been infused with lead. The slight movement caused pain to ratchet through my skull and the rest of my body. The source of the voice sat beside me, weeping and touching my face tentatively. 'Mummy, Mummy. Please don't die.'

I'd forgotten she was there. She'd witnessed our disgraceful behaviour. I felt shame wash through me. I should have just let things be.

'Daddy is different,' she'd said to me not too long after Gozie's return. She no longer ran to the door when he came home and the excitable screams of 'Daddy' had precipitously ceased, as though she sensed in him an indefinable and startling newness she neither understood nor liked.

Our living room was in disarray. I comforted my daughter, put on the TV for her to watch cartoons and started to clean up the room. Then, the twins began to cry.

For days, I stayed indoors, afraid for anyone to see the signs of my shame – the failed woman who couldn't keep a happy home. The damage couldn't be covered by makeup; the bruises were much too dark and the swellings were much too pronounced no matter how much ice I put on them.

When I heard a loud knock on the door during this time, I knew at once that the hand that produced it could only belong to one person – Ikechukwu. He always knocked on a door like he would have preferred to break it down and was only grudgingly bending to the dictates of civilised society.

'Uju. Open up,' Kelechi called.

I started to panic; I couldn't let my brothers see me this way. Perhaps if I stayed quiet long enough, they would assume I wasn't home and leave.

'Mummy, Mummy. Come and look at my homework,' Ego unwittingly called out from the room, loud enough for anyone outside our flat to hear. I had no choice but to go to the door.

'Uju!' Ikechukwu bellowed.

'I'm coming,' I called back, having no choice. I wrapped myself in a scarf and headed for the door.

I opened the door slowly, keeping my face averted.

'What took you so long?' Kelechi demanded impatiently, pushing his way in.

'Don't mind them. We were in the neighbourhood and decided to stop and visit you and the children,' Ugochukwu explained as they walked in. I could hear the smile in his voice. I still hadn't looked at any of them yet.

'Why are you wrapped in black? Have you changed religions?' Ugochukwu joked. I laughed nervously. Ikechukwu was eerily silent.

'Let me go bring the children,' I mumbled and tried to rush past them.

'Obianuju. Wait,' Ikechukwu said. I stopped in my tracks, my back to them, my head bowed. 'Remove that scarf and look at me,' he commanded. The other two were quiet as they waited for me to comply.

'Uju, why are you hiding your face? Remove that scarf, turn around and look at us,' Ikechukwu instructed again.

With shaky fingers, I pulled off the scarf, turned and raised my head. I winced as each one of them let out gasps of shock and fury.

Cool-headed Kelechi was the first to react. 'He is going to die,' he pronounced. 'Ikechukwu, take the children to Mama and come back to meet us. Tell her we wanted to take Uju out and could not leave the children alone,' he instructed immediately.

'Wait. Please wait, it's not what it looks like,' I pleaded.

'What is not what it looks like? Did that fool hit you or not?' Ikechukwu demanded.

'Yes, but please, it was my fault. I swear it was.'

I was squarely ignored.

'We warned him. We warned him,' was all Ugochukwu could mutter.

'Uncle, uncle, uncle,' Ego ran out screaming.

Fake smiles immediately transformed their faces, and they bent to fawn over her. I stood about nervously waiting, hoping they would change their minds.

I wasn't to have such luck. 'Ikechukwu.' That was all Kelechi had to say before my brother went into action. Within minutes, he had the children in his car, with Ego happily waving me goodbye – innocently excited at the prospect of seeing Grandma.

In his absence, I tried to plead with the other two. I was wasting my time, they said. Gozie was going to learn the hard way.

Ikechukwu had just returned when the sound of a Peugeot 504 driving into the compound interrupted us.

'Please,' I begged one final time as, moments later, the key turned in the lock, and Gozie pushed the door open.

He smiled, oblivious to, or purposely ignoring, the murderous glares my brothers sent his way. 'This is a surprise. I'm guessing you're here to see your sister. Uju, is there anything to eat? I'm hungry.'

His chatter was met with heavy silence. I sat there wringing my hands in apprehension. It was then he finally noticed our expressions. 'Is anything the matter? Is everyone okay? Mama? Papa?'

'Everyone is fine,' Kelechi ground out.

'Then what is the matter? Why are you all seated here like statues?'

'Chigozie, look at our sister,' Ugochukwu said. Gozie turned to look at me.

'Was this how she was given to you?' Kelechi asked, his voice deceptively calm.

'What did we tell you about touching our sister?' Ikechukwu demanded.

Gozie's eyes widened as comprehension hit him. It was like he'd somehow not noticed the ugly bruises I'd been carrying around for days. He was used to seeing me that way.

He began to back up towards the door. It was then they pounced on him. He was thrown into the boot of Ikechukwu's car and driven to Peter's apartment.

Peter had been Ikechukwu's classmate in secondary school, and they'd kept in touch even afterwards. Many afternoons, he'd come over to our parents' house for Mama's special pepper soup and bottles of chilled drinks. He'd always called me sister, and mirrored my brothers in size and temper. I followed their entourage on the back of an *okada*, crying hysterically. They were going to kill him. I was sure of it.

My prayers that Peter be out of town were clearly unanswered when we arrived and Peter's car was parked in its usual spot with Peter standing in front of his door, as if alerted to our arrival. He spoke to me first. 'Obianuju, what happened? Who did this to you?' he asked, his deep voice vibrating with barely controlled fury. And I knew I would not have an ally in him.

Ikechukwu threw the boot of his car open and pointed at a shaken Gozie. 'This is the animal that did this to her.'

'Bring him inside,' Peter instructed and turned on his heels.

Gozie was made to strip to his underwear, then, taking turns, my brothers and Peter beat him savagely, their fists pounding into every part of his body.

It was like a scene out of a Nigerian movie about terrible marriages and unbearable in-laws. And I – its main character – knelt close by, tears streaming down my face, wailing and begging for mercy, but they showed no signs of tiring.

'You're not sorry enough,' Peter announced several minutes into their thrashing session before disappearing for a few minutes and returning with a long whip. 'It's good we're in a military era,' he said, then chuckled, the evil sound rumbling in his chest. 'You can rest. I will continue from here,' he told my brothers and the beating stopped. Their chests heaved from the effort.

Peter turned to Gozie. 'Since you want to behave like an animal, you will be treated as one. *Oya* start frog-jumping. If you stop before we say so, this *koboko* will land on your back.'

'*Crack!*' was the sound the whip made as it connected to Gozie's back a few minutes later, after his weak legs had given away.

I screamed, grabbed Kelechi's leg and tugged with all my might.

'Please don't kill him. Please. My children would have no father. What will happen to them? I beg you in the name of God. I swear he won't do it again. I swear! Please have mercy!' I cried. Something about my plea finally penetrated the angry haze. Kelechi signalled for Peter to stop and Gozie was roughly pulled to his feet.

'You're very lucky that she is here to beg on your behalf. Or you would have died today. Idiot,' Ikechukwu spat.

'Next time. NEXT TIME. Touch her! And see if your ancestors don't welcome you that day,' Ugochukwu added.

'Left to me, he would be a dead man,' Peter grumbled.

Kelechi refused to look at Gozie. He turned to face me instead. 'Ikechukwu will bring your children back for you later in the day. We have to go now, because if we stay here . . .' He didn't have to complete the statement.

Ugochukwu dropped us at home. We stepped out of the car looking like survivors of a war. It *was* a war, a war I could never win.

'*Nkem*, take care of yourself and your children. We'll come back to check on you. Ikechukwu should be here soon,' Ugochukwu said without looking in Gozie's direction, then drove off.

Mama Ifeoma chose that moment to stroll by with a bucket in hand. She raised her hand to greet us, then froze. 'My God. Are you okay? What happened to you?'

Gozie's battered face transformed into a smile. 'We were involved in a small accident on our way back. We are okay, just a few bruises and cuts. My brother-in-law had to drop us off,' he replied smoothly.

'Sorry. I'll bring over some of the herbs and *abubu eke* my mother sent from the village. They will help with any injuries and scars.'

'Thank you. We'd really appreciate that.'

'These Lagos roads. May God help us.'

'My sister, may God help us,' Gozie echoed. I stood rooted in silence.

Mama came prepared this time. If I wasn't going to listen to her, Deacon Rapuokwu was going to talk some sense into me. An elder at my parents' church, Deacon Rapuokwu was responsible for counselling couples-to-be, newlyweds and those going through marital problems. Ironically, his name meant 'Avoid problem', and it was said that once Rapuokwu was called into your matter, your problems were really serious and needed to be avoided as soon as possible.

'Uju, your mother has come crying to me. My ears have heard some things and I don't want to believe they are true,' he started. We sat on the sofa in the living room. The windows were open to ward off the heat.

'Uju, your mother tells me that you reported your husband to your brothers, and that you got them to beat him up so bad that he had to visit the hospital. Is this true?'

I was silent.

'Is he not talking to you? *Ehn* Uju?' Mama interjected.

'Mama, what do you want me to say? You're talking about Gozie. Look at me. Am I not your daughter? See me, see my face, see my hands. Do I look like normal to you? But you're here talking about Gozie.'

Deacon Rapuokwu intervened. 'Uju, your mother only means

well. She's heard only one side of the story. Now we're here, we want to hear yours.'

'Hmmm. This is serious,' Deacon Rapuokwu said when I was done.

'This is the devil at work,' Mama concluded.

'You're very right, my sister,' he concurred.

'We will have to talk to your husband. Violence is never the answer. But since you're the only one here, we will talk to you first. Obianuju, your husband is the head of the home. No matter what happens, you're subject to him. If money is the issue, whenever money comes in, hand it over to him. You know he's a man, even if you're the one making the money. You have to make him feel like a man,' Deacon Rapuokwu said.

'But—but . . .' I stammered, unable to believe what I was hearing.

Mama raised her hand to shut me up. 'But nothing. Listen when your elders are talking to you. I've told you several times, this is the problem with you. You talk too much. You don't want to listen. Your mouth is too sharp. That is why your husband is always beating you. A man is going through financial problems, and all you do is talk and talk. Why wouldn't he react?'

They talked for hours after that, cautioning me to be submissive, to repent my ways and pray for forgiveness.

'As for your brothers, I will talk to them. They must stop interfering in your marriage. Even if you're quarrelling with your husband, must they add to the fire? It is why our people say, "One should not join a mad man in mad practices." If you were to become a widow, what would they do?'

# 16.

## *It was God. Or something like him*

'Obianuju! Obianuju!' Adaugo's lilting voice called from somewhere behind me at church in March '86. Casually, I turned around on my new platform heels.

'Uju. You're a big madam now. See me calling you and you're just rushing like you cannot hear me,' Ada said when she finally stood in front of me.

'I'm sorry, Ada. It's not like that; I was just rushing to get home as soon as possible. You know we just moved, and we aren't done cleaning and unpacking yet.'

'*Just moved. Cleaning and unpacking,*' she mimicked, smiling slyly, and we laughed. 'You're so lucky. In fact, I'm jealous. See you: new apartment, new car, new clothes. You're looking like a big man's wife now. I saw your blouse the other day in a boutique, and it was so expensive. In fact, I nearly fought with the woman selling . . .' She continued chattering, her head bobbing up and down animatedly, the heavy curls on her head bouncing in whichever direction she turned.

157

Ada had recently taken to perming her hair with the latest wave in style – jheri curls. The first (and last) time I'd escorted her to the salon to get her hair done, I'd nearly vomited when I got a whiff of the chemicals the hairdresser applied to her hair.

But Ada loved to be dressed head to toe in the latest styles, and I admired – even envied – her knack for always appearing like she'd stepped out of a foreign magazine. Our church's progression towards the modern age had helped too: scarves were no longer compulsory and skirts were no longer the only option available to women. The elders had disagreed, arguing that we were departing from the light, and 'going the way of the world'. But the pastor had insisted. He could not risk losing more members to the New Age churches.

I slapped her shoulder blithely. 'You're talking as if I don't know how well Uzondu's business has been doing. This blouse you're wearing can probably buy me a couple of pairs of shoes.' She blushed and laughed, stopping to adjust her outfit primly. Adaugo had never been modest about Uzondu's success in business; she wore it like a badge of honour.

'Even though we've never held a thanksgiving service in church like you and Gozie. Even the pastor came out to dance with you,' she replied.

'That's because Uzondu is hardly ever in town. He's always travelling to one place or the other for business.'

'No. It's because you and Gozie give so much to the church. I heard the elders are thinking of elevating his position. But some are saying he's too young to be a deacon.' She rolled her eyes. 'I really need to encourage Uzondu to give more to the church.'

It was the first I was hearing of such plans.

Adaugo pulled me closer. 'But the way your life has turned around, *ehn* – one day you were struggling and now you're doing so well. Who would have thought?'

'My dear, it's God o,' I replied, and we giggled gleefully.

It *was* God. Or something like him . . .

It was nothing new. Nigeria was home to multiple overnight millionaires – uneducated drivers who'd become local government chairmen, struggling civil servants who'd stumbled onto government contracts, tailors to top government officials who'd been gifted oil blocs. It was the way of the world we lived in. When the current government had ousted the former in a coup in late August of '85, we were already rather used to sudden programme interruptions followed by a rendition of the national anthem and redundant speeches to announce the exchange of power, to seeing soldiers braggadociously roaming the street.

Gozie spoke of returning to journalism. The papers weren't as restricted; he could investigate and expose corrupt officials. I listened silently. My opinion wasn't of any importance to him anyway.

Then one hot Saturday afternoon, Nasir came to visit. I stood with my door ajar, staring at the skinny man I could not recognise. Attired in a pristine white traditional Hausa kaftan and *babariga* – the gold-threaded detailed embroidery of the square neckline proof of the painstaking efforts of the weaver and the costliness of the clothing. His head was covered with a well-knitted *hula* and his feet with expensive leather shoes. He looked every bit the Northern aristocrat.

'Good day, madam. I'm looking for Chigozie Azubuike. I was told he lives here,' he said, smiling with the charm of one that was used to being – and expected to be – liked everywhere he went.

'Yes, I—'

'Nasir! Is that you?' Gozie shouted from behind me.

'Gozie the man!' Nasir boomed in reply.

I stepped back in self-preservation as Gozie ran over to embrace this man that was apparently his friend.

'I cannot believe this. Nasir at my doorstep,' Gozie said, ushering him in to sit.

'You better believe it,' Nasir responded, grinning from ear to ear.

'The only Hausa man in Nsukka! The only Hausa man in the East! It's been ages. How did you find me? How have you been?' Gozie asked when they were seated. I stood awkwardly in a corner, waiting to be introduced to the strange man in my house.

'My friend. I've been fine o. I saw Obinna the other day at a meeting on Lagos Island and I asked if he'd heard from you or seen you since we graduated from Nsukka. I was shocked when he told me you'd moved to Lagos and that you were married with children. But Gozie, you didn't do well; you didn't even look for or try to contact me.'

Gozie shook his head. 'See, my brother, it's not like that. You know once you graduate, life just takes over.' It was at that moment Gozie finally remembered I was still in the room. He gestured for me to come closer. 'Nasir, meet my wife, Uju. Uju meet Nasir. We were classmates at the University of Nsukka,' he said simply.

I smiled and extended my hand to Nasir. 'It's nice to meet you.'

'Nice to meet you too, madam,' he said, once again flashing his charming smile. He turned to Gozie. 'You're a lucky man. Your wife is beautiful. Does she have a sister?' he said, still holding my hand.

I giggled, trying not to blush. 'Thank you.'

160

Gozie smiled; his glance towards me, however, communicated just the opposite. My grin died immediately.

'But Nasir, see how you're shining. Come and tell me, what is the secret?' Gozie asked.

'My brother it is God o,' Nasir said smiling. And they both burst out laughing.

They sat together for hours laughing and catching up, while I scurried about, entertaining them with food and drinks. That way, I caught snatches of their conversation.

'But Nasir, you have to tell me: how have you done so well for yourself in such a short time? It cannot be from this same journalism I've been hustling since,' Gozie said after they'd chatted for a while.

Nasir let out a loud guffaw, then paused to take a sip from the glass filled with orange juice I'd placed on a stool by his side. 'Journalism? Under a military government?' He gestured to himself. 'Do I look like someone that likes to suffer? As I'm slim like this? You want me to die? One day in jail and they'll rush me to their hospital.'

Gozie grinned, a forced one. 'So what do you do then?'

'I do anything and everything.'

'Anything and everything? Hope you're not involved in criminal activities.'

Nasir looked offended that his friend would even suggest that. 'No. Not at all. Come on now, Gozie, don't you know me better than that? Or do I look like a thief to you?'

Gozie was immediately contrite. 'I'm sorry. Please don't be offended. You've always been a good guy. I just don't understand what you mean by "anything and everything".'

'I mean I'm a contractor. If you need a truck of cement, I can supply to you. If you need cars supplied, I can get them for you. Motorcycles? I'm your guy. Anything and everything, I do.'

'Really?'

'See, Gozie, leave everything they taught us in school. You have to be sharp. It is condition that made the crayfish bend. In this country, it is the poor that suffer. Or didn't you hear Fela's song? Life in this country *na* original sufferhead.'

Gozie gave it some thought. 'Hmmm. My brother, you are right. So how do you get these contracts?'

'Government,' Nasir replied.

'Government? Same government?'

'Yes. Government. That is where the money is now. Oil money is flowing, so the government is spending. They are buying cars and building houses. So I help them spend the money.'

'But how do you get the contracts?'

'I made some big friends in government and the civil service. They get me the contracts and I give them a cut of whatever I make.'

'Hmm,' Gozie said, brooding over what Nasir had just said.

Nasir leaned closer to him. 'Gozie, listen to me. Our work does not pay. It only leads to suffering and imprisonment, and in the worst cases, death. All the reporting that has been done, what has it changed? Leave this struggling and suffering. Come and take your share of the national cake. I can introduce you to some people, and within no time, you'll be living in a big house and driving a big car. Don't you want to live well? To be able to afford the good things of life?'

Gozie looked uncomfortable. 'But—but . . . is this right? Aren't you encouraging corruption, making money like this?'

Nasir laughed nonchalantly. 'See, if I don't take the contract, someone else will. I'm just making my money, and there is nothing wrong with that. If the government has decided to spend on useless things, why not help them? My not taking the money won't stop them or make them do the right thing. I have nothing to feel guilty about.'

Bending his head in concentration, Gozie took his time to think about it. His business intellect seemed to war with his sense of civic duty. Was he any less patriotic or integrous if he went along with what Nasir suggested? 'Hmmm. You're right. You're very right, my brother,' he said eventually. 'We need to do what we can to survive in this country. Our leaders don't care about us. Left to them, we can all die. Look at me, after all my noise about corruption and calls for justice in the newspapers, what has come of it? They're all still living well and fat while I'm here barely surviving after spending how many months in jail. All my supposed integrity, nothing inside my pocket. Those journalists that praised them are buying new cars and houses. This country is really not for all of us.'

Nasir looked pleased with his friend's conclusion. 'I'm glad you're beginning to see things clearly. These guys don't care one bit; we mean absolutely nothing to them. Even Fela sang it: few people are getting fat while the rest are hungry.'

Gozie laughed and jumped to his feet. 'I love that song!' It was the happiest I'd seen him in a long while.

Not disappointing his friend, Nasir got to his feet and closely imitated Fela's voice: 'Army arrangement.'

The seriousness of the conversation was forgotten as they sang and danced like young undergraduates in a university hostel without a care in the world.

Hours later, Nasir drove off in a shining grey Mercedes-Benz W126 – 'Army Arrangement' blaring out his car windows – after Gozie had promised to meet with him at his office first thing Monday morning.

Nasir was true to his word and overnight we were catapulted into the coveted upper-middle class. We no longer struggled to afford the basic things; we had food on our table – Gozie could finally have more than a piece of meat in his soup.

Nasir came to visit quite often and soon became 'Uncle Nasir' to my daughters. On occasion, he brought along his wife, Halima, and their three children – two sons and a daughter.

Halima and I were opposites in life, looks and disposition. She was timid and quiet. Muslim, she kept her hair constantly covered in colourful scarves that were always draped around her like a second skin. Her light skin and waist-length loose curls – visible only when she took off her scarf indoors – denoted her Fulani heritage. Later, with a contented smile, she would tell me about the foreignness in her blood as well; her grandmother had been from Yemen. Halima had been betrothed to Nasir young, but it was obvious in their smiles and subtle touches that they'd grown fond of each other and theirs had become a love marriage.

The transformer on our street blew up one day and Gozie decided he'd had enough. We were moving out; our little apartment no longer fit our status.

Our new flat was located in a newly built block in the heart of Lagos, with constant power and water supply, freshly painted walls and rooms so large it was difficult filling the bare spaces with our sparse belongings. The air of the surrounding community was fresh, bereft of the dank stench of overflowing gutters and rubbish that had become our constant companion. Somehow, I'd gotten so used to hardship, I'd forgotten there were other realities.

'By the way, we're having another prayer meeting today. You should join us,' Adaugo said.

'Which group is that again?' I asked.

'Expectant Mothers o. You know I'm the new president.'

I laughed, genuinely amused. 'Adaugo, Expectant Mothers? Since when? Haven't you expected enough?' Ada had been pregnant constantly for years now, giving birth to four children – all girls – within just over six years, searching desperately for that elusive male child. Each time, she'd returned home from the labour ward disappointed and eager to try again. Now, she had a constantly rounded look about her, her slim lithe figure of our varsity days long gone. I could never tell whether she was pregnant or recovering from a previous pregnancy.

Adaugo's face settled in disgruntled frown. 'Obianuju, don't start. Anyway, Easter is coming soon, and the women are thinking of doing somethi—'

Chinelo chose that moment to pass by, dragging her little son along. The poor boy looked fed up with his mother's after-church antics, much like I'd always looked as a child, following Mama. Mama had known everyone back then, from the pastor to the church gateman.

165

Ada turned her attention to the little boy clutching Chinelo's hand tightly, her gaze filled with open yearning. 'Hello. How are you?' she cooed softly at him before turning back to his mother. 'Chinelo. *Kedu*? I was just telling Uju that Easter is coming and that the women's group is thinking of planning something,' Ada said.

'Really? That is a good idea. When is Easter again?' Chinelo asked.

'*Odiegwu*. Where were you when the pastor was announcing the dates – or have you started dozing during service? Easter is the thirtieth of this month,' Ada replied.

'We should use Obianuju's new place for our planning meeting,' Chinelo suggested.

My welcoming smile died. 'Why?'

Adaugo smirked shrewdly, seeing an opportunity for immediate revenge. 'Yes! Wonderful idea. I will tell the women.'

'Adaugo, if you suggest my house to anyone, prepare to die.'

'Come and kill me first,' Adaugo said and stuck out her tongue.

Chinelo giggled at our bickering. 'Obianuju, you should share what God has given you with the world. You're now a big woman. I was just admiring your car parked outside this morning. You're so lucky.'

Mama had expressed similar sentiments during her last visit. 'See how lucky you are. You should be thanking me. I was the one that told you to marry him even when you were proving stubborn. Didn't I tell you he reminded me of Ikenna? Good and hardworking! See how you're enjoying now,' she said, her face alive.

I laughed – whether sardonically or in good humour, I wasn't sure. Something about my laughter must have disconcerted Mama because she uncharacteristically chose to change the subject. 'Your brother is bringing the woman he plans to marry on Saturday to meet the family. Hope you haven't forgotten o.'

'No, Mama, I haven't forgotten. I'll be there.' It was hard to forget, considering how often Mama talked about it – that was the fifth time she'd mentioned it that day alone.

'Good. Make sure you wear the wrapper we agreed on.'

'Yes, Mama.'

'Good, good,' she said cheerfully. I wondered if Mama was aware that Ugochukwu barely knew the young lady he was bringing over – having met her just a few months before – and was tying the knot just to put an end to Mama's constant harangues. Even hot-blooded Ikechukwu was planning on doing the same.

Mama let out a sigh of contentment. 'Everything is going so well. Finally.'

I was stopped on my way out of Ego's classroom two days after I saw Ada and Chinelo at church; now that we had some money, we could afford to send her to a private school with well painted walls, new desks, updated textbooks and smaller classes.

I'd just waved my daughter goodbye and was on my way out the door, when her teacher stopped me. 'Madam, I'm sorry to disturb you but can I please speak to you in private?' she asked as she closed the classroom door behind her.

'Sure. Is anything the matter? Is Ego doing badly in class?' I asked, already worried.

'No, ma, she's doing really well.'

'Then what is the matter?'

167

She took a deep breath before speaking. 'Your daughter is doing very well academically but her social behaviour is a bit worrying.'

'What do you mean?'

'Well, she keeps to herself a lot and hardly talks to the other children. Sometimes, we find her in a corner crying. The other day we asked the children to come up with a crayon drawing of their families and what she drew was rather unusual. I do not mean to intrude, but is everything okay at home?'

I stared at her blankly, unable to believe my ears. What was I to tell her? That my husband still beat me at the slightest provocation, and most times in the presence of my daughters? That my blood lined the tiles of our new home? That the heavy makeup I wore was to cover the heavy bruises underneath the layers? That I was mocked whenever I asked my husband for anything, even though I was no longer allowed to run my shop because it didn't fit his new status? That even the car I drove was given to me as a symbol of status and could be taken away at any time?

I was tempted to tell it all. Then I noticed the bareness of the second finger of her left hand. No. I wouldn't be the one to ruin her illusions. It was better to hope, for her sake, that hers – if she ever got the chance – was better than mine.

So instead, I said, 'Nothing is wrong at home. Thank you for letting me know and for your concern. She's probably just adapting to the new environment; you know it takes some children longer than others to adapt.'

If that was what it meant to be lucky, I could make do with a little less luck.

# 17.

## *Okenwanyi! Agunwanyi! Nwanyi Ike!*

We celebrated Chinelo's promotion at work at the end of '86 with wine stolen from Chigozie's home bar, wine so crimson and smooth it swished softly in the crystal glasses we raised in toasts, then transitioned seamlessly from our tongues to our mid-palates, the velvety currant flavour lingering at the back of our mouths long after we swallowed.

'Chinelo! *Nnukwu Ada!* Madam manager! You lead and we follow!' I saluted and mock bowed.

'*Okenwanyi! Agunwanyi! Nwanyi Ike!*' Adaugo shouted and refilled her glass to raise it again. 'I'm so proud of you, *nne*. Keep going. The sky is your starting point.'

Then we lost ourselves in the bottles, emptying their contents, hysterical with laughter at the most mundane jokes – enjoying the absence of our children, who were spending the weekend with our mothers.

\*

Nwamaka wouldn't stop crying in January of '87. Her little buttocks moved restlessly around her seat and her loud wails reverberated through the church auditorium. I could feel the irritated glances of everyone around on us, their judgmental stares.

Gozie stretched his arm behind me and moved closer, a smile plastered on his face. To anyone, he looked like a man who wasn't embarrassed by failures. I was used to it; the false displays of affection – the hugs, quick pecks, the possessive arm around the waist – that made people say 'Love *Nwantinti*' and giggle afterwards like little children watching a romantic movie for the first time.

'Make her stop crying. You're embarrassing us,' he whispered harshly through his teeth. His hand discreetly gripped my right shoulder to emphasise his point and I automatically flinched. The dark bruise I'd acquired during our 'discussion' the previous day was still too raw.

'I'm sorry. I'm trying,' I said.

'Try harder or take her out,' Gozie growled under his breath.

I nodded and smoothed the embroidered wrapper around my waist with shaking hands.

'Auntie Kamto bought me some biscuits,' Ego said looking at me. She was maturing fast, and not for the right reasons.

'Nwamaka, do you want biscuits?' I asked, hopeful.

'*Biskits!*' she warbled and nodded eagerly, her face immediately transforming into a smile. Ego pulled out a packet of biscuits and handed it over to her little sister. I felt Gozie's grip on my shoulder relax as Nwamaka's wailing ceased.

'Tell your sister thank you,' I told Nwamaka, sending Ego a grateful smile.

Nwamaka shrugged indifferently. Sometimes I worried she'd grow up to be like her father. 'Nwamaka!' I warned.

'*Tank chu*,' she mumbled. I sighed. Her speech had improved greatly but it was still mostly baby talk. There was still time. It had taken me years of practice to perfect my pronunciation and Uncle Ikenna had been the most patient, practising words with me, calling out the phonemes, explaining where I was unclear. I thought of the picture in the mail and wondered what he would have thought of my children, the sort of uncle he would have been. Mama always said he would have loved Nwamaka the most because she was stubborn just like I'd been.

Mama had written to the woman in London to thank her for the photograph, then she'd spoken with Gozie about getting it published in the newspapers. 'Someone might recognise him. You never know,' she said to me, eyes bright with hope. I drew from her well of hope and nodded in agreement.

An usher dressed in a dapper suit approached our pew at the front of the church. 'Sir, they said I should tell you that the bride is around,' he said to Gozie, but I knew he addressed the both of us. It was, after all, considered proper to address any issues concerning a family to the man of the house – all our correspondence, invitations and cards were addressed to 'Mr. Azubuike and Family.' I was the 'and Family' in the equation: a mere addendum.

'Thank you, my good man,' Gozie responded, promptly bouncing to his feet and adjusting the black cap on his head. The *isiagu* he wore shone bright, the intricacies of the embroidered gold designs blinding; heavy neck beads adorned his neck and he clutched a specially carved cane he did not need. His outfit was an announce-

171

ment to everyone; it said, 'See me – can't you see how rich I have become? I'm no longer the poor man of yesterday.'

But he could be excused today. Today was special; it was, after all, not every day a man gave his sister out in marriage.

Outside the church, the bride stood beside a jeep decorated with telltale colourful ribbons, gripping her bouquet.

Gozie's status as a man of the people meant we were invited to weddings often, not because our presence was appreciated, but in hope that the happy occasions would cause us to dip into our deep pockets. The invitations were handed out with ceremonious 'thank yous' – unabashed statements of expectation – and the collection, an implicit acceptance on our part to share what abundance we had. But no matter how many times I sat at the front of the church, a guest of honour with Gozie, I was never prepared for the first sight of the bride: the joy, the beauty, the excitement, the anxiety, the fear.

'Congratulations, Kamfeechukwu. You look so pretty,' I said to Gozie's sister, hugging her tight.

'Thank you, *nne*. You're looking really nice too o. Are you sure my brother won't pay another bride price to your people?' she said in return, and we laughed together like we'd been best of friends all our lives.

We hadn't gotten along in the earlier days of my marriage, but the years had helped us both mature enough to put our differences behind us. Adaugo had joked that perhaps Kamfeechukwu and her twin's years of singlehood had improved their dispositions. 'When a woman notices her market is not selling, she has to change what she's selling.' I'd laughed then but felt a nagging sense of guilt for finding the hilarity in such words. Why did we have to change our 'market'? To mould ourselves like clay, continuously transforming until we were in a form most pleasing.

'Kamfee, are you sure you're ready?' I asked the bride, half-serious.

'What kind of rubbish question is that?' Gozie interjected. I would not be the one to ruin his big day.

'I'm sorry. I was just joking,' I murmured.

'*Haba*, brother. She was just joking,' Kamfeechukwu interposed. 'Sister don't mind him. He's always too serious. I'm very ready.'

I smiled shakily; I'd just earned myself another beating, and my shoulder had barely healed. 'Where's your twin?' I asked, quickly changing the subject.

'She was here some minutes ago, but she went to talk to her fiancé.' She emphasised the word 'fiancé' with pride, letting anyone who happened to be listening know that her sister was soon to leave the doomed world of singlehood.

The ceremony was beautiful, but then, they always were – the blushing bride, the conjugal vows, the cheers as the couple shared their first legitimate kiss. It was repetitive and predictable, but it was in that that a poignant sweetness lay.

Afterwards, the pastor said, 'Let me tell you a story,' and launched into a tale of a son of the soil who'd married a girl who'd been raised outside the continent. She wasn't raised right, he said. She was unable to cook and clean and dared to challenge everything her husband did. As expected, the marriage hadn't worked out and she'd divorced him, taking all his money in the courts. It was one of those stories mothers told their sons to warn them of the evil of marrying foreign women. He stopped to commend Kamfeechukwu's husband for choosing a 'properly brought up' girl to marry. 'We know our sister here is very well behaved and would never do such a thing.'

Kamfeechukwu blushed.


Nasir and Gozie sat side by side on the high table, chatting and laughing as the wedding celebrations went on around them. Nasir, resplendent in his white *agbada* and embroided *hula,* was seated in his place of honour as the chairman of the occasion – a position reserved for those who had contributed the most to making the event a success. Gozie leaned closer to speak with his friend, a broad smile stretched across his face, and I was reminded of a time in October '86 when they'd been huddled up together wearing more sober expressions.

The day the news of the letter bomb broke, Nasir drove to our home looking frazzled; sweat drops gathered atop his upper lip, his kaftan looked like he'd pulled it out in a hurry and his head was without his signature *hula*. It was the first time I would see him with anything other than a relaxed smile.

'Madam, is Chigozie home?' he asked without preamble immediately I opened the door. I found it sweet that he always called me madam.

'Is everything okay?' I asked as I ushered him in.

'Yes, yes, everything is fine,' he replied without looking at me. 'Please just let your husband know I'm here.'

I rushed inside to get Gozie.

'Did you hear?' Nasir asked as soon as Gozie appeared.

'Hear what?' Gozie replied.

'He's dead. They killed him.'

'Who? Who did who kill?'

Nasir didn't respond, instead he grabbed the remote and switched on the television and turned up the volume. A snapshot of one of the country's most prominent journalists splashed across the screen. A letter bomb had been delivered to his home, and once opened, had exploded, fatally injuring him.

Gozie grabbed his head in his hands as the newscaster's voice droned on in the background.

'He'd been criticising the government a lot, you know. Maybe too much,' Nasir murmured.' They were rumours that he had some very incriminating information against some powerful people in government that he was about to publish. They had to shut him up for good.' Nasir shook his head, still in a state of disbelief. It was as though he needed a safe haven and Gozie was the only person he'd thought of.

'My God!' Gozie whispered.

The police were investigating his death, the newscaster said. But we all knew how those things went – nothing would be found; we would all move on and every year, people would write meaningless newspaper articles about his death and talk about the lessons to be learned.

'That could have been me, you know. I could have ended up that way,' Gozie finally said.

'You're right, my brother. You know it's good we left that profession. It's much too dangerous. Threats, killings, imprisonment, all to silence the truth.'

'Silencing the pen with a bomb,' Gozie murmured.

AIWANOSE ODAFEN

Nasir nodded soberly. 'But we're benefiting from this. In one way or the other we're equally guilty of contributing to what's happening,' Nasir said. I'd never heard him speak that way. If anything, he'd always been the one to assuage Gozie's doubts about their contracts and grafts.

Gozie turned to him, his eyes hard. 'We're doing what we can to survive. What is the point of dying for a country where no one will remember your death or at least make an effort to bring your killers to the book? Where they'll join them in drinking wine and dancing, and they and their children will go on to live long and comfortably? What's the point? Why should I risk my life for that?'

I wondered for the umpteenth time what had happened to the Gozie who'd been willing to go to prison – to die, even – for his beliefs. 'Na condition dey make crayfish bend,' Adaugo always joked.

'Nobody is above it; this country changes and humbles everyone. Did I think I would ever eat lizards? But war came and I ate even rats,' Papa had said to me once.

But I missed him, that Gozie who'd seemed somewhat more human.

Nasir tapped Gozie's shoulder gently. 'My brother, calm down. I'm sorry. I know you speak from personal experience. I was just thinking out loud.'

Gozie nodded calmly, summarily appeased.

Nasir turned his eyes back to the television. A re-broadcast of the news was going on. Photos from the dead man's house were shown and eyewitnesses were questioned. 'My only worry is if they succeed in silencing all of us, who will speak for truth?' Nasir said. 'Who will speak for justice? What then becomes of such a country?'

176

Nasir whispered into Gozie's ear and he guffawed loudly, drawing attention from members of the crowd of wellwishers at the wedding. It was hard to do so, but I had to admit to myself that I was jealous, jealous of Nasir in a way a wife was of a mistress, jealous of the brotherhood he'd formed with Gozie and locked me out of. It was like watching my husband take his childhood sweetheart as a second wife. Once, I'd asked Gozie about his former friends, the ones he'd worked at the newspaper and sung 'Zombie' with, and he'd responded that he no longer spent time with riff-raff who had too much time on their hands for idle talk.

I was seated on an aged sofa in my parents' living room a few days after the wedding. Papa was trying to make Nwamaka smile.

Papa looked old: oceans of grey now filled the once coal-black hair on his head and his once towering frame was now slightly stooped. He'd always been a god to me, an invincible and ever-present figure. The transformation from deity to mortal happened so suddenly. For the first time, the possibility of Papa passing away flashed through my mind, and despair gripped my heart so tightly it felt like a physical pain.

'She's so serious; she reminds me of your brother Ikechukwu as a young boy. He would only smile when I bought him biscuits or your mother gave him pieces of fried meat,' Papa said, interrupting my gloomy thoughts.

As if on cue, Nwamaka smiled, her tiny teeth glowing as Ego handed her a biscuit stick. Papa and I burst into laughter. 'Yes, she's definitely like Ikechukwu,' I said.

'Speaking of Ikechukwu, have you been to see him yet? His wife gave birth a few days ago.'

'Yes, I visited them and their newborn yesterday.'

'Ah, so you knew your mother was going to spend the weekend there,' he said and turned a suspicious eye to me. 'Is that why you decided to visit this weekend?'

I was unable to hide the guilt from my face. Papa's laugh was full of depth and knowledge. I smiled sheepishly and stared down at my fingernails. We'd never been able to deceive Papa as children, and as adults, his senses only seemed to have gotten sharper.

'You children are all the same. Even Kelechi that never darkens our doorstep came to see me this morning. You shouldn't avoid your mother, you know. She might have her faults, but she means well,' he said.

I stared at my hands.

Papa sighed aloud. 'You know, she wasn't always like this,' he said. I looked up at him. He'd never spoken such words to me before. I didn't know much about life in our household before I was born; the little I knew was from stories my brothers had told me.

'Life happened and she toughened up.' He sighed again. 'I didn't always help matters as well. I didn't make it easy,' he said, his voice filled with regret, then he fell silent. I stared at him, waiting for him to continue, to unwrap the mystery that was Mama. He didn't say any more. And for a while, we said nothing, the children's voices filling the vacuum.

I looked up at the pictures on the wall, focusing on its most recent addition, the smile that haunted me daily. 'Do you really think he's alive?' I whispered to Papa.

'I don't know,' he answered, but even that sounded patronising, like he was trying not to burst my fragile bubble of hope.

'Have you heard anything?' I asked. Papa shook his head no and my chest grew tight.

'I miss him,' I continued, staring at the picture still. 'Do you think he would have liked Gozie?'

Papa laughed. 'Truthfully? I very much doubt it.'

I smiled, understanding. 'You know, one time, someone tried to bully me and he came to pick me up from school. He marched me to the headmistress' office to complain, then he told me to point out the bully. He pulled him him by his ears and warned him that he'll be the one to face him next time he tried such nonsense.' Papa and I chuckled then I launched into yet another story of Uncle Ikenna. It was only with Papa I ever voiced my feelings about Uncle Ikenna's disappearance. With Mama, I had to be the anchor, resisting the overwhelming pull of grief so it didn't drag us under.

Nwamaka squealed and Papa turned his attention to the children. They were busy playing a game only they understood and were enjoying themselves quite a bit. 'The girls are growing really fast, like palm trees,' he said at last, turning to me with a smile. 'You weren't even as tall as the twins when you were five, and they are only three, and Ego looks like a ten-year-old child. Hopefully they stop growing so fast when they are older or it will be hard for them to find husbands.'

I laughed. 'Papa, how can you be talking about marriage now? They are still children.'

He smiled. 'It's never too early to talk about marriage. They are women, after all.'

# 18.

## *Ozoemena*

The journey to Kaduna in November '87 was long and arduous. We set out at 5 a.m. from the bus park in Ikeja and would not reach Zaria till 8 p.m. There were several stops along the way for food and to stretch our legs, and Mama complained that her joints were no longer what they used to be. The air transformed as we travelled up north, from the mild, somewhat humid harmattan of the south west to the frigid dry and dusty north-easterly wind from the Sahara.

In Kaduna, we lodged at a motel that looked like it had been around since the time of the British, with its colonial-style architecture. People chatted casually in Hausa as they went about their business and I could feel Mama grow more and more tense beside me by the second; she looked around often as though wanting to be assured of an escape route.

The man we had come to see resided at the edge of the city, just before the road to Sabon-Gari. He was an Igbo trader with businesses spread across the North. A woman in a scarf answered the door and Mama shook her head disapprovingly. He'd married one of them.

'I was a boy then, about twelve years old, but I remember him clearly. Captain Ikenna Ezemonye,' the man told us. He narrated his story in staccato, like a tape recording. 'When the war started, we were in Asaba then. My father was afraid that the war would soon come to our doorstep and so he started sending our properties to our relatives living deeper in Biafra territory. Then the Biafran soldiers occupied Asaba in August '67.

'They would come to our classrooms and teach us how to take cover and lie flat on the ground should the Nigerian army attack. Captain Ezemonye was one them. Everyone liked him because he was always very friendly, even our teachers.'

He sighed and shook his head. 'When the Biafran government started conscripting people into the army, my parents got scared and kept us at home. My mother asked Captain Ezemonye if I could be an attaché in the Boys' Brigade so I wouldn't be conscripted into the army because I was very tall for my age. He agreed. All I did was carry his things and run little errands on his behalf. He was very good to me.

'After the Federal forces retook Benin in late September '67, the Biafran soldiers fled through Asaba; they blew up the Niger bridge behind them so the Nigerian army couldn't pursue them. Captain Ezemonye couldn't go with them because he was injured; he had a very bad leg injury. My parents took him in and hid him in a small hut at the back of our compound to repay him for the good he did for us. He was badly injured but very much alive.'

Mama's face beamed with hope; earnest, desperate hope.

'A few days later, the Nigerian troops came. It was early October. We started hearing that they were burning houses and killing people for being Biafran sympathisers. Everybody was scared. My parents hid Captain Ezemonye in the roof of our house. The town leaders sent criers with gongs to announce that soldiers were in town and we should all come out for a peace rally to pledge loyalty to one Nigeria so they wouldn't kill us. My mother was scared for me and so she dressed me in wrapper and headtie to look like a girl and accompany her and my father to the parade. We were singing and dancing.

'The soldiers came out and separated us into men, women and children. Next thing their captain ordered them to start shooting. *Kpa kpa kpa.* Everybody scattered and started running. My father was killed immediately. I ran into the bush with my cousin but they were still shooting at us. My cousin suggested that we wait till it was dark before we left. He was a few years older than me – fifteen at the time. When it was dark, we snuck back into town (his family lived at the edge of the town), took his father's car and drove into the bush. None of us knew how to drive; he just turned the key and moved the gear and started going. We didn't even know where we were going to.'

He swallowed saliva slowly and his eyes filled. 'We didn't come back till after the war, over two years later. I went to our family compound but it was empty. They didn't burn it like many of the other houses, but it was deserted. Till today I don't know what happened to my mother. They said many women were raped and killed. And that people had gone the day after the shooting to identify bodies of their relatives and take them away in wheelbarrows to be buried, while others were buried in mass graves. Nobody was around to bury my father, so he was buried with the others.

'I asked about Captain Ezemonye but no one had seen him. I

asked if he was found and killed; they said they didn't think so. I never saw him again.'

When he was done, he cleared his throat and excused himself – to shed tears, I suppose; men didn't cry in front of others. Mama and I wept openly, swiping at our faces with handkerchiefs.

When he returned, he was more composed and there were no signs of tears. Mama asked questions; he answered.

Before we left, he introduced us to his wife. She smiled timidly and encouraged us to stay longer.

Her family had hidden his uncle's family during the riots and had safeguarded their property for them afterwards. That was how they'd met – when he'd moved to the North with his uncle after the war.

'She lost five of her brothers,' he told us at the door. 'They were soldiers in the Nigerian army even before the war started. May we never see such again.'

'*Ozoemena*,' Mama echoed.

Never again.

Life took on a routine in early '88: a sameness that was safe and comforting. Every day I woke the children in the morning to prepare for school. And each morning it was the same: Ego dutifully went into the bathroom while I chased the twins around the house to force them to do the same, the pitter patter of their tiny feet on the tiled floors echoing as they ran from me. 'Nwamaka, Nkechi! Come back here! Mummy is not joking; you have to get ready for school,' I shouted. And each time, their tinkling giggles would come back to me as responses like the shingles hung in front of ancient houses.

They hid in the strangest places – inside the cupboard in the dining area, underneath the chair, their tiny forms allowing them to squeeze into any space. Tired of the noise we were making, Gozie would come out of his room and yell at the top of his voice, 'Nwamaka! Nkechi! Get inside the bathroom and get ready for school now!' And they'd scurry out, like little insects, from their hiding places and into the bathroom. It irked me how readily they obeyed their father, without thought for question or debate – his word was the law – yet how easily they found it to shake their heads no, to laugh at me even when I told them I was being serious.

In the afternoons, I drove my maroon Volvo through the black iron gates of their school to collect them, waving as I passed by the jovial security guards. I always arrived five minutes before closing time and parked under the tall mango tree in the compound just so I could see their faces as they raced out the building in their green pinafores and white shirts, their eyes bright and their arms raised, grateful to be free of the clutches of education.

Then I would drive to Mama Sikira's house to check for Akin's letters. 'Uju, who is writing to you from America and why can't you give him your address?' she asked each time before handing over the same brown envelope.

He wrote to me often now, about his campus, his students, life in a foreign land. Our relationship felt closer, yet safer this way – over a distance, where nothing could happen.

He hated winters, that the biting cold made his fingers sting and penetrated the thickest clothing, that it got that dark at 2 p.m. But most of all, he hated the fact that he was Black. Not because of his skin-tone – he loved that – but the damning nature of it. To be

Black meant to be followed about supermarkets like a common thief, to be randomly reported to the police for merely existing, to have his voice glossed over in meetings. He'd never thought of himself that way before. Yoruba, South Westerner: those words he knew, prejudices he could handle. But this one, he could not understand it. We only ever spoke of Gozie in passing and he never probed further. He seemed to understand my unwillingness to broach the subject or perhaps he was just as eager to forget Gozie's existence.

On the way home, we listened to the radio. It was the only time the children stopped talking. We chorused along to LeVert on 'Casanova', begging the lady in question to believe they'd never been friends with Romeo, rocked with The Whispers on 'Rock Steady', switched voices between Aretha Franklin and George Michael on 'I Knew You Were Waiting', and worked on the 'Nightshift' with the Commodores. My favourite was when Whitney Houston's 'I Wanna Dance with Somebody' came on. I imagined myself dancing with her, wearing big curly hair, a leather jacket and fitted jeans, free of life's worries and responsibilities.

In the evenings, I worked with the children on their homework, holding Nwamaka and Nkechi's tiny hands as they learned to colour within the lines and practising grammar with Ego.

Occasionally, Gozie travelled. To where, I didn't always know, but it was always 'for business'. Before he left, we would exchange stilted words; we never bothered to fake affection when we were alone. Then he would count out the notes he thought sufficient to cover for his time away, pick up his bags and leave, as I said '*Ije oma*' to his retreating back. Sometimes, I wasn't sure if I really wished him a safe journey.

I rebelled while he was away, relishing my little windows of autonomy. I stopped to buy the roadside food he detested so much, food he'd eaten as a 'poor man' – the spicy *akara* and piping hot *puff-puff* with the steam coming off wrapped in old newspapers Mama Nike sold not far from Papa's house, the meat pie and rock buns Madam Kasi hawked from her show glass in front of the children's school, the picante *suya* Musa roasted with onions and portions of *yaji* at the junction at night.

I let the children play outside, something he never let them do; only children of the uncultured did that. I didn't shout when they laughed too loudly or complain when they ran around the house. The atmosphere at home was different. It smelled of freedom.

It was during one such time that Ada showed up at our doorstep one night looking like a woman who had just fought in the marketplace.

The sleeves of her dress were separated from the bodice and a jagged line ran from the hem to her waist. A dark bruise was forming on her right cheek and her lips were cut.

'Adaugo!' I screamed as soon as I opened the door. 'What happened to you?' I demanded, gripping her shoulders and pulling her in. It was then I noticed her children, small and silent behind her.

Ada sat on the red sofa, the one Gozie never allowed anyone else sit on – it was reserved for him and him alone – staring at nothing in particular; her mind in some faraway place I couldn't access.

I grabbed my car keys. 'Let's go to the hospital. You don't look good,' I said to Ada.

'No. I'm fine,' she said without looking at me.

'Adaugo, this is not the time to be stubborn. Even if you're fine, you should still get checked by the doctor.' When she would not say anything, I settled in a seat, defeated, and said, 'Tell me what happened.'

She tried to speak, then broke down, heavy, wracking sobs shaking her. Finally, she said something. 'Yesterday he came back from Aba. At least that's where he said he was travelling to.' I nodded, encouraging her to continue.

'I opened his box. I wanted to help him unpack; it's not like I was looking for anything. I was just being a good wife, you know? And then the whole thing reeks of perfume. And it's not his perfume. I know his perfume! It was a woman's perfume. His white shirts that I packed had lipstick stains on the collar. She must have packed his box and sprayed it so I would know.'

'Did you ask him?' I asked.

'I took the things to him and, can you imagine, this idiot started asking me why I was searching his things. So, I told him he was liar and a cheat.' She paused and turned to me, this time with venom in her eyes. I'd never seen Ada like that. 'He slapped me. Can you believe that? I didn't let him get away with it. *Agwo emeghi ihe o jiri buru agwo, umuaka ejiri ya kee nku,*' she said. If a snake doesn't show its venom, little children will use it to tie firewood.

I was afraid to ask, but I did anyway. 'What did you do?'

'I fought back. When he hit me, I hit him back; when he punched, I punched him back. The only way he was going to win was if he killed me, because I was ready for him and I told him that.'

I covered my face with my hands and for several minutes we sat like that, in silence. 'What are you going to do now?' I asked finally.

'I don't know.' There was pain in her eyes, raw and unfettered.

Two days later, the children sat in my living room happily munching on meat pies while Ada and I watched the television. We'd gone over to her place the previous day, when we were sure Uzondu wouldn't have been home, to pack enough belongings to last her and the children a while.

'That actress, what is her name again? Anyways, she can cry *ehn*! You would think they flogged her before they started filming. *Chai*. Some people are naturally talented with this acting thing,' Ada said. She was already sounding like her old self again.

Then there was a loud knock. 'Give me my wife and children!' Uzondu barked as soon as I opened the door.

'Good afternoon, Uzondu,' I responded calmly, shutting the door behind me. 'I have no idea what you're talking about.'

'I have checked everywhere, and I know this is the only other place she'll come to hide so you better produce her now before I do something drastic.'

'And what will you do? Do you know who my husband is?' I said and stared at him daringly. It was the first time I'd ever spoken that way to anyone and I felt a niggling self-disgust at my resort to common threats based solely on the identity of the people my husband knew. Yes, Uzondu had money, but Gozie knew people. And in Nigeria, connections were what mattered most.

I would use the same words a few days later when Nwakaego returned with palms flogged red by a teacher who'd accused her of being rude for questioning the validity of a comment he'd made; I'd raised her to always ask questions, to challenge opinions and the reasons behind them.

'Who did this to you?' I demanded, before marching to the school's staff room to raise hell.

I already lived in fear of retribution; my children were not going to do same.

# 19.

## *When you do these kinds of things, you shame us all*

I'd anticipated consequences, but not the form in which they came. A little over a week after Uzondu's appearance at my front door, Ada and I were in our hometown with our families to heed a summon. Summons were meant for the cesspool of society; the ones whose family could no longer control them, whose *wahala* had gotten so much that it had become absolutely necessary to engage higher powers. And overnight, I'd become part of that class.

Elder Ude's house was chosen as the site of the meeting; as the eldest of the elders and a distant relative of Ada's, his place was most appropriate for such matters. On the designated day, Ada and I showed up dressed in matching skirts and blouses of ankara material my tailor had made: a small sign of defiance and solidarity. Our relatives morosely followed behind like members of funeral procession.

They were seated – all four of them – in a semicircle on plastic chairs in the courtyard of Elder Ude's vast compound. It was what

I'd always assumed judgement day would look like; I'd just never imagined my adjudicators dressed in ankara.

'As you all know, we are gathered here for a very important reason,' Elder Ude said in Igbo after clearing his throat to gain our attentions. Bald heads moved up and down in agreement. I could feel sweat beads forming on my upper lip and I impatiently wiped them away with a handkerchief.

He paused for effect. 'A serious matter has been brought before us, and we have decided to call those involved to come and speak for themselves. Our people say that when a son of the land does something bad, he is forcibly dragged through his father's courtyard. If indeed you're in the wrong, we will not fail to reprimand you.' His fellow elders grunted in agreement.

Elder Ozoemena spoke up next, he always talked like he had a heavy tongue and needed time to lift it for each word. Our people considered it a sign of wisdom that came with age; only the young and foolish spoke like they had hot yam in their mouths. 'Adaugo, what Elder Ude is trying to say is that we have heard that you and your friend here have been giving your husband trouble. And that the both of you have connived to keep your children from seeing their father. Your husband has even spoken of returning your bride price to your people. So, we have called the both of you here to tell us why you have dared to do such a thing,' he said accusingly.

Adaugo responded first. 'My elders, I greet you,' she started tearfully, pulling out a handkerchief, and recounted the sequence of events that had led to that night. Slowly the elders' faces began to transform, gone was the open resentment and disapproval; in its place was earnest compassion.

'Adaugo, it's okay. Please stop crying. We have heard what you have to say,' Elder Udobata said once she was done talking, his tone gentle and comforting as if he were speaking to a weeping child.

'Yes. Why don't we hear from the person that brought this matter to us in the first place,' Elder Aghaegbuna interjected gruffly, clearly uncomfortable with Ada's display of emotion. 'Uzondu, now that we're all gathered here and you have heard what she's had to say, can you repeat before everyone what you told the four of us was happening in your home?'

When Uzondu was done, the elders excused themselves to go and deliberate in Elder Ude's *obi*. They returned not long after, wearing stern looks of resolve.

Elder Ude cleared his throat as soon as they were all seated; the gravelly sound he made was that of a man who'd taken too much snuff in his youth. 'We have heard what you have to say, and we have deliberated. Now it is our turn to give you advice. I advise you to listen closely to what we have to say,' he said as the other elders bobbed their heads up and down in agreement.

Elder Ozoemena leaned forward to speak. 'Adaugo, you are walking down a dangerous path that will only lead to the destruction of your marriage. The person that kills his plantain tree with his own gun forgets that he is destroying his own property. Why would you quarrel with your husband for having other women? Does he not feed you and your children? Does he not clothe you? Are you lacking in any way?' he asked, staring down at Ada, his voice rising with each word he spoke.

'You see, it is the white man I blame for these kinds of problems,' he continued. 'In our fathers' day, men took as many as twenty wives

192

and no one complained. Even my father, the late Mazi Obi, had six wives and my mother dared not say a thing. In fact, it was her duty to welcome the new wives.'

Murmurs of 'Hmmm' and vigorous head movements accompanied his words. Adaugo looked ready to cry.

'Even if you want to complain, try to do so in a gentle manner. Our people say, "If one sets the mouth properly and chews very hard palm fruit, it is like chewing softer palm fruit." Even the Christians say a soft answer turns away wrath. *Ehn* Ada?' Elder Udobata added gently.

Elder Aghaegbuna was not having it. '*Tah!* Why should she complain? It is probably because of her quarrelsome behaviour that her husband is looking outside. You should ask yourself what you're doing wrong,' he snapped, his face distorted in outrage.

'We cannot condone this type of behaviour! If we let this happen, our daughters will think it is okay to fight their husbands like mad women,' he continued. 'If your husband beats you, it is not your place to fight him and take his children away from him. If you have a problem, you report him to his parents or his people. You do not go about exchanging blows – or do you think marriage is a wrestling match?'

'Aghaegbuna, it's okay. I think she understands what you're saying,' Elder Udobata intervened. 'Adaugo, try as much as possible to live in peace. Apologise even if you're not wrong, if that will prevent quarrels from happening. Peace is the most important thing, especially for the sake of your children. It would not be good for them to grow up in a household where the parents are always fighting. Do you understand?'

'I understand,' Ada whispered, and Udobata smiled. 'Good.' He turned to Uzondu next. 'And as for you, Uzondu, please do not beat her. You should not be exchanging blows with a woman. If you want to fight, your mates are in the village square. You can go wrestle with them. Besides, you took an oath before the white man's god to be with only one woman; you should at least try to keep to it. Squeeze your face if you like but you know I am saying the truth. You better listen. Remember that it is the fly who does not have an advisor who follows the corpse into the grave.'

Elder Ude coughed in a poor attempt to hide his laughter.

'I agree with Udobata,' Aghaegbuna announced, sounding surprised by his own admission. 'You should be patient with your wife. You know how women are; they always talk anyhow. It is our job as men to be patient with them. If I had beaten my wife every time she annoyed me, she wouldn't be alive today.' The men chuckled; everyone knew how short a temper Aghaegbuna had. It was an irony that his name meant 'Do not kill'.

'As for you!' Aghaegbuna said forcefully, turning to me, all good humour disappearing. I'd hoped that they'd forgotten about my presence. All eyes present turned to me with hostility. 'Your friend came to you and told you she had problems in her home, and you decided that the best solution was to keep a man's wife and children away from him, *o kwa ya*?' he said.

'It is like a man with an eye problem approaching his friend to apply eye-clearing medicine, and instead he puts pepper in it,' Elder Ozoemena added, to the approval of the other elders.

'If you did not know what to do, you should have at least asked your mother. Is that not how things are done?' Elder Udobata said.

'I'm sorry, my elders,' I mumbled.

'Sorry for yourself!' Elder Aghaegbuna retorted.

Elder Ude intervened this time around. 'Aghaegbuna, it's okay. The child has apologised for her stupidity. I think we can move along now,' he said. Aghaegbuna let out a low hiss, dragging out the sound for all to hear, then turned away.

Elder Ude continued speaking. 'I think everything that needs to be said has been said. Let us not talk too much. Adaugo and Uzondu, we hope you have heard all we have to say. We do not want to hear about this kind of thing again. When you do these kinds of things, you shame us all.'

Soon, it was that time of the year again – when the weather gods chose to play mind games with mere Lagosians. When it was too wet to be the harmattan season and too dry to be the rainy season. I imagined them casually sipping gourds of palm wine and laughing as they waited for us to be complacent and comfortable with the dryness, to put our clothes out to dry and wash our cars, to set up canopies and cook food in outdoor *konga* pots on burning firewood. Then they sent the rains in full force, thundering and roaring, drenching everything in their path. The rains would disappear as suddenly as they appeared, and the scorching sun would return, but everything would have been ruined.

Gozie sat alone in the dining room in July '88, his head bowed in concentration as he prepared his sermon for the upcoming midweek service, the silence around him interrupted only by the sound of the ceiling fan blowing cool air across the space. Every now and then, he looked up to flip through the pages of his worn Bible or to write in an open notebook; the expensive fountain pen he used had been a gift from a government minister. He'd made sure to let me know exactly who had given him the pen. It was his way of reminding me how lucky I was to be married to such a big man.

I watched him from the living room – the excitement and anxiety, desperate to impress on his first try. Only the previous week, the pastor had announced a Mr. Chigozie Azubuike as a newly ordained deacon of the church and called him to the altar for blessings. It had not come as too much of a surprise to me – Gozie had just donated a huge generator to the running of the church and gifted the pastor a brand-new Mercedes-Benz.

The front door burst open and the children ran in screaming, their small heads bobbing up and down, scattering the colourful beads and rubber bands that had been painstakingly threaded into their hair all over the floor. I'd forgotten they were to return that day; too busy, as I was, enjoying the brief holiday I'd been gifted when Chinelo had offered to have them for a few days.

I'd taken advantage of the children's absence, sleeping more, eating more and screaming less, spending my time watching my favourite television shows, reading novels and relaxing outdoors with a cold glass of juice as Madonna's 'Holiday' played in the background.

'Mummy! Mummy!' they screamed in unison, eager to tell me just how much Aunty Chinelo had spoiled them.

'*Shhh!* Your father is working,' I said, trying to quiet them before Gozie would.

Gozie's pen banged on the glass of the dining table and the sound ricocheted off the walls into the living room. '*Ogini*! Can someone not work in peace in this house again?' he bellowed. 'Uju! Are you not there? And you're letting these children make noise like this?'

'I'm sorry. They're just excited,' I hurried to apologise for the children. They cowered behind me.

'Sorry for yourself. If it's to make trouble now, you'll be there front and centre. Idiot,' he said.

He still hadn't forgiven me for 'embarrassing' him and 'his people', as he put it, and brought up the incident at every opportunity he had.

I'd waited anxiously when he'd returned for someone to report me, to rid me of the trepidation I felt, like a child awaiting the punishment its father would mete out for its wrongdoings in his absence. And just when I'd begun to believe that fortune had shone on me and perhaps I'd escaped retribution, Gozie stormed through our front door one day, screaming my name at the top of his lungs and pushing the children – eager to greet him – out of his way.

'ARE YOU MAD?' he'd yelled in my face when I'd finally slithered out of my hiding place. 'I cannot believe a wife of mine would try to destroy a marriage! What if the church hears about it?' he screamed. This was followed by a resounding slap, then another and another, until I lost count. In that moment, I was grateful that Ego's teacher did not know the way to our house.

Months later, he was yet to let it go, convinced as he was that I'd been sent by the devil to deprive him of his bright future.

## 20.

### *You are now a man!*

It was August of '88 and Akin had a girlfriend. I'd never imagined him as the type to date an African American, much less a light-skinned one with hair permed so straight, it flowed limply over her shoulders. He'd hated my hair straightened. 'One day that thing will fry your scalp,' he warned every time I used a hot comb on my hair. Then he would pull at a strand and shake his head disapprovingly: 'So flat. Why won't you leave your hair the way it is? Stop stressing it so much,' he said, like my hair had feelings. And when I indeed burned my scalp and complained about the sting of the scabs, he chuckled and murmured, 'Good for you.'

I stared at the picture that had come with his most recent letter, not knowing how to feel. He had his arm around her waist and she leaned into him, eyes glazed with affection. They smiled winsomely at each other, as if sharing a private joke. I imagined them going to a club together; there was no 'Love Nwantinti' in America so they would dance to Will to Power's rendition of 'Baby I Love Your Way'. I wondered if he held her close when they danced, if his eyes twinkled the same, if they kissed to Marvin Gaye's 'Let's Get It On', if he planned to introduce her to his mother, to settle down and have children that looked like her.

By the time Christmas of '88 came around, Gozie was too busy preparing for our trip to his village to remember not to talk to me. 'Obianuju, are the wrappers we bought for the women complete?' Gozie asked a night before we were to leave.

'Yes, I've packed them already.'

'How about the bottles of wine for the elders that I bought? Hope nobody drank any of the bottles?'

I rolled my eyes behind him. 'Gozie, who would drink your bottles of wine? Is it me or the children?'

He turned to face me. 'I don't know. Maybe your useless brothers came to visit and you decided to share it with them,' he sneered.

'The bottles are complete,' I said, refusing to take the bait.

'Hope the children are ready to leave tomorrow,' he said.

'Yes, they are.'

'Okay.' It was a single word, but it was punctuated with venom.

The next morning, bags packed and vehicle fully loaded, we began our sojourn. Our journey was smooth sailing, the 'smoothness' interrupted by the occasional pothole on a road that the government had promised to fix but had abandoned, just like their predecessors and the predecessors before them, and our speed delayed only by the congested traffic in the bustling city of Onitsha.

It reminded me of the good times, when I was a child; every December Papa would ship our family to the village for the Christmas holiday. It had been my favourite time of the year. And I found myself longing for those days again – for the cool harmattan breeze that blew at night and made our skins flaky white, for the delicious pieces of roasted yam dipped in *ofe akwu* and the fluffy pounded yam crafted in ancient mortars that tasted nothing like the one made in the city; the village air lent its own taste to the food.

I missed how easily we climbed trees to pluck mangoes and *ukwa* and swam in the freezing brown waters of the village stream. I recalled the numerous gatherings – the dances with vibrant music, the traditional weddings with large parties and endless supplies of food, the entertaining communal assemblies, and the wrestling matches where the toughest men contested, their muscled bodies flexing with power and glistening in the sun – activities all somehow squeezed into the space of a few days.

Most of all, I missed the feelings of warmth and safety of being surrounded by family members – uncles who'd moved outside the country in search of better opportunities, cousins schooling in other parts of the country, relatives trading in Northern cities – all home for that one time in the year. We would sit together and talk for hours, eager to make up for lost time and to catch up on the details of the others' lives: who had a new house, a new car, whose wife was pregnant and whose wasn't, and who could no longer pronounce 't's and 'r's properly because they had stayed too long 'in the abroad'. Then abruptly it would all come to an end ushered in by the New Year, and we would say our tearful goodbyes with passionate promises to do the same the next year.

But this trip was different. This time I was going 'home' to Gozie's people whom I barely knew; the short visits we'd paid in the past had hardly given me any time to make any friends. And I couldn't help feeling a bit of anxiety at the uncertainty of it all, as our jeep sped past the small towns, thatched houses with iron roof sheets and unpainted brick houses disconnected from the electricity grid, reminding me that Lagos was but a mirage – a false representation of what and where the nation truly was.

At Sunday Masses, they chanted, 'Let Us Break Bread Together' during the Eucharistic consecration instead of '*Ezi Chukwu Nara Aja Anyi*'; hymnals were limited to ones written in the English Language and the occasional Igbo canticles the priest allowed. Christmas carols were the Igbo translations of the popular versions – '*Abali Nso*' in place of 'Silent Night' – and not the Igbo Christmas folk songs Father Amanze, the Catholic priest at my father's village's local parish, had insisted we sing. In this, I felt a strange fascination and enjoyment, and a feeling of superiority that we had done it better growing up. Had Mama felt the same way all those years ago?

We stayed at Gozie's late father's house. The mansion Gozie was erecting in the village was not ready, and it would take a while to be so. He wanted a structure that would have the villagers talking for years to come. And that required a good dose of time – and money, of course.

It wasn't too much of a surprise to me that Gozie would invest so much in a house we would barely occupy while we lived in a flat, albeit a luxury one, in Lagos. The war had made our people paranoid, and so we built homes at 'home' so that in the incident of a recurrence and the union of the nation falling apart, we had a place to return to.

Our children were never happier, and it was a strenuous task to get them to sit with me for more than a few minutes, disappearing this way and that with one cousin or the other, strangers who had now become family. Then at night, they would scurry back like little rats to amuse me with tales of their adventures.

Two days after the New Year of '88 was a Sunday and after Mass, Gozie stood in a cluster of men of comparable social stature, chit-chatting. We'd driven all the way to a nearby town to attend a service at the largest chapel in the area just so Gozie could socialise. It was always important to mix with higher-ups amongst our people, he'd reminded me.

I was in a cluster of the wives, not too far away, pretending to listen to the women whine endlessly about how hard it was to be married to wealthy men. I could hardly recall their names, even though we'd been introduced before.

'The other day, I sent my maid to the market and would you believe that she came back with cartons of *kpanla* fish instead of the croaker fish I sent her to buy? Who eats such cheap rubbish? I sent her back to the market immediately!' one said, adjusting her skyscraper head-tie dramatically. Her husband was the MD of an oil company in Lagos and one of the wealthiest men in the area.

'Mine nearly destroyed my expensive suede shoes the other day. You wouldn't imagine that the idiot used a rag soaked in water to wipe them, instead of the special polish I bought. I nearly killed her that day. Stupid girl,' another shared, her unnaturally fair skin turning a blotchy red. The near-translucence of her bleached skin reminded me of the girls in the university who'd mixed numerous toning creams to brighten their pigmentations in the hope of catching rich boyfriends and husbands. I wondered if her skin could withstand the physical abuse she apparently meted out to her help.

'A good maid is really hard to find,' a third lady quipped, her already large eyes bulged out for rather unnecessary emphasis. The others nodded thoughtfully as though she'd dropped words of profound wisdom.

'Uju. What about you? What has your experience been like?' skyscraper head-tie asked, turning to me unexpectedly with raised brows.

'What about me?' I replied, surprised they'd included me in their conversation despite my conscious effort to not contribute.

'Yes, how has your experience with your maid been?'

'Oh, we don't have a maid yet; maybe we'll get one soon,' I said flippantly. I wasn't yet ready to trust a total stranger in my home. Looks of horror met my comment and I had to stop myself from bursting into laughter.

'Really?' Big Eyes asked snidely.

'Really,' I replied with an edge in my voice.

Unnaturally Fair looked between the both of us anxiously. She did not like trouble. 'Did you hear that Chinwe gave birth to her second child some weeks ago?' she interjected, changing the topic abruptly.

'Which Chinwe?' Big Eyes asked, leaning in. She loved to gossip; this was her life – maliciously living daily off the tales of people's fortunes and misfortunes, hoping to distract others from the imperfections in her own life.

'Chinwe Okpara now! The one married to Amaechi Okpara that owns a big supermarket in Enugu,' Fair Skin responded.

'Really? What did she have?' This was from Skyscraper Head-tie. She said 'what did she have' like the answer would determine just how valuable the news was.

'A boy!' Fair Skin replied, grinning from ear to ear.

'*Hei*!' 'Thank you, God!' 'Finally,' everyone in the group remarked at once.

'Is that not her husband coming out of the church now?' somebody noticed, pointing at a large, pot-bellied man. And we all turned to look.

He stopped over at the men's cluster. 'Okpara! Okpara!' Skyscraper Head-tie's husband hailed.

'We hear congratulations are in order,' Gozie said. Okpara laughed and it came from his belly, the contented sound of one who had everything he wanted in life.

'Congratulations, my brother. You are now a man!' Fair Skin's husband boomed.

Gozie winced, but so quickly I thought I'd imagined it. Then he turned his head to stare at me meaningfully, and in that moment his pain became mine. He didn't have a son.

Before the service, he'd talked about working with the man who'd called Okpara 'a man' on a contract. I wondered if that had been jeopardised.

He turned away again, to smile and laugh with the men.

## 21.

### *Even the police look for convicts that escaped from prison*

I caught a glimpse of my reflection as I passed by the full-length mirror in my bedroom in April of '89, three days after that one night. Gozie was not back yet; he hadn't returned home since, and I was doing everything to distract myself from thinking about his return.

That night, I'd opened my eyes to find myself surrounded by the walls of my bedroom, and by Nwakaego holding my hands and weeping silently. I had no idea how long I was out for. My head felt light and my tongue heavy, as if weighed down by pyramids of sand. 'W-w-what happened?' I asked. My voice sounded croaky and adenoidal to my ears, like it belonged to someone else.

'Daddy, he beat you. All over ya body. Blo-blood ev-everywhere,' she said, tears flowing down her face, her spoken English, refined by years of lessons, falling apart.

Nwakaego began shaking violently and I gently rubbed her arm to calm her down. 'Everything will be fine. I promise,' I said over

AIWANOSE ODAFEN

and over. I would later learn that had she'd run out in the middle of the night to find a doctor after Gozie had left me in a pool of my own blood.

Gozie had come home later than usual that night and I'd stayed up to wait for him. At 3 a.m., I heard a bedroom door squeak open and turned to see Ego stagger out with sleep-bleared eyes.

'Nwakaego. Is everything alright? Why aren't you sleeping?' I asked as I made space for her beside me on the sofa.

'I don't know. I just woke up and can't sleep back,' she mumbled, rubbing her fists over her eyes.

'Did you have a bad dream?' I asked wearily, putting my arm over her shoulders as she relaxed beside me.

She nodded as her eyes settled on the clock, and realising how late it was, she asked, 'Daddy has not come back yet?'

'No, not yet,' I replied, taking care to keep my tone flippant, as though it were not something to be bothered about. 'He'll be ba—'

Gozie knocked on the door. 'See, he's here already. Please go in and try to sleep. We'll talk more tomorrow,' I said to her as I stood up to open the door.

He sauntered in with the slow gait of one who wasn't drunk but wasn't far from it.

'*Nnoo,*' I said as way of greeting. He grunted in response as he moved past me.

I thought about it for a second, then I opened my mouth to speak. 'Gozie. Please, I need to talk to you,' I started, and he stopped with his back to me. 'I know it's late, but I don't want to do it in front of the children, and we need to talk.'

It had probably been foolish to try to have a conversation with

206

him in that state. But I was at my wits' end. He turned around slowly to face me. 'What is it?' he asked, his voice gruff and impatient.

I wrung my hands nervously. 'You've been staying out late a lot these days, later than usual. And it is really stressful for me because I have to wait up for you to come back and still wake up early to prepare the children for school.' I said it all at once, eager to get it off my chest before I lost my nerve.

His body tensed as I spoke, until his face had calcified into a hard mask. 'Obianuju, what nonsense are you talking about by this time of the night? Are you trying to accuse me of something?' Gozie asked in a quiet voice laden with warning, and I felt the hairs on the back of my neck stand up.

My voice shook as I forged ahead. 'I-I-I'm not trying to accuse you of anything.'

He hissed dismissively in response and turned to walk away. I put my hand on his arm to stop him. 'Gozie. Wait. I—' That was all I said before my arm was grabbed and I was forcibly thrown against the wall, my head landing with a sharp crack.

*The mirror has a way of revealing one's true self,* I'd once read as a child. I finally understood what those words meant. And for the first time, as I stared into the gilded frame that hung in our bathroom, I saw who I'd become – a simpering, vacuous replica of the person I once was.

Battered and bruised, my face looked unrecognisable. Gingerly, I touched my right eye, which was almost swollen shut, and ran my fingertips over the dark bruises on my neck and arms. I started to cry – unrestrained sobs – for the person in the mirror, the one who I was now, even as I remembered the girl I'd once been: fearless, exuberant, dazzling.

Then I wiped my tears, dragged out the boxes Mama had given me on my wedding day – I hadn't had cause to use them in a long while – and started to pack my belongings. I had no idea where I would go, but I knew I had to leave and that I was taking my children with me.

At first, I left out the expensive wrappers, the ostentatious jewellery and other gaudy benefits of being married to a man of moderate wealth. But as I sat on the cold floor of my daughters' room arranging their clothes and shoes into boxes as fast as I could, I realized just how foolish leaving it all behind would be. So, I ran to my room and packed it all, every single thing. It was the least I deserved.

In the car, I turned on the radio to block out the thoughts that were running circles around my mind. I had no idea where to go or what to do. I had no money; Gozie had always made sure to never let me have too much money at once. It was his way of controlling and limiting the extent of my actions in his absence. But he always ensured I was dressed in the finest; a mannequin to showcase his affluence.

I couldn't stay with my friends; I did not want to burden them with my troubles. Asking someone to house three children (one a teenager) and an adult woman was a lot to demand of anyone, no matter how deep feelings went, and I did not want them developing issues with their husbands and mine.

Only one place came to mind as I navigated aimlessly through the avenues of Lagos – the one place where I was the one thing I wanted to be most at that moment: a child. I turned around – narrowly missing a tomato seller who had set up her kiosk too close to the busy road and was cursing loudly in typical Lagos fashion – and headed home.

The twins sat in the back seat, oblivious to the turmoil surrounding us. Ego stared out the window of the passenger seat, quiet and sober, lost in her own head. Then Felix Liberty's hit song 'Ifeoma' came on and we all put everything aside to beg the eponymous lady-love to marry him.

Mama did not bear the news well, and her reaction came in three phases. The questioning disbelief came first, starting as soon as I stepped through the front door, anxious and searching, eager to understand.

'Jesus! Uju, what happened to you?' she screamed, her eyes wide with concern. She followed closely behind as I dragged our luggage into the house, and hurled questions at the back of my head.

'Were you in an accident? Why are the children with you? And why did you bring all these boxes? Where is Gozie? Is he dead?'

I kept walking in the direction of the rooms that had been left empty when my brothers had finally moved out of our parents' home, taking with them the constant clutter and musty smell of manliness that clung to the walls like a second coating of paint.

Or maybe not. I could swear that a trace of Kelechi's perfume remained when I opened the wardrobes, and the mirror of Ikechukwu's bathroom still bore a hint of his spicy aftershave, the same one he'd been using since he turned eighteen.

'Uju, please answer me!' Mama shrieked when I still wasn't forth-coming. 'Is Gozie dead? Is your husband dead? *Ehn?*'

Already starting to panic, she turned to the children, grabbed Ego by her little shoulders and shook her with so much force her teeth rattled. 'Is your father dead?'

Ego stared at her through wide, confused eyes, then she turned to me as if to ask, 'What is happening?' She'd never seen Mama behave that way.

'Mama, please leave her alone. Can you not see that you're scaring her?' I said finally.

Mama wasn't listening. She was in full-on hysteria. She put both hands on her head and paced briskly about the room. '*Hei* God! Gozie? Dead? But he was still a young man. What will I do? What will we do? What will Uju do? My enemies! They have finally succeeded.'

She went on and on until I was forced to interrupt her. 'Mama, nobody is dead. Gozie is alive. Please stop behaving like that, you're scaring the children. See, Nkechi is about to cry. Please let's go to the living room and talk in private,' I said, pulling on her arm so she'd stop talking.

Mama put down her arms and turned to me. 'Nobody is dead? Gozie is not dead? Are you sure? Uju, you're not lying to your mother, are you?' she said, her eyes narrow with suspicion.

'Mama, I'm not lying. Come, let's go,' I replied, dragging her out of the room.

It was rare for Mama to be speechless. In all my years, I could not remember a time when Mama was without something to say, even if it was a simple 'My God' or a 'Jesus is Lord', but that is exactly what Mama was – speechless – as she stared at the worn carpet in the living room while I narrated the events. I described every detail – the constant beatings, the abuse, the torment – and with each word I inaudibly pleaded with her to understand, to take my side for once.

Mama stared at the same spot on the carpet for several minutes after I was done talking, saying nothing, as though searching for something only she knew was there.

'Mama,' I called after several minutes of unbroken silence.

She blinked, startled from her trance. 'Hmm?'

'You've not said anything.'

She sighed. 'Uju, these things you've said are quite serious. Are you sure you're not exaggerating?' she said, shifting in her seat, regaining some of her composure.

'Mama, how can you ask such a question? Look at me.'

'But a man cannot just wake up and act this way, Uju. Does it even sound reasonable to you? *Ehn*? Tell me the truth.'

'Mama, is that really what you're going to say?'

She waved dismissively as though flicking a pesky fly away. 'I'll need to talk to Gozie to get his own side of the story. He is a reasonable man. Smart. Hardworking. Cool-headed.' She shook her head disbelievingly. 'You must have done something. I know you. You've always had a sharp tongue. Was it not you that Ikechukwu used to beat every time when you were children?'

'Mama!'

'Don't "Mama" me,' she said rising to her feet. 'Every time I'm saying something important, it's "Mama, Mama". *Biko* leave me, let me talk. If you're thinking of leaving permanently, better remove that from your mind. You will not bring that kind of shame to this family.'

She stormed out of the living room, the *pitter patter* of her feet resounding long after she'd left.

When Gozie did not come to look for me after a few days, Mama became worried. 'Uju, what is happening? What have you done? Your husband has not come to look for you once! Once! Even the police look for convicts that escaped from prison.'

'Mama, what are you saying?' I asked, confused by her choice of words.

'What am I saying? You have left your home for another woman to take over and you're here asking me stupid questions.'

But I knew Gozie better than she did. He was calling my bluff, and I was determined to prove to him that I was truly done. A week went by, then two, and Mama became convinced I'd made a drastic mistake. And slowly, the questioning disbelief degenerated into assiduous pleading that was just as purposeful as the questioning. 'Uju, *biko*, listen to your mother. You're making a mistake. Think of your children, how will they grow up without their father? What are you going to tell them? Whatever your husband has done, forgive him.'

'Mama, where is the person you're begging for? I've been here for weeks. Where is he?'

'Maybe he is angry. You too, what did you do? You have refused to tell me what you did that annoyed him so much. Can't you swallow your pride for your children?'

212

'Mama, this is not about pride,' I said, walking away. I just wanted to have peace.

Another week passed, and Mama had had enough. Our people say, 'The child that does not make the mother sleep at night will not sleep either.' And Mama was determined that I wouldn't have any sleep. 'Uju, you've been around for a few weeks now. When do you plan to return to your husband's house?' she asked one afternoon. It was raining outside, the heavy drops making battering sounds against the steel of the roof, and the accompanying wind shaking the window glasses.

'Mama, not today, please,' I replied, exhausted with having a version of the same conversation every day. I was seated on a sofa by the window with a lurid romantic novel – the type that you had to hide the cover – looking out every now and then to enjoy the storm, something I'd always done as a teenager to escape my troubles. I'd gone looking for work earlier in the day, as I'd done the days before, office by office, determined to reclaim my financial independence, and had been either turned down for my lack of working experience or told to wait to hear back.

'What do you mean "not today"? This is my husband's house so I have a right to know when you will be returning to yours. If I had left here, would you have a place to return to hide?'

'Mama, please,' I begged.

'Answer me. Okay, if you're not going back, what do you plan to do?'

'I don't know.' I paused. 'I've been thinking of talking to Kelechi's friend. He's a very good lawyer. He can help me get a divorce.'

'Divorce? You want to get a divorce? What will you do after your divorce? Who will marry you? A thirty-one-year-old woman with three children. Girls, for that matter. You better get that rubbish out of your mind. It is not happening!'

'But Mam—'

'"But Mama" nothing! You're not getting a divorce. You will not bring that type of shame to this family. If everyone was divorcing their husbands for beating them, you think we would have any married people?' she said.

To escape Mama's hostility, I took my children out of the house more, stretching any money I had to the limit. I still couldn't find answers to their questions – *Where is Daddy? Why is Daddy not here? When will we see Daddy?* We took whirlwind rides at the amusement park, licked freezing ice-cream cones in the sun and munched sweetened popcorn and saccharine donuts on the sandy shores of Bar Beach. But even then, the heavy cloud surrounding us remained like a wet blanket. Our laughter was hollow; our smiles a little too bright to be genuine.

# 22.

## *Do you pray at all?*

We'd been nearly two months at my parents' house when I noticed a familiar car parked outside on my way back from the market one afternoon. I walked into the living room to find Gozie, dressed in a dapper three-piece suit, talking to my parents. A shiny black leather suitcase sat by his feet, perfectly matching his shoes. I remembered those shoes; I'd cleaned them several times after bringing out matching traditional lace outfits for us to wear to parties: hand in hand – the perfect couple.

He got to his feet quickly and rushed to my side. 'Uju. You shouldn't be carrying such heavy bags by yourself. Let me help you,' he offered.

I held on tightly to the bags as I eyed him incredulously. Since when did Chigozie Azubuike help me carry bags to the kitchen?

'I'm fine. Don't worry. Thank you,' I said sharply.

'Uju, let your husband help you,' Mama chimed, smiling at what she thought was hope of a reunion. Papa looked on, silent and studious.

I ignored them, walking around Gozie to go inside the room – away from them and the apprehension I felt sneaking into my bones.

215

I did not show my face until he was gone that day or the other days he visited after that, when Mama had run inside joyfully to inform me he had arrived. He could see the children, I told her; they were his, after all. But I no longer belonged to him.

'Uju, see what he bought for me and your father?' Mama told me one day, not too long after I heard his car pull away, grinning as she dropped two packs of matching expensive lace material beside me on the bed. I turned away, facing the wall, my back to her. 'He even bought foodstuff for the house, very nice-quality shoes for your father and plenty of gifts for the children. And for you, his beautiful wife, he bought the latest George lace.'

I remained silent.

'Obianuju. Are you sleeping?' she asked, prodding me in the back with a sharp fingernail. '*Ehn* Uju? I said your husband bought things for all of us and you're not saying anything?'

'Mama, I don't know what you want me to say,' I finally replied, turning to face her. I eyed the package in her hands. 'The wrapper looks nice,' I commented flatly.

'What I want you to do is to behave like a good woman and go and see your husband when next he comes to visit. Why are you behaving like this? Was this how I brought you up? Your husband has been coming to visit and each time you hide inside like a rat instead of going to talk to him. He has even apologised to me and your father and has promised to do better. Are you even a Christian at all? Can't you forgive? Marriage is about forgiveness!'

'Mama, please leave me alone. So, because Gozie bought some wrappers I should run into his arms? Why not just sell me to him? Since that's what I'm worth to you.'

My head was thrown to the side as Mama's palm connected with my cheek in a resounding slap. I turned my back to her and faced the wall again, and did not move until I heard the door close.

In the afternoon of the next day, Papa settled in beside me on the sofa in the living room.

'Good afternoon, Papa,' I greeted.

'Good afternoon, Uju. How are you?'

'I'm very fine, Papa.'

He nodded thoughtfully. 'Obianuju, I want to talk to you about something,' he started. 'You know I never like to put my mouth in your matters. You're my last child and I have always left you to handle your affairs, especially now that you're an adult. Culturally, as a married woman, I also shouldn't interfere in your marriage because you now belong to another family, but there are times that, as your father, I must advise you, and this is one of those times,' he said.

'Our people say, "What an old man sees sitting, a young person cannot see standing." Listen to me and take my advice. I know your husband has wronged you. But he has shown that he is very sorry for his actions. I'm not saying you should go back to him yet, but at least give him a chance to explain himself. Left to me, you can stay here for as long as you want, but we both know your mother would never let that happen. All I'm asking is that you listen to what he has to say for the sake of your children. Do you understand what I'm saying?'

'Yes, Papa. I understand you. I will think about what you have said,' I replied. It was the least I could do for Papa.

'Good. As for your husband, I will speak to him next time he comes around; he cannot continue to treat my only daughter like this,' he said as he stood up shakily. He shook off my hand and chuckled as I tried to help. 'Uju, your father is now an old man. My legs now complain when I sit for too long.'

Mama was on a mission, and I wasn't too surprised when my brothers all happened to visit at the same time just hours after Papa spoke to me.

Ugochukwu did not waste too much time getting to the crux of their visit. 'Uju, you have to go back to your husband,' he said as a way of greeting me.

'Ugo, that's not how to handle such matters,' Kelechi reprimanded him. 'Uju, come and hug me first. I haven't seen you in so long. How have you been? You're looking so fine o,' he said.

I laughed as I hugged him, disappearing in his large arms. He had a way with words; it was no wonder he'd had his way with women for so long. 'I've missed you too,' I said against his chest.

'Can we get to the reason we're here, please?' Ugo interrupted.

'Not until she greets me too,' Ikechukwu answered.

Ugo shook his head. When we were finally done, it was Ikechukwu who spoke first. 'Do you want us to beat him for you?'

'Ikechukwu!' Ugo and Kelechi shouted at the same time.

'What?' he responded, looking away guiltily.

'Can the both of you please let me speak? I'm the first son, after all, and it seems I'm the only reasonable one here today,' Kelechi said. He turned back to me with a charming smile. 'Uju, as you probably already know, we heard about what happened an—'

'I know why you're here,' I interrupted. 'Mama told you to convince me to return to my husband.

'Am I wrong?' I asked. None of them said anything. They were too proud to admit that Mama could still control them.

Ugochukwu spoke up. 'Uju, you know how these things work. Marriage is for life. We can talk or, as Ikechukwu suggested, beat sense into Chigozie; we can even take this matter to his people – maybe they can pressure him to be better – but you cannot leave. Moreover, think of your children. How do you think they will feel growing up without their father? How do you even plan to take care of them? Do you have the money? Have you gotten a job yet? You haven't worked in almost ten years. Who will hire you? Or do you plan to start a business?'

Kelechi added, 'Imagine the embarrassment of Papa returning your bride price after how many years. Where does he even start putting that kind of money together from? Think of his old age and the stress. And don't forget your husband is a deacon in his church. What if they hear of this? Why would you want to bring such shame to him and your family?'

I was quiet after they'd spoken, carefully contemplating what had been said. Then an image of the woman in the mirror flashed in my mind – the one with the battered body, broken spirit and empty eyes.

Deacon Rapuokwu was Mama's last hope. And he had gotten fatter since the last time I saw him, his neck now as thick as the trunk of a small tree, disappearing under the folds of his drooping second chin.

He held his Bible between his thickened fingers as he spoke. It had always fascinated me how he always seemed to have it on him, as if its presence reassured him of God's agreement with every word he uttered. 'Uju, it is a woman's job to build her home, not to tear

219

it down. Right now, what you are doing is tearing down your home by refusing to return to your husband. Have you read about the Proverbs 31 woman? And about her deeds? The Bible says, and I quote, "The heart of her husband doth safely trust in her, so that he shall have no need of spoil." Do you know what that means? It means her husband trusts and relies on her so much he wouldn't have any need,' he said in a solemn voice, his voice echoing in our living room. Mama nodded in agreement so vigorously beside him that I was afraid her head would fall off.

'Can your husband trust you not to need of anything that he would not go outside your home seeking for it?'

'Please tell her,' Mama said under her breath.

'Do you pray at all?' Deacon Rapuokwu asked.

'Sir?' I asked caught off guard by the question.

Mama responded on his behalf. 'He said, "Do you pray at all?" *Ehn* Uju? Because if you prayed at all, this kind of thing should not be happening to you.'


'Obianuju, I'm going to ask you the same question you asked me when I ran to your house,' Ada said some days later. 'What are you going to do? You have to have a plan. Chinelo, don't you agree?'

'Uh?' Chinelo answered, blinking. Her eyes carried the faraway look of one who was present in body but absent in mind.

'Are you listening to us at all? Where is your head?' Ada asked testily, pouting her very red lips. 'Anyways, as I was saying . . . Uju, what exactly do you think you're doing? You can't pack all your things and run to your parents' house.'

'But you left your husband, too, whe—'

'It's not the same,' she interjected. 'I did not plan to leave permanently. I would never do something that stupid.'

I flinched at the implication of her words. Chinelo spoke up on my behalf. 'Ada, did you come here to talk or to fight? When you had issues, Uju stood up for you but you're here attacking her. Is that how friends behave?' Then to me, 'Uju, don't mind her. I don't think what you're doing is stupid.'

It felt good to hear someone say it finally. 'Thank you,' I mumbled.

Ada appeared contrite. 'Uju, I'm sorry. I didn't mean it that way. But what are you going to do? Don't you love him? Isn't this the same Gozie that you didn't let us sleep because of him, back in the day?'

I sighed deeply. 'I don't know anymore, to be honest. I don't even know if I ever loved him or if I was just infatuated with who I thought he was, plus Mama really liked him, you know? He was so much like my Uncle Ikenna; we were convinced he was as good a person. I don't even think I recognise this Gozie; he's so different from the man I met.'

Adaugo shook her head pitifully. 'Obianuju! This is real life, not fantasy or those white novels you and Chinelo were always reading when we were in school. You forgive him and move on. For the sake of you and your children. That is marriage. You manage, I manage, we all manage.' She cackled at her own joke.

'Or Chinelo, am I wrong?' she asked. 'Chinelo!' she shouted when there was no response. And Chinelo squeaked like a startled mouse.

'What are you thinking about?' Ada queried. 'I don't blame you; it's because you have a perfect marriage. Christopher treats you so well; you even have a son, unlike the rest of us.'

'Is everything okay?' I added. Chinelo had been mostly lost in thought from the moment she'd stepped into the house.

'Yes, everything's fine. I just have so many things to do today,' she replied. We let it go. She would speak when she was ready.

Finding no hope of acquiescence on my side or support on Chinelo's, Ada switched to church gossip, filling me in on all I'd missed – who'd gotten married, whose daughter was pregnant out of wedlock, which family just moved into a new house in Ikoyi. On Sundays, I stayed home like the heathen that Mama now thought I was, while she dragged my daughters to Sunday school. 'I don't want you to become like your mother,' I heard her say to them.

'Remember Sister Adaure that was engaged to Brother Chibuzor?' Ada asked halfway through her chat.

'Was? They're no longer engaged?' I asked, surprised.

Ada clapped her hands dramatically. 'My sister, that is not even the story. The real gist is *why*. Would you believe that one Saturday morning Brother Chibuzor and Brother Abayomi were exchanging blows in the church parking lot? Not small blows o! Heavy-duty punches because of Sister Adaure.'

'Because of Sister Adaure? Why?'

'It turns out she was dating both of them and had promised them both marriage. It was when her engagement was read out during service announcements that breeze blew and the fowl's buttocks were exposed. Brother Abayomi was going to see the pastor, when he ran into Brother Chibuzor in the parking lot. Pastor tried to separate them and he, too, got a share of the punches. He had to wear sunglasses to preach his sermon the next day.' Adaugo cackled long and loud.

'*Ewo*! People lack the fear of God o,' I said.

Ada continued to laugh. Then she thought of something and paused. 'But you won't believe that the story that two church brothers fought over one Sister Ada spread round the church. People started approaching me to ask me questions. Imagine! A whole Adaugo like me. I had to tell them that it's not my own Ada, before my husband will go and hear such tales. She's Adaure, I'm Adaugo. Why would such a nonsense person share names with me *ehn*?'

'Serves you right,' I said, and laughed in Ada's frowning face.

When the sun started to shine brightly through the windows to warn us of the coming evening, Ada hurried home. Her husband was returning from a business trip that evening and she needed to go prepare a special meal for him. She stepped out the door, anxiously patting her hair and arranging her embroidered blouse; she'd taken to dressing even more elaborately than normal. 'These women outside want to take my husband from me. After all my hard work and suffering? *Tufiakwa*. I will not let it happen.'

Adaugo turned to me apologetically. 'I may not visit any time soon. Uzondu does not like me spending time with you. I only came today because he travelled. He says you're a bad influence, especially now that you've left Gozie.' She rolled her eyes. 'Men and their upside-down thinking. Do I tell him what friends to keep? But what can I do? I cannot spoil my marriage over such a small matter. *Nne biko*, don't be angry o. I'll come to visit when I can.'

'It's okay. I understand,' I replied with a genuine smile before pushing her towards her car. It looked new. Uzondu's business must be doing well.

## 23.

## *You must not wash your dirty linen in public*

Kelechi, the great philanderer, was finally leaving the congregation of single men in December of '89, and Mama couldn't have been happier. It was at his wedding that I decided it was time to return to Gozie.

'My God has done me well!' Mama had shouted excitedly when Kelechi had introduced Anwulika – the fresh-out-of-university twenty-year-old with supple fair skin and a timid gap-toothed smile – as his wife-to-be.

The day of his traditional wedding, Mama was like a spirit – here, there and everywhere, some sort of omnipresent deity. I'd never seen her that excited, not even at my wedding. 'My life is complete now. All my children are finally married. I can rest and enjoy my old age and wait for my grandchildren,' she boasted to her friends later that evening. They were seated in our family compound, still dressed in their party attire, chewing pieces of fried meat and downing bottles of soft drink, the celebratory mood from earlier permeating the air around them.

The women hailed her, tapping and high-fiving her cheerfully, some adding out loud how lucky she was, and how they could not wait to get there.

'But they haven't done the church wedding yet; that is the most important one,' one woman said. I recognised her at once as Mama's distant cousin. Her youngest daughter was yet to marry, and Mama always joked the girl was becoming as old as the trees in her father's compound.

'Why are you speaking like a newcomer, Oluchi?' Chinelo's mother reprimanded in Igbo, unwilling to let anyone spoil her friend's joy. 'Since when did the white wedding become more important than the traditional rites? Before the white men came, were our people not marrying themselves and living happily?'

'It's okay. I'm sure Oluchi meant well,' Mama interjected good-naturedly before the conversation could degenerate into a full-blown quarrel; the women were already eyeing each other combatively. She really was in a good mood.

'You're lucky o. If only my foolish son will come and see his mates getting married and do the needful,' another woman seated beside Oluchi said, directing the discussion back to its beginnings. 'That your daughter-in-law is so young and fine. With her fair skin like *mammy water*.'

'*Asa nwa!*' Mama Chinelo chimed in.

Mama giggled like a girl in secondary school.

'And she looks like a good girl too. Well behaved and soft-spoken,' Ada's mother added.

'She is a good girl,' Mama said with authority.

'But how do you know? You only just met her a few months ago,' Oluchi challenged.

'I know,' Mama asserted, then leaned forward and gestured for the other women to do so. 'My son told me she's a virgin,' she whispered theatrically.

'*Hei*! Wonderful! Your son really chose well o,' one of the women said.

'That is rare in this day and age where these young girls are jumping up and down,' Mama's other cousin added.

Mama nodded. 'My sister, very rare,' Mama chimed, her voice taking on a sing-song quality.

'She will have healthy sons,' Mama Ada predicted.

'Amen,' they all said in unison.

Two weeks to the white wedding, my brothers and I were seated in our parents' living room, drinking bottles of beer, laughing and reminiscing about the days of old, and throwing endless jabs, at Kelechi in particular.

'Remember Chibuogu?' Ugochukwu asked with a smirk, referring to one of Kelechi's former girlfriends.

'The one with the big ass?' Ikechukwu responded.

'Yes! Yes!' I shouted clapping. 'I remember her. She always walked like this.' I got up to demonstrate, rolling my waist slowly, this way and that, like she had always done, as if she was carrying excess baggage behind and needed to move with care. We all shouted with laughter, Ikechukwu falling back on the sofa and Kelechi shaking his head in mock exasperation.

'What about Kasarachi?' Ikechukwu asked the group.

'The one with the very large . . .?' Ugochukwu replied, using his hands to describe the size of her bust.

We all broke into peals of laughter.

'But Kelechi, I won't lie: you surprised us,' Ikechukwu said, wiping tears of mirth from the corner of his eyes. 'After dating all those well-endowed women, when it was time to marry, it's that slim girl you chose. What happened?'

'That is not even what surprised me,' I said. 'I was expecting to see someone close to my age, but I had no idea that Kelechi would go and hustle with university boys to collect a wife from their class-rooms.' Lower-octave chortles followed my statement.

'But Kelechi, talk true, you're over forty. Isn't your wife a little young for you?' I asked, half-joking. I wasn't lying when I said I'd been surprised by her age.

The voice that responded wasn't Kelechi's but Mama's, and it was neither jocular nor carefree. 'So this is what you're doing instead of facing your own problems? Trying to scatter another person's marriage? How is it your business if she's twenty or fifteen? At least she's married. Look at you, thirty-one years old and living in your parents' house with your children after scattering your marriage, and drinking beer like a drunkard. Have you no shame?'

With each word she spoke, I could feel her revulsion and disdain. I was a disappointment, a physical embodiment of some failure on her part. How else could I have turned out the way I did?

'Mama, it's enough,' Ikechukwu intervened.

'Mama, calm down. She was just joking,' Kelechi added.

'Don't "Mama" me. Talk some sense into your sister!' Mama said, then she walked out, most likely to her room to stare once more at the beautiful sequinned wrapper and blouse she planned to wear for Kelechi's wedding. It was something I'd seen her do a few times when she was in a bad mood, and each time she'd come out of her room singing cheerfully about what the Lord had done.

But for those of us still seated in the living room, the good humour was gone, snuffed out like a breeze to a candle flame. In its place was shame, a deep-seated shame for the person I'd become. And it remained long after she was gone, settling in my stomach like a rock at the bottom of a river.

Gozie was at the wedding, adorned in a shining royal blue – the official wedding colour – kaftan, matching the blue wrapper and head-tie I had on. Mama must have invited him.

I'd finally given in and agreed to see him, and since then, his visits had become more frequent, each time bearing a gift and begging me to return 'home' to 'where I belonged'. He'd do better, he said, never lay a finger on me, remain faithful till the day we died, take better care of me and the children. All I had to do was give him another chance to make things right.

But even though the physical scars had healed, others remained underneath the surface of my skin, festering, easily awakened by the slightest memory of my ordeal.

He cried during one of such visits, his head bowed as he let out heart-rending sobs pleading for forgiveness. I'd never seen Gozie cry in all the years I'd known him, and seeing him broken down gave me no satisfaction. I felt like the witch Mama often said I was – stubborn and hard-hearted. But with each tear, I felt my resolve waver, disintegrating like slow-thawing ice.

And so, at the wedding, when he smiled cautiously, I smiled in return. I returned the hugs he gave and shifted to create space in the pew for him to sit beside me and the children, who looked on hopefully.

He held my hand during the vows, gently massaging the knuckles as if to remind me of our own vows, and turned to me during the couple's first kiss with a twinkle in his eyes, asking me to remember our first kiss for the awkward hilarity it had been. And as I gazed into the warm, chocolate hue of his eyes, I could no longer recall why I was holding back or what exactly I was holding back for.

Mama was right. I was a thirty-one-year-old woman who'd run away from her husband's home and was living with her parents with her three children. I had almost no money. I'd applied to several organisations, but no company wanted to hire a woman with out-dated skills who hadn't worked in ten years; even Papa's connections could not help in getting me a position better than a clerk or a secretary and Mama swore she would drag me back to my husband's home before she let me take such a job. I'd sold most of my expensive jewellery and clothes to pay for the children's private school fees, too proud to ask Gozie or any other person for fear of sneers or further urges to do as they said. A part of me suspected that Gozie hadn't offered to pay in hopes that I would run back to him in desperation. The children were my weakness and he was well aware of that.

Even the wrapper and head-tie I had on had been given to me by Kelechi after he'd turned down my numerous offers to pay for the wedding uniform. 'I know you're a big man's wife now, but you're still my baby sister,' he'd said, chucking me playfully under the chin, but we'd both known that was not why he'd done it. No matter how I tried to hide it, I was struggling, and it was clear for all to see.

In that moment in time, Gozie's hand covering mine as Anwuli and Kelechi professed their love for each other, I decided I had nothing to lose, hanging all hope on the promises that he would change.

I waited for weeks to tell anyone, wanting to be sure, searching desperately for signs of change, and holding on to anything I could get – a smile, a hug, a calm response where there would have been screaming in the past – telling myself that I wasn't making a mistake. Then one day I told Gozie – in a shrill voice that didn't sound like mine, high with excitement I didn't feel – that I and the children would leave with him the following weekend. I felt my feet leave the ground as I was lifted by my thighs, his joy child-like. I laughed out loud, my head thrown backwards.

That same evening, I told Mama and Papa. I waited until I was sure they were together watching the evening news between hisses and lamentations on the state of Nigeria, eager to be done with it once and for all, and to temper Mama's reaction with Papa's soothing presence.

'I'm leaving on Saturday,' I announced without preamble, to neither of them in particular.

Mama stopped midway through her rant on the military government to face me, her eyes piercing and suspicious. 'Leaving? To where?'

'Uju, where do you plan to go?' Papa added, his countenance disturbed.

'Obianuju, I hope you're not planning to do something stupid, because I will not let it happen. Not in this house. Or is it whoever you've been sending letters to? You're cheating on your hus—'

'Obiageli, let her speak!' Papa said, sternly interrupting Mama's tirade.

For a moment we were all frozen; even Papa seemed stunned at his outburst. It was the first time since I could remember that he'd spoken to her that way. Mama shut her mouth and folded her arms like a sulking child.

I blinked. 'I'm going back to my husband's home. I told him today,' I said, answering their questions.

'My God has done it!' Mama screamed, and jumped to her feet.

The children had a similar reaction when I finally told them, jumping up and down like rabbits with springs in their heels. They were going to spend Christmas with Daddy.

Except Nwakaego; she only stared at me, frozen in silence.

The morning of our departure, Mama walked into my room solemn-faced, covered only by the yellow night wrapper tied across her chest, as I sat on the bed zipping up boxes and bags. I looked at the small table clock seated on the desk in the room, the same one I'd used as a student to study for exams. It was just 6 a.m.

'Good morning, Mama,' I said, before continuing to squeeze one last pair of shoes into the small *ghana-must-go* bag I was zipping up.

'Obianuju. Good morning. How are you?' she replied.

'I'm fine, Mama.'

'You're returning to your husband's house today, *shey*?' she asked, as if to verify that she hadn't been dreaming when I'd spoken of returning to Gozie.

'Yes, Mama,' I replied, not looking up.

'Very good,' she said as she made space for herself beside me on the bed, pushing the folded clothes aside. 'There's something very important I want to talk to you about before you go back.'

I sat up quietly, schooling my features not to show my irritation.

She smiled, adjusted her wrapper and shifted to make herself more comfortable. 'Uju, as you return to your husband's house today, I want you to please behave like the woman I brought you up to be. Do not quarrel with your husband; when he is angry, apologise. When he is hungry, give him food to eat. If he wants to visit your bed, don't push him away. Are you hearing me?'

'Yes, Mama,' I replied, determined to keep our conversation brief.

'Please, let this be the last time you run to your father's house when you and your husband have issues. Any problem you have, settle it there. Don't bring it here. You're no longer a child. *Inugo?*' she said, pulling at her right ear.

'Yes, Mama.'

'Good. Do you see me running to my family compound whenever I and your father quarrel? Or you think I don't have a family?'

'No, Mama.'

'Also, I don't know who it is you're always writing to and always receiving letters from, but as your mother, I'm advising you to stop if it's a man. Whoever this person is is distracting you from focusing on your family. Do you understand?'

I said nothing.

'Be strong; you're a woman. *Jisie ike.*' She stood to leave, pulling her wrapper up her breasts by its folded top.

'Let me know if you hear anything,' Mama added. I didn't need to ask what she was referring to. I nodded quietly.

We were yet to receive any new information about Uncle Ikenna. Every time the mail came, we'd both run to the gate in hope that someone somewhere knew something that could help us. Since our trip to Kaduna, we'd gone to Asaba several times and spoken to survivors and witnesses of that fateful day, but we'd been unable to find anything new.

It was the only time Mama and I never argued or disagreed – when we spoke about him – our love for him the only binding force powerful enough to surmount our prodigious differences. It didn't matter how long it took, how many years of silence in between, we would find him. Our hope burned on, like the last embers of an eternal flame that refused to be put out.

Just as she was about to step out the door, Mama turned to look at me. 'Before I forget, how many people did you tell about this?' she asked.

'About what, Mama?'

She waved her hand impatiently. 'About you leaving your husband?'

'Nobody, except Ada and Chinelo,' I replied slowly, confused at the question.

'Good. Don't tell anyone else. If they ask, tell them you went to spend some time with your parents because they were ill, and your husband was travelling a lot. You must not wash your dirty linen in public. Your husband is a big man; you cannot afford to embarrass him. *Inugo*?'

'Yes, Mama,' I replied humbly.

'Good. You can continue.' She smiled as she sauntered out of the room, undoubtedly pleased at my easy acquiescence. I was slowly becoming the daughter she desired.

By the time Gozie arrived, our belongings were all packed and arranged at the front door, ready to be put in the trunk of the car. My brothers had already appeared earlier to help me carry my bags and boxes out of the house. 'You're doing the right thing,' Ugochukwu said, patting me gently at the side of my face. I was like a new bride leaving for her husband's home for the first time, or a relative departing for abroad.

After many months away, I stepped onto the polished terrazzo-tiled floors of our flat.

'I plan on buying a bigger house for us soon. So please just manage this for now,' Gozie said as we walked in. He hadn't stopped talking since we'd driven off from Papa's compound: about the new expensive coating of paint he'd had done on the walls of the house, the new dresses he'd bought for the children and the new car he planned to buy for me.

I smiled at him encouragingly, remembering Mama's words to keep him happy, and hanging on to his words as signs of the fulfilment of his promises that he'd once again become the man I'd fallen in love with.

The next morning, I wrote to Akin to let him know I could no longer continue our correspondence.

*I will always be grateful for our friendship, but I have to put my children's needs before mine. My family has to come first.*

He never responded, and I didn't expect him to.

# PART 3

# TOMORROW

## 24.

## *A worthy woman who can find?*

The church was hot that day in February '92, too hot. So hot that I could feel sweat drip down the crevice of my breasts, past my stomach and to my legs under the thick, heavy material of my sequinned blouse and matching wrapper.

'Pray!' Sister Ndidi screamed into the microphone, the veins in her neck screeching out of her skin along with her voice.

The crowd broke into a chorus of discordant rumblings. 'Father Lord!' the woman beside me screamed before dissolving into an avalanche of words I could hardly decipher. Another rolled on the floor, on the small pathway between the pews, her headscarf, dislodged and rumpled, lying forgotten by her side.

We were at a prayer meeting, the crowning finale to a four-day marriage programme organised by the church's Christian Women's Association, the second held in three months. The church was packed with a sea of faces and had been that way for the past seventy-two hours.

We began each assembly in the same way: with a drawn-out opening prayer followed by twenty minutes of singing and dancing.

Then it was testimony time – when fellow worshippers took to the pulpit to share embellished and dramatic versions of the miraculous events that had taken place in their lives, while a church attendant held the sole microphone to prevent and cut short ramblings.

'Brethren, I want you to help me thank God,' a sister said into the microphone held to her mouth on the first day. She looked not much older than thirty. I couldn't recognise her as a regular; a church member must have invited her. She let out a sound, something between a hiccup and a sob, before continuing. 'This time last year, I was single. I didn't have anyone to take care of me or for me to take care of. My enemies had already begun to laugh at me. They said, "Who will marry you? At your old age?" But look at what my God has done,' she said, waving the back of her left hand at the congregation, where a distinct gold band gleamed on her ring finger. The crowd roared in approval. I wondered how long she had waited to share her testimony, practising the words she would say over and over, and when it eventually happened, choosing the perfect clothes and jewellery – wanting to shame her enemies just right. And I imagined her husband, if he was there, beaming and adjusting in his seat, his shoulders a little higher, his back a tad straighter.

Another woman walked gingerly to the pulpit, clutching a small boy, not more than three months old, to her chest. Three little girls were by her side. She cleared her throat and leaned into the microphone. 'I want to thank the God of Abraham, Isaac and Jacob for saving my marriage and removing shame from my life. For years, my in-laws were trying to chase me out of my husband's home because I could not have a male child. But my God, the one that shames our enemies, has done it!' she said, raising the infant triumphantly like a trophy. The cheers from the congregation were deafening. 'I just want to say, don't lose hope. The God that did my own can do your own too.' I spotted Ada, seated much closer to the front, screaming and jumping, waving a white handkerchief above her head.

'You should jump too,' I told myself. But my feet would not move. She'd referred to her daughters as 'shame' in their presence and my heart hurt for them.

After the testimonies, the ushers, led by Sister Seun, passed offering baskets round while the choir sang 'Give It Shall Be Given unto You'.

Deacon Esomchi taught the message that day, titled *Maintaining a Good Home*. An elder in the church, and having been married for twenty-five years, he had been unanimously chosen by the planning committee to give the opening sermon.

'Let us all open our Bibles to Proverbs 31, verse ten,' he announced in a solemn voice as he flipped through the huge Bible that he rested on the pulpit. He was not a very tall man – his wife towered over him by several inches – so his head barely got above the top of the wooden column. '"A worthy woman who can find? For her price is far above rubies. The heart of her husband trusteth in her. And he shall have no lack of gain. She doeth him good and not evil. All the days of her life."' He paused meaningfully to let the words sink in, looking round the faces present. His all-knowing paternal gaze made me feel as though he could see every person present and every sin they'd ever committed. Then he bowed his head and shut his eyes. 'Let us pray. Father, as we're gathered here today, let every word spoken touch hearts and change our ways.'

'Amen,' we echoed.

Over the next hour, Deacon Esomchi espoused the virtues of

becoming like the Proverbs woman. '"She doeth him good and not evil . . . She riseth while it is yet night. And giveth food to her household." Some of you women are too lazy. By 7 a.m. you're still sleeping, snoring in your beds! You're supposed to be up, taking care of the home. As a woman, you're a cook, a teacher, a nurse, a counsellor, an alarm clock. That is your duty! But many of you are following the ways of the devil in the name of modernisation.'

He stopped to turn a page in his Bible. '"She perceiveth that her merchandise is profitable . . . Her husband is known in the gates." Her merchandise is profitable and her husband is known. Some of you women, once you make money, your husband won't be able to speak again in his own home. You start talking to him and treating him like your houseboy. And you wonder why you are not happy in your homes.' He took a sip from a glass of water before continuing. 'I will give you the example of my wife, and I would like to encourage you women to be like her. Many years ago, she was earning more than I was at her place of work. Everyone thought she would start carrying her shoulders about the house, even I thought so too. But every month, she would take all the money she was paid and give it to me as the head of the house. Then she would kneel and ask me to give her money for anything she needs. My wife is here so you can ask her if you don't believe me. Brethren, that is a humble and virtuous woman, and I am glad I married her.'

Women and men alike rose to their feet to applaud such a rare gem. I looked over to where she sat, to check for signs of embarrassment or discomfort, but she beamed, the skin of her fair face illuminated as though kissed by the sun itself.

And so it went – each day, someone would come preach the same message as the day before but in a different light, the words and expressions interchanged for euphemisms and synonyms: 'Ladies, learn how to be quiet – some of you talk too much', 'Women, submit to your husband', 'Women, learn to talk about things other than the market and tomatoes so your husbands will want to talk to you', 'Ladies, be peaceful at all cost. If your husband insults you or tries to quarrel with you, hold your peace. That is the only way to maintain a happy home.'

Occasionally, a word was thrown in for the men and unmarried amongst us: 'Men, love your wives.'

One speaker talked about the book he'd specially written for married women – *My Husband Must Prosper* – and encouraged everyone present to pick up a copy after the service. 'As a woman, you have to stand by your husband; protect him from outsiders,' he taught. 'Protect him; hide his shame! Let your chaste character transform him. Don't fight; let God fight for you. Crying will not help you. Reporting your husband to the extent that you've become better than a news reporter will not help you. Stop talking to outsiders about your marital problems. Pray! Leave your husband alone. Many of you women harass your husband when you discover that he's seeing someone outside, instead of changing things around you. Men like attention. Are you giving your husband attention? Are you changing your hairstyle and your wardrobe? Are you looking good for him? How do you know the other woman hasn't used charms on him?' He went on to tell the story of a woman whose husband had returned to her after several years after she'd lost a lot of weight and begun to dress better.

Sister Ndidi had a special message for the spinsters in the house. 'A lot of you unmarried women are single because you're too picky. You want a brother taller than you or one that has money. You sisters have become too greedy. In our day, we married no matter what the men had. As long as a man is working, marry him. No matter what he is earning. The money will come. Some of you are sleeping with men you're not married to. Don't you know that when you give yourself to a man before marriage, you cheapen yourself? A man will respect you more if you're a virgin when you marry him; love you more, treat you better. Take note. You're also leading these men astray, like Delilah led Samson to his death with his head on her lap . . . Single women, slap your legs and say after me: "My lap shall not be the graveyard for any man."'

'We will be taking questions today. If you have any questions, please step forward,' Sister Ndidi announced at the end of her sermon on the third day, and within seconds, a queue was formed.

Sister Cynthia was the first to go. Petite with a squeaky voice that sounded more mouse than human, she'd been married for a little over two years. From the size of her belly, she was expecting a second child soon. 'Thank you for the sermon. I have a question. Why do men change so much after marriage? Before marriage, they take you out, buy you things, try to help out around the house. But the moment you marry them, they don't want to do anything at all! I know you have said we should take care of the home, but we take care of the home, take care of our children, take care of family members. Please, what are the men doing? Shouldn't they contribute somehow? That is my question. Thank you!' Women hollered encouragement as she marched back to her seat. I could tell that she had been waiting for an opportunity to speak, the stress and discontentment had choked her for far too long. I looked over to where her husband, an usher, stood at the back of the church; his bow tie had suddenly become too tight.

'Pastor, you asked yesterday about why brothers in the church are not getting married. I have come to answer the question,' Brother Afamefuna said. He was the oldest unmarried member of the congregation. 'There are no more quality women in the church, women like our mothers. Women willing to respect and take care of their husban—'. He'd chosen the wrong crowd to air his views. Before he could finish, a large proportion of the congregation hissed in synch, like members of an in-tune choir, and those that didn't hiss were too busy booing or shouting him down. 'There are no quality men too!' one woman yelled from the back. 'Go and marry your mother!' another woman screamed from the other end of the auditorium.

Sister Ndidi was forced to intervene. 'Sisters, sisters,' she called into the collected microphone. 'We're in the house of God. Let us behave ourselves please. To avoid further disturbance, we will move on to the next person.'

A young woman stepped up as Brother Afamefuna stalked off the stage. 'Good morning, church. I am a single woman looking to get married but I have a question, and this is one the reasons I've been fearful of marriage. Why is it that men like to beat their wives? Even if there is a disagreement, why not talk it out like two adults? Why resort to blows? That is my question. Thank you.' The women in the audience screamed in applause.

'I will answer the first question and Deacon Esomchi will answer the other, then we will continue. Our sister asked why men change after marriage. We are all human. Even you – I'm sure you have changed since you've gotten married. You are probably not as slim

243

as you were. About helping at home, women it is our duty to take care of the home. The men can help out every now and then, but it is our duty. Men, please try to help out at home; it is not easy for us women,' Sister Ndidi said and handed the microphone to Deacon Esomchi.

'The second lady that asked the question, you said you are not married. So how do you know? You see this is how many of you don't help yourselves. You hear things and believe all, hook, line and sinker. Yes, some men beat their wives, but let's be honest, you women have razor-blade mouths. Before your husband says one, you have said ten, then you come and complain when he beats you. Let us all look inwards. You might be the source of your problem,' Deacon Esomchi said.

Sister Ndidi grabbed the microphone before it could be handed to the next questioner. 'Sisters, I know some men can be very bad-tempered but with prayer, honour and trust in God, even the most terrible man can become a saint.'

'Hmmm, but some men really have bad character o,' I heard a woman sitting in front of me say to her friend.

'My dear, it is okay for a man to have a bad character as long as he is a man,' her friend replied.


Nkechi tugged hard at my wrapper, bringing me back to the prayer service. 'Mummy, I want biscuit and sweet,' she said with a lisp from the space where her front teeth had been just a few weeks ago.

'Yes, Mummy, we want *biscuith*,' her twin concurred through her own tooth-gap.

'*Shhh*. Mummy is praying,' I whispered.

'But we want *biscuith*,' Nkechi near-shouted.

I frowned, beginning to get annoyed. 'Behave yourselves. Close your eyes and pray.'

'About what?' Nkechi asked in a sing-song voice.

I sighed. I really should have left them with Mama but I'd been avoiding her since our last family meeting, where she'd demanded that Ugochukwu's wife issue her a formal apology for forgetting their pre-planned market appointment. When Ugochukwu had tried to defend his wife in her absence, she'd silenced him.

'But Mama, she already said sorry, what formal apology again?' I'd simply said, and Mama had reminded me that I had more important problems to deal with in my home, like the marked absence of a son.

'Go and ask Ego for biscuit,' I said to the twins. Some sort of tacit communication seemed to take place between them and they skittered off to meet Ego at the other end of the pew.

'Mummy said we should come and collect biscuit from you,' I heard the both of them say in unison.

'I don't have any. Let's go and buy some outside,' Ego said, and got up to take them.

I watched them traipse out of the auditorium and a warm feeling settled at the bottom of my stomach. It was still jarring to me just how fast they were growing. Ego bent to listen to something Nwamaka said, and then burst into laughter. I was happy to see her still laugh that way, not the timid tinkle sound she'd begun to make.

'My English teacher said I don't behave like a lady,' she'd announced one afternoon as we settled down for lunch.

'Don't behave like a lady? How?' I asked as I continued spooning mounds of white rice into the porcelain dishes I'd laid out.

'He said I laugh too loud, and that I'm always playing sports with the boys.'

I dropped the spoon and turned to give her my full attention. 'There is nothing wrong with your laughter. And there is absolutely nothing wrong with playing with boys. I used to play with my brothers when I was younger, too. In fact, I still play with them. Who is this teacher? I need to go and talk to him.'

She shook her head vigorously and rubbed her palms together in a pleading gesture. 'Ah. Mummy, please. No. Everyone is still talking about the last time you came to school because of what Mrs. Afolabi did. Please don't come. I'm begging you.'

I'd paid a visit to the headmaster's office and demanded to know what sort of school he was running when Ego had told me her Mathematics teacher, a Mrs. Afolabi, had punished all the male students for 'allowing' a girl to top the class when Ego had gotten the highest score in a test.

I hissed, long and hard. 'They should talk about me very well. They will see me time after time if they try any more nonsense. Just look at all the money we're spending on school fees every term. Is that what they are supposed to be teaching you people there?'

Every day, I sent my daughters out encouraging them to be themselves in a way no one else could, to be different from what was expected, and each day, the world around them to returned them to me with minds replete with questions and doubts, telling them that all their mother had said was a lie.

# 25.

## Let them live and enjoy jare

Adaugo threw a birthday party for her second daughter when she turned ten, in January '93. *You're cordially invited to celebrate with the Okafors on the momentous occasion of our daughter turning a Glorious Ten,* the invitation said, the words surrounded by pink and purple flowers. *Glorious Ten.* I chuckled at the words; Adaugo, dramatic as ever. Were the years before inglorious?

The cumulous sleeves on Zina's frilly gown bubbled as she reached for the glassy purple ribbons in her hair. Her mother slapped at her wrists. 'Zinachukwu stop pulling at the ribbons. You want to spoil the hair I spent hours making?' Adaugo said.

'It's not even my birthday. I don't know why I have to dress like this,' Zina grumbled.

Adaugo eyed her with irritation. 'It's your sister's birthday and you have to dress like you own the party, not a visitor.'

'How do visitors and party owners dress, Adaugo?' I asked, laughing as I pulled the twins with me into her compound.

'You're here,' Adaugo said, turning to look at me, her face brightening

247

in a smile. 'Don't mind her, always complaining about her clothes,' she continued, dismissing her first daughter with a wave of her hand.

'Good afternoon, Aunty Uju. What ab—'

'Good afternoon, Zina. And you don't have to ask – Ego is coming behind; she's helping me lock the car.'

She did not bother to say thank you as she ran out the gate.

'You cannot even say "thank you",' Adaugo shouted at her back and glanced at me apologetically.

'You sound like my mother,' I mocked.

'And you're early. I see you did not leave this your first-to-come behaviour in your Gozie-chasing days,' she retorted, and we giggled.

Hours later, the compound bristled with people and activities – the children arrayed in colourful party dresses dancing non-stop as the party MC announced winners of mini-competitions, the pitched screams coming from the blown-up bouncy castle, the smell of jollof and fried chicken coming from the back of the compound, where caterers worked non-stop.

'Uzondu must have spent serious money o,' Chinelo commented, her eyes taking in everything from our seats under a canopy. She'd come in an hour after me and her children were amongst the dancing competitors.

'Adaugo doesn't do things by halves,' I said.

The DJ changed the song and Wreckx-N-Effect's 'Rump Shaker' blared from the speakers. I frowned in disapproval. 'Don't you think this song is too mature for a children's party?' I complained.

Chinelo threw her head back and laughed. 'When did you become a prude, Obianuju? Do they even know the meaning of the lyrics? Let them live and enjoy *jare*.'

She pointed at our eldest daughters in the middle of the dancefloor. Zina was saying something to Ego and Chinelo's daughter Eriife was howling at whatever it was, just like her mother. 'They're going to be just like us,' Chinelo said.

Adaugo bounced into a seat halfway through the party, looking flustered. 'Sorry I haven't been able to keep you company. Are you minding that stupid party planner? I don't what's the point of hiring a party planner if you're still going to be running around.'

'Do you need any help?' Chinelo asked, already making to stand.

Adaugo placed her hand on Chinelo's shoulder, pinning her to her seat. 'You're a guest today. You too, Obianuju; you better not stand up from that seat or we will fight.'

I raised my hands in surrender.

'What were we talking about?' Adaugo asked, shifting to settle comfortably.

'Where is Uzondu? I don't think I've seen him today,' I said, looking around to confirm.

'He said he had a meeting or something; I don't know,' Adaugo replied flippantly. She was used to his absence at functions.

'How many husbands can you see here today?' Chinelo said. 'You too, where is your husband? Where is my own?'

'My child is not the celebrant,' I joked before Adaugo asked us if we'd seen the flyer for the upcoming women's meeting at church and we flowed in our usual banter.

'Are you still in touch with him, by the way?' Adaugo asked out of nowhere and I stared at her, perplexed.

'In touch with who?'

'Dr. Ajayi, of course. Your mother said you were always hiding in a corner to read letters when you were at your parents' place and I assumed it was him. Who else would you be sending letters to?'

'That was years ago and I know other people you know,' I answered guardedly.

'You didn't answer the question, Uju,' Chinelo murmured, focusing on me with immediate intensity.

I looked between the both of them. 'Is this an interrogation or something? Can't I have friends again?' I was being defensive, I knew.

'I know I encouraged you back then, but you're married now,' Chinelo said.

'Yes!' Adaugo supported. 'The Bible says we should flee from all sorts of sin, including adultery.'

'Adaugo, please. I know what the Bible says about adultery,' I snapped.

The letters had started coming again in '91, after he'd watched the video of a Black man named Rodney King getting assaulted by the police on television – they'd battered him with batons, fists and kicks. He felt fear for the first time since he'd arrived in America, Akin said. Crushing fear that it would be him, and no one would care because he was an immigrant from a poor country. These things happened in Nigeria but this was America; America was supposed to be different, and I was the only one who could understand. He would write me again in April '92 (it reached me in July), when the officers were acquitted. The fear had become rage.

A lot had happened since my letter. For one, he was no longer sure – about America or becoming a professor. He was an associate professor now; his department head had called to congratulate and assure him of his path to professorship. His colleagues had organised a dinner to celebrate. But as they'd drunk white wine over sushi, he'd felt a teeming uneasiness, an unsettledness in his bones he could not shake.

He'd separated from his American girlfriend, and from that I felt a morbid joy that made me ashamed. His mother hadn't liked her; her son would not marry a foreigner. But that was not why they'd broken up. She was ready to settle down and had begun hinting at marriage – her prime years for childbearing were passing – but he wasn't ready. It surprised me that American women felt the same pressure we did; they were said to be more liberal, less bothered by such archaic thinking.

I was tempted to reply, to say, '*Why aren't you ready to marry? Are you not old enough Mr. Man?*' He missed me, he said, the warm assurance of our friendship. But I'd promised Mama that I would not be distracted, and for my children's sake I was going to keep my word.

'You have another letter, Obianuju,' Mama Sikira informed me whenever she spotted me on my parents' street, and I thanked her each time, collecting the letters and tucking them at the bottom of my handbag, where I was sure Gozie never looked.

His last letter had come with a picture – he wore a medium-top fade and a biker jacket. I thought he looked like a rapper.

Adaugo left us again, in the middle of their questioning, when her help ran to our midst wringing her hands nervously. 'What? What happened?' Adaugo demanded to know, jumping to her feet.

'Madam, the caterer talk say jollof rice don finish,' was all the girl needed to say before Adaugo ran off in the direction of the back of the duplex.

In Adaugo's absence, Chinelo and I sat in awkward silence. I could tell she was contemplating on whether to continue their questioning but decided to let it be. And so we remained together but alone in the comfort of our silence, saying nothing but not having to.

We stayed that way for several minutes before Chinelo said suddenly into the stillness, 'I can't have any more children.'

The world tilted in my head. 'What?'

She picked up the bottle of soft drink in front of her earlier and held it close to her face, contemplating the dark cola. 'I can't have any more children,' she repeated.

I jumped in my seat, realising I'd heard right. '*Chineke!* What? How? Why?'

'They say my heart is too big, that I have something called cardiomegaly.' She paused and squinted her eyes in concentration, trying to recall the exact words the doctor had used. 'Hypertensive cardiomegaly. It's dangerous for me to have any more children,' she said in a deadpan voice – devoid of inflection and affection, anguish or pain, just one of disbelieving acceptance – staring still at the bottle.

'Hyper what?'

'Hypertensive cardiomegaly,' she repeated.

I could tell she'd said it several times before, over and over, until she, who'd had issues pronouncing basic illnesses when we were Biology students in secondary school, could say it without a single pause or inflection.

'My God. I'm so sorry, Chinelo.' I didn't know what else to say; words had fled the periphery of my mind.

'Promise me you won't tell Adaugo; she will worry too much. She already has a lot going on with her family; I don't want to burden her any further.'

I agreed to be sworn to secrecy.

I asked the most important questions that came to mind. 'Does Christopher know? What did he say?'

She nodded slowly, a wry smile on her lips. 'His people want me to quit my job to focus on having more children.'

'Why? You already have two children, a boy and a girl.'

'I am not from their place; I have only one son,' she responded as if the reasons were obvious to see.

'At least you have one!' I insisted.

She gave a small smile to communicate that I couldn't understand. 'The other day I heard his sister tell him that if only one of something is remaining, it is as good as finished.'

'Jesus Christ! What sort of nonsense talk is that?' I exclaimed.

She turned to face her bottle.

She didn't say anything for several minutes, not to respond to me or to say any more about the situation. When she finally turned, there were tears in her eyes, and they spilled down her fair cheeks.

'Uju, what do I do? I don't know what to do,' she said.

'This is for the mummies and daddies in the house!' the DJ announced over the sound system and the Bee Gees' 'Staying Alive' came on.

*

Nwakaego wanted a birthday party after that.

'I've never had one, you know,' she said to me, a twinkle in her eyes. 'My birthday is in March. Pleeeaaasseeee?'

She'd never had a birthday party mostly because I'd also never had one. Papa had promised me a large birthday party for my tenth birthday, just like Sikira down the street had had.

For Sikira's tenth birthday, her mother killed two goats and cooked a bag of rice. The whole street was invited, and we turned up wearing our finest party dresses. Sikira shone in our midst in a pink dress of organza and sparkling sequins. Her mother had used a hot comb on her hair and arranged it in an elegant updo. Two ringlets danced by the side of her cheeks.

On the gramophone, they played the black records of Sunny Ade, Obe and Dele Abiodun, the marinated sounds of juju music and Afropop causing even the adults with us to break into dance. When evening began to dawn and everyone had eaten to their fill and all the party games had been played, Mama Sikira brought out an enormous frosted cake with ten candles burning brightly at the top and we gathered to clap and sing 'Happy Birthday' as the celebrant blew out the flames.

For days, all everyone could talk about was the magnificent party and Papa promised to throw me one just like it. I imagined the perfect dress of organza and sparkling sequins just like Sikira's but in iridescent purple, and Uncle Ikenna promised to place a special order for it.

But war came the year I turned ten and I spent my birthday in a bunker, surrounded by exploding bombs, brightly burning buildings and haunting screams.

'I'll talk to your father about it,' I promised Ego, and she beamed.

'What's the purpose of such frivolities?' Gozie said when I mentioned it to him.

'You throw and attend parties all the time, Chigozie; it shouldn't be too hard to have one for your daughter. She really wants it.'

'I've never had a birthday party,' he countered. 'Not as an adult, and not as a child. I didn't even know what parties were when I was her age; we were too busy trying to survive.'

I sighed. 'Gozie, please.'

'What has she done to deserve it? Is she even doing well at school?'

'She is doing very well, and you would know that if you bothered to even check her results.'

'I'm sure whatever her grades are, she can do better. Every time I come home, I see her in front of a television,' Gozie said.

'You don't know anything about your daughters, not Ego, not Nkechi, not Nwamaka. All you do is criticise and criticise!'

I did not know when we started screaming at each other at the very top of our voices or how long we'd been doing so before Nwakaego barged into her father's study and pulled me forcefully by the arm.

'Mummy, it's okay; please let's go. I don't want a party anymore. Please,' she begged, her voice cracking as she dragged me towards the door.

I made sure to deliver a parting insult before I acquiesced. 'Nothing will ever be good enough for you because you know deep down that you yourself will never be good enough.'

'Get out before I really lose my temper!' Gozie yelled as the glass nameplate he kept rather unnecessarily on his desk crashed against the door behind us.

# 26.

## If I believe, it will happen

'Christopher wants us to move to England,' Chinelo said to me in my living room a few weeks after Adaugo's party.

'England?' I asked, fearful that I was about to lose my friend in a way I'd never imagined.

'He said we wouldn't have to deal with family pressure over there and I would have better treatment options.'

I nodded, understanding. 'He has a point,' I said.

'I'm not moving,' Chinelo said with finality, the same stubbornness she'd shown in marrying Christopher.

'Why?' I asked cautiously.

'If we wanted to move, we should have moved years ago. Where would we start from? We're doing very well here – he just made associate director and I'm a senior manager. Why should we go abroad and become second-class citizens and start worrying about things like papers?

'But—' I tried to interject.

'My children will soon be teenagers; you want me to take them to that place where those *oyinbo* people have no home training? Next thing they'll become drug addicts like Obiefune's son that is now in prison.'

'Chinelo, but many people go there and do very well. There are so many opportunities there and they have a working system.'

'Well, that is their business,' she said. 'We went to see a specialist together the other day; I've started treatment already. We have good doctors here; our system just doesn't reward them.'

Chinelo chuckled and said, 'Christopher cried when the doctor read out the diagnosis. And I was the one comforting him. Me, the person with the illness o. Maybe it's because I've seen childbirth.' Then she laughed some more. But I could see that behind the false bravado that Chinelo was afraid. Afraid of death.

By May '93, it had become painful to watch Chinelo. She sprung from her seat during a church service when Sister Ndidi began the prayer for good health and then for children, her hands stretched high, head thrown back and eyes closed, tears streaming down her face as though she could somehow push herself closer to the heavens to collect that which she desired most.

I turned away. It hurt just how much she wanted this, how desperate she was for it. And the emaciated version of herself she became as nothing happened still, shrinking within like a withered leaf, worry lines appearing on her delicate, fair skin as though carefully drawn in by an oil painter, each line representing a disappointment.

'If I believe, it will happen. I just have to believe. I don't believe

257

enough yet, that's why it hasn't happened. Pastor and Sister Ndidi said so,' she'd told me with tears in her eyes the last time we'd spoken about it.

She attended every service and breakthrough programme now. 'They said a powerful man of God is coming and once he prays, everything will be fine.' 'I heard one sister was healed when she swallowed two spoons of anointing oil. I've bought my own o.' 'My miracle is coming; I can feel it.' She'd become a mini-Ada of sorts, but she lacked the spirit, enjoyment and enthusiasm with which Adaugo did these things.

Adaugo's eyes were bright after the service, as though someone had turned on the lights in them. 'Adaugo, why are you running? A whole big woman like you? Are you trying to spoil your reputation?' I teased, even though she'd just been walking a little too quickly, screaming my name in order to be heard above the din of the noise around us.

She laughed, her bosom, still heaving, raising the top of her blouse. 'You're an even bigger madam now, that is why a big madam like me was running after you, because I don't know where you're rushing to.' We laughed, comfortable in the balmy embrace of our banter.

'What did you think?' she asked when we'd stopped laughing
'About what?'

'About the service now. Or were you not here? That prayer was powerful! I could feel the spirit moving.'

'Yes o! It was awesome. I saw you in front, jumping and waving your handkerchief,' I said with feigned enthusiasm.

'My sister! I had to claim my own miracle.' She raised her arms to demonstrate the way she'd done it earlier.

'Adaugo put down your arms; you're not a student,' I reprimanded.

'I'm a student o, a student of God,' she rejoined.

'I really like this your gown o. Did you buy it or did a tailor make it?' I asked, admiring the embroidered purple *jalabiya* she had on, changing the subject.

She smiled wider, her face glowing; she was so beautiful, even after all these years. 'My new tailor made it o. One of Uzondu's friends' wives took me to her shop when I asked her where she gets her dresses. This one isn't even as fine as some of the others she made. Do you want me to take you to her shop later this week?'

'You must take me there. You cannot be shining alone; we must shine together.'

She giggled, an airy sound of delight, and I wondered if Uzondu still complimented her like he used to. 'Are you coming for the women's meeting on Thursday?' she asked.

'Yes, you know I have a committee meeting just before the meeting. There's no way I'll miss it.'

Ada nodded in understanding. 'What about the "Woman on Her Knees" prayer meeting on Friday? And the Prevailing Women's meeting on Saturday?'

'Yes, I'll be there. Sister Ndidi has talked about it so much that I'll probably dream about her if I don't come.' We howled and clapped our hands together like juveniles.

'But you know the power of a praying woman,' Ada said, grinning.

'What about the men? Don't they pray? Why is there no "Prevailing Men"? Every time praying woman, intercessory mother.'

Ada cackled and shook her head slowly. 'Obianujunwa! When will you change?'

'Not anytime soon,' I retorted.

'By the way, I've been meaning to talk to you about something,' she said, lowering her voice and darting her eyes side to side to make sure we were not being heard by someone else. 'I think something is wrong with Chinelo.'

'Why?'

'Haven't you noticed that she's been acting strange?'

'Strange how?'


Four years later and it was still strange to me how easily I'd fallen back into the endless flow of activities, doing something, anything, to be away from home. On Mondays I had prayer meetings, Tuesdays, Bible Study, Wednesdays, we gathered for Women's meetings, Thursdays were for Marriage Council meetings and Fridays for Intercessory Prayer meetings. Saturdays were the days for every other programme and when I joined the Sanctuary Keepers to sweep and mop the floors of church premises in preparation for Sunday's service while Sister Ndidi shouted 'Make sure you mop the altar very well; that is where the message and power will flow from.'

'You need something to get you out of the house. Other people to spend time with. That's what you need,' Adaugo and Chinelo had recommended when I had returned to Gozie feeling adrift and muddled.

That Sunday, I was taken to see the woman who held the church in the palm of her hands: Sister Ndidi. No one knew how old she was; she could have been as old as Methuselah for all we knew, but we were aware that her husband was dead and her children were all grown up, married and living outside of the country. So powerful was she that even the pastor could not question her judgement. 'Ah. You want her to remind him of where she was when he was just a boy?' Ada had quipped when I'd asked why.

Up close, Sister Ndidi was shorter than I'd expected, the top of her head not getting past my shoulders. For some reason, she'd always seemed taller; an unyielding giant, standing at the altar, issuing commands, making announcements, providing guidance for the lost souls amongst us.

'You're welcome, my daughter. It is good you have finally decided to participate more in church activities. There is always space for another servant in the house of the Lord. I've always wondered how your husband could be so active and be a whole deacon, and you so quiet, doing absolutely nothing. But it is good to know that you were just focusing on bringing up the children, like you have said; that is your most important job as a mother, you know,' she said after we'd explained the purpose of our seeking her exalted audience.

'Thank you, ma,' we said in unison, even though she'd spoken only to me. And with that, I was welcomed with open arms.

'You should join the Sanctuary Keepers and the Intercessors,' Chinelo suggested.

'And the Women's Fellowship,' Ada appended.

Sister Ndidi had other ideas. 'I will recommend you to the Marriage Council. I think you would be a good addition to our team. You've been married for over ten years, and you're Deacon Azubuike's wife. We need people like you to share your knowledge and experience. That is the only way marriages will continue to last in the church.

'You can never advise them to leave their marriages, no matter what you hear. If they want to leave, you tell them to stay. "God hates divorce. You cannot break your marriage, no matter what happens!" That's what you should say. Do you understand?' Sister Ndidi said to me the first time I was finally allowed to counsel a couple. I looked over to where the pair sat, a tall, big boned man looking around the room as though searching for an escape route and a timid, average-height woman who couldn't seem to stop looking at her fingers – whether it was shame or fear she felt, I could not tell.

'Yes, Sister Ndidi,' I replied. It was the way we all answered her – *Yes, Sister Ndidi*. I was yet to hear someone argue with her or utter the forbidden words: *No, Sister Ndidi*. I was almost certain that the day that happened time would freeze, the Earth would cease to turn on its axis and the world would end.

# 27.

## Witch!

'You're a witch! Witch!' Gozie screamed in March of '94.

He was like a madman, grabbing anything and everything in his path of destruction, intending, brazenly, to do damage. Tears raced down my cheeks, mixing freely with the catarrh dribbling out of my nose, and flowed down my chin into the seams of my dress. 'I'm sorry!' I cried, even though I knew it was useless. Begging had never worked, fighting back had never worked – nothing had ever worked.

Nwamaka and Nkechi wailed, forgotten in a corner.

'Daddy, please stop,' Ego's voice implored in the background. I thought she sounded choked, like she was close to tears. But Daddy wasn't listening. I watched her gather her siblings and take them to the living room upstairs, the one with large windows and a lot of fresh air, to play cartoon video tapes on the big television. She turned the volume up so loud that their little worlds could remain undisturbed by the war raging about them.

Gozie continued to stalk me. 'You're a witch! You want to ruin me. I should have known you were evil all along. After everything I have done for you. You ungrateful bitch!' he raged.

'I'm sorry,' I moaned from where I was crouched.

'Hope you're happy with what you've done. Hope you are very happy. If I'm not able to clear my goods at the port, this house will be too hot to contain the two of us, just know that.'

I cackled then, the deranged sound of an asylum patient. The house would become too hot, he said. From where I was, it was blazing as bright as the furnace of hell itself.

'I didn't do anything. I swear I didn't do anything,' I lamented to the ceiling. It was true. I hadn't done anything to warrant this sort of punishment. I cursed Ejike. Ejike with his slimy smile and sweaty hands and consistently dry lips. Ejike, who'd run away with Gozie's money.

Gozie had brought him to the house the previous October, Ejike wearing an oversized t-shirt and baggy jeans.

'He's my brother, Ejike. My great uncle's grandson,' Gozie said, his arm around the young man's shoulders. I'd become used to the sudden appearance of people claiming to be related to him one way or the other; money had a way of thickening blood ties and creating ones that never existed.

Instantly, I knew I didn't like him. His eyes were hungry, consuming everything around him – the marble tiles on the living room floor, the gleaming leather of the sofa, the twinkling chandelier dangling from the ceiling. I could see the numbers running around in his head, coming together to estimate how much each item cost, and I knew that, given the chance, he would put everything in the worn travel bag he carried and run to the nearest market and sell it all. But for half of what the things were worth, because he was not very smart.

'You're welcome,' I said. I smiled, a brief movement of the lips, polite yet aloof.

Later, Gozie took Ejike and his dusty travel bag to the boys' quarters to stay. He would work with him at his business.

'Ejike said he knows someone that works with the port authority so we won't have to pay as much as we do for clearing our goods at the port. That Ejike is such a hardworking boy, always looking for ways to help the business. I'm happy I brought him to the city,' Gozie offered, unprompted, several months later, rather uncharacteristically.

I turned from my position on the stool in front of my dressing table with the pink polished wood and wide looking glass to stare at him. 'Don't you already know someone there?' I asked.

He frowned. 'Yes, of course I know someone there. But apparently, my contact has been cheating me because he thinks I'm a big man. You know how all these people are. Ejike says his contact is willing to collect much less.'

I paused to think. 'Hmm. Are you sure? How did Ejike meet him anyway? Didn't he just come to the city in October?'

'What sort of rubbish are you saying, Uju? Do you know how many millions of naira this will save me? I'm saying my cousin has found a way to save my business money and you are here asking stupid questions.' The vein at his forehead began to throb with warning.

I altered my tone, filing around the edges so I sounded neither threatening nor suggestive.

'I'm just saying that I think you should be careful so you don't lose money in the process of trying to save some. You don't know who these people are; you can't trust them too much.'

The vein throbbed even harder. 'Are you trying to accuse my brother, my own blood, my family, of being a fraudster, Uju?'

'No, I'm—' A thick book cut my words shut, hitting me right in the face. I said nothing more, turning to face the mirror as though nothing had happened.

When Gozie came home one night, screaming for Ejike at the top of his voice, I pretended not to notice, my attention fully committed to giggling at the antics in *Tom and Jerry* on the television set with Nwamaka.

'Obianuju!' Gozie called just when Tom grabbed Jerry by his murine neck.

'Yes?'

'Have you seen Ejike?'

He looked frazzled: his flaming red tie was loosened, lying limp against his chest, his jacket was folded across his arm, and the sleeves of his shirt looked like they'd been hastily rolled up. I shook my head emphatically. 'No, I haven't seen him since he left for your office this morning. Is there any problem?' I responded calmly.

'Uju, I've always told you to stop asking me foolish questions. Of course there is a problem. Why else would I be shouting his name?'

'Sorry.'

'Sorry for yourself. Idiot.'

When the sun had long disappeared from the sky and Ejike still hadn't returned, Gozie went to search the boys' quarters. 'Maybe he came in and the gateman forgot to tell us,' he said. I nodded glumly. But the boys' quarters were empty, the room in disarray as though its occupant had left in a hurry – the closet was cleared and old shirts were strewn nonchalantly across the mattress. Most telling was the absence of the dusty travel bag.

Still, Gozie did not believe that Ejike was gone. He sat at the dining table, his head in his hands. And I sat with him, waiting and waiting, but Ejike did not come. When the clock struck two in the morning, and my eyelids began to stick together, I trudged up the stairs to our bedroom to sleep. Gozie was in the same position when I came down the next morning.

'Are you going to eat something?' I asked when it was noon and he still hadn't gotten up.

He didn't respond. Instead, he got to his feet and walked slowly to the door and out of the house. I watched him leave, perplexed as to what was happening, then I heard the start of a car's engine and the stuttering creak of the gate opening.

We did not see or hear from him, or Ejike, until that day – that day when he'd unceremoniously barged in. Then the punishment had started. It did not matter to Gozie that I'd never met Ejike before he'd brought him to our house or that I'd not been involved one way or the other in their business dealings. All that mattered was I'd actualised the happenstance into being by uttering the words in the first place. And for that reason alone, I was a witch.

'From frying pan to fire,' was what Gozie had said at the conclusion of the political chaos of '93: the months of unrest, the cancelled election results, the interim government and finally the new military government.

267

Gozie paused to roll a ball of pounded yam and dip it in a dish of *ogbono* soup, before swallowing it in a gulp. 'We should have just stayed like we were, *jeje*. "Democracy, democracy," we were shouting, as if we didn't know how our people are. Now look at us,' he lamented.

Nasir shook his head from side to side and the traditional Hausa *hula* he wore somehow remained fixed to his head like an appendage. 'It was too good to be true in the first place, my brother,' he said, voicing my thoughts. 'We should have known that the military liked power too much to stay out of our affairs for too long. There is nothing wrong with wanting democracy – of the people, by the people and for the people!'

'But even the democracy that we had before, what did we do with it? Corruption! Wasteful spending! Up and down,' Gozie retorted.

Nasir roared with laughter, his head thrown back against the chair he sat in. I expected his cap to fall finally, and patiently watched for it, but still it did not move an inch. 'Chigozie Azubuike! How times have changed. You of all people against democracy? So the last military government was full of saints, *ehn*?' he said, when he was finally able to talk. 'You're talking as if you have not benefited from the same corruption you're lamenting about.'

Gozie looked away, his face twisted in a sulk. Nasir continued to chuckle. 'Come on, my friend. Don't act that way. It is the way of our country. We must all survive somehow. As long as we don't pretend to one another.'

Gozie was slightly pacified. 'Hmm. All I know is we need to do something. We cannot continue to be fully dependent on government contracts for our businesses. We must branch out. Because we don't know when something like this will happen again, and next thing you know, all our businesses will collapse.'

Nasir rubbed his bald chin with his clean hand as he ruminated over what Gozie had said, the other hand still roaming around the pieces of meat in his soup. 'I see what you're saying, my brother. But the government is the richest and biggest spending institution in this country, the surest source of income for us. And with the government we can charge almost any price we want for our goods; everybody knows those budgets are padded. Like I told you before, governments can come and go, but civil servants will remain. As long as we keep those connections, we're fine. But still, I see what you're saying. There is no harm in looking for other sources of business.'

Business multiplied after that. Using the proceeds from their government contracts, they traded everything in from generators to frozen foods, installing massive cold rooms mounted on wooden pallets in the city's biggest markets.

With each success, Gozie's reputation spread like oil in water. It wasn't too long before everyone wanted to know, and be associated with, him. The business-column writers were curious as to how he'd managed to thrive in the midst of recession; the society magazines were eager to know what his wife looked like, what kind of clothes she wore, and how often we travelled out of the country for holidays. Nasir preferred to remain in the shadows, known but unseen by the rest, like a godfather, referred to namelessly as 'the business partner'.

Abruptly, I was thrown into a spotlight I didn't want to occupy, forced to attend elaborate functions and parties I had no interest in.

Always dressed in the best, I'd sit at tables with the wives of the haut monde and idly chatter about the latest fashion and business escapades of our significant others, while the lights above us glinted off the cascade of jewellery on our arms, necks and garments and the crystal glasses at our tables.

Mama never failed to remind me how none of it would be possible if I hadn't returned to my husband. 'So, you would have left all this for another woman to enjoy? *Ehn* Uju? Thank God that I serve a living God, and that you recovered your senses. If not, I would have dragged you back here to your husband's house by myself to apologise,' Mama said as soon as she stepped into the compound of our new house in Ikoyi. Adjusting her wrapper, she slowly turned to take in the majestic black gates, three-floor edifice and spacious compound with five cars, all the latest models. The hedgerows were perfectly even, the ixoras blooming and purple hibiscus trees intertwined in a breathtaking ornamental play. At the centre of the courtyard was a fountain of alabaster: a winged angel held a jar at its centre and crystal water gushed down to the pool below.

Inside, the house was even more grandiose, with polished marble floors and surfaces, spiral staircases with gold-plated railings, spacious rooms and lucent hanging chandeliers. Oriental rugs lined different parts of the floors, expensive paintings decorated the walls and gold-embroidered curtains with tassels hung from the windows.

'Jehovah,' Mama whispered reverently, her mouth hanging open, just before she turned to imprison my arm in an unyielding grip. 'Obianuju, you must not let him go o. Hold him tight. Guard your husband with jealousy. Now that your husband is very wealthy, other women will start eyeing him. Don't let another woman steal him from you and reap the fruits of all your labour. Do you hear me?' she said.

'Yes, Mama.'

'Good.'

## 28.

## *Let me see him and have peace*

Kelechi's wife was barren by the end of '94, at least that's what Mama said. 'How else do you explain her not having children after how many years? Ugochukwu's wife has three children including a son. Ikechukwu's wife even has all sons. Yet, after almost five years of marriage, nothing. Not even a miscarriage to show that she was fertile, that she even had the ability to conceive. Look at Oluchi: even her old-as-trees daughter that just got married already has a child. Was Kelechi sure when he said that girl was a virgin?' Mama said one day as we sat peeling *egusi* seeds that would be grinded for soup later. The weather was hot, so we sat outside on small stools, a large tray of dry seeds on the ground between the both of us.

I shook my head in dissent. 'Mama, you can't talk like that,' I said.

'Why can't I talk like that? Her mates that are having children, do they have two heads?' she asked, her eyes squinted. I still remembered how ecstatic Mama had been when Ugochukwu's wife had given birth to her son, Mama's first grandson; her excitement

272

had bubbled like a pot of boiling rice. 'I have a grandson. I am a grandmother to a man,' she'd said with joy, raising the tiny bundle, and then turning to Ugochukwu's wife. 'Akudo, my daughter, you're a true woman.'

'Mama, Anwulika is not God, who gives children. It's not like she doesn't want to have children herself,' I said, cracking a seed between my fingers.

Mama hissed, a drawn-out insulting sound. 'How do you know she wants children herself? For all we know, she could have destroyed her womb before she got married with her promiscuity!'

'Mama, these kinds of things are not always the woman's fault, you know. They should go and see a doctor; Kelechi might be the one with the problem.'

Mama jerked; the bowl of peeled naked seeds in her lap shook, on the verge of tipping over. 'God forbid! How can you say such about your own brother?'

'But you too, how can you say such about somebody's daughter? We're not living with them; we don't know what is going on.'

Mama raised a brow. 'Does it matter? Is it not what my eyes are seeing that I'm saying? Is she your sister? Or did you become related without telling me?'

I chose not to reply. Instead I quietly continued to peel the seeds, taking my time to separate the thin shells from the fawn-coloured seeds, then rubbing the naked seeds gently in my palm before placing them in the bowl on my lap.

I felt a sort of solidarity with Anwuli. We'd started trying again, Gozie and I – not that we ever stopped, but now it seemed more purposeful, willing the outcome we wanted into being. Nothing

273

happened, despite the numerous visits to various hospitals and experts, and the reassuring words that we were both fine from doctors in blanched overalls and stiff stethoscopes coiled around their necks like delicate pets.

'Just keep your wife relaxed and happy sir, and a baby will come,' the youthful doctor had said on our last visit. I could tell he was not long out of medical school, not too far removed from the days of spending sleepless nights sipping black coffee from insulated mugs, flipping through bulky textbooks and dazzling girls with his wide grin.

Gozie had smiled in response, the charismatic smile of one used to charming others into his aura. 'Ah, doctor, she's very well rested,' he said, squeezing my hand tightly, daring me to disagree.

With each appointment my anxiety grew that one day Gozie would get tired of the intrusive tests, the continuous poking and prodding: that he would listen to the numerous voices buzzing about him like flies telling him to take another wife, to find a fertile ground that would give him the male offspring he so desired.

But Mama did not understand; she just couldn't comprehend why a woman, a true God-fearing woman, could not bear healthy children of both sexes. Then Kelechi stopped bringing his wife home to see Mama and Papa, and she became even more relentless with her demands.

'Kelechi, where is your wife? Why have you stopped bringing her to our house? Are you hiding her? Am I a witch, that you'll be protecting your wife from me?'

Other times, she was even more caustic, discarding all restraint and decorum. 'Kelechi, what is the difference between your wife and a man? You're there sleeping with a man, thinking you have a woman. Tell your wife to produce my grandchildren. Tell her that her evil plans will not work. If she has used *juju* to blind your eyes and that is why you cannot see that it is wrong for you to be as old as you are and not have any children, tell her I said her charms will not work! You have a praying mother who serves a living God.'

When I tried to intervene, I was sternly told by Mama, 'You, that your marriage is standing on one leg, you want to speak on another person's behalf? Better go and find a solution to your own problem. How do you know they are not negotiating a new wife for your husband as we speak?'

Then Kelechi stopped coming to visit altogether, and Mama whined endlessly about how all her children hated her, after she'd sacrificed all her life for us.

Mama's frustration was rooted in something else, blowing below the surface and ready to lash out at the slightest provocation. Seven years had passed since our visit to the man in Kaduna and despite all our efforts, our search trail had grown cold. We'd hit a dead end – Asaba: we couldn't seem to go beyond that fateful day.

Gozie continued to expend his vast funds keeping the newspaper ads running. Some leads had come forward but with nothing concrete, and the more time passed, the more we feared that we were most likely not to hear anything. Time passing meant fewer people alive had witnessed the horror of those years, and those who had were ageing and soon to succumb to nature's eventual call, their stories locked up with them for eternity.

'Mama, I think it's time we stop searching,' I said one day. It was something we had all been thinking for a while but hadn't the courage to approach her. Even Papa had stopped writing letters seeking assistance and Ikechukwu no longer took advantage of his government job to search through war records. And so, on a day we were alone together once more in my living room, I told her, with a heavy heart, that it was time to move on. 'We've done everything possible. There's nothing else we can do but find the strength to come to terms with it and move forward. It's been twenty-seven years. We're just reopening old wounds. He was a good man; he'd understand.'

Mama's face hardened with conviction. 'He's not dead. He's alive somewhere. I'm sure of it.'

'Mama—'

'Stop! I don't want to hear another word. Is this what you invited me to your house to come and say?' Mama fumed, her eyes accusing me of betrayal. 'You didn't know him. You think you did but you didn't. Did you watch him grow up? Run around your father's compound? Come out best in his class?' Her voice broke in a cadaverous waver. 'The whole village put money together to make sure he sat for the government scholarship that took him to England because he was too brilliant to waste away; everybody loved him. Everybody! I see his face every night when I sleep – do you know that? Do you?'

'At least let me know what happened to him. Don't you want to know what happened?' Her tone had become one of piteous pleading. She was begging me not to leave her alone in this; I'd always been the only one who understood. 'Even if he's dead, let me know how he died, where he's buried. Let me take his body home to be buried with his people. Let me see him and have peace.'

Gozie was out for a 'very important meeting' the morning Mama Ifeoma and Mama Bidemi came to visit, but then again all his meetings were. The gateman knocked on the door, three cautious raps on the wood, followed by a single light press of the doorbell.

I opened the door. 'Yes, Usman? Any problem?' I said, patting the expensive Chinese weave on my head.

'No vex, madam, but two women, one dark and the other fair, *dem dey* gate say *dem wan* see you, that *dem* be your friends from *tay tay. Shey* I go let *dem* enter?' he asked, anxiously shifting his weight from foot to foot. I wondered what I'd done to make him scared of me.

'*Wetin* be their names?' I asked in a low tone, trying not to further frighten the skinny man.

'Erm something like Mama Ifyooma and Mama Bi . . . I no too get the second name like that.'

Excitement flowed through me. 'Bidemi?' I asked.

He smiled, thankful that he didn't have to finish the name he'd obviously forgotten. 'Yes, madam.'

'Bring them in! Quickly!' I shouted, and Usman jumped, instantly startled.

'Y-yes, madam,' he stammered – and ran to the gate, his rubber slippers almost falling off his feet.

We hugged at the door, crying and clinging tightly to one another, and for a small moment the years we'd been apart fell away like old garments, and we were back in the compound chatting and relaxing in the evening breeze.

They even smelled the same: Mama Bidemi like fresh, locally churned shea butter and Mama Ifeoma like unrefined coconut oil, tiny shaves of coconut still floating at the top.

Mama Bidemi had not lost her penchant for storytelling and once we settled in the living room, she began narrating how they had come about paying me a visit. 'Mama Ifeoma saw your pictures in a magazine and brought it to my flat shouting, "Come and see Uju! Come and see Uju!" like a bush woman.' Mama Ifeoma wrinkled her nose at her in mock annoyance.

'I was like, "Ah, our small Uju of yesterday? We must go and look for her and pay her a visit." We went to your former house first; even to find that place *sef* was hard. If not that I remembered your description, maybe we would still be checking because this one here could not remember anything. When we now found the place, the new people there told us you had moved o, and to Ikoyi for that matter. I said "Ah, Ikoyi is far. Uju is now a big woman o; only big people stay in Ikoyi." So, we collected your address from them and came here. We were just passing fine, fine houses on the way; this Ikoyi is not a small thing at all. When we saw the house, we were saying "Hope we're not at the wrong place," especially after your Hausa gateman refused to let us in. He said he must talk to his madam first. I was even afraid you wouldn't know who was looking for you; the way he was pronouncing our names, I was wondering if it was Ifeoma he was saying or Ifeyinwa.'

Mama Ifeoma and I laughed, not immune to Mama Bidemi's humour.

We talked for hours, exchanging stories and experiences, grasping desperately to draw the years apart together, like two ends of a loose knot, but intrinsically aware that we were different people, the very essence of our selves shaped by those years.

Mama Ifeoma was rounder, with a plumpness that came with the birth of children and the passing of time. Her hips were corpulent, defined in their fullness; her upper arms thick and fleshy. Like Mama would say, she had the shape of a real woman. Her once very fair skin was tanned, darkened, I could tell, not just by the fiery rays of the Lagos sun but by the hardship of city life. There were new lines, on her face and by the side of her mouth.

But Mama Bidemi was the same as she'd been all those years ago, the only indication of her ageing the full head of white hair that had once been a light sprinkle. Her ebony skin was unchanged, effulgent as ever in its darkness, and I imagined her the same in a hundred years, watching others wrinkle away around her, as she remained frozen in time like the vampires in the American movies shown on our new satellite television.

'You would not believe it! His people came all the way from their village to drive her out of her husband's home, and his body was not even cold in the ground yet. God will punish them! All of them!' Mama Bidemi said hours later, her anger and frustration apparent. Mama Ifeoma and I shook our heads with sympathy.

Mama Bidemi's youngest daughter, Bidemi, had lost her husband and life had been difficult for her ever since. 'Such shameless people, coming to clear everything Bidemi and Kunle built together. They said it's their brother's property, so she owns nothing. Can you imagine the rubbish? What kind of way of thinking is that? What do they want her to use to feed her children? *Ehn*? I'm retired; my husband is retired. Or should she go and beg her siblings, who have their own problems they are dealing with? She stopped working at the accounting firm because their children were still young and she wanted to focus on bringing them up. If she had not left her job, they are the same people that would have said she was a bad wife. How was she supposed to know that her husband would die in an accident just how many years later? My poor daughter.' She brought out a handkerchief to wipe the stray tears that had slipped out as she'd spoken. Helpless as to what to do, Mama Ifeoma and I murmured empty words of comfort, fully aware they did little to help.

'Maybe you should hire a lawyer. I'm sure a lawyer can help her,' I suggested hopefully.

Mama Bidemi cackled, acrid and hollow. 'In this country? My second son, Sunkanmi, is a lawyer; you've forgotten,' she said. I had forgotten this important fact.

'Her husband did not leave a will behind, and all their properties were in his name. According to Sunkanmi, our law does not say that the properties he owned must transfer to her. And if we go to court, we can be there for years. You know how these things are. I know a man that has spent over ten years dragging his father's lands with his brothers, and the case is still in court. We don't know what to do. If she remarried now, they will say she is the one that killed her husband with *juju*. She's staying with us now, with her children. We're just praying that her old company will take her back, even if it means her starting from a lower position, just so she can have money to eat and take care of those children.'

'*Nawa*. What kind of country is this?' Mama Ifeoma asked no one in particular. Mentally, I made a note to ask Gozie if he could do anything to help. He loved situations like this, opportunities to be benevolent, not out of goodwill but a desire to be seen as a sort of god, with the ability to do and undo at will, to transform lives with the stroke of a pen, and the money would mean absolutely nothing to him.

'How is your husband?' I asked Mama Ifeoma carefully later. She'd spoken about everything and everyone but him, skirting round any mention of him with the finesse Ego displayed when playing dancing chairs at her school's Christmas party.

'He's fine,' she said tightly, the small smile at the side of her mouth disappearing. And I wondered if a small part of her wished to be freed by an act of the universe from the vows that bound them together.

'Does he still work at a factory?' I asked, hoping to lead the conversation on.

'Yes, he does,' she replied, looking around the living room as though she was just seeing the opulence surrounding her for the first time. I thought about how it must all seem through her eyes – she with the husband who was a poor factory worker, her world unchanged after all the years of endurance and patience, and me, the one whose life had seemed hopeless, with the husband who could afford to live in such a house. And not for the first time, I pictured how life might have been had Nasir not found us. Perhaps Gozie would have been eventually forced to find work in a factory like Papa Ifeoma, and perhaps I would have been like Mama Ifeoma, stuck in the unending grind that was the poor Nigerian's life, with no clear hope of anything better.

Just before they left, we exchanged hugs; Mama Bidemi's arms enveloped me – tight and assuring, with a promise, but Mama Ifeoma's embrace was cautious, ensuring to keep enough distance between her ankara blouse and the top of the embroidered purple *jalabiya* I had on, as though afraid that with a hug, she would transfer some of her bad luck to me.

## 29.

## *This your daughter is like a man*

When Mama called in December of '95, I assumed it was to ask about Gozie – her favourite son-in-law, as she called him, even though he was her only one. 'Take good care of him o. There are many women waiting to take him from you o,' she always said.

Or that she had called to gossip about Anwuli and Kelechi's refusal to give her a grandchild after almost a decade of marriage. Or to complain about either of Ikechukwu or Ugochukwu's wives. The last time we'd spoken, she had been upset about the size of watermelons Ikechukwu's wife had brought her from the market. 'That girl does not know how to go to the market. The watermelons she bought look like large oranges. What nonsense. She should have just told me she didn't want to go; my legs are still working. Is it now a sin to send your daughter-in-law on an errand?'

Our telephone bills were high, and the NITEL man would always stroll in jauntily, a knowing smile on his lips, to deliver the slip of paper with exorbitant naira sums.

I didn't expect Mama to to sound suffocated that day, like someone had her throat in their hands or to scream at me in discordant Igbo, 'Uju! Obianuju! Your father . . . your father is dead.'

'What?'

'I said your father is dead!' she screamed and broke down into hysterical sobs, her voice hoarse with uncontrollable grief. Then the line was disconnected.

For what seemed like hours, I stared at the phone in silence. It was one of those old-fashioned phones, an antique that Gozie had purchased for a ridiculously high price because it made him appear sophisticated to our old-money guests.

Papa? Dead? What did Mama mean? Papa could not be dead. I'd spoken to him just the day before. We had talked about the military government, and the rumours that a special killer squad had been assembled to get rid of political dissidents; there were even whispers of people disappearing mysteriously. Now, people muttered curses behind raised palms, convinced that God would surely punish the administration for its evils. Papa had told me to make sure Gozie had no plans to write any articles this time around, and to hide any political writings I found lying around the house.

Then we had talked about the famous Ogoni Nine. The case reeked of corruption and the dark fumes of oil money; even the defendants' lawyers had resigned in protest, leaving them to fend off the storm alone and to their inevitable fates. When the verdict had come, no one had been surprised. Guilty. Their execution had been televised for all to see. Papa said he could not understand what kind of country would choose to waste such brilliant citizens for politics and money, and that we deserved all the international condemnation and sanctions we were receiving as a nation. 'Oil money has been our undoing. May God help us,' Papa had said.

'Take care of yourself, my daughter.' Those were his last words to me; it was how he'd always ended our calls. *Take care of yourself, my daughter.*

Suddenly, my legs could no longer bear the weight of my body and I collapsed onto Gozie's favourite settee.

Papa had been a good man, and when good people died, the world gathered to mourn them. Our house was full when I arrived, men and women everywhere, shaking their heads and wiping away sorrowful tears with the edges of their wrappers. The air was covered in a blanket of grief so heavy it weighed on us all.

At the centre was Mama, surrounded by women like guards, patting her shoulders and back and whispering futile words of comfort. Others sat on the floor at her feet, wailing at the top of their lungs and asking the heavens why they had taken Papa, crying more than the bereaved, Papa would have said. I spotted Chinelo's and Ada's mothers amongst them.

Mama looked like I'd never seen her. She was dressed in a blouse and wrapper made from a rough black material. Every few seconds, she ran her fingers hurriedly through her hair and scratched the scalp like a mad woman, clumps of hair falling from her crown. Had she always had those clothes? Or had her tailor hastily sewn them together? Or were they the same ones she had worn when *Nna'm Ukwu* had passed away?

When her father, *Nna'm Ukwu*, had died, that first harmattan season not long after I had turned five, Mama had wept for days – but even then, she had not looked like this. She raised her head in my direction, white streaks of dried tears like tribal marks on her face as I cut through the crowd of comforting hands to reach her.

'Obianuju,' she called in a frail voice when I finally stood in front of her. 'Obianuju, your father . . . your father has left me all alone. What am I going to do?' Her voice cracked under the weight of tears, coming in floods now, and I knelt to gather her in my arms as I struggled to shed the tears that would not come.

Weeks later, we were in Papa's village to bury him like a proper Igbo man, the true son of the soil he was; only an *efulefu* would be buried in foreign soil.

Papa's house in the village was full before we even arrived. My brothers had made sure to announce the burial ceremony far and wide; posters were put up, flyers printed, ankara materials with Papa's picture stamped on them were distributed to be made into clothes to be worn for the burial, family members we hadn't heard from or seen in years were called and letters mailed to them; Ikechukwu even purchased a full-page announcement in a popular newspaper daily. Everyone had obeyed the clarion call to come home to give Mazi Nwaike a befitting burial.

Gozie walked beside me as we entered Papa's compound, clutching my hand tightly in his. He hadn't left my side since I'd called his office to instruct his secretary, a skinny woman with a honeyed voice and a penchant for tight clothes and the grating words '*Oga* is not on seat', to inform him of Papa's demise. '*Oga*

286

is not on seat but I will let him know when he gets back,' she'd responded in that voice of hers, as if I'd told her the dry cleaner had just delivered Gozie's clothes. She was the type Adaugo would call a Delilah and warn me to be careful of, the type most likely to snatch a man from his family.

Hours later, the tyres of Gozie's jeep had skidded into Papa's compound. Then the performance had begun. He'd picked Mama off the floor and comforted her like a child till she'd stopped weeping. When Kelechi, Ugochukwu and Ikechukwu arrived, he offered to pay for parts of the burial. But they'd refused his help; they were men after all and their pride would not allow it. 'We can handle it,' Ikechukwu had said, his face a tight mask of disdain.

Anwuli ran out the front door of Papa's house, her gap teeth exposed in a wide smile, to welcome us before we could get to the door, and I wriggled out from under Gozie's arm. As our bodies drew together, her stomach, unmistakably flat, met with mine and I clasped my arms tighter around her slim physique as my heart clogged with pity for her.

The *ili ozu* was held a few days later, just as the sun was rising across the horizon, the gentleness of its blooming coral rays casting a soothing light on our sorrowful gathering. Before the ceremony, I went to the room where Papa had been laid. He looked the same but for the slight greyness that had started to appear on his skin – an indication of the chemicals he'd been embalmed with – and the cotton wool stuffed in his nose. I stared at the still form, the head rested on the silk and cotton-stuffed pillow, the body dressed in Papa's finest Sunday clothes: his favourite *isiagu* and wrapper, and his black walking stick resting peacefully beside him like an extra limb.

It had been weeks since it happened, and I was yet to shed a single tear. 'This your daughter is like a man o. She hasn't even cried once!' I'd overheard one of our relatives tell Mama. Mama had turned to cast a weary glance my way, then looked away. She knew; she understood that the tears were gathered in my chest, frozen into a solid mass that refused to be dissolved. At times, they wafted up and gripped my throat till I felt like I would choke and join Papa where he was.

With my eyes, I willed Papa to sit up, to laugh that gruff laugh of his and call me his Uju, to say it was all a lie, that the past few weeks had been nothing but a spectre of a nightmare. But he lay there, still, his soul long gone. Defeated, I left to join the gathering outside.

Kelechi, Ugochukwu, Ikechukwu and our cousin Ikemba carried the casket by its palls, their bodies swaying slightly from the weight of the gleaming bronze chest and the body it contained as they led the procession to the burial site. The professional mourners wept loudly and shouted Papa's lineage for all to hear. I looked around at the people with us, dressed in different shades of black, and I knew they could never understand what it felt like to lose Papa, our pillar. We were surrounded but alone with our grief.

Papa had been a Christian, so instead of kola nut and libation to the ancestral spirits to escort him to the other side, the local parish priest said a prayer from the Pocket Ritual asking God to accept Papa's soul. But I did not want God to accept Papa's soul – I wanted him to return it to us.

The casket was lowered into the freshly dug earth after the prayers, the wailing around the grave rising to a crescendo as the casket slowly

disappeared into the ground. Mama screamed and had to be dragged
away from the edge so she would not jump in. I turned to look at
who had pulled Mama back; it was Ikechukwu, part of his face
hidden under a pair of dark sunglasses. He did not cry like the
others, even though I could tell he wanted to, neither did Kelechi
nor Ugochukwu. They were men, and real men did not cry, no
matter the circumstance. It was feminine to show any form of weakness, to feel. And for a while, I was one of them. A man. Until the
first shovel of red earth landed on the casket, and it hit me like a
blow. And I crumpled to the ground wailing and screeching like a
child, but Papa did not come to comfort me like he'd always done;
Adaugo's and Chinelo's hands lifted me from the dust as I continued
to scream for him. But he remained buried underneath the rising
heaps of red dirt.

Hours later, we congregated once more, this time to conclude the
planning of Papa's *akwamozu* – the burial rites and celebration of
his life; the only way he could transition smoothly to join his kinfolk
on the other side. It was compulsory for a man's sons to give him a
proper burial or they, too, would not be accorded the same honour
upon their death. There was a popular story of a young man who
had been forced to perform the funeral rites for his great grandfather
and grandfather when his father had died because his father and
grandfather had failed to do so, and tradition had to be fulfilled;
they had to be ushered into the spirit world before his father could
receive his own befitting burial. According to the story, by the time
he had finally done what was required, he'd had no money left to

289

bury his father and had left the responsibility for his own son to bear upon his death.

The family compound reeked of animal excreta from the cows and goats tied to wooden pegs, and the stores were overflowing with tubers of yam and cocoyam, bottles of wine and hot gin, and crates of alcohol stacked on top of each other till they touched the ceiling; the *akwamozu* would take place over several days, and sufficient food was needed to feed the mouths of the several family members, friends and well-wishers that were expected.

The *nche abali* was the first of the festivities, held throughout the night for the spirits to escort Papa to the other side. On the designated evening, the *umuada* danced into the compound, singing at the top of their voices. They wore the materials with Papa's face we'd distributed but they looked starkly different from the yards of simple fabric they'd been given, transformed into an array of eclectic styles and matching head ties.

Cows and goats had been slaughtered and their forelimbs sent to Papa's maternal home as per custom, and the remains had been cut and cooked in an assortment of forms – boiled, roasted, fried. Plates moved about in trays – pounded yam, *fufu*, *eba*, accompanied by bowls of soups thick with garnishings of vegetables, dry fish and stock fish.

The first group of dancers stomped their feet in the sand, waved white handkerchiefs and shook their waists vigorously until the beads at their waists jumped in rhythm to the music and a cloud of dust rose from beneath their feet, nearly obscuring them from our view. Other groups carried out elaborate acrobatic moves: jumping over one another, spinning in the air and landing on their forearms like wild creatures. With each performance, I worried for my brothers. Did they have the money for such a lavish display?

At midnight, gunshots were fired to inform Papa's spirit that tradition had been fulfilled.

# 30.

## *Please say something. Anything*

It was the night before we were to leave the village. In the afternoon, we'd organised a thanksgiving service at the local parish for a successful burial, and Father Amanze had sprinkled Holy Water as blessings and protection.

Mama sat as still as death as Aunty Achebe put the local razor close to her scalp and slowly set about scraping off every strand of her hair. On the floor beside them was a heap of hair that had been sheared off. Aunty Achebe was one of the *umuada* and a widow herself; she, too, had had her hair shaved when her husband Anozie had passed away.

I watched the strands settle on Mama's face, covering most of the skin there, and on top of her rough black blouse, leaving her scalp frosty and exposed. That Mama had agreed to have her hair shaved off was still a shock to me; Mama's hair had always been her pride, the one body part she'd always flaunted without caution or care.

I stood up, unable to watch any more, and wandered through the side door into the frigid harmattan air. The only signs of the erstwhile merriment were discarded pure-water sachets and sweet wrappers scattered about like residue of multicoloured confetti. It was the first time in days I'd had any time alone, and I cherished the absence of the constant screaming and wailing, of sympathetic pats on the back and feeble reminders that Papa had gone to a better place.

The letter hidden underneath the wrapper tied at my waist had come by Express Mail. Mama Sikira had pulled me aside to hand it over when she'd come over to pay her condolences weeks after Papa's passing. 'It came yesterday,' she whispered, looking over her shoulder to check for Mama.

'Thank you, ma,' I said, tucking it in the bra of the drab black gown that flowed well past my ankles and dragged on the titles.

I'd left it in my handbag, weighed down by all that was happening, mentally unprepared for whatever would have made Akin send a letter by Express Mail. But I was ready now, to feel something other than grief.

*My dearest Obianuju,*

*I ran into your old friend Sally in New York. She hadn't seen you in years but somehow found out that you lost your dad. And I knew I had to write you right away. You always talked about him, your unyielding love and admiration for the man who'd let you be you.*

*I still remember that day at the park. Remember? You'd stretched your hair again, and it blew behind you like a scarf as we tried to settle for our picnic. You said only white people and foreigners had picnics but I'd insisted because what better way to relax than outdoors with a good book? I even managed to get you to take bites from the sandwiches we bought at Kingsway. 'Who eats bread in the afternoon?' you complained.*

*Your eyes shone as you spoke about him – your hero. He'd insisted you go to university, even when your mother had argued it was a waste, bought you your first book, listened to you talk about your ambitions. He'd said you could have it all. I was a little jealous of him, you know, this man that made you glow like that and I wished for a day that you would speak of me like that, with that look in your eyes.*

*I'm so sorry Obianuju, so so sorry. My first thought was to take the next flight to come be with you but I realised just as I arrived at the booking office that it would only make things worse for you. Then of course, there are my commitments here. I'm a professor now. A professor. I still can't believe it.*

*You told me I would do it, all those years ago in Unilag, told me you believed in me. On my robing day, all I wanted was for you to be there to see me and be proud of me. My mum asked after you, 'That girl that was always in your office.' I had no way of telling her that that girl wouldn't speak to me anymore. I wish I could fix this. Tell me, how can I fix it? I'll do anything to make it better.*

*I miss you terribly Obianuju. I know it's not right for me to say these things but I've stopped caring about what's right or wrong. We've never done anything wrong; why do I have to let go of you? Why can't I be your friend at the very least? The one who just listens your problems and your joys, who reminds you to stop stretching your hair and to always wear yellow because it looks good on you. Your sounding board, remember? Why can't I*

*have that feeling of excitement again when I pass my mailbox,*
*checking, waiting to hear from you? Smallie please say some-*
*thing. Anything.*

   *Love Always,*

   *Akin.*

'Obianuju, are you okay?' Ugochukwu asked behind me and I hurriedly tucked the letter in my wrapper waistline and wiped my face with my palms.

Ugochukwu settled on the floor beside me and stretched out his long legs with a tired sigh. 'You don't have to pretend with me, Obianuju. Cry as much you want,' he said, and put an arm across my shoulder and pulled me closer. 'I know you miss Papa; I miss him too.'

The phone rang again, several weeks later, jangling loudly in its cradle. Every time I heard the sound, I jumped with excitement, thinking it was Papa. Then I would remember: Papa was gone. I still had trouble sleeping at night thinking that maybe, if I'd been there when the heart attack happened, he wouldn't have died.

Mama was on the other end of the line. Her voice had gotten stronger, regaining some of the timbre it had lost in the days after Papa passed. 'Obianuju. How are you? How are your husband and children?' Mama called my full name and I knew she wanted to talk about something important.

'We're all fine, Mama. How are you?' I was genuinely concerned. Even during the worst of times, I had never imagined Mama without

Papa or Papa without Mama; they were fused together in my mind, one inseparable unit.

'I'm fine o. Thank God. Your brother Ikechukwu came to visit with his wife and children today. That his son is a frog. You should have seen how he was jumping up and down the house; he tried to climb to the top of my wardrobe.' She giggled, light and airy, it was good to hear her laugh again.

'I had to remind Ikechukwu that he was just like that as a boy or he would have given that boy a good beating yesterday.' She cackled this time, stronger with bass.

I smiled. 'Mama, how are you? Are you really okay? Are you eating well? Should I bring some food from our store for you?'

Mama sighed, and when she spoke again, her tone lost the feigned laxity she'd started the call with. She sounded bone weary. 'Obianuju, I'm not fine, but I'm trying to be fine. That is one of the reasons I called you today. Your brothers say that there's no money. They spent most of their money on your father's burial and are still trying to recover from it. Uju, *biko* since your father has decided to leave me all alone to fend for myself, don't let your mother die of hunger. Your brother Kelechi's business has been affected by this fuel price increase, Ikechukwu is not earning much as a civil servant and Ugochukwu said his company has been owing salaries for months. Help us out with some money or talk to your husband, if he can help us out with something.'

'Something.' It was the word we used when we asked for favours, to evade mentioning specifics, to leave the decision to the giver so we did not ask for less than they'd intended to give.

I wished Mama had just called Gozie directly – that way he would

TOMORROW I BECOME A WOMAN

have been forced to help. How was anyone supposed to believe that the wife of an affluent man of Gozie's stature didn't even have a bank account to her name? They saw the clothes, the jewellery, the cars, the frequent trips out of the country, the pictures in the expensive winter jackets surrounded by the white man's snow.

Gozie had become a god unto himself, his money the double-edged weapon via which he exercised his power. He had been unhappy the day I'd told him I needed something to do. 'Uju, what type of nonsense are you saying this afternoon?' he'd replied, looking up from the leather-bound notebook.

'I said that I need something to do. Even if it's a business. I don't have any money of my own. I can't even buy a sanitary pad or fuel for my car without asking you.'

He eyed me, like one would at an ungracious child. 'What do you need money for? Do I not provide enough for you and the children?' He'd put out his palm and counted on each finger. 'You eat good food in this house, you wear clothes from the best designers, you can – if you want to – travel to countries that your father could not afford to even visit.' I'd flinched as he mentioned Papa. 'What do you need money for? You just want to do whatever you want and be misbehaving up and down Lagos, right? Well, I will not allow it, not when I'm alive. God forbid. If that is what you came to discuss with me this early Saturday morning, you can leave my study. As you can see, I am very busy doing actual work that will make sure you can have food to put in that ungrateful mouth of yours.' Then he'd hissed slowly – my brothers would have said 'like a woman', and it was never a good thing when a fellow man said you did something 'like a woman'.

I stared at the back of his head and contemplated breaking a vase on it, not one of the cheap ones, but the expensive ones he kept in a special showcase in the living room to impress his visitors. How dare he mention Papa? Instead, I turned to leave the study.

'Close the door behind you,' he barked to my back.

'Obianuju, you're not saying anything. Can you help us or talk to your husband to help us?' Mama said in my ear, her voice high with anxiety. I could tell she was on the verge of tears.

'Don't worry, Mama, we will help. I'll talk to Gozie when he comes back. Everything will be fine. Don't cry. *Biko*,' I reassured her.

'*Daalu nwa mu nwanyi*. God will bless you.' She hung up.

## 31.

### *Useless or not, a husband is a husband*

The women's meeting started out normally in August '96, the calm before the chaos. Sister Bose led the opening prayer. She took her time, touching on every prayer point that could possibly concern the women present: desire for children, misbehaving husbands, spirits of foreign women and mistresses, struggling businesses, career progression, harassment at the office. The bright-red pucker that was her lips moved with astonishing speed as she hopped from prayer point to prayer point amidst loud choruses of 'Amen'.

Sister Ezichi made announcements next. She went over the general ones first – the meetings and upcoming events being organised by the fellowship. Then she jumped into the crux of the matter: membership dues. Women snickered behind their hands like little children, others averted their eyes to avoid contact with Sister Ezichi's and some suddenly had something they had to find urgently at the bottom of their handbags. It was the timeless game of cat and mouse we played. Sister Ezichi, the accountant and unofficial 'tax collector' of the fellowship, would ask for dues, and we would pretend not to hear her until it was time to collect our wrappers or to participate in group activities and we had no choice but to pay up. She was known to waylay sisters after church – at the snack stand as they tried to buy *puff-puff* and meat pies – and demand that they pay the dues they were owing for the month.

'As mothers within the church, we have many activities we need to carry out. There are children within this church that need to go to school – we need to pay their school fees, we have to buy books for them – and most importantly, our annual bazaar and party will be coming up in a few months. All these things can only be done with money!' she continued, and seeing that many were still not taking her seriously, she dropped a final warning. 'I also hope that we're aware that we only attend the burials of our members that pay their dues.'

'A dead man does not care who comes for his funeral!' a disembodied voice shouted from the back. The room broke into peals of laughter as Sister Ezichi huffed in annoyance and handed the microphone to Sister Ndidi, who took her time admonishing the innominate degenerate who would 'do such a thing in the house of the Lord'.

Sister Aderonke, the self-appointed fellowship choir mistress, went up next to teach the women the new song she was proposing as our fellowship anthem: *Lord make me a virtuous woman this is my earnest plea, That I be the crown of my husband and Christ be the head of the home.* She went through the song, emphasising each word with great effort so no one would have an excuse for not knowing the lyrics at the next meeting.

Finally, it was Sister Bolatito's turn to share the sermon, and it was at that moment that the chaos began. There had been rumblings for weeks, like a volcano waiting to erupt, rumours circulating that Sister Bolatito was in the process of divorcing her husband and had moved out of her marital home into a new home (some said with a new man). Thus, the campaign had begun to have Sister Bolatito removed from the leadership council of the fellowship. Of course, there were many amongst the disgruntled who saw this as ample opportunity to exact revenge for personal issues in the past; Sister Bolatito had always been forthright, unafraid to speak her mind, and had stepped on several toes in the process. She'd studied abroad; it was the American way of doing things.

The noise started when Sister Bolatito took the microphone from Sister Ndidi, a collective whispering so loud it was like a buzzing beehive. Sister Bolatito pretended not to notice. Instead, she shifted the open Bible in her palm and began her sermon. 'Today, we will be talking about leadership within the church, and how we as women can lead by example,' she said in that distinct accent of hers that was somewhere between Nigerian and American, the foreignness never truly leaving her despite the years that had passed since she'd returned to the country after studying abroad. She flipped the tissue-like pages of her Bible. 'Please open to the book of . . .'

Sister Enitan, a short woman with shrewd eyes, stood up to properly interrupt Sister Bolatito's teaching. At first, it seemed Sister Bolatito would ignore her, but Sister Enitan folded her arms across her chest and continued to stand, until eventually Sister Bolatito turned to her with bored eyes and asked in a droll voice, 'Yes, Sister Enitan? Is there something you'd like to share with us?'

Sister Enitan pulled herself to her full height, which wasn't much, and nodded emphatically. 'I believe I speak the mind of many amongst us when I say we cannot accept leadership lessons from someone who cannot even keep her marital home. It is very hypocritical to stand there and preach at us when your home is in a shambles,' she said, unable to keep the venom in her heart from her tone. This was personal. The buzzing started again, this time in assent with the speaker. 'Even in the Bible, God told Hezekiah to go and put his house in order.'

'Amen!' someone from the group behind her shouted.

Sister Enitan put her hands on her waist and bent forward. 'Sister Bolatito, is your house in order?'

Shouts of '*Oho!*' followed.

'I do not see how that has anything to do with today's sermon. If you will just wait till the end of service, we can talk about it . . .'

I was surprised Sister Ndidi still hadn't said anything. She looked shocked, transfixed in her seat, but whether it was about Sister Bolatito's divorce or Sister Enitan's behaviour, I could not tell.

'Wait, *gini?*' Sister Udo, another member of the disgruntled group, shouted jumping to her feet, her rather generous bosom jumping up with her, almost connecting with her chin.

'We are not waiting for anything! We must address it now!' she declared, pointing to the ground and stomping her foot.

Before Sister Bolatito or Sister Ndidi could respond, Sister Abike, one of the older women in our midst, stood up and adjusted the wrapper at her waist. Her children were grown up and she owned one of the biggest shops in Lagos Island market. She pointed at the troublemakers. 'Enitan, Udo. Sit down!' Things had gotten ugly, 'Sister' was only dropped in two circumstances: outside the church and when you believed the other person had behaved in such a way that you could no longer be associated with them in the body of Christ.

Sister Enitan and Sister Udo were flummoxed. 'Sit down! What sort of nonsense is this? How can you interrupt our meeting like this? Especially you Enitan, a Yoruba girl. I am disappointed. *Se o leko ni*? You people don't have home training?' Sister Abike continued. Several women shouted in support of Sister Abike.

Sister Udo did not care. 'Sister Abike, we will not sit down. Home training or not, this woman has no right to be a leader in this fellowship! She is not living by example.'

'Yes!' the women behind her chorused.

'You're one to talk,' a voice murmured, so low in our midst that it was almost sibylline that it would be the one to be heard amid the pandemonium.

The room went quiet as a mortuary as Sister Udo's eyes turned to slits. 'What did you say, Sister Uchechi?'

Sister Uchechi got to her feet slowly, like a queen aware her subjects were watching her every move. She arranged her ruffled white blouse with manicured fingers and dusted her jean skirt before speaking. 'I said, "You're one to talk," Sister Udo. You're here talking like your marriage is perfect, like we all don't know your husband spends his evenings at the university's parking lot pursuing young female students. Wasn't it you I saw on the street the other day fighting a small girl that you claimed was your husband's mistress? Were you setting a godly example when you and your friends stripped her naked on the street?'

Oohs and ahhs echoed throughout the room; even Sister Abike's mouth hung open. Sister Udo's fair skin flushed in embarrassment.

Sister Uchechi turned slightly to address Sister Enitan, and Sister Enitan moved back a step, tottering dangerously on the back of her heels. 'Don't even let me start with you, Sister Enitan!'

Sister Udo recovered from her sudden muteness. 'Witch! You're a liar!'

'And you're a fool!' Sister Uchechi responded.

*Kpa!* Like two palms meeting in a clap. That was the sound of the blistering slap Sister Udo replied with. I did not know if it was Sister Abike that returned the slap or if it was Sister Enitan that grabbed at Sister Uchechi's hair. But all of a sudden, the gathering erupted into a fiery explosion of flying wigs and torn blouses. It was the end time the biblical ancients had foretold: sister against sister, up in arms seeking to deliberately harm the other.

Sister Ndidi tried to intervene. 'Sisters! Sisters! Please let's behave as is befitting of Christian women. If you're acting like this, what should your children do?' But it was too late. Nobody was listening.

Ada's place was the meeting point where we gathered to dissect the day's gossip. And after the catastrophe that was that women's meeting, Chinelo, Ada and I were more than eager to assemble.

We drove into Ada's compound looking like casualties of the war we had escaped; my blue ankara blouse was ripped down the middle, my bra peeking out of the ruin, Chinelo's wig teetered at the edge of her head, waiting for the brush of the slightest breeze for it to fall off, and Ada's newly relaxed hair (she'd long abandoned the jheri curls, referring to them as 'old school') looked as though she had just strolled through a typhoon.

Inside the house, I stared at the familiar surroundings. Ada turned on the television and adjusted its antennas until, finally, a clear picture filled the screen. Hanging on the wall in the corner was a long calendar with '1996' printed in bold black ink at the top. Dates were circled in red, with scribblings at the side: the children's birthdays and school activities, I assumed.

'Receive your miracle today!' the pastor on the air screamed.

'Amen!' Ada shouted in response, still standing in front of the television. 'Sorry, this is my new favourite programme and I don't want to miss it.' She was smiling sheepishly.

The pastor stretched out his right arm – an expensive gold wristwatch glittered across the screen – blew air into the microphone, and people began to collapse like the Lego towers Ego used to put together as a child. 'He's a very powerful man of God. Sister Tinuke – remember her? The one in the choir that just gave birth? Well, she was telling me the other day that she got pregnant with her son after having five girls, after she watched his miracle service once. Just once! Can you imagine? His speciality is the fruit of the womb. You people should watch it too. He's very powerful, his church is always full, and many people are always sharing their testimonies. If not that his church is in Edo state, I would have started going there every Sunday,' Ada said.

'Adaugo, come and sit down; let's talk. We can discuss that one later,' Chinelo replied impatiently. I stared at her, surprised. Ada turned down the volume of the television, high enough that she could turn to it every couple of minutes to shout 'Amen', but low enough that we could still hear each other.

'Wonders shall never end. What was the meaning of what happened today?' Ada asked rhetorically through smeared lipstick, then clapped her hands, leaned back in an armchair and picked up a magazine to fan herself.

'My sister, are you asking me? I was just trying to separate them and see the blow they gave me. I just hope I don't go blind,' Chinelo said, pointing to the purpling bruise around her right eye. 'After that, I carried my bag *jeje* and went to my car. No be me kill Jesus.'

Adaugo clapped her hands slowly. 'Do you people think what Sister Enitan and Sister Udo did was right? Because, I mean, even if they didn't agree with Sister Bolatito or didn't think she should have taught the message, why not wait till after the meeting to raise your concerns, or better still go to Sister Ndidi afterwards to complain? Why create that kind of drama?'

I hissed, making a *mtchew* sound where my tongue met the roof of my mouth. 'Are you minding that Sister Enitan? No manners whatsoever, always acting like a market woman. If you ask her now, she will tell you she went to school. Was she not the one that came to meet me the other day during service to tell me to go home and change my trousers to a skirt because, according to her, they were ungodly, too tight and were tempting the brothers in the church?'

'*Chineke!*' Chinelo exclaimed.

'When did this happen? I would have given her a piece of my mind,' Adaugo said.

'I hear she wasn't even the one that asked for the divorce o,' Chinelo added.

'Chinelo, you know something and you did not tell us?' I asked in an accusatory tone. There was an unwritten code between us that any gossip obtained intentionally or accidentally must be passed unto the others.

'Two sisters behind me today were talking about it, even before the drama started, and they had the full gist. I was just doing *amebo* and listening to everything they were saying.'

'So, what did they say?' Ada asked, leaning forward eagerly.

'Well, according to one of them, Sister Bolatito's husband found one small girl he wanted to take as a second wife, and when Sister Bolatito refused, he asked for a divorce. Can you imagine?'

'*Ewo*,' Ada and I chorused.

'That is not all o. According to them, he even wanted Sister Bolatito to give him the money to marry the wife. Can you believe that? Just because her family has the money. She pays the children's school fees, buys their clothes and the food in the house. Her family even set up his business for him.'

'What sort of useless man is that? So what was he doing?' I asked.

'*Amam*. I don't know, *nne*,' Chinelo said raising open palms to the ceiling.

'Useless or not, a husband is a husband. Having a man around is good, even if it is just to look responsible,' Ada said.

'But what if the "useless" man decides to leave? Should she hold his legs?' I countered.

'Well, you have a point,' Ada conceded.

# 32.

## *Love is for those that have finished eating*

Chinelo rubbed her belly when we had discussed the meeting enough, and Adaugo was quick to spot it. 'Chinelo, is there something you're not telling us?' she asked, a curious tilt in her smile.

Chinelo glowed with the answer, as she carefully draped her arms around her belly, creating a barely visible bulge like a full belly after lunch. 'Yes. The doctor told me last week: I'm nine weeks pregnant,' she announced.

Gut-wrenching fear descended around my heart like a wraith hand, wielding it in an unyielding grip so tight I could not bring my mouth to utter the word expected of me: congratulations.

'You . . . you're pregnant?' I asked dumbly, just to be sure I'd heard well.

Her smile widened. 'Yes, I am,' she replied, rubbing her belly joyfully once more.

Ada jumped up from her seat and rushed over to pull Chinelo into a long embrace. 'Congratulations! *Nne*, I'm so happy for you!' And I could tell she truly meant it.

Ada returned to her seat, still smiling. 'This is good news o. Right, Uju?'

When I did not say anything, she finally noticed the dread that had crawled its way from my heart to my face. She frowned. 'Uju, what is the matter? Why aren't you smiling? Are you not happy?'

I fixed my face into a smile. 'Yes. You're right, Ada. Congrats, *nne*.'

Adaugo left us not long afterwards to change her clothes and put food on the stove.

I turned to Chinelo immediately when she was out of sight. 'Are you not sick? Did the doctor not say you have . . . what did you call that thing? Hypertensive something? And that you should not have any more children? *Ehn*?'

'I've stopped taking my medicine. I feel better. I'm healed. I have faith. Do you know how long I've been praying for this? If God can give me this baby, that means he plans to make me well enough to take care of it.' She refused to look me in the eye, choosing instead to stare at her belly, the source of her hope. I was fear. I was reality. And she would not face that.

'What did the doctor say? Did he not run other tests? That's standard antenatal care.'

She frowned. 'He advised that I get an abortion, that the pregnancy is too high-risk – apparently the law allows for abortions in such a case.'

'And?'

'I refused, of course! What do you expect, Obianuju? Do you know how long I've waited and prayed for this? You think I would throw away such a gift from God?'

'Chinelo, please!' I tried to calm myself down. 'Okay, okay. Have you told Christopher?' I asked.

'Not yet. I want to wait a while. I want to surprise him. He'll want me to remove it; he's too fearful.'

'What if you die giving birth to that child? Who will raise it? You think he won't be pressured to marry someone else?'

Ada walked in then, carrying a small clear bag filled with ice in one hand and a plate of green apple slices in the other. She'd wiped the tarnished makeup off her face, changed her torn clothes and swept her hair up in sleek bun.

She handed the bag of ice to Chinelo. '*Nne*, put that on your eye so it won't swell up too much,' then she set the plate of apple down on the centre table. 'The rice is on the stove. Please help me manage this one for now. Hope you people will eat jollof rice because that's what I'm making, with fried plantain and chicken,' she said before settling back into her armchair. 'Uju, are you sure you don't want to change your blouse before you go? I can borrow you one of mine. It's not good for a woman of your stature to be going about like that,' she added lightly, smiling.

'I still can't believe what happened today in church. The next meeting will be hot o. I won't be surprised if Sister Ndidi calls for an emergency meeting after Sunday service. What happened was disgraceful,' Adaugo said.

My mouth tasted like bile as I tried to feign interest in the conversation. 'I wonder what Sister Bolatito's husband's family have to say about this.'

'Apparently his family were the ones that brought the second wife,' Chinelo said.

'It's like those two sisters know everything happening in that

310

church. *Biko*, what are their names? So that I can sit in front of them at the next meeting,' Ada said, and we all laughed.

The sound echoed hollow in my chest.

Outside, the gate creaked open and a car zoomed into the compound, just as we'd switched the discussion to families.

'These men,' Adaugo said. 'The way they act, you would think we don't have families too. Their brothers come first, their mothers' word is law, what their dead uncle or grandmother said is more important than any nonsense you say now. Everything their family says is right, but if I listen to advice from outsiders, I'm trying to destroy my marriage.'

Chinelo nodded quickly in agreement. 'You're so right, my sister.'

'Of course I'm right! The things these my two eyes have seen since I married Uzondu *ehn*,' Ada responded, pointing at both her eyes dramatically. 'Every time he and his brothers quarrel, next thing I hear from their mouths is that Uzondu's wife is putting poisonous thoughts in his mind; she wants him to abandon his real family and spend all the money on her and her children. It is always my fault. Sometimes I even beg him to settle with them, just so they can leave me alone. You won't believe that Uzondu has stopped me from managing one of his shops, all because one of his brothers said he heard from a reliable source that one rich man's wife in our market is building a house somewhere without her husband's knowledge. Can you imagine? Me, Ada? I had to ask, "Is it me Ada or another Ada?" Am I even the type of person to do such a thing without making noise? You will live with somebody for how many years and think the person would at least know you a little. Not much o, just a little. He has now handed over the business to his brother that did not even finish Form 4 and has never run a business in his life. Good luck to them. I'm here and I'm watching; let us see what will come of it.' She hissed bitterly.

'When we marry, everyone – our parents, uncles, aunties, siblings – tells us over and over again that we no longer belong to their family,' Adaugo continued. 'That we belong to our husband's family. We even change our last names and advertise in the newspapers, but to these men and their families, we'll always remain foreigners, intruders even, in their family affairs.'

'But Uzondu was not like that when you married him,' Chinelo said wistfully.

Ada cackled so loud I was sure her voice carried outside the compound. 'See Chinelo sounding like a lover girl. You think you're still in the university?'

'You can't really blame them. Our society puts so much pressure on the men to make money and provide for their families, so they forget everything else. Is that not why most of our men are marrying later than our women?' I said.

'It's true o,' Chinelo said, after giving it serious thought. 'Uju, see when you married; see when your eldest brother married.'

'You see what I'm saying? Sometimes life's stress and pressure from this our society can make someone forget about love. Love is for those that have finished eating,' I said.

Chinelo chortled until she began to cough, and Ada hurried to get her a glass of water from the kitchen.

'Uju, I understand what you are saying,' Ada said, relaxing in her seat when she returned, 'but there is life changing your behaviour and there is three-sixty transformation.'

Chinelo set the glass down to poke fun at Ada. 'You mean after all the "hard to get" that you did for Uzondu, he does not treat you like a queen?' she said.

'You're talking as if we were not there. Weren't you the one that consumed most of the *suya* and ice cream he bought that time? Is that "hard to get"?' Ada teased in return, but the smile disappeared from her face soon after. 'Uzondu that acted like he couldn't kill a fly. He used to say I was too serious. Now, I can't remember the last time I saw his yellow teeth. One day, I asked him why he had changed so much. You won't believe what this man said to me.'

'What?' Chinelo and I asked at the same time.

'"Does the hunter set food in the trap after catching the bush meat?"'

Shrieks of laughter followed naturally and we fell back in our seats as water ran out of our eyes.

Chinelo was the first to recover and she raised her hand slowly, like a pupil asking its teacher for an opportunity to speak. 'Wait, so you're telling us that all those gifts Uzondu bought – including the *suya*, ice-cream, *puff-puff* – everything was a trap to catch you, the bush meat, *ehn*?' she asked, before succumbing to another bout of laughter so contagious, we joined her.

'With his fair skin like overripe pawpaw,' I said.

'My children! They're back early today and the food isn't ready!' Ada shouted when she heard the car, jumping to her feet. She'd become a mother again. It was never far away, that cloak of motherhood, like a handkerchief hidden in a handbag, ready to be pulled out and worn whenever necessary, transforming her into a totally different person. When we went out to eat, she ordered extra packs of food for her children; when we went shopping, she remembered her first daughter needed a new pair of shoes. It wasn't just her, it was all of us.

Zina was the first to walk through the door, a heavy-looking school bag on her shoulders as she clutched her youngest sister's hand. Behind them, the five other girls followed, clutching colourful school bags, water bottles with drawings of Mickey Mouse and Donald Duck and food flasks.

They greeted us as they passed, sending tentative smiles our way and mumbling shy 'good afternoon's. The youngest let go of Zina's hand and ran over to her mother, the colourful glossy ribbons in her hair bobbing as she bounced up and down in excitement shouting, 'Mummy, Mummy!' Ada smiled contentedly as she bent to lift her up and fit her tiny legs around her waist. This had always been her dream: to be a mother and wife. All that was missing was the son to provide perfection.

She walked behind her children as they logged their schooling luggage upstairs, screaming about homework, dirty clothes, baths and house chores.

For several minutes, Ada floated about like a forest nymph – inside and outside, upstairs and downstairs – in a flurry of activities, staunchly refusing any help we offered. She could handle it all, she said. She was used to it.

When she finally let herself sit again, Chinelo and I were ready to leave. Just as we were getting up, Zina ran down the staircase with such speed, I suspected she had been eavesdropping. Black earphones hung from the slim Sony MD Walkman she held in her hands, and I smiled, imagining she'd probably been listening to 'Wannabe', the new song by the British girl band Spice Girls that my daughters had adopted as their anthem.

She returned the smile sheepishly, and it struck me just how much she resembled her mother at that age, despite her inheriting her father's bright complexion.

'Aunty Uju, please can I come with you? I want to see Ego, we—'

'Jesus Christ! What are you wearing?' Ada exclaimed, turning around in her seat to look at her eldest daughter properly. 'You want to go out of the house wearing that?'

Zina frowned and put her hands on her waist. 'What is wrong with it?' she challenged, staring down at her outfit – low-rise jeans and a bright-yellow crop top. My smile stretched wider; she had spunk, this one.

'"*What is wrong with it?*"' Ada mimicked. 'Are you blind or you cannot see that what you're wearing is indecent? Who would see you and think you're from a decent home? *Ehn?* Before I blink, better run upstairs now and go and change. And make sure you carry your books with you to study!'

Zina stalked up the stairs muttering under her breath.

'Ada, loosen up; you sound just like your mother. She's only coming to my house,' I said once Zina was out of listening range.

'Uju, please, she should go and change. If her father should see her, he would say I'm letting her dress anyhow. I'm always to blame whenever these children do anything wrong. Their mother this, their mother that. I know you raise your children like they live abroad and Gozie doesn't care because he's always busy, but let us be honest, this is Africa.' Mama had said same to me when I'd complained about what others said to my children, sending them home to me with questions – like the Home Economics teacher who'd asked Ego if she planned to feed her husband with books when she'd mentioned that I hadn't started teaching her how to cook. I was raising my children for the world I wanted, and not the one that we lived in, Mama had said. I'd driven to Nwakaego's school the next day and given the teacher a piece of my mind. Now, she and the other teachers greeted me with cautious respect.

'Nobody would see her walking on the street like that and think she is a decent girl. When she's ready to marry and they ask around about her, people will say she's promiscuous. I cannot let them spoil my daughter's name like that,' Adaugo continued.

'But she's still fifteen,' Chinelo countered.

'Her father wants all of them to marry early. As soon as she turns eighteen, he plans to marry her off.'

'In this day and age?' I asked, shocked.

'He must be in a hurry to collect bride price,' Chinelo joked.

Ada did not smile. 'My sister, even me I don't agree with it. I've talked and talked, but he has refused to listen. He said they can finish their studies in their husbands' houses. What can I do?' she asked. *You can fight*, I thought, *You can fight for your daughters*. But then again, who was I to speak of such things?

'If I fight, my marriage will scatter,' Ada said, as if in response to my thoughts. 'They are his children and he has the final say. You should see how he monitors everything they do. The other day he personally watched her as she ground pepper with the local grinding stone – he has refused to buy a blender o – for the soup he told her to make for only him, so he could test her cooking skills.'

'At least your husband cares about your children; Gozie acts like ours hardly exist. He just drops money and goes,' I said. I did not add that I feared my daughters would grow up feeling they were inadequate, that they would desperately seek the love their father had failed to give them.

'Oh, they all do that,' Ada said, waving her hand as if to say it were to be expected. 'They put money down, buy one or two things around the house and leave everything else to us, then they come home and wonder why we're always tired.'

'Christopher can be like that sometimes,' Chinelo said. 'Before we got a driver, I was the one dropping the children at school and picking them up every day. The day he went to pick them up, the teachers thought he was a kidnapper until the children themselves told them he was their father. I go for all their PTA meetings,' Chinelo said. I smiled at the mention of PTA meetings; it was like a secret cult all the mothers were a part of, joining hands together to harass the school management into doing what we wanted. The few men in our midst were praised and treated like rare, endangered species.

Zina came down at that moment, dressed in an oversized flowery gown her mother approved of and clutching a bag of books to her side. 'If you like, frown your face,' Ada said to her daughter. 'My grandmother used to say that the goat that frowns its face does not prevent it from being sold in the marketplace.'

In the car, Zina screamed along to 'Wannabe' on the radio in the passenger seat beside me. She'd taken off the gown in the car, assured of my loyalty to her freedom; Aunty Uju would never tell her mother.

## 33.

### *Earth to earth*

' . . . earth to earth, ashes to ashes, dust to dust.' The pastor read out loud from the Book of Common Prayers in his open palms into the cool early-morning dew of March '97. It would be hot soon, humid, with sweat trickling down our backs – it was that time of the year. Above us, a small bird flew by, making cheery chirping noises as it passed, contrasting with the gloom of our ceremony.

A piercing scream rang from the small crowd gathered at the graveside. It wasn't mine, this time. The scream came again, more insistent, and I watched helplessly from under the protection of the large sunglasses concealing the crimson redness of my eyes as Mama and Mama Ada struggled to pick up Chinelo's mother from the sandy grounds of the graveyard. 'Chinelo! Chinelo! My daughter! You cannot go like this; you cannot leave your mother here,' she cried in heart-rending Igbo, her knees on the ground, her body bent over in anguish. Had she known?

Mama and Mama Ada gave up trying to lift her from the floor;

instead, they joined her, falling to their knees and circling her in a protective embrace as her gut-wrenching cries were muffled.

I felt the tears coming again, and I did not try to stop them.

Another cry came, hoarse and dolorous. It still wasn't mine. I recognised it, even before I turned away from the image of Chinelo's mother to look.

Adaugo. We hadn't spoken since that day at the hospital, since that day when life had shattered the fragile nonsense that was our world into tiny splintering pieces, the shards piercing our hearts as they scattered.

'She said to call you,' Christopher had said into the line, with that unique blend of excitement and anxiety that overcomes a man when his wife is in labour, but Christopher's had something else – a hint of fear. 'She wants you and Adaugo to be there when the baby comes.'

I felt a rush of panic. Was everything okay? Did she feel like something would go wrong? I'd pestered Chinelo so much during her months of pregnancy that she'd threatened to stop picking up my phone calls and letting me through the front door of her home. 'Uju, you worry too much. I'm fine. Look at me; don't I look fine?' she'd always say, stretching her arms wide for me to evaluate for myself. And each time, no matter how hard I examined, I saw the same thing – a growing bump, and a glowing, rosy-cheeked Chinelo, who had never looked happier.

At the hospital, we waited and waited and waited. Soon, Christopher paced the floors of the waiting area like a lunatic, his shoes wearing out the smooth surface of the floor tiles. What was going on?

I knew things had gone south when the nurses and doctors started running in and out of the theatre she was in hurriedly, like firefighters frantically trying to quench a raging inferno. I felt the glass around us cracking then, craggy lines of doom appearing on its fragile surface. They made *kr kr* taunting sounds in my head, and I feared I was going mad.

Ada and I grabbed each other's hands and held on as we murmured desperate prayers for an intervention to bring Chinelo and her child out of the room alive. Somewhere at the back of my mind, I knew it was futile. The die had been cast, but still I hoped that someone somewhere would have mercy on us all, on the child and, most especially, its mother, who hadn't done any of it for herself.

A doctor came out from the theatre finally, surgical cap in hand. Sweat was dripping down the side of his face. His loafers were noiseless on the hospital floors as he walked towards us, but I could hear the hopelessness in every step he took.

'Mr. Christopher Makama?' the doctor asked.

'Yes?' Christopher responded.

'I'm sorry, we did everything we could but—'

My heart stopped. 'Nooooo! Nooooo!' I screamed before the doctor could finish what he was saying. There was no need; I already knew how it was going to end. I'd watched it on television many times, and I'd never once imagined that I would be on the receiving end of those words.

Chinelo, my Chinelo, was gone.

From a distant place, with a self that was not mine, I could hear the doctor continue speaking and I saw Christopher respond to him, as Adaugo collapsed on the floor in tears. She wailed, she rolled on the tiles, not minding the dirt that might have accumulated there. She shouted for Chinelo, then she shouted for God.

'I advised her against this,' the doctor said to Christopher, sounding defeated. 'With her heart problems, it was dangerous for her to be pregnant in the first place. Even normal women are at risk of death during childbirth, talk less of a woman with her condition.'

The doctor shook his head. He seemed upset, frustrated and sad at the same time, like he wanted to yell at Christopher, to ask him why he'd put his wife at risk, but realised there was no point to it. 'I'm really sorry. The baby is healthy and in good condition. Once she is ready, after all the necessary tests and clean-up, the nurse will inform you that can see her. We tried our best to save your wife. I'm really sorry for your loss.' He put a comforting hand on Christopher's shoulder then turned to walk away dejectedly.

'Heart problem?' Ada asked, surprised, through tears, looking between mine and Christopher's faces and the retreating doctor's back. 'What heart problem? I did not know about any heart problem. Since when? Uju, did you know about this?'

I didn't answer. What was I to say? That I'd known and not said anything because Chinelo had asked me not to? That I could not share a secret that wasn't mine in the first place? Or that I'd hoped and believed that Chinelo had been right all those times she'd said she was okay? That I'd looked at how happy she was and convinced myself I was being too cautious; paranoid, even?

'Uju, did you know about this?' Ada asked again, staring at me with a rage that dared me to lie.

'Ada, please can we talk about this later?' I pleaded, painful tears pouring down my face.

Ada wiped her face hastily with the back of her hands. 'No, we must talk about it now. Uju, did you know about Chinelo's illness and did not tell me?'

Looking down at my hands, I nodded, refusing to meet her accusatory glare.

Suddenly, Ada grabbed me by the top of my blouse and twisted it in a tight grip like a woman on the verge of lunacy. 'You knew Chinelo could die and you did not tell me?' she yelled in my face.

I shook my head side to side forcefully. 'No. No. Please it wasn't like that. She said I should not say anything. Please understand, please don't be angry with me,' I tried to explain, tears blinding me. 'She told me she was fine, that everything was okay again. I did not know she would die like this. I swear I didn't know. If I'd known, I would have said something.'

Christopher put his hand between us and tried to loosen her grip on my blouse, but it would not slacken, strengthened as it was by grief. 'Leave me alone! This is all your fault!' she yelled in his face. From the corner of my eyes, I saw two nurses rush over to try to separate us.

'Ada, I'm sorry. I'm really sorry. I didn't want her to die. I swear, I didn't want her to die, either.'

'Madam, you can see the baby now,' one of the nurses interjected in a shaky voice, apparently hoping that would separate us. We ignored her.

'You let her die,' Ada screeched in my face. Still gripping my blouse, she turned her head to Christopher. 'The both of you let her die and God will judge you for it.' She let go of me then, throwing me away like a rag doll against the wall, and stormed out of the hospital.

'You can see the baby now,' the nurse repeated nervously. She was young, inexperienced and uncomfortable with such situations, I could tell. Christopher glanced at me apologetically before following the nurse quietly, his head bobbing dejectedly as he went. I remained where I was, staring into the space Ada had just occupied. I wasn't ready to see the child. I wanted to see my friend.

I covered my face with shaking hands.

Uzondu pulled Ada into an embrace as she continued to sob uncontrollably, her frame vibrating with the sheer force of it. He whispered some words into her ears, and she quieted, just a little. I imagined it had something to do with the growing bump I could detect under the black boubou she wore. He had probably told her to think of the baby's health, what could be their last hope of having a male child. I was surprised he'd even let her come. I continued to stare at her, hoping she would look my way and she'd come to me, hold my hands and hug me, then tell me she'd forgiven me. And even if not that, that she would at least say she understood why.

When a third cry interrupted the pastor once again. I didn't have to turn to see who it was.

It was mine. 'Chinelo! *Chi mo*!'

# 34.

## *You cannot abandon the living because of the dead*

Gozie did not understand. He could not just understand why I would grieve one person's death so much. 'What was the meaning of that nonsense?' he yelled at me in the car, on our way home from Chinelo's funeral. We'd just driven past the Three Wise Men that welcomed visitors to Lagos. 'Are you the first person to lose a friend that you would go about acting like a mad woman? You're an embarrassment.'

The back seat of the car was deathly quiet as he spoke; the children were making careful efforts to not attract his attention; even Nwamaka, who had been crying for Aunty Chinelo, had stopped her sniffling.

I turned away from him to look out the window as our SUV moved through the street. We passed two women in colourful *aso oke*, chatting excitedly, probably on their way to a party. One of them reached out a hand to brush off a particle on the other's face and I felt my throat close up once more.

324

Life lost its colour, the world around me descending into lugubrious shades of grey. I couldn't comprehend how the world outside could move on – how the sky still shone blue, the birds still sang, breeze still blew, the stars danced out at night. What was the meaning of our very existence if the universe continued so smoothly when we were gone, as though we never existed?

The sadness would not leave; it remained like an ever-present companion, following me everywhere I went. At night, I was haunted by dreams of Chinelo's funeral. Other times, I was in the coffin with her, banging on the lid and pleading to get out, but no matter how hard I screamed, the voices of ceremonial prayers around me droned on, and when the dirt landed, it penetrated the enclosed space and filled it until I was completely covered, and tears, mixed with the sand, suffocated me.

And so I stopped. I stopped sleeping, I stopped going out, I stopped eating, I stopped bothering to dress in anything other than black. I just stayed home all day and cried. Maybe it was because I blamed myself for her death or perhaps it was because I'd lost my father and my best friend. A piece of me had accompanied them to the grave.

Gozie tried everything; he screamed, he cursed, he threatened, he even throttled. But I stayed the same, unchanged in the slightest. Eventually, he gave up and called the one person I'd never known to give up, the one he hoped would bring me back to my senses.

Mama appeared like an angel on an infernal assignment, still in the same black clothing I'd come to see as her second skin. Her hair was a mini Afro now, full, dark and lush. 'Obianuju. What is this I'm hearing about you?' she started as soon as she walked through

325

the door, her sandals making slip-slap noises on the marble floors. A small black handbag was clutched to her side.

'Good morning to you too, Mama,' was my sardonic response as I shut the door and followed her to the living room.

'Don't greet me,' she said, choosing a comfortable seat. She dropped her handbag on it, balanced her backside on its edge and leaned forward to clasp her hands together. 'The morning is not good. How can the morning be good when I'm hearing that my own daughter has gone mad? Please tell me.'

'I'm not mad, Mama, as you can see,' I said, relaxing in a settee on the opposite end of the room.

'If you're not mad, you're not far from it because only a mad person would do the things I've heard. And why are you still wearing black? Did your husband die without my knowledge?'

I turned my face away.

'Obianuju, look at me. What is going on? This is not the Obianuju I know. Is it because of your friend that died? But you were not like this even when your father passed away. Talk to your mother.'

'I don't know,' I said desolately, staring down at my hands, giving in to the maternal concern I heard in her tone. 'It's everything: Papa, Chinelo. Everything! I'm always sad, I can't eat, I can't sleep, I can't think. I think I'm depressed, maybe I should see a psychologist.'

Mama cackled so loud, I stared at her in bewilderment till she was done. 'Uju! You sound like these white people; it's like you really let this schooling enter your head. Do Africans get depressed? Don't let them and the devil deceive you! You want to pay good money to someone for them to sit in their air-conditioned office and listen to you talk about all your problems and personal business, then they'll speak big English and give you advice your mother can give you for free?' she said when she could finally contain her amusement.

'This is what I've been trying to tell you since you were a child. You're too soft, and as a woman, you can't be soft and expect to survive this life. If your husband dies now, what would you do? Jump out the window? This thing is up here,' she said, pointing at her head. 'If you can control this place, you'll be fine. They're gone, they're gone. There's nothing you can do about it. You think I'm not sad that Chinelo died? She was like a daughter to me, but if God has decided to take her, what can I do?'

I did not tell Mama that God hadn't taken Chinelo, she'd walked into her own death.

'It's okay to cry, but you've cried and now it's enough. You cannot abandon the living because of the dead. All these things cannot bring them back; nothing can bring them back. Put them behind you. Your husband is alive; your children are alive. Look at them and remember why you have to live. Force yourself to, even when you don't want to. *Inugo?*'

'Yes, Mama.'

'And please try to eat; you've become too thin. Your waist has almost disappeared and that space at the bottom of your neck can carry water. Have you not heard our people say "*e lewe ukwu egbue ewu*"?' I smiled for the first time in a long while: *A buxom waist that makes her husband kill a goat for her when he looks at it.* It sounded like something Mama would say.

We talked some more before she left, about Ugochukwu's wife, who was expecting another child, about Ikechukwu and his civil service job, about everything but Papa, Chinelo and Kelechi. We carefully circumvented those topics like expert navigators.

Before she left, Mama said to me, 'Obianuju, you and your brothers are all I have left. *Biko*, pity your mother. Take care of yourself.'

'Yes, Mama.'

Then Fela died not long after, and I watched Gozie silently grieve for a man he'd never met. For days, he would not eat, so much so that the steward stopped preparing meals for him. He just lay in the second living room upstairs, drinking bottles of beer as the distinctive melody of Fela's Afrobeat music played around him non-stop.

Chinelo, *enyi m*, it was never supposed to end like that. We were to grow old together, watch our daughters fall in love and plan their weddings together. We said we would switch for our daughters' *omugwo* – Chinelo would go for Ego's and I would go for Eriife's, that we would watch our grandchildren together and tell them the same stories our mothers had told us at moonlight as children: the cunning tortoise, the hawk and the hen. Your favourite had been the one of the girl who'd married the skull. You always said, even though it hadn't ended well, at least the girl had followed her heart.

## 35.

### *What is done in secret will be revealed in the marketplace*

The child was beautiful in May '98, just like its father; even the plump cheeks of smooth, moisturised, chocolate skin couldn't hide the resemblance. There was no mistaking whose son it was. It looked about six months old; its face was so strikingly epicene that, were it not for the fact that I knew it was a boy and had been painstakingly dressed as one to remove any doubt, I would have simply assumed the opposite. I smiled wryly, thinking such beauty would have been better fit on a female.

It was almost unimaginable that such a beautiful creature would be the source of so much pain. The child squealed with glee and threw his rattle up in the air, blissfully unaware of the tension around him. His mother – a dark-skinned slender woman not that many years older than Ego – caught the toy, handed it back to him and bent to murmur indecipherable words that made him squeal even louder. My eyes caught hers as she sat up straight again; adjusting the shoulders of her loose gown, they darted away immediately. Fear? Shame? Or wonders of wonders, was she possibly shy?

'My husband is not around,' I said to the mother and the man seated beside her on our living room sofa, most likely her father or uncle. 'He travels.'

Gozie had left that morning for his village. He had a meeting with his peers, he'd said. I hadn't questioned him further. I preferred him gone anyways.

He was a titled man now – an *Ozo* title holder – and by peers, I assumed he meant his fellow titleholders. He'd met the number-one silent criteria for all *Ozo* title aspirants: to be wealthy. As our people said, *ichi ozo bu maka ndi ogadagidi* – taking the *Ozo* title is an affair for the high and mighty.

Gozie's father had died a titleless man – a nobody, as Gozie constantly put it – and Gozie had been determined not to allow a similar fate to befall him. He contributed extensively to his community – built schools, offered scholarships to the university, set up businesses that employed the agile youth and tarred the roads the authorities had abandoned. Everywhere you went, the young and old spoke of the goodwill of Chigozie Azubuike.

When the time was right, he approached the head of the title-holders – the *isi nze* – with his intentions, and with a customary consultation fee of tubers of yam, kegs of palm wine, kola nuts and some bank notes. Apprised of his ambitions, the titleholders promised to deliberate and get word to him when they were done.

Not many days passed before a list of requirements was sent to him, detailing what needed to be done before he could be accepted into their fold. First, he had to rebury his parents, they told him – properly this time. The appropriate ceremonies hadn't been carried out. His parents' spirits hadn't been appeased; the villagers had not danced and eaten in celebration of the lives they had lived. Gozie's father had passed away when he was but a boy barely out of primary school. The burial had been swift and utilitarian, and his family had struggled to survive. His mother, the third and youngest wife, had been more worried about where her children's next meal and school fees would come from than the interment of an old man to whom her penurious parents had married her off. His older sister had been quickly married off, and her dowry used to take care of the other children, and even that had been barely enough.

The first wife, whose children would have been old enough to perform such rites had they lived beyond infancy, was childless, the second wife's children were just a few years older than Gozie. And when Gozie's mother had died from a late cancer diagnosis, he'd been a poor university student working and struggling to send himself to school.

Next, he was to host the other titleholders at a sumptuous feast of food and drink where their leader would announce the four title names Gozie would take. Afterwards, they would gather round and advise him on the conduct of a titled man. Only then could he begin the process of taking the *Ozo* title.

The process happened in many stages. Each stage, lavish and elaborate in nature, entailed joyous feasting and merriment, including the *ula mmuo* that required him to host all *Ozo*-titled men, his age grade, his mother's patrilineage, all young boys and married daughters of his kindred, in-laws and friends to a grand feast. None of that was of import to Gozie; nothing was going to stop him from obtaining that which he desired.

On the day of his coronation, I danced with him in my place of honour as his wife, smiling and wriggling my waist vigorously to the rhythmic tempo of the *ufie* music until the beads at my wrists and ankles rattled and new ones made of sweat formed on my forehead and dripped down the sides of my face.

For his title names, Gozie settled on four he considered befitting for his status: Akunwata – the child's wealth, to announce that he'd acquired his riches of his own efforts; Akukwesili – the bearer worthy of his wealth; Akajiugo – the hand that holds the eagle, to demonstrate his high position in society; and Omeluora – the one who does charitable deeds for his people.

And I was his wife. His wife!

I adjusted the new beads around my wrist that declared me the wife of an *Ozo*-titled man, sat up straighter in my seat and stared at the people. I'd worn them that morning for no particular reason, but if anything, it signalled that my spirit person was in touch with the universe happening outside of it.

'Madam, as you can see,' the man said, moving his forearm in a misshapen semi-circle that encompassed the array of large *ghana-must-go* bags and the other people, besides the girl and her child, that had accompanied him, 'we've brought our daughter to her husband's house. That small boy you see there is her husband's son, his only son, and this is his house by right. We're going to wait till her husband is back.'

I laughed, out and loud. He was a joker, this one.

'*Ihe di woro ogori azuala na ahia,*' I heard Papa's voice whisper in

my ear – *What is done in secret will be revealed in the marketplace.*
Gozie's secret had been exposed at last.

'I'm sorry, I have no idea what you're speaking of, but my husband
isn't home,' I said in the most formal-sounding English I could muster,
emphasising the 'band' in 'husband'. 'When he returns, you can come
back, hopefully without your bags this time, and tell him whatever
you have to tell him. But I can assure you that he will return. Till
then, please can all of you to find your way out of my house.'

'Madam, all this English you're speaking doesn't concern us; we're
not going anywhere,' one member of the group said, folding his arms
tightly to emphasise his point. The girl looked nervously between
us.

I leaned forward, locked my fingers together and looked him
straight in the eye. 'Don't make me call my security guard and the
police, because if I do, I will not listen to any apologies then. Get.
Out. Of. My. House. Now!'

They passed looks between themselves as if contemplating the
severity of my threats and the likelihood I would actually execute
them. I marched to the front door with determination, threw it open
and yelled for our security. 'Usman! Usman!'

Their feet scattered as they hurriedly jumped to their feet, grabbed
their luggage and ran past me. Usman stood outside with his baton,
ready to react if any of them misbehaved.

The girl was the last to leave. She adjusted the child carefully on
her shoulder as she rose to her feet, and and he gave me a grin as
she passed by, a wide toothless one. I returned the smile wistfully.
If only he were mine.

\*

Mama was further away than usual, the roads leading to her house were tighter and longer. I drove and drove, manoeuvring my way through the melee of vehicles and stopping ever so often to wind down my window to scream out my frustrations at other drivers, until finally Mama's house appeared through my windshield.

My brothers and I had tried to convince her to move in with one of us – we didn't want her to be alone – but she'd refused. 'Please let me enjoy my freedom. This is the first time I've truly had it. You, my children, are grown and married with your own children; my husband has passed away and left me alone. When I'm old and sick and about to die, I will call all of you,' she'd said.

We hired Ngozi, a thick-set young woman in her early twenties from our town with a loud laugh and strong hands she loved to use to sew beautiful blouses, to live with Mama and help out with anything she needed. In the evenings, she took adult classes at a nearby school; she hoped to get into the university someday, she'd told me.

Ngozi opened the gate with a smile that quickly disappeared once she caught proper sight of me.

'Good a—Aunty, is everything alright?'

'Where's Mama? Is she around?' I asked, abandoning regular pleasantries.

'She's in her room,' she responded, pointing at the house, her eyes wide.

I ran inside without looking back, holding my wrapper by the waist so it wouldn't fall off. I hadn't bothered to tie it properly in my hurry.

Mama glanced up with a smile as I burst into her room, then

returned her gaze almost immediately to a bundle of shiny cloth on her lap she was smoothing over with her palm. 'Obianuju, thank God you're here. I was planning to come visit you later today. Come and see this very nice material I bought from Mama Chidera. Remember her? The welfare officer at our *Ndigbo* women's association. Her first granddaughter is getting married next month and we all want to wear this. What do you think? If you like it, you can buy one as well – I'm sure they'll have extra.' She looked up at me, her hand still moving over the material, like it was an animal she was petting.

Mama saw my face then, and almost immediately she jumped to her feet, leaving her precious cloth to tumble, neglected, to the floor. 'Obianuju, what's wrong? What happened?'

'Mama, how could he?' My breath came in short, hurried gasps, as tears clogged my airways. 'How could he do this to me? How? After everything?' I sat on the floor of Mama's bedroom, put my head between my legs and wept.

It would take a while before I could gather my wits enough to tell Mama what had happened.

Mama blamed me first. 'I told you! I told you we should go and see that man Mama Ezinne said helped her daughter get pregnant with a son, but you refused. You said you were tired of trying. Now, see. You don't know this thing is a war; you can't close your eyes and sleep – your enemies will attack. Just make sure you don't let that girl stay in your house. Don't you know one son cancels out five girls? Oh God! What are we going to do now?' She placed both hands on her head, and paced the floor so fast that I worried she would dig a hole with her feet, as she thought of what to do next.

But Mama couldn't think of anything, so she told me to go home and wait for my husband to return; she would visit me later. Hopefully she would have thought of something by then.

I drove to the church instead, deciding on a whim to see the pastor and seek counsel, and questioned the wisdom of that decision as soon as I parked my car in the lot of the church compound. What if I caused a scandal?

I wiped the nervous sweat on my palms against the skirt of my gown and dusted imaginary dirt off it, then I looked in the rearview mirror, applied a cherry shade of lipstick and adjusted my face enough so that I could get into the pastor's office without too many questions from nosy parishioners.

The pastor stood up from behind his large desk to receive me, welcoming me with 'Ahh, Sister Uju . . .' and a wide-toothed smile, the kind that embraces you without doing so. I returned a crooked replica.

'Sister Uju, this is an unexpected visit. How are you? How are your husband and children?' he asked when we were both seated.

'Very fine, pastor,' I replied with a shaky voice.

He tilted his head to the side as if to say, *If everyone is fine, why are you here?* 'So you want to see me . . .' he said, more a question than a statement.

'Yes, I do,' I said. I didn't know what else to say; my mind was blank, my tongue stiff and I could feel sweat gathering at my temple, palms and under my armpits. I rubbed my hands together. I peeped at the door, ready to bolt.

Pastor smiled. 'Sister Uju, please relax, feel free to say what's on your mind,' he said to calm me. Perhaps he'd noticed my glance at the door.

I cleared my throat. 'You see, my husband . . . my husband . . .'

'Yes? What happened to your husband?'

My throat closed as I pushed out the words. 'He had a child with another woman. A son. I'm tired; I don't think I can do it anymore.' I couldn't look him in the eyes. I'd failed. I'd failed as a woman.

Pastor's eyes widened. 'Brother Gozie Azubuike? Are you sure of what you're saying?'

I nodded mutely, struggling to control the fresh barrage of tears burning through my chest. I swiped at a tear that leaked out the corner of my eye.

'When? Why? What happened?'

I narrated what had happened, how two women and three men had shown up at our gate with their luggage, ready for a stay at their 'in-law's place', the child whose looks validated their claims, the woman young enough to be my niece, if not my daughter. I didn't stop there – I spoke about the years of pain, of constant abuse and emotional and mental torture and trauma. 'I can't do it anymore. I really don't think I can,' I concluded, wiping the corner of my eyes again.

Pastor shook his head. 'Don't talk like that. Marriage is for better or worse. You have to stand strong; you have to pray for your husband. He has lost his way. You and Brother Gozie have been members of this church for many years, and are an example to so many around you; you're even a member of our marriage council.

'Listen to me,' he continued. 'The things you've said are very serious and must be addressed. The moment your husband gets back, ask him to see me. But I don't want you to quarrel with him. Be calm. Most importantly, pray. Refuse to give up on your marriage.'

Drained and incapable of response, I turned my eyes to the side to stare at a painting on the wall of the office: a painting of Christ – a man with pale skin, blue eyes and almost straight, auburn hair. I wondered if he would tell me to do same, to accept my life as I'd come to accept the popular painting: a lie as the truth.

# 36.

## *We took an oath before God and man*

Ego came home that weekend I found out about the child, a back-pack around her shoulders and a pink flower-patterned duffel bag in her hand. She hardly visited home since she gained admission to the university to study law, running, as she was, from the turbulence in our household. Some days, I drove by her hostel just to see her face and make sure she was okay.

'Mummy! I'm around,' she screamed from the door that afternoon as soon as she threw it open. I laughed for the first time in days.

'This one that you came to visit us today; hope we're not owing your pocket money for the month. Or did you forget something?' I joked as I walked down the stairs.

She laughed, the same boisterous laugh she'd had since she was a teenager. 'We finished our tests for the semester; we have a short holiday before classes start again. You always complain that I don't come home. Where's everyone?'

'Your father travelled to the village and your sisters are with Mama for the weekend; you know she likes to spoil them,' I said, arriving at the ground floor at last and walking quickly to pull her into a warm embrace.

I didn't add that Mama had thought it best to take the children away so I could properly think about what to do next. 'You have to do something, anything. If your husband returns this weekend, try to get pregnant,' she'd said.

'I missed your trouble,' I said, letting her go and gripping her shoulders with a smile.

She laughed again and opened her mouth to respond, but something about my face stopped her. Her smile disappeared immediately and she squinted into a frown.

I touched my face self-consciously. 'What? Why are you looking at me like that?' I asked.

She dropped the duffel bag – it made a heavy thud where it hit the floor – and stared at me a little longer before she asked, 'What did he do this time?'

We both knew the 'he' she was referring to. Ego was older now, old enough to understand all that was happening around her, to understand what those childhood memories signified – Mummy in a pool of blood, Mummy spending days at the hospital, the long holiday with Grandma and Grandpa. The many questions I'd left unanswered had been exposed by maturity's dawn. For that she resented her father deeply, but I knew that somewhere in the recesses of her heart she reserved some resentment for me, for staying in spite of it all.

She planned to never marry. 'I don't see how it benefits women in any way,' she'd said one holiday as we relaxed in the garden. 'You leave the comfort of your father's house for a man; you give everything, sacrifice yourself, your ambitions, put your body through the pain of childbirth and he doesn't appreciate it. What's the point? We've been brainwashed to want it more when they benefit from it the most.'

'Not all marriages are that way; there are some good ones, you know. You read too many books,' I'd said quickly. Guilt gnawed at me like the sharp teeth of a rabid dog. It was my fault my daughter was this way. I'd touched her arm. 'I know your father and I haven't set the best example for you, but I can assure you that it's not always this way.'

'It's not just about you and Daddy. You know I have friends with parents too, right? And I listen to what people say every day. We want women to put in everything and be okay with getting almost nothing in return. I'm not going to live like that.'

There was nothing I could say to that. I'd always wanted her to be different; I had to accept whatever came with it.

Ego repeated her question, but with added rancour. 'What did he do this time?'

I waved her question away, picked the duffel bag off the floor and walked towards the staircase. 'Nothing, nothing. You're imagining things. Let's drop these things in your room then I'll ask the steward to make you some chicken pepper soup; I know how much you like it. Then later this evening I'll make jollof rice by myself, just the way you like it. You're looking too thin. I hope you don't spend all your time reading and speaking big English; you have to take care of yourself too.'

She grunted behind me as she followed me up the stairs. I sighed, thinking, with relief, that I'd avoided her curiosity. I'd tried to protect my daughters from the turmoil in our home, but it was almost impossible to do so in the face of such open aggression. And every now and then, I would pass by their rooms and overhear conversations that let me know they knew; they just pretended not to, to make me happy. How was I going to hide a whole human being from them?

Later that evening, we chatted in the dining room as Ego shoved spoonfuls of jollof rice in her mouth and regaled me with tales of university life. '*Nne*, calm down, the food is not running away. You'll choke eating like that,' I warned as I poured water into a glass for her.

She swallowed quickly and sighed with satisfaction. 'I missed your food. It's been long since I ate good food like this. I never have the time to cook anything besides white rice or beans and warm the bowls of stew you usually bring to school for me. You know those restaurants cannot make food like this. And when do I have the time to fry plantain or chicken when I have so many assignments to finish?' She picked up the drumstick from the plate and tore into the meat with her teeth.

I smiled. 'Try to eat well in school, *biko;* I don't want you to fall sick.'

She laughed. 'I won't fall sick; almost everyone eats like that in school. I'm sure it was like that in your day as well.'

'It was like that o. Mama was always complaining that I was too thin to catch a husband. In fact, Adaugo, Chinelo, and I—' I froze, realising what I'd just said. The pain of the loss hit me again. Adaugo still wouldn't talk to me, even after all those months; she wouldn't even look in my direction when we crossed paths at church. Chinelo had been the glue that bonded us together, and in her absence, we'd fallen apart irreparably.

342

Ego gently rubbed the arm I'd stretched out on the table. 'It's okay, Mum; you don't have to talk about it. I know you miss them.'

I grabbed the used plate and utensils and walked swiftly to the kitchen. Ego followed silently behind me, rested against the counter and watched quietly as I viciously scrubbed the dirty items.

Suddenly, I felt her arms wrap around me from behind. 'You can cry, you know; you don't always have to pretend to be strong because of us.'

Slowly, I turned around and returned the embrace. 'Are you going to tell me what he did now?' she whispered in my ear.

She held me tighter as I tried to pull away; we were the same height now, and somehow she'd gotten stronger, or maybe I'd gotten weaker. We stood that way for what seemed like ages before she let me go, and we walked to the living room in silence.

'I'll tell you, but please I want you to promise me that you won't do anything about it,' I said. She didn't respond for a moment, then finally, reluctantly, she nodded.

'You should get a divorce,' she announced as soon as I was done talking. 'I know Grandma won't agree but she's old-school; people get divorced nowadays. You can talk to Mama Bidemi's son – he's a lawyer – or I could talk to—'

'No, Ego, stop it,' I interrupted her. 'You're not going to do anything; neither of us is going to do anything.'

She glared at me like I'd lost my mind. 'You mean you don't plan to talk to him about it?'

'It would just cause another argument. I'm tired of fighting. Those people were probably lying anyways. You know how peop—'

'Mummy, you're lying to yourself and you know it. You said it

343

yourself that the baby looked exactly like him! The least you can do is challenge him about it. How dare he do something like that to you? If you're not going to ask him, I will!'

Cold fear washed over me, chilling me to my bones. 'No!' I exclaimed, then quickly recovering myself, I lowered my tone. 'Please, no. I'll talk to him myself, but please don't say anything. *Biko*. I don't want him to take out his anger on you. He still pays your school fees and gives you pocket money. Do you have money to pay your own fees?'


When Gozie returned from the village, days later than expected, I was ready to face him, buoyed by the prospect of Ego challenging him in my stead if I failed to.

I waited till he'd showered, eaten and taken a nap. He was stretched out on the large sofa in the living room watching the news when I walked in.

I cleared my throat. 'Gozie, please, I'd like to talk to you,' I mumbled.

He ignored me. 'Gozie, I'd like to talk to you,' I repeated, louder this time.

He rolled his eyes towards me before turning down the volume on the television.

'Yes?' he asked with irritation as I sat on the edge of the adjoining sofa.

'Some people came to see you when you were gone.'

He sat up slowly. 'I'm listening.'

'A woman, her son and some of her relatives.'

He shifted uncomfortably and that minute act alone wiped any residue of doubt I had in my mind. 'How could you?' I whispered. 'How could you do this?'

He didn't bother to pretend. Instead, he decided denial was the best route to follow. 'Whatever they told you is a lie. That child is not mine.'

'Do you think I'm a fool? Or that I'm the same naive girl you married almost twenty years ago? That child looks exactly like you!'

'You should get your eyes checked,' he declared and turned his attention back to the television.

I could feel my temperature rising with each second, and when he commented on something he saw on the screen – 'Unserious government' – I stomped over to the television, turned it off and stood in front of it.

'Obianuju, move! Now!' Gozie bellowed.

'I am not moving till you respect me and speak to me like a human being! Have I not given enough? Have I sacrificed everything to make sure we stay together? How could you do this to me?'

His face twisted into a sneer. 'What was I supposed to do? Was I supposed to sit and wait until a barren woman like you gives me a son? I'm the only son of my father!'

I was used to his bile, his insults, his name-calling. So I was barren. What else? 'We took an oath before God and man. You should be ashamed of yourself!'

'What did you say?' His eyes narrowed precariously as he slowly got to his feet and walked the distance between us in the cavernous living room.

I should have been scared, terrified even, by the look in his eyes, but I didn't care anymore. I was tired – tired of being scared, tired of living like a fugitive in my own home. 'I said you should be ashamed of yourself! How old is she? Nineteen? Twenty? That girl is young enough to be your daughte—' Those were the last words to leave my mouth before the first blow landed, and the second and the third and the fourth, and the ones after I stopped counting.

Underneath the pounding, I heard the sound of feet running down the stairs and towards us, and all of us sudden Gozie was knocked off balance, giving me the space I needed to escape.

'Leave her alone!' Ego commanded, pointing at her father. 'Haven't you done enough? Aren't you tired of treating her this way? Will you wait until she's dead before you stop?'

'Ego, please go upstairs. Please, in the name of God, go upstairs!' I pleaded through bleeding lips.

'No! I'm sick and tired of this. When will he stop?' She pointed at him again. 'You got another woman pregnant; you should be begging her not to leave you!'

I grabbed her arm and pulled for her to move. 'Ego, please go upstairs. Go to your room. Think of your school.' But she stood firm, and so I pushed to my feet and stood in front of her instead, a human shield.

Gozie sneered again at the both of us. 'Obianuju, hope you can see for yourself the kind of mother you are; just look at the type of daughter you raised: rude and mannerless! No wonder you were not blessed with a son, and you were wondering why I found another woman?'

'You have no shame!' Ego yelled before I could conjure a response.

It happened so quickly it felt like a flash – one of those moments

346

that remain with you for the rest of your life – and suddenly I was flung into stiff air across the room. The last thing I saw just before my head banged against the wall was Gozie's hand at our daughter's throat and his other raised to strike the first blow.

## 37.

## *We women have to stick together*

The walls of the hospital were yellow, a yellow so faint I could almost see the drab grey of the plastered centre underneath. It had been a long time since I'd been in one of these – a government-owned hospital, where the hallways and corridors were packed with the sick, seated and standing, waiting to be attended to by poorly compensated, overworked and sleep-deprived doctors. Outside the building was an ambulance, parked up because there was no fuel to keep it mobile.

It was a harsh slap to reality. I'd gotten used to the hospitals in Ikoyi with decorated marble floors, foreign workers, locals with foreign accents and well-mannered nurses who didn't shout at a patient that they had other people to attend to when they wouldn't stay still for the prick of an injection needle.

I didn't know how long it had been since I'd passed out, but when I opened my eyes, Gozie was nowhere to be found and our daughter was unconscious in a pool of her own blood. Quickly, I crawled over and called her name. 'Ego! Ego! Wake up!' She didn't budge. I jumped to my feet, ignoring the wave of dizziness that attacked immediately, and ran up the stairs to get my car keys.

'Where's your *oga*?' I asked the gateman as soon as he appeared, referring to Gozie.

'Madam, I no know. He drive out since he never come b—'

'Okay, please help me. Help me carry her to the car,' I cut in, pointing to Ego. Usman's eyes moved in the direction of my finger and widened as they focused on Ego.

'Hurry! Please! There's no time,' I begged, to prompt him into action. Carefully, he lifted her in his arms, and her head lolled to the side as though her neck was made of jelly. The blood on the floor had formed a strange shape, like a map of some forgotten country, the end a curve where her head had lain. And for a second, I stared at it, willing it to disappear into a dream, then I hurried after Usman, locking the front door behind me.

I headed straight for the general hospital, not the family hospital where we were known; it would have been too much to answer the questions. Most importantly, even though I'd finally opened a bank account, unknown to Gozie, and started making savings off sales of my old items, I knew I didn't have enough to afford their extortionate bills.

At the hospital, the car had barely come to a halt, the tyres screeching in protest, as I leapt out of the vehicle and screamed for help. Almost immediately, a stretcher raced after me, and within a few seconds Ego was pulled from the back seat of the car and wheeled into the hospital.

I paced the floors of the hospital hallway as I waited anxiously for word from the doctors, beads of sweat dripping down the sides of my face and forehead and into my blouse. Ten minutes passed, then fifteen and twenty and I began to panic.

'Extradural haematoma,' a doctor said to me after thirty minutes of waiting. He was an elderly man of experience, the greys of his hair almost the same colour as the white of his coat.

'What's that? What does that mean?' I asked with apprehension.

'The bleeding in the dura mater of the brain as a result of severe head trauma. We need to carry out surgery immediately. Please make the deposit at the desk over there so we can proceed at once. If we waste any more time, she might lose her life. As it is, we cannot be certain that she'll fully recover from this.'

I felt my blood pressure rise. I swallowed. 'How much is the deposit?' My head spun on the numbers he answered with. 'I don't have that kind of money with me now, but if you can start the surgery, I can go and—'

'Madam, I'm sorry that is against our hospital's policy.'

'But you can't let her die. Please! I promise I'll pay.'

He shook his head, 'I'm sorry, madam,' he said, and turned around to leave.

I grabbed at the sleeve of his coat in desperation. 'Wait! Please wait!' I begged. My voice shook as I placed my car keys in his hand, closed his fingers around them into a fist and knelt beside him. 'Th-that's my car key. It's a Mercedes-Benz sedan. My husband got it brand new this year. You can hold on to it as surety. I'll find the money; I'll pay. Please, she's my first daughter – don't let her die. Just don't let her die.'

He stood still for what felt like forever, his face not betraying any emotions, then finally he nodded and pulled me to my feet. 'Go to the desk over there and fill out the necessary forms,' he said, pointing at a desk at the other end of the room.

While the doctors operated, I called the house with a phone at the hospital desk reserved for emergencies. Gozie answered the phone; he must have used a spare key to get in.

'Hello?' he said in rich, polished tenor, ever the suave businessman.

'Hello, Chigozie, it's me, Uju.' He hissed. 'Nwakaego is unconscious. They said she was bleeding in her brain; they're operating on her now. Please, I need some money to pay for the operation. I had to beg the doctor in charge to carry on with the surgery before payment. Can you please send someone with the money first thing tomorrow morning?'

'Obianuju, that is your business.'

'What?' I'd expected him to ask how much. Even though he'd never shown any feelings of affinity towards our children, he'd always provided for their needs, no matter the cost.

'I will not pay for the treatment of such a rude and idiotic child. If she's going to die, let her die.'

The hand that held the telephone shook violently and tears ran down my cheeks. 'She can't die. Please, ple—'

He hung up. I thanked the nurse in charge of the phone, pretending not to notice her look of concern, and sat in a corner to try to stop the shaking. I was losing my mind; I could feel it, the slow unravelling of the knots that held my sanity together. Was this how it happened? How seemingly stable people crossed the line to insanity in plain sight of everyone, balancing the thin line and juggling the weights, until one day the final thread was cut and they plummeted into a strange world where the abnormal took on the cloak of normalcy, and unseen voices lined the walls?

I took a deep breath to try to calm myself. I couldn't fall apart, not now; I had to be strong for my children. I squeezed into the corner of the old wooden bench and tried to think of someone who could come to my aid. Mama did not have her own money; if anything, she depended on my brothers and Gozie for her upkeep. My brothers had their own families to take care of, school fees to pay and clothes to buy, and I couldn't think of a single scenario where making them aware of all that had happened would do more good than harm.

'Mrs. Azubuike,' the doctor called, interrupting my thoughts. I hadn't noticed him walk up to me. How much time had passed?

I scrambled to my feet. 'Y-yes? Please, how is she?'

'We just came out of surgery. It went well. She's stable at the moment. We'll just have to wait and see how she recovers.'

'Will she be okay?'

He shook his head gravely. 'I cannot assure you that she will ever fully recover from this; we aren't even very sure of when next she'll be conscious. But we've done the surgery and it went very well. We'll just have to wait and keep monitoring her progress.'

I nodded eagerly, trying to hold on to the small ray of hope. I grabbed his hand and clutched it tightly in both of mine. 'Thank you, doctor. Thank you so much. God bless you.'

'No problem, madam. You're welcome.' He pointed at the right side of my head. 'Do you want treatment for that? A nurse can dress the wound and get you something for the swelling.'

'For what?' I asked, confused, feeling the side of my face his finger

352

called attention to. It was then I noticed a gash on the side of my forehead that must have been created when my head hit the wall, and the swelling of my face.

I lowered my head and used my hand to conceal the injury. 'Yes, thank you.'

For a second, he stared at me like he wanted to ask more questions – to understand why a woman of my stature had shown up at a general hospital in that state with an unconscious bleeding daughter – then seemed to decide against it and turned to leave. He stopped to talk to a nurse, and minutes later I was directed to a small room where a nurse in a white uniform and a matching nurse's cap attended to me.

Days passed and Ego wouldn't regain consciousness. During the day, I went about trying to sell off enough of my personal possessions to pay the hospital bill and spoke with the twins on the phone to make sure they were eating well and going to school, and at night I kept vigil by Ego's bedside, and begged God not to take my wealth, my Ego, from me.

I sang to her – lullabies I'd sung to her as a child, the same ones Mama had sung to me, hoping my voice would infiltrate the oblivion and bring her back to me.

After a few days, some nurses took pity on me and prepared a small bed for me beside hers so I could rest at night. I thanked them, even though I knew I wouldn't sleep.

Sister Bolatito parked right outside our gate as I was waiting for a taxi to take me to the hospital. I hadn't seen her in a while; she'd stopped teaching and had been less involved in group activities since the confrontation at the women's meeting. Now, she slipped in and out of meetings stealthily, like a hunted criminal avoiding the hammer of the law.

She stretched across the passenger seat, wound down the glass and smiled at me from the driver's side. 'Sister Uju! Good evening o.'

I bent at the waist to speak to her; I was genuinely pleased to see her, despite all that was happening. 'Sister Bolatito, how are you? I'm surprised to see you here.'

'I noticed you weren't at the women's meeting again, so I decided to come and check on you. Are you going somewhere? Come in, let me drop you.'

'Thank you,' I said once I was seated in the comfort of her Porsche.

'It's no trouble at all. Where are you going by this time? And why aren't you taking your car?' she asked as she turned on the ignition and pulled away from the concrete.

'I'm going to the general hospital at Victoria Island. My daughter, Ego, isn't feeling too well. I had to leave my car at the hospital.'

'Hope it's nothing too serious,' she replied. She probably assumed it was malaria or typhoid fever.

I faked a nonchalant smile. 'No, nothing too serious.'

We moved in intermittent silence. Every few minutes, Sister Bolatito would bring up a topic she thought would interest me – church, the weather, politics – and we would chat for a few more minutes, but soon enough I grew quiet, drawn to the world inside my head.

At the hospital gate, Sister Bolatito stopped her car and turned off the engine, and I thanked her. As I turned to leave, she touched my shoulder, causing me to pause. 'You can talk to me, you know. Something is wrong. You said you fell down the stairs, but I know that's a lie. I have been there. I want to help you. We women have to stick together; we have to help each other.'

Something about those words penetrated the false walls of strength I'd built around myself. The tears didn't come softly, but in a torrent like heavy rainfall after a drought. I covered my face with my hands and gave in to my emotions.

Sister Bolatito rubbed my back gently in silent comfort as I cried. When I was done, she handed me a handkerchief to wipe my face and listened patiently.

'I'll help you,' she said immediately. 'I'll give you the money for the bill.'

The tears came again, but this time they were ones of relief.

She was the miracle I'd prayed for.

Ten days later, I walked into the hospital lounge to find the doctors gathered round a television. I peeked at the clock: it was eight in the morning. I moved closer to the group to find out what would cause them to gather around so early in the morning.

On the screen was a uniformed officer in front of the State House building in Abuja; martial music played in the background. When the music stopped, he leaned into the microphone to make his announcement.

The head of state was dead.

The small crowd in the lounge erupted into shouts of joy, doctors and patients clapped, strangers hugged and high-fived each other, others danced to imaginary music, and a few doubting Thomases stood by the television waiting for a rebroadcast to reconfirm the news. Someone produced a cassette player and soon highlife music filled the hallways; even the sick did not look so ill anymore, a pep in their steps as they danced into the doctor's office.

I managed a small smile and returned the hugs and handshakes good-naturedly, though my heart was incapable of any feeling besides sadness. I walked to the ward wearily, afraid to give up hope yet fearing holding on to hope and then becoming disappointed in the end.

She was staring at me when I arrived. Still disorientated, eyes foggy, as though she was still trying to absorb her strange surroundings. At first, I thought my eyes were deceiving me, that all those days and nights of crying and praying had finally run me mad. Then a smile appeared on her face, one so innocent it reminded me of her as a child, when I'd gone to pick her up at school. She would smile just like that before running at top speed to grasp my legs.

Tears filled my eyes and my voice shook. 'Nwakaego?'

'Mummy.'

The doctor discharged us two weeks later in June '98, with a bag of medication and a warning that the worst might be over but we still had to be careful.

I pulled away from the hospital in my car with Ego in the front seat, her sisters in the back, and our belongings in the boot of the vehicle.

I wasn't sure where we were headed, but I knew we were never going back.

# 38.

## *He was a man just like the rest of them*

'Obianuju, I want to tell you a story,' Mama said in January '99. It had been six months since I left Gozie and Mama was yet to come to terms with it. She'd cried, she'd begged, she'd even threatened to disown me, but still I wouldn't budge. I wondered when she would finally tire of trying and accept things as they were.

'Yes, Mama, I'm listening,' I said warily, bracing myself for what I expected to be another tirade.

She cleared her throat before speaking. 'You see, I never told you about this because I know how much you loved your father and how close you were to him, but I think it's time I told you some hard truths. It might help you; who knows?' she said.

My brows came together in a perplexed frown at the direction of the conversation.

'You're probably wondering what I'm talking about. Well, I'll tell you,' she said.

She started from when she'd come to Lagos as a naive teenager to meet the man her parents had chosen for her as a husband. He

357

was doing very well for himself in the city and was from a good family, they'd assured her. When she first met him, she was fascinated, she admitted, by this tall handsome Igbo man that had whiter teeth than those of the unrefined men in her village and spoke unaccented Queen's English. She was lucky to have such a husband.

Papa barely paid attention to his new wife; he was a young man in his prime. She was a bearable burden, a necessary inconvenience so his people would let him be after they'd insisted he settle down. Every other thing was just an added perk. Mama worked to make her husband happy and build a home the way her mother had taught her. She cooked, she cleaned, she picked up after him, she found where the nearest market was and learned how to haggle with the Yorubas so she could get the best for the least. She was going to win her husband over and make him love her with her perfection of womanhood.

But Papa carried on living his life like he had done before she'd made an appearance – freely and in the midst of women. Mama struggled to endure it, but when she couldn't any longer and she challenged him, she was thrashed thoroughly every time.

Kelechi was born within a year of their marriage, and Mama was overjoyed with hope that his coming would keep Papa at home more. It did, but only for a while. Within months, he was out and back to his old ways. Then Ugochukwu came and then Ikechukwu, and each time, the cycle repeated itself – he would stay home for a while but then he would resume his normal lifestyle. Mama gave up hope of having the life she'd always wanted – it had all been a lie, a fallacy sold to young girls to help them dream sweet dreams at night, to make them bubble with excitement as they journeyed to their husbands' homes. This was reality; this was life.

Then I was born.

'You should have seen how he stared at you at the hospital, like he was seeing an angel from heaven. He said you looked like his late mother. I didn't argue with him,' Mama said with a small smile at the side of her lips, her eyes cloudy as she gazed into a time long gone.

Overnight, Papa became a different man. He stayed home more and put an end to his string of affairs. Of course, he would never love Mama, but at least he stopped beating her and actually acknowledged her existence. But by then, Mama had undergone a transformation of her own: she had been hardened.

I was in a pool of tears by the time Mama was done telling her story – for her, for the woman she'd been, and for me. I struggled to marry the image of the Papa I'd known and loved to the man she'd just described. I went over the images of my childhood in my head for signs of that person I might have missed. And suddenly, it all became clearer. The moments he'd shut Mama up with a hard stare when she'd spoken too much. The days he'd given Mama strict instructions to follow as though she were one of his children. The many times I'd wanted to do something Mama disapproved of and he'd simply overruled her decision as though her opinion was irrelevant, and those times, I'd danced with glee that I'd been able to do what I wanted.

I'd gained my freedom at the expense of Mama's.

'I'll help you pack,' Mama said, wiping the tears from her face with the edge of her wrapper as she rose to her feet.

I stared at her as though she'd suddenly lost her senses. 'Pack? To go where?' I asked.

'Your husband's house of course. Where else?'

I sighed loudly. 'Mama, but I already told you I'm not going back to Gozie. I meant what I said – I am not going back.'

'Even after everything I just told you?' she asked, surprise colouring her tone.

'How does that have anything to do with this?' I replied, squinting at her in confusion.

'Are you deaf? Or can't you see that I was trying to show you that even your father that you loved so much changed for the better with time? He was a man just like the rest of them, but I stayed and persevered, and see how he calmed down with age. See how he treated you and your brothers. You cannot abandon your marriage just because of little problems like this.'

'Mama, Gozie had a child – a son – with another woman and he nearly killed Ego. How are those little problems?'

'And so? Don't you know there are women going through worse? These are just some of the things that you can experience in life as a woman. You must be strong, learn from them and move on. You know, this has always been your problem – complain, complain, complain. You have never learnt to accept your lot in life. You're a woman not a man. The sooner you accept it, the better.'

In a way, Mama was right. Somehow, I'd just never managed to be good enough as a woman – strong enough, pretty, meek, softly-spoken, quiet, sober, selfless, long-suffering, willing to bend for others – and perhaps that was why my life had ended up that way.

'Mama, this isn't normal; it shouldn't be normal. I won't have my daughters grow up thinking it's normal. I am not going back to Gozie,' I said with finality.

'So, what do plan to do? Stay here while another woman reaps the fruit of your labour? Or do you think you can remarry at your age? No man will marry a divorced woman with three children – all girls, for that matter. Your husband has apologised several times. He is even willing to take you back as long as you've not had any affair since you left him, and I know you haven't, so what is the problem? What exactly do you want?'

I chuckled at the irony of Gozie's declaration.

Mama's face twisted with rage. 'You are so selfish,' she spat out. 'You're only thinking about yourself. You're a disgrace to this family. What about your children? Is this how you want your children to live? In this nonsense, struggling to survive when their father has a mansion? Don't you know your daughters will have issues marrying because they're from a divorced home? Don't you know they will be insulted with it by outsiders? And what about your brothers? Where do you expect them to raise the money to return your bride price? Don't you know they have their own families and problems? What is wrong with you?'

I sat in silence after Mama was gone, thinking about what she'd said, her ominous parting words in particular. 'You will die alone and your children will have no inheritance. Your father must be rolling in his grave!' Even then, knowing all Mama had shared, it pained me to think that I might be a source of shame to Papa. I'd always wanted to make him proud, to hear him say, as he had always done, 'Yes, that's my Uju.' I was angry at the realisation of the man he'd been, that he'd been responsible in part for the woman Mama had become. But he was gone and I had no one to channel the hurt and confusion to. I loved him still; I would always love him, but what was I to do with the memory of the man I'd known?

I looked around the living room of the compact two-bedroom flat I'd only just managed to rent. *Nonsense*, Mama had called it, but for me it represented peace and freedom – emotions I'd long forgotten existed and could belong to me.

I'd driven to Sister Bolatito's house from the hospital with nowhere else to go. I called Mama to let her know I was fine but would not reveal my location to her, for fear of her reporting it to Gozie.

For weeks, we lived with Sister Bolatito until I finally found a small apartment that I could afford for us to move into. I sold everything I had, including my sedan, to pay the rent; what was left went into our upkeep.

Our lifestyle was economical, far from the flamboyant one it had been with Gozie, and my children weren't used to economical. They made conscious efforts not to complain, but I could feel their discomfort in the way they forced down the repetitive meals I made, when I put off the generator so we could conserve fuel for later, and when they had to make use of public transport. Other times, the twins were vocal in their discontent, too lost in their teenage frankness to fully comprehend all that was happening. Nkechi complained that her classmates made fun of her means of transport to school – they still attended the expensive private school because Gozie had paid for two years – and Nwamaka talked about her former home with wistful longing. I feared they would resent me one day for snatching them from that life, and many nights I stayed awake, riddled with guilt that I'd left for my own selfish reasons at the expense of my children's comfort. I wondered what I would do when the school year ended and I could not afford the fees for the following year. Perhaps I should have stayed longer, endured until they were done with school at least. But then I would think of Ego and how I'd nearly lost her.

Our injuries healed, slowly and then quickly, the scars disappearing into our skin. 'Mummy, I'm okay,' Ego would say with a small smile whenever I stared at her carefully for signs of that dark time in the hospital. I purchased a medical textbook and read up on long-term effects of haematomas and watched for symptoms, but even as she assured me she was fine, I knew other wounds remained underneath the surface, etched deep within our blood, that would never heal. They were alive in the way we jumped when we heard the neighbour's doorbell ring, mistaking it for ours, and in the quick tempo of my pulse whenever a car like Gozie's passed me.

I found a job as a clerk at a government parastatal. Ego resumed her studies at the university, and when a new school term started, I moved the twins to a cheaper private school closer to where we were staying. A sense of normalcy returned as we settled into our new lives.

'You smile more these days,' Nwamaka commented one day as we sat together watching a movie, surprise written on her face and in her tone.

'And I haven't heard you laugh like that in a long time,' her twin added.

For months, Mama pestered me every time I contacted her from a call centre near my office to reveal where we lived. Other times, she begged that I return to my husband. It was strange, but I missed him sometimes, the force and power of his presence. I could no longer use the words 'Do you know my husband?' when I found myself in a fix. Every so often, I thought of the good times, in the early days before and during our marriage.

Then I slipped. I gave in one day and recited our new address to Mama quickly over the phone. I was tired of hiding, of feeling like a fugitive on the run, and of her constant pressuring and emotional blackmail. I pleaded with her to come alone.

She came alone the next day, but the day after that, Gozie showed up at our door and he wasn't alone; a small squad of policemen formed a line behind him. I was charged with kidnapping, put in heavy handcuffs and taken away to the police station. I was officially listed as 'Awaiting Trial' – that death-knell tag instituted by our judiciary system to justify the locking-up of thousands and to indicate that their release depended on an unknown future date. That night, I curled in ball in a corner of the cold, hard floor of my cell, surrounded by other inmates and the rank and stale smell of body fluids, and shed tears of fear and sadness.

Days later, I was released on bail. The charges had been dropped.

It was a warning, Sister Bolatito, who'd taken care of my daughters in my absence, advised me as she drove me home from the police station, a clear indicator – if there was ever a need for any – of how far he could go to make my life impossible for leaving him. And that I should be thankful he hadn't taken my children away. I knew there was nothing to be thankful for; I was the one he was after. I was his property, and Gozie never liked to lose his possessions.

At the flat, I found a note pinned to our door, the words 'You will not get one penny out of me' were scrawled in distinctive handwriting. I unpinned the piece of paper, carefully folded it into squares until it was no larger than a tiny eraser and threw it in the bin.

The gossip columns came next, with pictures of Gozie and me, jagged lines running between us, and with words like 'The End', 'Rumours Have It' and 'Popular Businessman and Wife Split' written in bold letters. The stories from a 'reliable source' had informed them that I'd abandoned my husband and run away with my much younger boyfriend.

I thought of Papa, who'd lived by the mantra 'A good name is worth more than silver and gold', of Mama, of my brothers struggling to make ends meet for their families. Then I thought of my daughters: the twins still trying to fit in at their new school, Ego exerting herself at the university. I imagined the questions they would all have to answer, the looks and whispers they would have to endure as a result of my decision, and I felt shame – guilty shame.

## 39.

### *I have apparently failed in my God-given assignment*

The Lagos Island market was the last place I'd expected to run into Salome after two decades. It was several weeks after my release from prison.

Bodies brushing in a Lagos market was expected, a foregone conclusion as people bustled back and forth within the narrow lanes – it was why you never wore your best clothing to the market. And so, when a woman's shoulder grazed mine, I barely glanced in her direction as I mumbled an apology and quickly moved forward.

'Obianuju,' a voice called as I rushed past and I froze. Names were hardly used in a market; you heard things like 'aunty', 'fine girl', 'come and buy', 'I have your size', but not names, never names. I turned slowly. 'Obianuju, is it not you? Don't you recognise me?' the woman said, a wide smile on her face.

I squinted, trying to focus on her face and recall where I'd seen it before. Then it clicked. She looked nothing like she used to but it was definitely her. 'Salome Agboga? Sally?' I shouted.

'Obianuju! I knew it was you!' she exclaimed as we moved quickly towards each other for a long embrace.

I stared at her when we finally pulled apart. Gone was the sultry siren with the full Afro, heavy makeup and daring outfits, and in her place was a mature, sophisticated woman; her makeup was barely noticeable, her Afro had been subdued under a long, wavy Indian weave-on, and her clothing was the most appropriate I'd ever seen it. Some things hadn't changed, however – her curves were as arresting as they had always been, perhaps even more so, and when she spoke, I realised she hadn't lost her cynicism – if anything, it had become sharper and dryer, like the air during harmattan season.

We abandoned our shopping and found an eatery nearby to sit and catch up.

'Wow! You've really changed,' I said when we were seated. 'I almost didn't recognise you.'

'I hope you mean that in a good way,' she commented in that characteristic tone of hers.

I laughed. 'Of course I mean it in a good way; you look good!' I enthused.

She chuckled. 'Well, that's a relief. And I must say you look the same after all these years. It's almost impossible to believe you've had three children – if the grapevines are to be believed, of course,' she said with a wry smile.

My face – and spirit – fell a little as my mind wondered what else she'd heard from 'the grapevines.' A waiter chose that moment to interrupt us to take down our order.

'So, what have you been up to?' I asked once the waiter was gone.

'Mostly work,' she drawled, flicking her left wrist, and it was then

I noticed she had no ring on her band finger. She was single. I'd assumed that Sally would succumb to societal demands eventually, mellow down and become the version of a woman that mothers would accept as suitable for their sons, but a part of me had always known she would never bend; her back was too straight. Once, she'd referred to the girls who'd followed their boyfriends around campus every day doing their every bidding as 'cowering secretaries soon to be wives'.

'Tell me about your work,' I said eagerly, wanting an insight into perhaps what my life could have been like.

Although she tried to downplay success, I could tell Sally had done well for herself. She was a high-powered executive at one of the nation's largest and oldest banks.

'Wow! You've really done well for yourself.' I said, voicing my thoughts. 'But what were you looking for in the market? Why didn't you just send someone? I know you can afford to.'

'Thanks. I don't know about "done well",' she said with a cynical smile. 'Those guys stress my life so much; I hardly have time for anything else. I barely have any friends. And let's not even go into the hell they give me because I'm a woman; they act like I gatecrashed their boys' club, which brings me to your question – I didn't send someone to the market for me because every now and then, I need to see somewhere besides my house and my office.'

I nodded thoughtfully, unsure of the right response to give to that. 'I guess that explains the changes in your style,' I said lightly.

She laughed. 'Yes. That. They will never take you seriously as a professional when you're dressed too much like a woman or your makeup is noticeable; it's almost like they don't want any obvious reminders of your gender. And of course, there's my mother.'

'Your mother?'

'Yes, my mother! She's convinced that I have to dress a certain way to attract a husband; she can't believe I've reached this age without catching a single man or given birth to any children.'

'Marriage is not all that it seems,' I said, thinking of mine. Gozie had taken to constant harassment to intimidate me into doing as he wanted, and he had just the tools required in a society like ours – money and power. If it wasn't a police officer randomly knocking on my door, it was my car being towed for breaking some unknown parking rule. I'd sent a letter – I was still too scared to face him – pleading with him to let us be. He'd responded in kind; I was suddenly transferred to a government ministry office on the outskirts of town where the walls were unpainted and goats roamed the ungated compound.

'Tell that to my mother! According to her, a woman's true purpose is in companionship and childbearing, so all my career accomplishments are for my pocket; I have apparently failed in my God-given assignment,' Sally said, and I wondered if her mother's perception of her accomplishments had coloured her own view of her achievements, making them appear smaller and her efforts inconsequential.

'Personally, I'm just sick and tired of the harassment,' Sally continued, 'and I'm at a point that I'm willing to take any man available as long as he has hands, legs and a functioning brain, just so that I don't have to receive a call every birthday from my mother crying about how old I am and how I have not given her grandchildren even though she's quarter to the grave.'

I giggled; her mother sounded just like mine.

She paused in her rant, placing a finger on her chin. 'On second thoughts, I would take any man as long as he has hands, legs, a functioning brain *and* doesn't hit me. I can take many things, but I will not let any man born of a woman put his hands on me. The last boyfriend I had slapped me once during an argument and I broke it off immediately. You should have seen my mother's face when I told her the reason I no longer talked about the rich oil – company executive boyfriend she had already begun to refer to as her son-in-law. She looked like she was about to have a heart attack. Imagine breaking up with such a man in this day and age, when men are scarce, just because he hit you once?' She cackled riotously, obviously recalling her mother's reaction, and it took her a moment to realise I'd gone deathly silent.

My head was bowed ever so slightly as I struggled to hold back the tears that had suddenly welled up like a reservoir tank in my chest.

Sally put her hand over mine comfortingly. 'Did that bastard hit you?'

I couldn't respond; I knew the moment I opened my mouth, the tears would come.

She placed a second hand over my one. 'I'm so sorry, I had no idea; that was so insensitive of me.'

'I saw the magazines, you know,' Sally said suddenly, and I felt my body stiffen further.

I cleared my throat to move the tears so I could speak. 'What did you see?'

She sighed. 'Everything: the various tales, the stories that you were sex-crazed and had run off with your boyfriend.'

I nodded silently.

Sally pinched my hands. 'If it makes you feel any better, I don't believe them. You were never the type to do such; those stories sound more like something I would do. I mean, who doesn't want better sex?' she said.

We both burst out in laughter, then carried on chatting as though the last few minutes hadn't happened.

'What do you plan to do next?' Sally asked after we'd exhausted tales of our classmates and their lives now.

I appreciated that she didn't ask what had happened, didn't force me to relive the horrors. She knew I would tell her if I wanted to, but also she only cared about my future. 'I'm not sure,' I said glumly.

'Want to talk about it?' she asked quietly.

I hesitated for a moment, then told her everything. I watched her closely for reactions as I spoke; there were hardly any. She listened with rapt attention and a straight face. I realised then that I wanted Sally's approval – craved it, even. I just wanted one more person to think I'd done the right thing.

'You should talk to a lawyer,' Sally said once I was done, rational and quick-thinking as ever.

Until then, I'd hesitated to take any action. Any move would have been an acknowledging that it wasn't some Kafkaesque nightmare but my new reality. But most of all, the fear and irrational hope wouldn't go away.

'And I know exactly who you should talk to,' Sally continued. She reached into her bag, pulled out a stack of yellow sticky notes and a fancy ballpoint pen. Did she carry that everywhere with her? She tore the top one off and proceeded to scribble rapidly on it with the pen. 'Here's his name and address. He's one of the best in the business. I'll call him once I get home and tell him to expect you. And don't worry about the fees; I'll cover them. Don't even think of arguing,' she said, raising a hand to shut off any protests I had.

'I don't know how to thank you,' I said, embarrassed by her goodwill.

'Thank me by inviting me to your house to eat that village rice you used to make for me when we were in school. I'm still yet to meet anyone that makes it the way you do, even my cook no *sabi*. Speaking of school, I couldn't believe my eyes when I visited our department to give a career talk a few weeks ago. Everything is either broken down or exactly how we left it after all these years. Even the cafeteria doesn't serve the rich meals they used to. What is happening to this country?'

## 40.

# *We must defend our lives or we shall perish*

Our car journey to the east was shrouded in silence in February '99. Occasionally, the stillness was disrupted by the sound of tyres battling through the broken tar of dilapidated roads or the horns of other motorists. I gazed out the window thinking about my children and the upcoming fees for the next school term.

Ugochukwu had made several attempts to ease the tension within the vehicle until he'd finally given up, when neither Mama nor I would cooperate, and faced the roads. He'd volunteered to take us on this journey without a question. I turned to give him a small smile of gratitude. He winked in return, and I wondered how I'd never noticed he was just as handsome as Kelechi.

He'd always been the middle brother – the one we easily forgot about. Kelechi was the first son, the repentant playboy with the charm and silver tongue, and Ikechukwu was the recalcitrant hot-tempered last son – two overwhelming personalities. It was easy to overlook responsible and dutiful Ugochukwu and his reticent charisma. He'd always done what he was meant to do – he'd been the first to marry of the three, the first to have children, the first to have a son, the one to graduate with the best grades. Above all, Ugochukwu was a born follower, the one who listened when Mama spoke and who followed Kelechi's word like it was law, even though only a year and a few months separated them.

Ugochukwu had come to look for us at the new apartment, like the others, to convince me to return to my matrimonial home but he'd been the only one to provide support when I'd refused to do as advised. He first came with a bag of rice and a carton of cooking oil – 'for the children', he'd said, but I'd wept that day like an infant. He brought his wife the next time, with their children, and she'd given me a warm hug at the door and offered to look after the children whenever I needed to take care of personal matters.

It was Ugochukwu who told me about the man whose father hadn't spoken of the war for many years until he'd fallen ill and thought himself close to death, then narrated what he'd assumed was his final autobiography to his son. The son was Ugochukwu's co-worker, who'd been aware of our search for Uncle Ikenna.

And now we were on a journey to get the closure we'd craved for thirty-two years.


The main house was an old-style bungalow with large wooden windows in the middle of a vast communal compound deep in a small village. Pa Ezuma met us in a wheelchair at the entrance of his *obi*. 'You're welcome. I've been expecting you. These terrible roads make the journey longer than it should be,' he said with a smile. 'If only they'd rebuild the River Niger Bridge.' His help brought us kola nuts and bottles of soft drink and he motioned for us to help ourselves as we exchanged pleasantries and light talk about the journey, his son Chiazo leading the conversation.

'I was already a man when the war came,' Pa Ezuma started later. His eyes took on a distant look, the same one they all wore before they began talking about the war, as though entering a portal in their minds they kept shut.

'I was a simple villager. My father was a farmer and I followed in his footsteps, feeding off the land. In fact, I was still living in his compound then. My new wife had just given birth to our son when everyone started returning home in '66. They said they were killing our people in the North and that we were no longer safe in Nigeria. Then our leader announced that we were separating and becoming Biafra – I listened to it on the radio. Everyone said war was coming. And so when it finally came, people volunteered to fight; I was one of them.

'We were trained at Abakaliki Garisson. That was where I met Ikenna – always speaking English that one. I used to tell him then that he should speak Igbo more. He was very tall and handsome; some of the female officers used to drop notes on his bunk while we were out training.' Pa Ezuma laughed fondly.

'He always spoke about his family, especially his sister and her children – one Obianuju was his favourite.' My heart burst with emotions at the words. Uncle Ikenna had thought of me. Ugochukwu poked me in the side playfully like we were still children fighting for Uncle Ikenna's attention.

'We were moved to Nsukka after our training. Then he met Nneka in Nsukka and I didn't hear word again. Mr. Lover Boy.'

Pa Ezuma went on for a while about their time together in Abakaliki and Nsukka, before the real war – the fighting – began for them, and I suspected he was not ready to delve into the darkness.

'The war came to meet us in Nsukka,' he said eventually with a resigned sigh. 'At the beginning we didn't even have sophisticated weapons like the Nigerians who were being supplied by the foreigners; it wasn't until months into the war that we received external support. Many people went into war with machetes – we used to ambush the enemy and take their weapons. We created our own explosives, too – Ogbunigwe explosives. It was tough, very tough.

'After the enemy took Nsukka, Ogugu, Ogoja and some other towns, we invaded the Midwestern region to distract them from marching into Enugu, our capital. Your brother was with me then. We were in the 18th Battalion under Major Humphrey Chukwuka in the Niger Delta. But the Nigerian army was too strong; we had to escape for our lives and many of our comrades died.

'Ikenna suffered a terrible leg injury; we tried to take him along with us, but eventually we left him in Asaba to recover because dragging him with us meant we would die along with him. Our comrades blew up the Niger Bridge to prevent the Nigerians from pursuing. We didn't see or hear from Ikenna for months, and when we heard what happened in Asaba, we assumed he was dead.'

Mama leaned forward eagerly. This was the part we'd been waiting to hear about for years. What happened next.

Pa Ezuma cleared his throat and drank from a glass of water, and I impatiently counted the number of swallows he took. 'Ikenna appeared in Onitsha in December '67, over two months after we last saw him. We were so shocked; we all thought it was a ghost.

He said he'd been hidden by a family in Asaba and he'd somehow been able to disguise himself as a civilian and escape through the bushes until he'd reached a town where he could be treated, and then he'd snuck back into Biafra. I honestly don't know why he didn't just leave the country entirely; he was too patriotic that boy.' He shook his head.

'We continued fighting; we were used to death by this time. In fact, we were close to death so many times ourselves. We defended Onitsha till it fell in March of '68. Then we fought side by side in Owerri, then Aba and Umuahia. We kept moving. Food was scarce then; we ate whatever we could find – snakes, lizards, crickets. You name it.

'In the final battle, just before Biafra surrendered, we were under heavy attack, running, fighting and hiding. Someone threw a local grenade towards the bush path we were taking cover in. Before we could escape, *gbua!* It exploded.' Pa Ezuma demonstrated the explosion with his hands.

'The next time I opened my eyes, I was in a hospital, one of those ones run by the Red Cross then. That was how I ended up in this wheelchair.'

'What about Ikenna?' Mama asked, her voice high with anxiety.

'He was right beside me, as he'd been for all those years.' Pa Ezuma shook his head sadly. 'He'd been closer to the grenade so his injuries were more serious.'

He paused and his eyes welled with tears that he let slip down unashamedly. I knew what he was going to say even before he did. 'He died two days later.'

'Noo! Nooo!' Mama screamed, a deranged sound.

'It's not possible!' she continued, her voice shaking now. Ugochukwu put his arms around her to calm her. 'He can't be gone. Are you sure it's my Ikenna? Maybe it's another Ikenna *ehn*.' She pulled at Ugochukwu's shirt, her eyes pleading with him to say she was right before she dissolved into helpless tears. I wept silently with her.

Pa Ezuma stared at her sympathetically then he seemed to think of something and wheeled himself towards the main house. When he returned, he had a black and white photo in hands. 'Your brother loved you very much,' he said, holding out the picture to Mama.

It was Uncle Ikenna sometime during the war. He was dressed in a crisp uniform with the Biafran emblem at his shoulder. He smiled brightly into the camera, the same smile he used to give Mama, with the mischievous twinkle in his eye.

Mama stared at the picture for several seconds, then she held it to her chest and allowed the flood of tears to flow.


The drive to the cemetery wasn't in silence. Pa Ezuma spoke at length of the time after the war and the struggle to return to normal life. He'd lost it all – his family, his property, his body. His wife had been killed during an air raid and his child had been taken as a refugee to Gabon, lost to him forever. He'd remarried and created a new family.

They were asked to deposit all Biafran currency and were given twenty pounds in return; no matter how much they'd owned before the war, they were to restart their lives with twenty pounds. Papa had had to do same; I'd just been too young to realise it then.

'No compensation, nothing. At least I have a family to take care of me. Many of my fellow disabled veterans are lying in dilapidated homes.'

'I have no regrets,' Pa Ezuma said when we were close to the cemetery. 'None at all.'

> Beloved homeland of our brave heroes.
> We must defend our lives or we shall perish
> We shall protect our hearts from all our foes;
> But if the price is death for all we hold dear,
> Then let us die without a shred of fear.

He sang from the Biafran anthem, with the gusto of a much younger man.

Mama's muffled weeping continued in the back seat. I moved closer and put my arms around her.

The cemetery was overrun with weeds sprouting discordantly. Some were proper graves with stone slabs and names and years – the more recent ones. Others had wood stuck in sand and scrawled details; the unlucky ones had no identification at all. We followed behind Pa Ezuma and he wheeled through the narrow path until he reached a stone slab.

'I had it replaced recently; it used to be a plank before,' Pa Ezuma explained. 'When he died, the war had just ended and so everywhere wasn't settled but I wanted him to have a proper burial, not in the mass graveyard.'

'I should have tried to find you,' he said to Mama apologetically. 'But I wasn't even sure you'd survived. I only knew his sister's name was Obiageli; I never got to know your married name. I didn't even know how to start without my legs. Your brother was a good man with a good heart.'

Mama nodded to show she understood.

Pa Ezuma put his hand out to collect the broom we'd brought along from his son. Painstakingly, he dusted the top of the stone slab until the writings were clearer.

*Here lies*
*CAPTAIN IKENNA EZEMONYE*
*He lived and died with honour.*

# 41.

## *Let's Get It On*

I blinked when the secretary called my name not long after we returned from the East.

'Ms. Obianuju Nwaike,' she repeated and looked up from her notepad to study the faces in the vast waiting lounge.

My chest swelled with pride and a feeling I couldn't identify. Joy? Relief? Obianuju Nwaike. Nwaike, my father's name. It was the first time in over twenty years that I'd been called by that name. It had taken a moment for it to register even though I'd penned it down that way, when I was yet to file for a divorce.

I planned to swear an affidavit – when it was all done – and then place an advert in the national newspapers in the 'Declaration of Change of Name' section along with several others, mostly newly married women who'd taken on their husbands' names and others (men and women) who'd chosen to change the names given to them by their forefathers for religious or superstitious reasons; no one wanted to bear the names of idol gods, names that brought bad luck or names that declared them descendants of slaves or *osu*. It would read: *I, formerly known and addressed as Mrs. Obianuju Azubuike, henceforth wish to be known and addressed as Ms. Obianuju Nwaike. All former documents remain valid. The general public should please take note.*

'Yes?' I called in response, jumping up to my feet, my handbag clutched in my hands.

The secretary eyed me with something between exhaustion and irritation at how long it had taken me to respond. I smiled apologetically. 'Please come with me,' she said and turned to lead me in the direction of her employer's office.

Barrister Daniel Ogbu stood up to welcome me with an outstretched arm. His head remained slightly bowed, even as I took his hand and shook it slightly. *It must be the outfit,* I thought, peeking down at my cashmere double-breasted blazer jacket with gold buttons and pencil skirt. Pearl earrings hung from my ears and a Swiss silver watch from my wrist. They made up the handful of items I'd kept for occasions such as this – I looked every inch the wife of the rich man I'd abandoned. Or perhaps his show of reverence had nothing to do with me or my appearance but was a transfer of the one he had for Sally.

'Please have a seat, madam,' he said, gesturing to the chair on the other side of his desk.

'Thank you,' I said, doing as he'd asked.

'I have spoken to Ms. Sally, so I already have an idea of why you're here,' he began. I nodded silently; I trusted Sally enough to know she would have given him all he needed to know without saying too much. 'But I would like to hear from you myself exactly what you want and how I can be of help to you,' he said.

'I want to get a divorce from my husband,' I responded – it felt good to say the words out loud – before giving an abridged rundown of all that had taken place in the past years. The room was quiet as I spoke, except for the scribbling sound his pen made as it moved on paper.

'Hmm,' Barrister Ogbu said when I was done, shutting his leather-bound notebook and capping his pen. 'I'll be very honest with you, Mrs. Azubuike: this won't be an easy case. Your husband is a very powerful man and so I'm sure he will come with a stellar team as well. Our laws aren't very favourable to women in the event of divorce and do not enforce spousal compensation or child support payment, so it may be almost impossible to get anything financially out of your husband. In fact, I've seen a case where a wife of over thirty years was given just two thousand naira by the court to pack her things out of her husband's house.

'About your children,' he continued. 'Should your husband pass away without a will, it is also very unlikely that they'll inherit his wealth as our laws are not very clear on female inheritance, and in many courts customary law still supersedes statutory law on inheritance, and so your husband's relatives can still take you to court on the matter. Are you sure you don't want to reconsider and resolve matters with your husband instead, madam?'

I gaped at him, overwhelmed by the barrage of information he'd just offloaded on me, and the fact that he'd referred to me by my married name.

He sighed, reopened his notebook and uncapped his pen. 'I understand that this is a lot to handle at once, but I just needed us to be clear on the facts of the case, and to be sure that you truly intend to go ahead.'

'I do,' I said simply. *I do.* It seemed rather prescient that the words that had created my marriage would be the ones to end it.

'Good. Let's begin, then,' Barrister Ogbu said without reaction.

'If you don't mind me asking, do you have an idea of what you plan to do afterwards?' he asked much later with a hint of worry, after several minutes of interrogation and scribbling – the first sign of emotion he'd shown that morning.

For the second time that day, I blinked rapidly. 'Plans?'

'Yes, you know: what you intend to do when all this is over. Travel out maybe? Do you have an international passport?' he asked, as though the thought had just occurred to him.

'Yes, I do.'

He nodded in approval. 'Good, or else it would have been almost impossible to get one before the divorce is finalised. You know under our current laws a married woman cannot be issued a passport without a written consent letter from her husband . . . So, what next?'

I was silent – I still did not know the answer to that question, and I felt inadequate for not knowing.

I was able to answer the question when Akin asked it. 'Live. Be happy,' I breathed into the telephone's mouthpiece.

He was quiet, absorbing my words and those I'd left unsaid. 'I understand,' he said eventually in an all-knowing tone, and I knew he truly did understand.

'Do you still talk to Akin? I've run into him a few times in New York and Massachusetts,' Sally said to me one day. She'd called him

*Akin* and not *Dr. Akintunde* as she'd always done in the university. I wondered if those run-ins had led to the blossoming of something between them. He'd said he liked her once; she was *cool.*

My face must have reflected my thoughts because Sally burst into laughter. 'Don't look at me like that. It's absolutely nothing like you're thinking. As if he would look my way. All he does is ask if I've heard anything new about Uju. Uju Uju Uju.' She laughed some more.

'He's only ever had eyes for you, you know,' she said seriously. 'He's been in love with you for as long as I can remember. I can't believe you didn't see it.'

*Love.* I weighed the word in my mind and wondered if I still believed in its existence.

Sally scribbled his phone number on a page of her yellow sticky notes and forced it between my fingers. 'Call him,' she instructed. But I couldn't; I just couldn't.

I took an *okada* to the call centre – I still couldn't afford a phone – the afternoon in May '99 I found Akin's first letter from so long ago tucked between the pages of the old Bible Mama had given me just before my wedding. I hadn't gone looking for it that weekend when I finally unpacked the last of my boxes – in acceptance of my resolution not to run – and found the embroidered Bible hidden underneath everything else. The scriptures were written in Igbo, 'So you don't forget who you are and where you're from', Mama had said back then. I casually flipped through the pages in nostalgic recollection of simpler times, then the letter dropped out and found me. The sheet was browned by age and the ink of the words were fading but legible still.

He answered on the third ring. 'Hello?' he said in the same rich voice as the last time we'd spoken, as though so many years hadn't gone by in between.

'Hello Akin. It's me, Obianuju,' I said cautiously, and waited for him to hang up. It was the least I deserved.

For several seconds, there was heavy silence, then finally he spoke, his voice was raw with emotion. 'Obianuju, it's been a long time. How are you?'

'I'm sorry,' I whispered, not knowing what else to say. I had no explanations or excuses; I was just sorry. And as always, he forgave without question.

At first, our conversation was light as we caught up on the years and I asked about his work and life. Then he asked to know what was 'really happening' with me, and I told him, not in full detail – it was not the time for that – but a sort of glazing over of all that had happened; I didn't want my marriage to taint our first conversation. The divorce wasn't through yet but at least a court date had been set.

He told me he could help us leave the country if we no longer felt safe and if I was eager to explore new opportunities outside, or he could get in touch with the current department heads at our old university – some of his former colleagues remained – if I wanted to go back there instead. I promised to think on it and to let him know my decision as soon as I could.

'You know we will soon become a democracy again; you can also come back if you want to. Elections were held, and we voted. The government has a huge celebration planned for the handover on the twenty-ninth, our new democracy day,' I said just before the call ended.

He chuckled. 'Shouldn't you wait for it to happen before you start inviting people back? It wouldn't be the first time the military has promised and failed to deliver. How did our last attempt at democracy work out for us anyways?'

I smiled as I handed the phone back to the operator. I'd missed his laugh.

Adaugo danced to the front of the church auditorium with the vigour of a young woman in her prime many weeks after my phone call with Akin. Beside her, her husband, mother, mother-in-law and several well-wishers contorted their bodies with enthusiasm and joy to the music. Every so often, her mother paused to adjust the small bundle in her arms. Their prayers had been answered – Adaugo had finally given birth to a son, after seven daughters.

'Praise the Lord!' Ada shouted into the microphone when their procession arrived at the altar.

'Hallelujah!' the crowd responded.

'Brethren, I have a testimony,' she began.

I gazed at her from the back of the hall. Looking at her, it was almost easy for me to doubt the story Ego had brought to me a week before. But Ego never lied to me, and so I believed her. Zina was missing.

Adaugo's first daughter had run away from home to escape marriage to the man her father had chosen from her. Uzondu had placed the blame for her disappearance right at Ada's doorstep – she was a bad mother who'd raised an irresponsible daughter and put ideas in her head to disrespect and disobey her father.

Adaugo's testimony ended and Uzondu proceeded to share his version next, with his arm slung around his wife's shoulders.

I stood up to leave. A reception was planned for afterwards, but I was neither invited nor interested in attending. I'd come to see Ada for possibly the last time, just in case I decided to accept Akin's offer to leave the country. I longed for the days when things were different between us; when I would have been at the front of the church dancing with her and worrying about Zina, and when she would have been the first to know that the judge would decide on my divorce case the next day – that tomorrow could become my own democracy day. There were days I wished I could turn back the hands of time and change how everything had turned out, perhaps told Ada about Chinelo's illness before it was too late or prevented it from happening altogether, but those days are no more as I've long accepted that our relationship died along with Chinelo, buried with her deep in the earth's core.

It still puzzled me that life had chosen us for this path that we'd never asked for or desired, but whenever I was tempted to be discouraged or worry about tomorrow, I held on dearly to Papa's words: *O te aka o di njo, emesie o ga-adi mma.* Things will eventually improve despite the present difficulties. And for our sakes, I hoped he was right.

There were petals on floor of the apartment complex hallway when I returned from Adaugo's thanksgiving service, bright red calyces strewn around like discarded tissue paper. Our neighbour must have had a visitor over again, I thought. He had them over often, and when they came, flowers, chocolates and the smell of good cooking

accompanied them, and later the sound of rough lovemaking perco-
lated the paper-thin walls.

The petals continued in a line, a studiously created velvety path,
until they stopped at my neighbour's doorway. I smiled, remembering
the Mills and Boon novels Chinelo had loved so much.

Nwamaka answered the door, an awkward smile on her face, like
she was hiding something. The room behind her was shrouded in
the dim lighting of the setting sun; there was no power and our
generator had just enough fuel to run the next morning for school
prep.

'What's going on?' I asked. 'What are you children up to now?'

She rolled her eyes dramatically, moving from the door and
allowing me to enter. 'I've told you several times Mummy, I'm no
longer a child. I'm a teenager now.'

'Well, you'll always be a child to me; my child.'

'Erm, Mummy?'

'Yes? *Oya* confess, what trouble have you caused? I can't promise
I won't punish you but you won't die.'

'Someone came to look for you today. A man,' she said slowly,
watching my face.

'What man?' I asked carefully. She wouldn't refer to her father as
'a man'.

'He didn't say his name but he left something this behind; said
you'd know who it was from,' she said, handing me a card.

Cautiously, I opened the card and read the words:

*See you soon Smallie,*
  *A*

I stared at the familiar handwriting disbelievingly, and slowly fell into a seat to absorb the shock. 'Nwamaka, please turn on the television. It's almost time for the news,' I said, immediately searching for a source of distraction.

She didn't move, but instead stared at me in silent confusion.

'Sorry – there's no power. I meant the radio,' I corrected.

The radio presenter's voice came over the airwaves, smooth and charming. 'Just before the news at six, we will be playing one more song. This is for all the lovers out there – have a good night.'

The electric guitar came first, then the clash of a crash cymbal with a drumstick. Then the arresting tenor of Marvin Gaye's voice as tears clouded my vision:

> *I've been really tryin', baby*
> *Tryin' to hold back this feeling for so long*
> *And if you feel like I feel, baby*
> *Then, c'mon, oh, c'mon*
> *Let's get it on*

# Glossary of Words and Phrases

*Abeg* — Pidgin English for 'Please'

*Abi* — Pidgin English for 'Right?'

*Abubu eke* — Igbo for 'Python fat'

*Agbada* — a flowing wide-sleeved robe worn by men in West Africa

*Agunwanyi* — Igbo for 'Tiger woman'

*Agwo emeghi ihe o jiri buru agwo, umuaka ejiri ya kee nku* — Igbo for 'If a snake doesn't show its venom, little children will use it to tie firewood'

*Ahn ahn* — A popular local expression. Could mean several things depending on the intonation of the speaker

*Akara* — Igbo for 'Bean cake'

*Akuko abughi nri'* — Igbo for 'Storytelling is not food'

*Akwamozu* — An Igbo traditional funeral rite that ensures the passing of the spirit of the dead to the other side

*Ala* — A female deity in Igboland, she's the god of earth, morality, fertility and creativity

*Amam* — Igbo for 'I don't know'

391

AIWANOSE ODAFEN

*Amebo* — A popular local expression for 'A gossip'

*Asa nwa* — Igbo for 'Beautiful girl'

*Ashawo* — A local term for 'Prostitute'

*Aso ebi* — A Yoruba term for coordinated outfits chosen by a group of people for a particular event e.g. birthdays, weddings, burial.

*Aso oke* — A hand-loomed cloth woven by the Yorubas and sewn into various styles.

*Asun* — A Yoruba delicacy made up of goat-meat fried in pepper sauce

*Atarodo* — Yoruba for 'Scotch bonnet'

*Babariga* — A traditional outer gown for men

*Chi* — The personal spirit of a person or his identity in the spirit land given by *Chukwu* that determines his destiny

*Chi mo* — Igbo for 'My God'

*Chin chin* — A popular fried snack made from flour, butter, eggs, sugar and water

*Chineke/Chukwu* — Igbo for 'God'. In Igbo cosmology, he's the sovereign God above the other gods

*Daalu nwa mu nwanyi* — Igbo for 'Thank you, my daughter'

*Dem* — Pidgin English for 'Them'

*Dey* — Pidgin English for 'Are' or 'They'

*Dokita* — Igbo for 'Doctor'

*Don* — Pidgin English for 'Has' or 'Is'

*Eba* — A staple food made from cassava flakes

*Efulefu* — Igbo for 'Worthless person', 'Lost Soul' or 'Sell-out'

*Egusi* — A local soup made from ground melon seeds

*Ehya* — An expression of sympathy

*Eje boci* — Mashed grain meal local to the Nupe people of middle-belt Nigeria

*Ekaro o. Oloshi ni gbo gbo yin* — Yoruba for 'Good morning o. You are all foolish'

*Ekwe* — A hollow Igbo musical instrument made out of wood

*Ekwensu bu onye asi* — Igbo for 'The devil is a liar'

*E lewe ukwu egbue ewu* — A buxom waist that makes her husband kill a goat for her when he looks at it

*Enyi m* — Igbo for 'My friend'

*Erimeri na adi mma erimeri e. Erimeri na adi mma erimeri e. Onwu egbule nwanyi n'af'ime k'omuora anyi nwa, tara okporo, nuru mmii ngwo* — An Igbo song for celebrating the arrival of newborns, meaning 'Merrymaking is good, let death not claim pregnant women, so that they can deliver babies, so that we can eat and drink'

*Ewo* — An exclamation

*Ezi Chukwu Nara Aja Anyi* — A popular Igbo hymnal by Obieli Udoka

*Fufu* — A staple meal made from cassava

*Garri* — Cassava flakes

*Ghana-must-go bag* — A travelling bag given its name in referral to the mass deportation of illegal immigrants in the country, most from neighbouring country Ghana during the 1980s

*Gini* — Igbo for 'What'

*Hula* — Traditional embroidered cap worn by Hausa men

*Ichafu* — Igbo for 'Head-tie'

*Ichaka* — An Igbo musical instrument made by covering a closed dried gourd with beads or cowries woven into a net, making a rattling sound when shaken.

*Ichi ozo bu maka ndi ogadagidi* — Igbo for 'Taking the *ozo* title is an affair for the high and mighty'

*Igba Nku* — Igbo for 'Traditional marriage'

*Ihe di woro ogori azuala na ahia* — Igbo for 'What is done in secret will be revealed in the marketplace'

*Ije oma* — Igbo for 'Safe journey'

*Ije uka nwa* — Igbo for 'Child dedication'

*Ikuaka* — Igbo for 'Door-knocking', when a groom's family formally informs the bride's family of his intentions

*Ili ozu* — An Igbo funeral rite that involves the actual burial of the dead

*Inugo* — Igbo for 'Do you hear me'

*Isiagu* — An embroidered velvet shirt worn by Igbo men of Eastern Nigeria

*Isi ewu* — Igbo for 'Goat head pepper soup'

*Isi nze* — The head of the *Ozo* title holders

*Iya alase* — Literal translation from Yoruba is 'Madam of cooking'. A woman that rents out her services to cook for others during their celebrations

*Jalabiya* — A loose gown native to the Nile Valley

*Jeje* — Yoruba for 'Easy'

*Jisie ike* — Igbo for 'Hold on to strength', used to tell a person to be strong, to wish someone luck; thus, it can also mean 'Good luck'.

*Juju* — Local term for 'Charms'

*Kedu* — Igbo for 'How are you?'

*Koboko* — Pidgin English for 'Whip'

*Konga* — Large pots used for cooking on firewood

*Kpanla* — Local term for 'Hake'

*Kpuchie gi onu ebe-ahu!* — Igbo for 'Shut up'

*Kudi* — Hausa for 'Money'

*Love Nwantinti* — Igbo for 'Serious Love'

*Mammy water* — Pidgin English for 'Water goddess'. Also used to refer to an extremely beautiful woman

*Na my type get sense* — Pidgin English for 'It's my type of person that has sense'

*Na your type dey spoil marriage* — Pidgin English for 'It's your type of person that scatters marriages'

*Ncha nkota* — Local soup made from palm oil

*Nche abali* — Igbo for 'Wake Keep'

*Ndigbo* — The people of Igboland

*Ngwanu* — An Igbo expression, can mean 'Come' or 'Come on' depending on the context

*Nkem* — An Igbo endearment meaning 'My own' or 'Mine'; can also be a name

*Nnam Ukwu* Igbo for 'My grandfather'

*Nna-anyi* — Igbo for 'My husband'

*Nne* — Igbo for 'My sister', can also mean 'My daughter'

*Nnoo* — Igbo for 'Welcome'

*Nnukwu Ada* — Igbo for 'Great/Mighty Ada = first daughter'

*Nwanyi Ike* — Igbo for 'Superwoman'

*Nzu* — Igbo for 'Calabash chalk'

*Obi* — A room/structure separate from the other parts of a house within a compound, for the male head of that household, usually for the purpose of entertaining guests

*Obodo oyinbo* — Igbo for 'Overseas'; literally translates as 'The land of the white man'

*Ode* — Yoruba for 'Stupid'

*Odiegwu* — An Igbo exclamation, can mean several things depending on the use and situation

*Odinma* — Igbo for 'I'm fine'

*Ofe akwu* — Igbo for 'Palm kernel stew'

*Ofe nsala* — Igbo for 'White soup', a dish made from pounded yam, habaneros, catfish, beef, crayfish, *utazi* leaves and seasoning

*Ofe oha* — Igbo soup prepared with the leaves of the *Pterocarpus soyauxii/Pterocarpus mildbraedii tree*, known traditionally as *oha*

*Oga* — Pidgin English for 'Chairman' or 'Boss'

*Ogbono soup* — A dish prepared from the ground seeds of African bush mango

*Ogini* — Igbo for 'What is it?'

*Oja* — A type of flute local to South Eastern Nigeria

*Oloriburuku* — Yoruba for 'Cursed person'; literally means 'Owner of a bad head'

*Okada* — Pidgin for 'Motorcycle'

*Okenwanyi* — Igbo for 'Great woman'

*O kwa ya* — Igbo for 'Is that so?'

*Omalicha* — Igbo for 'Beauty'

*Omugwo* — Igbo traditional after birth care where the mother of the new mother moves in for a few months to ensure she and the baby are well taken care of

*Onu nwa* — Igbo for 'Child celebration', a ceremony held months after a child's birth to celebrate its coming

*Onye iberibe* — Igbo for 'Idiot'

*Onye jee obodo a n'ebe nti, o bere nke ya tinye* — Igbo for 'If one goes to a land where they cut off ears, he should cut off his own and contribute them', aka 'When in Rome, act like the Romans'

*Ookan* — Yoruba for 'One'

*Osu* — Igbo for 'Outcast'

*O te aka o di njo, emesie o ga-adi mma* — Igbo for 'Things will eventually improve despite the present difficulties'

*Oyinbo* — Pidgin English for 'White man/person'

*Ozo* — The highest and most important social title in Southeastern Nigeria

*Ozoemena* — Literally translates to 'Another one should not happen.' Could also mean 'Never again'

*Pikin* — Pidgin English for 'Child'

*Puff-puff* — A deep fried dough pastry made from flour, sugar and yeast

*Sabi* — Pidgin English for the verb 'To know'

*Se o leko ni* — Yoruba for 'Don't you have home training?'

*Shakara* — Pidgin English for 'Pose', 'Pride', 'Show-off' or 'Haughtiness'

*Shekere* — An Yoruba musical instrument, similar to the Igbo *ichaka*, made by covering a dried gourd with beads or cowries woven into a net, making a rattling sound when shaken

*Shey* — Pidgin English for 'Right?' or 'Is it so?'

*Sisi, obo yin ko* — Yoruba for 'Young woman, how is your crotch feeling?'

*Suya* — Roasted spicy skewered beef

*Tay tay* — Pidgin English for 'Since'

*Tokunbo* — Pidgin English for 'Second-hand'

*Tufiakwa* — Igbo for 'God forbid'

*Ube* — *Dacryodes edulis*, a fruit tree native to Africa

*Udu* — An Igbo traditional spherical and hollow pottery drum, provides a bass element

*Ufie* — An Igbo large slit drum

*Ugu* — Igbo for 'Pumpkin leaf'

*Ukwa* — Igbo for 'African breadfruit'

*Ula mmuo* — A stage in the *Ozo* title-taking process that requires the aspirant to host all *ozo*-titled men his age grade, his mother's patrilineage, all young boys and married daughters of his kindred, in-laws and friends at a grand feast.

*Umuada* — A group for daughters of the same lineage, clan, village or town

*Utazi* — The tropical plant *Gongronema latifolium*

*Wahala* — Pidgin English for 'Trouble' or 'Problem'

*Wetin* — Pidgin English for 'What'

*Yaji* — A spice made from ingredients including ground pepper, ginger, peppercorn, garlic, cloves and salt

*Yeye* — Pidgin English for 'Nonsense'

# Acknowledgements

As a first-time author, it is impossible to begin this without first acknowledging that I'm actually writing the acknowledgements for my very own book; at one point this seemed like a far-away and rather unrealistic dream. It still feels surreal. It is only appropriate that I start by thanking my wonderful agent and advocate Cathryn Summerhayes. Everyone says their agent is the best one, but I really do believe Cathryn is the best. Thank you for finding a beautiful home for this book, for believing in me and for always assuring me that you have my back.

Jess Molloy, Lisa Babalis and everyone at Curtis Brown. Thank you for being so good at what you do that I'm often quite overwhelmed by just how good you are.

Kaiya Shang, for having such indefectible faith in a new, unpublished author and being so lovely to work with. As someone who's not the biggest fan of editing, I must say you've made this a really enjoyable process. Thank you for your incisive edits that have helped improve this book to the state it's in now and for being a friend I can chat with anytime about music and everything else. Thank you to Tasha Onwuemezi for the copyedit brilliance. A special thanks to everyone at Scribner/Simon & Schuster UK for your efforts on this and for all the lovely messages letting me know just how much you've enjoyed reading this; they mean so much.

Mrs. Henrietta Ngumezi, my secondary school English teacher that made me fall in love with literature. I thought of you often during this process. Thank you for going far beyond the calls of the teaching profession, for exchanging books with me and being so strict in your corrections. It is because of you and other wonderful teachers like you I met along the way that I'm here.

It was at the Purple Hibiscus Writing Workshop that I finally figured out where to take this book after several months of wandering in the depressing confusion. So, it is only right that I show my gratitude to all the wonderful facilitators and friends I made there – Chimamanda Ngozi Adichie, Lola Shoneyin, Novuyo Tshuma, Eghosa Imasuen, to name a few. This would have been impossible without you.

My deepest gratitude goes to my family and friends. It is almost impossible to enunciate just how much your love and support has carried me through this process but I'll try.

Diligence Inubuaye Omimi, for reading the very first draft of this and telling me just how bad it was, and giving me the prescient advice to 'describe more, tell us if the walls are pink'. I'm deeply grateful. My smallie.

Ayo Arikawe, my dear, dear friend, for taking the time in the midst of building the future of agriculture in Africa to listen to my rants and buy so many lunches. I still remember the conversation we had in November 2015 that made me blurt out in anger, 'I'm going to write about it!' And here we are. Who would have thought?

Gabriella Njiokwuemeni, my trusted manuscript reader. You're the best friend a person could ask for. For being one of the very few people to not look at me crazy when I decided to become a writer. For crying and laughing with me through it all. You told me it was going to happen eventually. I love you.

Mofe Adeniyi, for being a source of encouragement and a hype master.

Ifeanyi Ekpunobi, for reading versions of this and correcting my Igbo phrases and translations. *Daalu.*

David Chukwuma, for telling me I'm a genius even when I didn't feel like one.

Similolu Adejumo, for your patience, love, encouragement and support.

Tobi Olaitan, for always letting me know just how much you couldn't wait to read my book. Knowing I had at least one confirmed reader was enough motivation to keep writing.

Emmanuel Omokhamion for the video games I don't know how to play, friendship, and endless arguments and laughs.

Salome, Oseiga, Ireneosen, Sona and Gideon Odafen. My siblings that continue to inspire and push me. For seeing me how I don't see myself. You often told me to believe. I didn't always believe, but you did in my stead. I love you.

My grandparents, Pa Joseph Taiwo and Ma Romula Elizabeth Moses, for your prayers and old copies of Shakespeare.

My parents, Mr. Ehimhanre and Dr. Mrs Sarah Odafen, for inculcating a love for books at an early age, for encouraging me to question everything, for being a constant source of strength and support, a place to run to. I've always joked that if anything happens, at the very least, I can always run to my parents' home. That remains true. We may not always see eye to eye, but your love for me has remained unshakeable. I'm forever grateful.

To everyone that I've been unable to mention that has contributed in one way or the other to this work and/or the person I am today, I express my deepest gratitude.

I prayed and cried often during this process, and so it is only right I thank my God, who has been a source of unwavering assurance that all things do indeed work together for good, even when they don't feel like it.